I0818164

MAP

The Claw
Ice
Andal
3212 mi
Dragonspine
5890 Miles
Achernar
Ice
N
E
S
W
Old Reefs
349 Miles
Viridia
6719 mi
Shelt
Anchor
7826 Miles

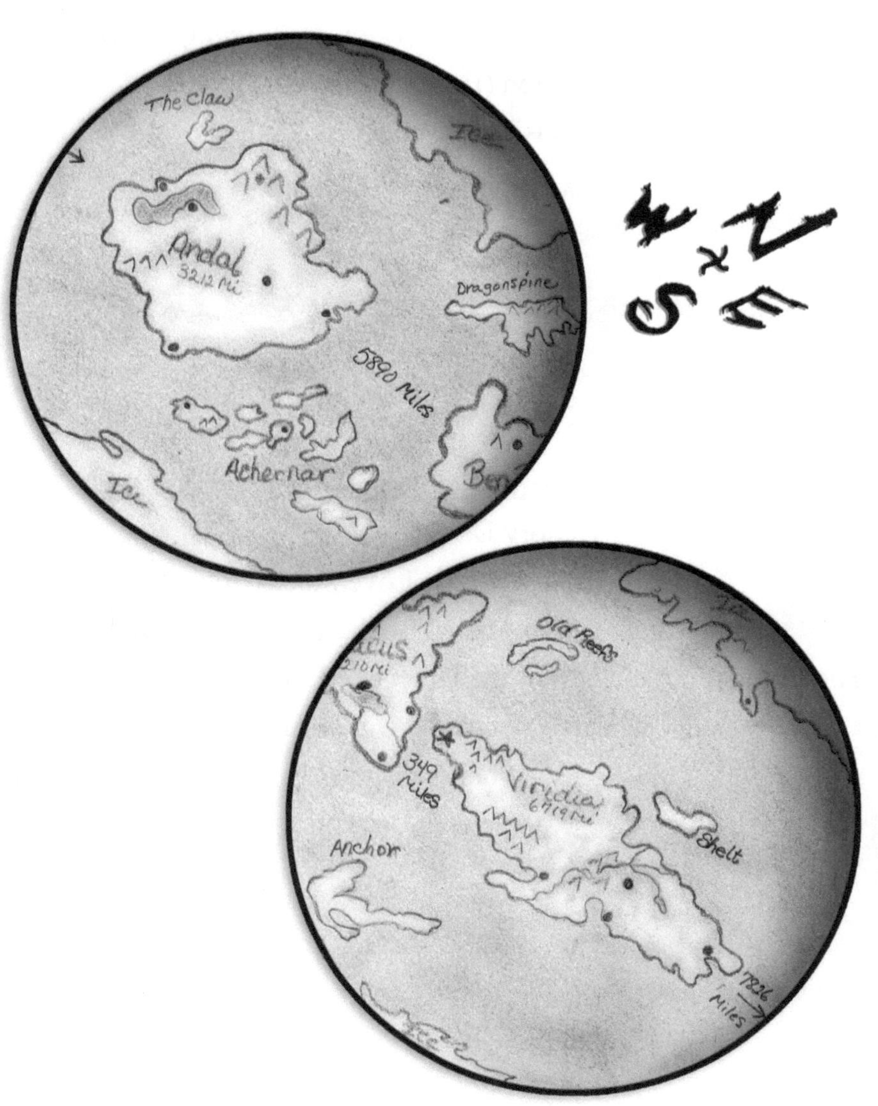

EQUUS

<u>Dragonhorse Chronicles</u>:

Dragonhorse Rising (Book 1)

Conscience of the King (Book 2)

Peace on Another's Terms (Book 3)

A Lopsided Colorwax Heart (Book 4) *(Coming Soon)*

Spirit in Motion (Book 5) *(Coming Soon)*

Visit our website at

www.dragonhorserising.com

<u>And for this Author's Peter Aarons Books</u>:

Glory Days (Book 1)

Another Man's Wife ~ A Love Story (Book 2)

Home Again Home Again (Book 3) *(Coming Soon)*

The Converging Objects of the Universe (Book 4) *(Coming Soon)*

Oh, Baby! (Book 5) *(Coming Soon)*

Visit our website at

www.peteraarons.com

Showandah S. Terrill

CONSCIENCE OF THE KING

BOOK TWO OF THE DRAGONHORSE CHRONICLES

SHORT HORSE PRESS

This book is a work of fiction, and any references to historical events, real people or real locales are used fictitiously. Other names, places, characters and incidents are products of the author's imagination, and any resemblance to actual events or locales or persons, living or dead, is purely coincidental.

Published 2020 by Short Horse Press.

Original Artwork by Edwin M. Pinson

Book Design and Shorthorse Press Logo Design by Jeremy T. Hanke

The text for this book is set in times New Roman, 11 point

Manufactured in the United States of America

Library of Congress Control Number: 2019902979

ISBN: 978-1-7328052-3-1 (hardcover)

ISBN: 978-1-7328052-4-8 (paperback)

ISBN: 978-1-7328052-5-5 (e-Book)

CONSCIENCE OF THE KING

"I have no desire to be pregnant by a man I do not know, nor to raise a child in a country strange to me. But I have no desire to die a failure, either. I have no desire to die at all, as a matter of fact."

-Princess Eridi

This book is dedicated to my editor and dear friend
Jeremy T. Hanke
Who said, "Yes, you can!"
(Then added, "And I will help you.")
Without his love, patience and considerable expertise I would forever have written in darkness.

And with love and appreciation to:
Jo Ann Safranek
Carrie Stevenson West
And the multi-talented Edwin M. Pinson

CHAPTER 1

Perhaps it was worry about the harvest, or the Lebonathi delegation, or his mother and her political agenda, or the whereabouts of Senator Konik. More likely, it was the certain knowledge that he'd stalled off going to Mountain hold for just about as long as he dared, and the equally certain knowledge that another heat cycle would soon be upon him, that made his first night back in the royal apartments less than restful for the Thirteenth Dragonhorse.

He lay staring up into the high, ornately vaulted ceilings above the sleeping platform, listening to his wife's even breathing and trying to quiet the thoughts milling around in his head. Perhaps a horseback ride would be enjoyable. All seven of the moons were up this night, and it was nearly as bright as day, though the light was a cool blue and the shadows deep. Even a walk to the stables might get his mind off things enough to sleep. Ardenai rose, slipped into a long-sleeved tunic and loose fitting trousers, and carrying his boots, made his way past the bathing pools and out onto the private balcony which overlooked the sleeping city of Thura.

He put his boots on and went up the stairs to the top of the hill into which the royal apartments, indeed the whole of the Great House had been carved thousands of years before. He stretched, and yawned, taking in a long drink of the fragrant night air. Maybe a walk through the wooded gardens would cure his sleeplessness. He decided to try that first, since a walk to the stables would necessitate going back through the apartments and out through the main entrance of the Great House. If Lionel heard him opening the apartment doors he would come charging out from under Gideon's covers and bark, and the household would be awake. If he tried to hush the puppy up, or worse yet, leave him behind, he'd howl with indignation, a fact already proven to the detriment of everyone's sleep. He nodded to himself, stretched his arms back until his shoulders popped, and began to follow one of his favorite paths around the crown of the hill.

He had gone perhaps a hundred yards into the gardens when he became aware of grief, deep and heartfelt, emanating from somewhere close by. He followed the palpitations and on a bench in the shadows beneath a myrianotus tree he discovered the source – a small figure bundled in a heavy white robe, arms clutched tightly around her middle, rocking, sobbing softly, staring at the ground.

Ardenai hesitated a moment, not wanting to frighten her with the suddenness of his presence. Staying back several feet he went down on one knee to be at eye level and said, "Ahimsa, I wish thee peace, my lady."

Her head jerked up, and the motion allowed her hood to slide off her shining white hair. She had skin so pallid it seemed to be lighted from within, and her colorless, slightly bulbous eyes with their huge pupils blinked at him, squinting as though they were adjusting to strong light. They had an odd glow to them, like a lithoped's eyes in the dark. A Lebonathi. She rubbed the palms of her hands across her eyes and nose, and looked back at the ground in what seemed to be embarrassment.

"I didn't mean to startle you, and I didn't mean to intrude, but I thought you might be in need of some help, or at least of some company," Ardenai said. "It doesn't seem like you're enjoying your stay on Equus very much."

"I hate it here," she said bitterly, and her words spilled out in a rush. "I have never been so cold for so long in my whole life. I can't stay awake in this light. It's a world of peasants. There are no rules of conduct, no protocols, no one respects authority. No one has offered us a single bite of decent food to eat...." She caught her breath, shook her head and made herself look at him. "I didn't mean that," she amended, and he could see that her teeth were chattering a little. "I apologize. I did not mean that. This is a beautiful place, and the air is wonderful. You can see so far into the distance. It's just... very different than what I'm used to."

"How so?" Ardenai asked, not moving from where he had knelt. He was tempted to offer her his cloak, but refrained. She was very young, and Lebonath Jas was not like Equus. On Lebonath Jas there were people who might take advantage of such a situation. Ardenai gave her room enough that she didn't feel threatened by his proximity.

"It's light here, all the time," she sighed. "Even at night. All I want to do is sleep when I should be preparing myself."

Her answer surprised him a little. Frankly, he'd expected to get an ear-full about the peasantry or the food. "For what?"

"Tomorrow night I am to be sacrificed to the Firstlord of Equus."

Ardenai looked no less distraught than she did. "What?" he squeaked. "What do you mean, sacrificed? Surely they're not going to..."

"No," she said, and either her phrasing or his reaction must have struck her funny, because she laughed, exposing even teeth with a double set of small, sharp cuspids. "I didn't mean to say that, either. I am to be gifted to him. I will spend the rest of my life here as his consort. I may never see my planet, or my mother or friends, ever again. It is a selfish thought, I know, but right now, it is all pervasive."

"If it is not your wish to be so given to a stranger..." Ardenai began, and a wave of her hand cut him off.

"You don't understand. While it may not be my desire, it is my destiny. It is what I was born to do, and what I was raised to do. I have spent my whole life knowing that I was to be the greatest offering of peace my planet could make. The most beneficent gesture. The giving of the flesh of the royal line of Lebonath Jas to the imperial flesh of the Great House of Equus."

Ardenai's first thought was one of indignation, but he remained silent. He remembered the joy of being a creppia nonage teacher, of spending his days with tiny children clustered about him, discovering the wondrous order of things; the pleasure of being a simple keeplord with crops to tend and horses to train. The adventure of being an ambassador for a while, and the joy his travels had brought him when they brought him his beloved Ah'ree as well.

He remembered all too well that morning he'd put a list from his mother into his trousers pocket and gone off to the city for a meeting of the Education Council – a simple meeting of the Education Council squeezed in before his one hundredth birthing day celebration. He'd requested a late afternoon sail with family and friends, and was hurrying to get through lunch with colleagues on the council when, at the stroke of midday, the great Equi drums had begun to sound until all the city shook and the very pavers throbbed with their thunder, and the doors of the council chamber had been opened very slowly, as if there were a dragon being loosed upon the city, and Ah'krill had entered with her retinue behind her. When all the council members rose in her presence, she had come to him and knelt at his feet, and held up the slim gold coronet of the Firstlord on a horsehair pillow. "Thou, Ah'rane Ardenai Krush, art this day become Ah'krill Ardenai Morning Star, The Arms of Elohim, the Thirteenth Dragonhorse, and thou art rising to be Firstlord of Equus and her affined worlds."

And had he thrown up his hands in dismay, or refused the office, or sputtered, *But, but, but ... I'm going sailing this afternoon*! No. He had not. He had raised her to her feet, and allowed her to put the circlet with its seven gold chevrons about his forehead, and he had gone with her to be stripped of his clothing, his routine, and life as he knew it. He had stood in a device many thousands of years old and been clamped in place while molten metal was poured into the forms they'd placed on his biceps, marking him for all time as Firstlord of Equus. He'd fought the terrible pain of the burns, nausea from the potion he'd been given to drink, grief, exhaustion, confusion, fear and revulsion. He'd mated with the priestess who would carry the next high priestess of Equus in her belly – a child Ardenai would not even see for fifty years. He hadn't seen his family or his world again for seasons after that. He knew the meaning of duty, and he understood the truth of her words. Not desire, but destiny. Well put.

She was aware that he'd fallen silent, and gave him a questioning look, to which he responded with a slightly sad, tight smile. "Are you afraid?" he asked.

"Yes," she admitted, "though I've been told by the people here that the Firstlord is a kind man, and a forward-thinking one. And he's a very old man, a hundred years old, so I don't imagine he's too..." She considered her words, and Ardenai chuckled softly.

"You do realize the High Equi have a lifespan of two hundred and fifty years," he said.

She gave a tiny shrug and looked baffled, and he realized that such a lifespan was beyond her ken. She probably thought he was joking. She paused a moment and picked up her thought. "It is within the history of our people that seven hundred years ago when Kehailan Firstlord, the Twelfth Dragonhorse rose to power, a delegation was sent with a fleshgift, and it was repulsed by him. She was killed, though not by him I don't think, but because she became a being without purpose, and an object of shame. A reminder of how futile it can sometimes be to try to make peace on another's terms."

She didn't say that her own people had killed the girl, but the implication did not escape Ardenai, who, with some alarm, filed it away for safekeeping, along with the still fresh and painful memory of his unborn daughter, Ah'leah, whose destiny it had been to be the next high priestess. She, too, had found herself without purpose. He took a deep breath and firmly, gently, pushed her memory to the back of his mind.

The girl sighed and studied the pavers as she studied her words. "I have no desire to be pregnant by a man I do not know, nor to raise a child in a country strange to me. But I have no desire to die a failure, either. I have no desire to die at all, as a matter of fact. We have an old expression about burning bridges, and building bridges, and that's how I feel right now, like a bridge, either to be useful in the intercourse between our two peoples, or to be burned in the sort of destructive act which leaves only rubble, and strange, garbled legends which surround the wreckage. Do you understand what I'm trying to say?"

"All too well," Ardenai responded.

He was nodding thoughtfully when there was a sudden shout, someone calling, "My Lady Eridi? Princess?"

She rose hurriedly, smoothing her robes and wiping at her eyes. "I shouldn't have slipped out. No one is supposed to see me until the ceremony. I must go at once," she said, brushing past him as he rose. She paused, and turned, giving him a gracious smile. "Thank you for listening to me bemoan my fate," she said. "I...don't suppose I shall see you again."

"Don't be too sure," Ardenai replied, shooing her off toward the sound of approaching voices. "And Princess Eridi," he added, "No harm will come to you, I promise."

Just then two men and what, from the features, seemed to be a woman, appeared abreast in the path, breathless, their eyes blazing with aggression and worry. Immediately the two men stepped forward, allowing Eridi to pass and closing the gap behind her. She was seized by the woman and dragged away, being shaken and scolded at every step. "And you," one of the men said, taking a step forward, "what have you to do with Princess Eridi?"

Ardenai shook his head and smiled. "We were just passing in our moonlight walks and paused to exchange pleasantries, nothing more."

"Well, she's not for the likes of you," the man said. "If I find out you've laid hands on her..." he paused, wondering which teeth to apply to the threat, since he himself was unarmed and the Equi in front of him was a head taller and considerably broader in the shoulders.

The Firstlord courteously hid his amusement. "Your princess is untrammeled," Ardenai said. "If you'll excuse me, I'll continue my walk."

There was a long moment's glare before the same man growled, "Go on, then," and turned with his companion back toward the royal apartments.

Ardenai continued his ramble and considered the words which the princess had spoken. Was it true? Had the Lebonathis approached the Twelfth Dragonhorse with overtures of peace in the form of a young girl like Eridi? He took a sharp breath of annoyance and shook his head. He needed to take himself to Mountain hold for his time of solitude and study. If he'd gone when he was supposed to, he'd have had this information at hand. He'd know what his birth-sire's reasons had been for not accepting the overtures.

If he'd heeded tradition, he'd have left for Mountain hold directly after his rising ceremony, but instead he'd taken off across half a dozen sectors with Sarkhan panting after him. He knew one thing for sure, he didn't want to go into a heat cycle, especially not an Imperial Dragonhorse cycle, here, and though it was still too early, it was once again close upon him – he could feel it – that creeping unquenchable fire. His last heat cycle had been kraalish in its intensity, and he wanted the isolation, the expertise, and maybe the tempering which his physician had implied Mountain hold could afford. He made up his mind that, no matter what was or was not settled regarding the disappearance of Ah'ria Konik Nokota, no matter whether his birth mother was speaking to him or not, once the Lebonathi delegation had departed, he was going to Mountain hold.

It was nearly dawn when he crawled back in bed and realized his wife was awake. "Out for a sorting walk?" she murmured.

"Um hm."

"And you met someone interesting."

Ardenai chuckled. "Do I smell like a Lebonathi?"

"Um hm."

"I met Princess Eridi. She's a child, and rather a young one. Apparently they're giving her to me tonight."

Io was now sitting up. "That's obscene, Ardi. What did you tell her?"

Ardenai sighed and sat up beside her. "First, you need to know what she told me, so we can act accordingly and not jeopardize the child's life. She is, just a little girl. I'm hungry. Let's go have this conversation over breakfast, shall we?"

Io groaned, but she nodded and crawled out over him as she headed for the lavage. "You are going to owe me for this, I just know it."

"You have no idea," her husband sighed, and over hot tea, fruit, and grainy, nut filled pastries redolent with cinnamon and orange marmalade, he told her and Gideon the story of his late night encounter, ending with his determination to go to Mountain hold as soon as possible. "Besides, I do want to speak further with Taki," he said, and his wife nodded her agreement. It was barely daylight and she was already dressed in the silver-green tunic and black riding tights of the horse guard. "I take it you're riding today?"

"Yes," she said. "We're drilling for tonight's ceremony welcoming the delegation from Lebonath Jas."

"And which will you be?" her husband twinkled, "Primuxori of Equus, or retiring Captain of the Horse Guard?"

"I thought I'd do both," she said blandly. "You can carry my dress in with you and drape it over my seat. After the opening ceremonies, I can just walk over and put it on over my uniform. Nobody will notice, I'm sure."

"I'm sure they won't," Gideon chuckled. "Are you going to clomp across the floor in your boots, or just vault off your horse and into your chair?"

Io shot him a look across the table. "And what are you doing today, Prince Gideon?"

"I was thinking there was going to be school, but I'm betting there won't be, not with the Lebonathis here, so I can put off steeling myself to attend." He felt his father's eyes and hastily added, "I will go, though. I promise."

"Now. What are your plans now?" Io persisted.

Gideon blinked. "Well, after breakfast I was thinking I'd try to teach Lionel not to jump up on people."

"In other words," Io said, "You have no plans, since the dog is obviously beyond teaching. Good. You can come with me to the stables."

Gideon looked from left to right, trying to figure out how the conversation had turned so quickly. Then his mouth opened, and he ventured, "I...you have plans for me, don't you? I can see it in the gleam in your eye."

"Absolutely," she grinned. "I can't be in two places at once, and obviously my place is at my husband's side this evening. But you, on the other hand, fine rider that you are, could represent the family in the saddle, couldn't you?"

"No!" Gideon gasped, "I could not! I only know how to ride Tolbeth, and she's at Sea keep. My saddle is at Sea keep. I'm not even a member of the Horse Guard."

"I can fix that," Io said, waving one eating stick like a magic wand. "Zimbim, you're an honorary member of the Horse Guard. Go put on some riding clothes and let's get going."

Gideon looked pleadingly at Ardenai, but the look he received in return was not encouraging. "Oh, all right," he sighed, and got up from the table. "I'll have to drop Lionel off with Criollo or Ah'brianne on our way to the stables, unless you want to take care of him, Sire."

"Even that chore sounds more inviting than what I am about to do," Ardenai sighed. "As it is, I am determined to make some sort of peace with Ah'krill before this evening, lest the Lebonathis sense division amongst us and use it to their advantage."

"How would they do that?" Gideon frowned.

"I have no idea," Ardenai replied, "But after finding out that they make gifts to strangers of their most precious children, I have my concerns about them." He set aside his napkin, drained his cup, and stood up from the table. "When you see Criollo and Ah'brianne, tell them I wish them to join us at the ceremonies this evening."

Gideon nodded and headed for his chambers to change, but Io gave him a questioning look. "Any particular reason?" she asked.

He bent, pulled back her heavy mane of hair, and kissed up the side of her neck. She tasted good, and smelled good, and it was an effort to take his lips from her earlobe. "I just think some young faces on the royal dais might be comforting."

Io turned her head and scowled at her husband. "Comforting?"

"Welcoming," he amended. "Welcoming. We know we are welcoming a child. What is more welcoming to a child than other children? I must go. My mother awaits me in her chambers." He thought a moment, and continued. "Have you spoken to Jilfan?"

"I have," Io said flatly, and tossed her napkin down beside her plate. "He has informed me that as long as I am married to you, you priestess-abusing beast, he will not be able to see his way clear to keep company or council with me." Her mouth smiled, but her eyes did not. She bobbed her head and strode off after Gideon, saying "Good luck with your mother, Beloved. I'll see you later in the day if you survive the encounter."

"Thanks," Ardenai replied. He stood for a few minutes, watching the fountain in the main hub of the apartment, finding its rhythm, quieting his own thoughts and clearing his head. Then he straightened his simple, woolen tunic, took a deep breath, and let himself out through the huge doors and onto the main concourse. Their apartment cornered the cliff at the front so it had windows on two sides, but it was slightly dim in the corridor as he looked away from the window and down the seemingly endless hallway toward his mother's apartments.

Because the Great House was carved from the living stone of the mountain, light came through only on the ends and the front of the building, where windows could be cut to the outside. Other than that, light came from skylights – tunnels really – their light source high above on the top of the cliff, where Ardenai had strolled and pondered the night before.

Upon arising, Ardenai had made inquiries as to which guest accommodations the Lebonathi delegation was occupying. He'd wanted to make sure they could make it as dark as they desired. He'd been assured that it was one of the inner chambers, and black as ink with the skylights closed. Again he thought of Eridi, and hoped she'd gotten some sleep. No, some awake time, so she could think, and prepare herself for the next great adventure. How hard this must be for her. He wondered as he walked what it would be like to live in a world where everyone slept all day and worked all night. If that was what they did. Were the rumors true? Did they all live underground? Maybe it was just that her planetary clock was flipped. The High Priestess would know – she who was his birth mother.

His thoughts took him to Ah'krill's door at the opposite end of the concourse from his own apartments, and he nodded to the two priestesses flanking the entry. They nodded back, bowing deeply as they opened the doors, and Ardenai stepped into chambers much like his own. There was a fountain in the center of the entry court with a skylight above it, and off to one side and a few steps down a more intimate space where friction fires danced on the hearth and overstuffed lounges invited repose and conversation. In front of him and to the left broad steps led down to the huge, formal dining room. To the right, steps curved up to the open balcony which housed the bathing pools and bedchambers, as well as down to what Ardenai assumed would be a study and a meeting room. On the level where he stood was an expanse which, in his apartment, held musical instruments and comfortable chairs, but in this apartment held a large gong and several dozen floor cushions. Opposing it was the space designated for formal yet private audiences. It was from this space that a priestess hurried, and gestured him in with a nod and a smile.

He was moving the beaded curtain aside when Jilfan brushed past him, neither nodding nor speaking, his chubby face a mask of studied indifference. Ardenai felt his hackles go up, but he refrained from saying anything, leaving that for another time. Right now, he wanted to make peace with his mother if he could.

She was sitting in a silver-green chair which was set at such an angle that she could both see out the window, and back into the room. Beside her there was a table with a tea service on it, and next to that, another chair identical to her own, except that it was deep purple, the color of the secular ruler. She nodded to him without rising, and gestured toward the chair. "Please," she said, "be seated, Dragonhorse."

"Thank you," Ardenai smiled, touched to his lips the languid hand she held out to him, and took his seat. "I wanted to bring you up to speed on what I've discovered since last we spoke."

"That would be very nice," she said, and returned the smile. She was a beautiful woman, and when she smiled, she could be disarming indeed, a fact not lost on her only son. "Have you breakfasted?"

"I have. We just finished. And you?"

"I have eaten, and I would prefer a stroll through the gardens or the streets to sitting here like two horses vying for the same manger."

"I would be more than happy to escort you," Ardenai said, and rose, offering her his arm. "It may be cool. Would you like a warmer wrap?"

"You may carry one for me," she said, gesturing a wrap from a nearby priestess into Ardenai's hand.

Having shooed off the acolytes who had immediately gathered to attend them, they went out through the doors, down the lift, and out through the main hall into the busy streets of the capital city.

It was a beautiful morning. The pavers gleamed white with bright patches of gold where the leaves from the Myrianotus trees had fallen, and for a while they walked arm in arm in silence, speaking to passersby, and enjoying the sensory input which such a day provided.

"You were going to report to me," Ah'krill said, and Ardenai nodded.

"I was, but when I think about my immediate needs, I'd rather you reported to me instead. Tell me, please, what you gleaned from your visit to the Lebonathi worlds."

Ah'krill nodded and thought. She stopped to accept a flower from a vendor, and twirled it as she walked. Ardenai noted that she wasn't wearing all the rings she usually did, and it made her hands look slimmer, and younger. Almost, he could feel a fondness for her. "Let's sit over there for a bit," she said, pointing with her chin to a bench near a fountain. Ardenai put her wrap around her shoulders and they settled themselves in a conversational pose.

"Too many ears at my end of the Great House," she said. "Well intentioned ears, no doubt, but entirely too sharp. When you have been in office for a few years, and the ranks around you have swelled as they inevitably do, you will find the same problem, my son. We did not visit Lebonath Tras, nor were we allowed anywhere near it. There are some strange and grusome tales surrounding that place. As a matter of fact, it was all a little strange." There was a pause. "And gruesome." She laughed softly. "My time on Lebonath Jas taught me that they are both eerily familiar and truly, truly foreign. They have extremely limited and inferior technology. I'd guess they've had rudimentary space travel for a hundred years or so," Ardenai stopped listening for a moment to digest that observation. His mother went on speaking, "yet they seem, from the few conversations I had on the subject, to go nowhere and make very few contacts outside their own world. They are incredibly suspicious of outsiders, and of each other. I felt this deep fear of something. Everything." She shrugged delicately and readjusted her wrap. "They go through terrible bouts with diseases of different kinds, including Cradle Bumps."

Even the term made Ardenai shudder. That particular illness had nearly killed him a few weeks back, and the memory of the burning fever and the blistered flesh and the endless thirst was still all too fresh for his liking. "I shouldn't have mentioned them," Ah'krill said, and patted his hand sympathetically. "But, as you know from hard experience, Cradle Bumps, while fairly innocuous in children can be deadly in adults, and they lose a good many of their elderly to just such diseases. They struggle with Influenza, and poxes. All sorts of things. They're an odd people, really. Very homogenous in their thinking, and fairly uniform in appearance within classes, at least the ones I saw. Their world was probably beautiful once, but nearly unlivable during the day because of the heat. Many if not most of the animal species have died because of intense planetary warming and loss of habitat. But these things you know from the historia we brought back with us."

"Yes," Ardenai nodded. "Tell me something I don't know." He wanted to say, *Tell me how, if they've been space travelers for only a hundred years, they managed to send a delegation to the Great House seven hundred years ago.* It was a thought he kept to himself for the time being. He didn't want to be explaining how he'd come by the information in the first place. Perhaps too, it was something Eridi would know.

"I got the feeling that they are a violent people. I never saw them strike one another, nor the men strike the women, but there was this uneasiness all the time, as though it was always a possibility. The males speak to the females and to one another in demeaning terms, and take pride in brute strength for the purpose of inflicting harm on another. Their sports are brutal, and draw large crowds."

She sighed and knit her brows in concentration. "I can't put my finger on a single incident, nor can I offer any proof, but I think the Lebonathi are a people with something missing in their culture. Something, but what is it? It almost feels as though they were given bits and pieces of technology from an outside source, and that they're still trying to tie all the pieces together into a fully functioning network. As though they are a relatively primitive people with technology that is beyond them. Perhaps another culture intervened with machines and materials, as we have done on various planets when they were failing, but instead of keeping them close and making them tribute worlds, they stepped back, thinking they'd done a good thing. In this case, the people do not yet have the native intelligence to properly and constructively use what has been given to them. Does that make any sense at all to you? It doesn't to me. Perhaps you should ask Senator Dahman. He went with us. You know who he is, don't you?"

"Yes, I know him very well," Ardenai nodded.

"He visited some of their schools, and saneceres. They call them lazarettes. Senator Sarkhan was part of the mission. I can see by the look on your face you didn't know that. He met with the politicians and wasn't really of much use overall – spent most of his time in private conversations and didn't have much to report afterward. My main interest lay with their religious practices, which I found to be fear-based, sexually biased and backward. Dahman got out into the countryside, and into the issues of pollution, and planetary warming, and that sort of thing. Talk to him."

She was growing impatient with the subject and it was beginning to show, so Ardenai graciously thanked her. As they rose once again to walk, he spoke of his concerns for Konik without telling her that all of a sudden he had a pretty good idea where Konik was. He needed to think about it before he discussed it with anyone – even those he trusted. She didn't know that the Telenir delegation had been taken to Mountain hold, and he didn't tell her that, either. It made him feel slightly devious, but still, he kept the information to himself.

He wondered about that as they continued their stroll through the city. He'd scoffed at Pythos' notion that Ah'krill was up to no good, and yet, when it came to telling her about certain things – the fact that Ah'nora of Calumet carried a son for Ardenai and the Great House, where the Telenir had been secreted, his meeting up with Eridi in the gardens – he kept his silence. He wondered what else he'd deliberately neglected to tell her, and how she'd react when the information finally came out. Interesting, this new practice of being both the only son of the High Priestess of Equus, and the Firstlord of Equus at the same time. Perhaps this in itself was a test. He chuckled to himself, and put his arm around Ah'krill's shoulders as they walked.

Ardenai had taken refreshments with her, then taken leave, and was nearly to the huge, vaulted entry doors leading out from her apartment when Jilfan came from the hearth room and headed in the direction of Ah'krill's audience chamber. He stuck his nose in the air, swung his head to one side, and would have passed in silence, but the Firstlord's big left hand wrapped itself around his upper arm and brought him to a halt.

"I would speak with thee," Ardenai said quietly.

"I am not interested in what you have to say," the boy replied, still not looking at him.

"Being interested in what I have to say is not a requirement," Ardenai said, "being polite to me while I say it, is a requirement. You will face me, and you will look at me."

Jilfan thought about it for a few moments, but the ominous rumble in the usually gentle baritone had already told him he was on shaky ground, so he turned, and looked upward for what seemed like a very long way into the smoking eyes of his stepfather. "You are Dragonhorse. I will listen," he said, and Ardenai released his arm.

"I am an Equi citizen, Jilfan. That fact should dictate your politeness, not the fact that I am Dragonhorse. No one deserves to be brushed off, nor spoken to harshly, nor ignored altogether. Not me, and most certainly not your mother, who loves you dearly. Now, if you have a problem with me, I would suggest that you come to me and discuss it. You are a prince of the Great House, and as such you must always be setting an example in all that you do. That includes how you act toward those whom you do not like. Here are my instructions to you in this matter. You will not use my relationship with your mother as a pry-bar. You will not use your relationship with my mother as a pry-bar. You will not ignore Io, you will not ignore me, and you will not ignore your stepbrothers. Do you have any questions about what I've said to you?"

The boy eyed him. "No," he said at last.

"Do you have anything you'd like to say at this point?"

Again the boy gave it some thought. "I…you'll never take my sire's place," he said, and there was a tiny gleam of defiance in his eye.

"I would never attempt to take Salerno's place in your affections, I have told you that. I am me, not him. If you want me to be a father to you in my own right, I will try to do that, and be happy in doing it. If you want me to be a friend and confidant, I will try to do that, as well. My only requirement is that you be civil to me for your mother's sake. You do owe me that much, simply because I draw breath."

"I will be civil," the boy said, emphasizing slightly the last word. He paused, then added, "May I go?"

"One thing more," Ardenai said, "I will expect you in my chambers this evening to walk with your mother, your stepbrothers, and me for the welcoming ceremony. When we stop to greet the High Priestess and her retinue, you may join them if you so desire."

Jilfan replied with a gracious nod. "As my Liege Lord wishes," he said, and walked away.

Ardenai just shook his head, and as one of the priestesses opened the door for him, he caught her crimping a grin. He glared at her from under his eyebrows, and she giggled, which made him laugh, and he was still laughing as he headed for the main stables of the Great House of Equus.

An amazing place, the Great Stables. Ardenai never grew tired of them, never failed to crane his neck and look about in wonder as he entered them. Like the Great House, they were carved out of living rock, and were entered by a pair of wide, sloping corridors which led down, one from inside the Great House itself, one from the avenue to the south of the main building. In part, it had been a natural, alabaster cavern, or it could never have been so huge. It had been shaped by the ancient Equi until none of the sense of a cave remained, but only the space, towering nearly as high as the Great House itself, and larger by slightly more than a third at its base.

A multi-leveled maze, it opened out at the lower end onto a natural outdoor parade ground, lower than the level of the city, higher than the level of the sea against which it abutted. Inside, in addition to apartments for those who worked in the stables, there was room for another, smaller parade ground, three training rings, a dozen tack rooms, storage for wagons and carts, a saddle-making shop, a huge forge, spacious stalls for over six hundred horses, and ample space to store the vast quantities of fodder they required.

Within its confines, a whole industry throve, with smithies working under Master Farrier Landais, and saddle and tack makers plying their trade under the watchful eye of Saddle Master Maremmano. The grooms, and those who kept the stalls and aisles clean, and those who fed, answered to Eider, who was Master of Distribution. When the Horse Guard trained on foot, they answered to Seglawi, who was Captain of Arms, and when they trained on horseback they answered to Teal, who was Master of Horse, and, until very recently to Io, who had been Captain of the Horse Guard. For the purposes of this night's entertainment and at Teal's request, she was Captain again. Over it all, as master of more than nine million statute square feet of the Great Stables, was Master Pottuck, who had been there since Ardenai was a boy, and who still ran every level, every aspect of the operation with an eye for detail which was the envy of every keeplord on Equus, including the Dragonhorse himself.

Ardenai strode into the midst of the activity, breathing deeply of horses and fine leather and waving to the people he knew, which included most of them. Over the ring of hammers he heard someone shouting his name, and turned to see Master Farrier Landais beckoning him over. "Have you come for that polo match you owe me?" the man called.

"I wish it were so," Ardenai hollered back, modulating his tone as he drew closer to the smithy. Unlike the prototype of a farrier, Landais was a small, rather slender man, but he had not an ounce of fat on his body, and his muscles bulged as though his tunic were stuffed with rocks. "Actually, I'm looking for my wife and my son. Have you seen them?"

"I have," Landais nodded, and pointed with his chin toward the parade ground. "Io is drilling the Horse Guard from the ground, and Gideon is riding in her place."

Ardenai studied the smithy's open, humorous face. "How are the others taking it?"

"Taking what?"

"Having Gideon riding with them instead of Io."

He shrugged. "Fine."

"You're sure about that?"

Landais snorted and shook his mane of dark hair, looking for all the world like the horse he stood next to. "Listen, Dragonhorse. Everyone down here adores your wife, and they adore that newly adopted son of yours no less. He's good natured, and he tries with all he's got to do what he's asked to do. He never lords it over anyone else, no more than your wife does. If she wants the boy riding in her stead so she can stand with you for state occasions, nobody here's going to have a problem with it. If they do, they'd best not say so around me."

"Thanks," Ardenai said. He gave the Master Farrier a slap on the arm, and went off in the direction Landais had pointed.

It wasn't hard to spot Gideon, blond and fair among the dark haired Equi, but his riding was improving to the point where he seemed no less accomplished than they, and Ardenai settled himself with a sigh of pleasure against the rail to watch for a bit.

There was an agitated whimper close by, and Ardenai found Lionel, safely shut in a pigeon carrying cage. He was watching the horses, and the many feet which passed him by, and trembling with excitement. Ardenai crouched beside his cage for a few moments and let the puppy lick his fingers, then gave him a little scratch under the chin and returned to his vantage point beside the main gate to the parade ground.

He wished he were down here to play polo with his old school friend, Landais, or out there drilling with the Horse Guard. Ordinarily, he would have saddled a horse and joined them, but this cadence was being orchestrated for a certain number of riders, and his presence would be distracting. At least if he were on horseback it would have been distracting. On the ground, he might as well have been a set of clothes draped over a fencepost for all the attention he garnered. His wife was totally focused on her task, which was precisely what made her a great military strategist, and the men and women under her command were nearly as focused as she was, because she demanded it of them.

Ardenai noticed that Gideon was riding Io's pinto mare, Kimmis, brought from Calumet along with Gideon's bay mare Tolbeth, and Ardenai's grey stallion. A wise choice for the young man. If he got confused all he had to do was drop his reins and let the mare do the rest. Gideon was smart enough to know that, and twice in the next ten minutes, Ardenai watched him let the mare take the lead. *It's a wise man who trusts a wise horse*, Ardenai thought, bringing the old proverb to mind with a smile.

He could have spent the afternoon there and gladly, but he knew that the senate committees and councils would soon break for lunch, and he wanted to catch Dahman. He gave the puppy's little chin a farewell scratching and jogged easily back up the cobbled passageway into the Great House seconds before the gong sounded to dismiss the morning sessions. Letting himself into one of the individual council chambers he hailed a tiny, thickset man with wild grey hair and bright black eyes, who was heading out the opposite door. Everyone stopped short, spun to face him, and there was a respectful silence which left the Firstlord momentarily nonplused. No more barging heedlessly from room to room hollering for people, Ardenai realized. He was Firstlord of Equus. His mother would have sent for the man and held audience in her chambers, not chased him down and cornered him in a public place. For a few seconds he felt ten feet tall and as broad, and his face felt hot with embarrassment.

He reminded himself that, one, this was the council on which he had served for years, and two, he was not his mother. He recovered quickly, and said, "The rest of you, please, go on to lunch. Dahman's the one I want to speak to right now."

"But Dahman's the one most interested in lunch," someone joked.

"I'll see that he gets fed," Ardenai replied, and the other committee members filed out, leaving the two men alone in the chamber.

"You want to talk about that trip to Lebonath Jas, don't you?" Dahman said very quickly, fixing his bright, round eyes on the Firstlord's face. He carried his hands high and up front, bespeaking his Taraxian heritage. He had a luxurious, close-cropped beard and little pink ears, which were set very high on his head, and his quick, almost furtive movements always reminded Ardenai of a spinklemaus. "Your mother said you probably would."

"And when did she say that?" Ardenai asked, losing the grin which seeing Dahman had brought him.

"Ah, yesterday, I think. Yes. Definitely. There were a couple more of us on this committee who went to Lebonath Jas you know. Yes. You could talk to all of us if you'd like. You could do that. We made it a point to be here today, all of us, just in case. Your mother said we should do that. She said you'd want to talk about that trip. It wasn't political, you know. It was a humanitarian junket, as part of the SGA's war on childhood diseases. Are you hungry? I certainly am. Would you like to talk to us?"

Ardenai resisted the urge to shake his head and sigh. Outmaneuvered again. "When would be convenient for you?" he asked, and Dahman gestured impatiently toward the door.

"Now would be good. Yes. I asked them to set a table aside for us in case you showed up, but we need to get a move on, or the salad will be wilted and the butter won't melt properly on the rolls, and all those wonderful little vegetable stuffed pastries that they make for us on Scoligyre will be gone. Is that what you'd like to do, eat while we talk? Or talk while we eat? Either one? Ardenai Firstlord? Ambassador Drakkyus is shameless in how he heaps his plate with those little pastries. One would think they don't feed their people on Potami at all. Those wonderful little pastries. They'll be gone soon. Very soon."

"Lead on," Ardenai said, pinching firmly at the corners of his mouth, and Dahman flipped his long tail over his back and scurried away toward the dining room.

Three others were holding a table for them, two men and a woman, and as they ate, they discussed the mission of their delegation. While Dahman appeared slightly dithery, he missed very little. He was devoted to the environment, and to the good of children everywhere, and despite the fact that he tended to fling food around when he got excited, he was a fascinating and informative companion.

"I'm Taraxian myself, you know," he was saying between savage little bites of pastry. "Of course you know that. Of course you do. Yes. Taraxia's none too forward thinking in a lot of ways, but the Lebonathis..."

He blew out through his lips like a horse for emphasis, and a fine spray of pastry flakes traveled in all directions. "Well, I'm a creppiatrician. Yes, I am, and you of course, Ardenai Firstlord, you're a teacher of the wee ones, or at least you were until you became Dragonhorse. You know how to spot when a child is healthy, and happy. Doesn't matter what species they are, Equi, Caspian, Taraxian, Lebonathi, Terren or newborn foal, for that matter, the signs are there. And I tell you this, the girl children on Lebonath Jas are not happy, and they're not particularly healthy, either. Air is nearly unbreathable for the sulfur and the carbon monoxide. Completely dependent on petroleum, they are. Yes. And dreadfully overpopulated in the oddest sort of way." Again, there was a fine spray of pastry flakes. "I've never seen a society more bent on destroying itself, except maybe the Declivians. Yes. They're bad, too. Of course they do have a bigger planet, and they didn't really have any choice in the matter. Being overrun by Terrenes and everybody else in the galaxy didn't help their case, no, not one bit, being pacifists and farmers and all. They may make it yet, not as a race of course, because most of them are dead. No offense to Gideon. Fine young man, that one. Healthy as a horse, or so I hear, and devoted to you and Io. Where were we?"

Ardenai resisted the urge to duck the pastry flakes, and kept his eyes fixed on the senator. "Tell me why you think it's only the girl children who are unhealthy."

"I don't think I said that, did I? All the children suffer from smoke inhalation, and that hole in their atmosphere," *another spray,* "that's why they've had to take to their burrows during the day. But the girls? Why they're more property, chattel, than they are children. Marriages are arranged with no say from the female, and so young, yes. Property, that's all they are. Just property, and their religion condones it. Very odd, fear-based religion. Full of gods who have lots of rules and no mercy, who eat people, and burn them alive and flay their skins off and such like." He shuddered, and comforted himself with another pastry, which he turned quickly in his hands, nibbling around the crust while his big bright eyes darted from face to face.

"Personally, I think..." *munchmunchmunch,* "...that's what happened to their planet. Their religion." *Munchmunchmunch,* "that's what happened. They kept thinking their gods were going to come and save them from themselves, instead of saving themselves from themselves."

"We have arranged matings," sniffed the raven-haired woman in the robes of a priestess, and Ardenai cringed inside. He'd figured it was coming in one form or other. They'd been at odds for years on the council. She had said a dozen times that she loathed the idea of a Dragonhorse, and now she had him at her mercy in a room full of people who had been his peers for decades.

He steeled himself to reply, but it was Breton, Master of Education for the Great House, who shook his grizzled old head and growled, "There is a great deal of difference between an arranged mating, and an arranged marriage, Priestess Ah'ti. There is a difference between being loaned briefly to the good of your people, and owned forever for the benefit of your master."

"Is that the man's perspective?" Ah'ti shot back. "We are no less chattel than they. If the Firstlord summons us to the bench to set his head against us and settle us with child, we go. We have no choice in the matter. He is no less our master than their husbands are theirs."

Ardenai felt his ears starting to pin back, and folded his hands to stop them from balling up. "Ah'ti, if you are summoned to bend under the weight of the Dragonhorse, it will not be me who does the summoning. It will be a bloodlines specialist from the Great House, and it is not only you who will be summoned, but myself, as well. Do you think I can pick and choose? No. I serve the Great House and its traditions, just as you do. I will do the duty I was born to, just as you do your duties for the ultimate good of our people. As to the matter of you being chattel, I can assure you that you are not. All you have to do is say, no, and I guarantee you, you will not be touched, or in any way violated if that is how you view it. No one's agenda can change my mind on that." He bit down on his next words.

Ah'ti had always been arrogant and narrow-minded, and how she'd ever made it into the inner circle of the Eloi was a mystery to the Firstlord. He reminded himself that the High Priestess had briefly considered this woman as a wife for him, and spent a moment thanking the Creator Spirit he hadn't had to have that particular discussion with his birth mother. Of course Ah'ti hadn't made even the first cut, which meant Ah'krill was aware of both the woman's personality and her ambition. He took a deep breath and forced his shoulders to relax.

"And that is the Equi perspective," Master Breton smiled, giving Ardenai's thigh a brief, quieting pat under the table and going on with the conversation as though the Firstlord hadn't interjected anything. "Respect for duty, and modesty in performing it. It is the secular perspective as well as the religious perspective. We have no separation of religious and secular thought. Science and religion agree. No one asks an Equi what things his religion believes in. No one has to. The mental, material and moral values of our ideal community are holy and immortal. For eleven long generations Equus is ruled by a High Priestess, by the Eloi, only every seven hundred years does a secular leader arise. He rules a mere one hundred and fifty years. We live our faith, and our faith is the very life of Equus. You represent that faith, Ah'ti." His tone was quietly disapproving, and the woman was quick to notice.

"The Eloi do not rule alone," Ah'ti said stiffly. "They rule with the guidance of a council. Most of that council is made up of men. The Dragonhorse is not so trammeled. His authority cannot be challenged. Is that because he is a secular ruler, or because he is a male?"

"Do I detect a note of bitterness?" Senator Hirzai chuckled, and dropped Ardenai a sly green wink from behind his tea cup.

Ah'ti's already ramrod straight back became yet straighter. "Do I note that the second the subject of males being the only absolute rulers comes up, the subject is changed? Why do we have such a dichotomy of leadership within a powerful government? It is unnecessary and unseemly. And there you sit, Ah'krill Ardenai Morning Star." Her lip curled slightly at the words, and she glared across the table at Ardenai "You, who spoke so eloquently in this very council about how the Equi had outgrown the need for a Dragonhorse. But when that exalted mantle landed on your shoulders, you began singing a very different tune. Now it is apparently a selfless and glorious calling, and every male in the room would agree. You know why that is?

Three wives to warm your bed and eleven worlds to adore you – that's why."

Ardenai sat watching her as she spoke and carefully veiling his own, uncharitable thoughts. He gave her a brief, cool smile. "The more I learn about my job the more it gives me pause," he said. "When I didn't know so much about it, judgments were simpler. More experience, fewer opinions, I suppose."

Master Breton put down his eating sticks and his eyes hardened, though his voice remained calm. "Ah'ti, need I remind you that we are a people of tradition? Much of what we do, we do because it is traditional to do so, and more importantly, we do it because it has been proven to work. We are a planet without civil war, largely without poverty, nor hunger, nor abuse, nor rampant crime. We are wealthy, beneficent, and the most powerful Affination of planets in the Seventh Galactic Alliance – the most powerful single planet in the United Galactic Alliances. Our system works, and it will continue to do so. Our tradition of rule stretches back ten thousand years, and it will stretch forward another ten thousand."

"Well said," Hirzai smiled.

Ah'ti exhaled sharply, brought her fists down on the table and spoke through teeth that were clenched in anger. "Tradition? Is that what you choose to call it? It's folly! Surely someone has to have noticed that it is only as the males rise that we have wars and insurrections. For generations we live in peace, and then another Dragonhorse rises. And what was the first thing that happened this time? *You…*" there was both emphasis and a sneer, "ran like a criminal from your own coronation, leaving your whole planet in upheaval, lured another man into chasing you across however many sectors and into a meaningless confrontation and then hurled a knife with the force of a crossbow bolt through his heart! Everyone on Equus saw the images before you ever got back here to take your office. That is what males offer us. And where does murdering Senator Sarkhan land you, Ardenai? With accolades in the history books, that's where."

Ah'ti's voice was raised and openly challenging, and there was a quick intake of breath from the surrounding tables, which had grown hushed as the diatribe progressed. "You nearly got your new bride killed, and you did get your unborn daughter killed. You dragged home Konik, who is a traitor. You adopted that unclean, rag-tag boy whore and made him a prince. How dare you abuse your power in such a manner! You have no judgment at all!"

At that point Ambassador Hirzai's fists joined hers on the table and she glared and blurted, "If we are so traditional, so bent on tradition, then why is it that we sit now in the presence of Ardenai Firstlord, when he should traditionally be at Mountain hold?" She leaned back in her chair, folded her arms across her chest, and dared the men with her eyes.

Ardenai refused to let the pain of her words register on his face, though his hands were clenched and shaking. He cleared his throat to test his voice. "Konik saved my life, and the life of the High Priestess," he said quietly. "It was his hand that turned war into peace – dishonor into honor. Now he is missing and his wife is dying. Gideon is a child, who had no choice in what was done to him, which seems to be the very crux of your argument, Priestess. He saved my life when he had no reason to do so. He traveled with me, was put to the lash with me. His courage, his intelligence, his wisdom inspires me every day that I am with him. What Dragonhorse, what man, would be so foolish as not to surround himself with courageous, honorable people like those two? As to why you sit in my presence, it is because I seek your council." The pounding of his heart began to quiet. "I believe we were discussing the Lebonathi?"

"Yes, and I took us off the subject," Master Breton said. "My apologies."

"Please," Ardenai smiled, "Do not apologize. You taught me as a boy, and again today I am instructed. I am grateful for your words."

"But you would like to continue discussing the Lebonathi?" Dahman smiled, only the slight twitch of his luxurious tail where it lay against his neck indicating that he, too, was angry.

"I would, if there is anything more to discuss. Did anyone at all besides Sarkhan spend time discussing politics?" Again he felt that twitch of intuition, that spark of knowing what had happened to Konik. Had anyone heard anything, seen anything that might confirm his suspicions? Had

Sarkhan sought to use the Lebonathi as a stepping stone to power, and had Konik gotten caught up in that web somehow?

As if in answer, Hirzai shook his head. "The subject was strictly off limits, at least in theory. I think perhaps High Priestess Ah'krill made some inroads, though. You know how subtle she can be in her inquiries."

"Oh yes," Ardenai nodded.

"Perhaps you should talk to her."

Ardenai let the suggestion go by. To say he'd already talked to her would be the same as saying he'd been gullible enough to allow himself to be misdirected, and Ah'ti, who was still smoldering across the table, would immediately rise to the occasion. Instead he said, "Tell me a bit about this fear-based religion."

"Much ado about sin," Dahman said with a knowing nod. "Yes. Much ado about what the gods want, and the punishments they'll exact if you don't toe the line. The usual rules and regulations designed to keep the priesthood in power and the people in chains." He glanced at Ah'ti and made a little gesture, half capitulation, half annoyance with his hands. "Metaphorically speaking, Priestess. Metaphorically speaking."

"Sounds rather vague," Ardenai said, giving him a hard look.

"And with good reason. The trip was orchestrated," Hirzai said. "Start to finish, it was orchestrated. Their leader is very religious, singularly odd, and I didn't trust him one bit. We saw what we were supposed to see, and heard what we were supposed to hear. It was vignettes and short speeches. At no time did it flow naturally, nor were we able to enter into a real dialogue. Did we come away with the notion that they had some real needs? Definitely. Did we come away with the idea that they were actually going to let us help them? No, we did not. Sarkhan seemed satisfied. The rest of us were just frustrated. At least I was."

"That makes no sense at all," Ardenai scowled.

"No, it doesn't, does it?" Master Breton sighed. "They're an enigma. An odd, enigmatic people, with a beautiful, ruined planet, and an overweening pride in something that doesn't exist anymore. What do you suppose they'll have to say tonight?"

"I think," Ardenai said, swirling the tea in his cup and speaking thoughtfully, "that tonight we may get the answer, or at least the terms surrounding Hirzai's second question. I think tonight, we'll find out whether or not they're actually going to let us help them, and what it's going to cost us to do that."

CHAPTER 2

When Io arrived back at the royal apartments she found Ardenai sitting on the balcony, long arms wrapped around his updrawn knees, staring glumly out over the city. She sat beside him and laid her head over on his shoulder for a bit before speaking. "Difficult day, Beloved?"

Ardenai took a deep breath, and rubbed his cheek gently against her hair. She smelled so good, of horses, and well-tanned leather, and somehow it deepened the ache in his heart. "I'm just not very good at my new job. When we were on Calumet, and I only had to do one thing at a time, it didn't seem so bad, but now..." a shrug punctuated the thought.

"What happened?" she asked, draping her arm across his thigh and shifting about to get more comfortable.

"Today I went to see Ah'krill, prepared to have it out with her. I told you I was going to do that. Well, she immediately charmed and disarmed me, and made me feel all warm and accepting, and she had her way with me. She played me like the finest floor harp on Equus. What was supposed to be a hard, fact-based discussion, became a chat, with me naively believing everything she told me. Then, at her suggestion, I went to talk to Dahman. I went loping heedlessly into the Council Chambers, hailing him like a mannerless lout. I embarrassed myself, and I'm afraid I embarrassed him. Then I met with the delegation that went to Lebonath Jas with Ah'krill a couple of years ago, and they referred me right back to my mother. Ah'ti was less than charming. She accused me, and rightly so, of breaking with tradition by not going to Mountain hold." He flipped his hands out in frustration. "I've wished half a dozen times today that I had in my possession the information that place holds for me. I just...I've never felt so unsure of myself in all my life, Io." He dropped his hands, hugged his knees, and settled back into gloom.

"Why don't you just boot everybody out and start over again with a new council, new committees, new everything? You're Dragonhorse. It's your right."

Ardenai turned his head enough to scowl at her. "I'm the one at fault, here, not them. They're doing their job, and they know more about their jobs than I do about mine. Getting rid of them to save myself embarrassment would do Equus not one bit of good."

"A wise decision," she grinned. "See, there's one wise decision today. You're not such a bad leader, after all."

He shot her a glance out of the corner of his eye and drew his knees in closer, rocking a little with annoyance and pent-up frustration. "Precious Equus, how did I end up in this position, anyway? Teal should have been Firstlord. He's the one with the military background."

"This is not the post of a soldier," his wife said gently, "nor did Teal spend five hundred years in the womb of one of the dragon physicians of Achernar being schooled for the challenge. You did."

Ardenai's head snapped around and he gave her a look askance. "How did you know that?" he gasped. "Nobody knows that!"

"Nobody but you and Teal, and your father, Pythos," she murmured, placing her palm against his cheek and smiling to reassure him. "When you were so sick and feverish, you rambled in your head. It wasn't hard to make the connection."

"Does Pythos know?" he asked warily. He remembered that morning on Calumet when Pythos had told Ardenai how he'd carried him as an embryo, and ultimately placed him in the womb of Ah'krill to be born as the Thirteenth Dragonhorse. Ardenai's son, Kehailan, had overheard the conversation, and Pythos had wiped his mind of it in a nanoth of a second.

"Yes, Pythos knows," she said. With a quick, graceful movement she half-rose, and ducked under his right arm to sit astride him, using his updrawn knees as a backrest. "And he didn't feel it necessary to wipe my mind clean, and he didn't say anything about having me killed if I told anybody. I know better than to do that." She leaned forward on him, laced her fingers behind his head and kissed him lingeringly on the lips. "You're entirely too serious, Ardenai Firstlord. You need some recreation before this evening's pomp and circumstance."

"Mmmmm," he replied, kissing her throat, "what did you have in mind, my lovely blossom bat?"

"I thought perhaps ... a little canter?"

"With my usual rider?"

"Um hm," she said, and slid her tongue between his parted lips. She could feel his phallus as it dropped from its protective sheath and thickened beneath her, and she peeled off his tunic and pushed him down flat on his back biting gently at his nipples.

He groaned with pleasure, and allowed her to continue for a minute or so before murmuring, "I'm wearing riding boots, and these britches have no fly."

She looked up from her teething and smiled. "I'm wearing riding boots, and these britches have no fly. What unromantic soul designed the uniform of the Equi Horse Guard, I ask you?"

"Someone who thought sexual energy was best channeled into other outlets?"

"Well, they were wrong," she said, and kissed him again, long and deep.

From flat on his back he caught her under the buttocks, bent his knees tighter, and just stood up with her, a feat which made her gasp despite her passion. All her life she'd known this man, and still he amazed her. Every day, he amazed her. He carried her into their bedchamber and dumped her unceremoniously onto the huge bed.

"It's going to be like that is it?" she grinned, tossing her boots across the bed onto the floor. "Have it your way. At least we'll have it your way the first go-around. Let's get out of these clothes and into something more comfortable."

"If by that you mean you, by all means. Where's the boy, and that obnoxious little dog? I still want to know who's behind that dog. And why is it the size of a baby shoe? It's half the size of Mikilosh. It could curl up and sleep in a soup bowl. I've stepped on it twice already." As he spoke, Ardenai was jacking off his boots. He tossed riding tights and tunic after them and tumbled onto the bed beside his wife, pulling a fleece over them both. The season was advancing and the old palace was growing colder.

"That feels good, though I didn't realize I was getting chilly," Io smiled, snuggling up against him. "Gideon is with Criollo and Ah'brianne, I suppose. And where Gideon is, there also is Lionel."

"Good," Ardenai murmured. "How may I bring you pleasure, my wife?"

"Your weight, and your warmth, would be most welcome," she said, sliding her arms around his neck.

"Your wish, is my fondest desire," he responded, entwining his legs with hers to spread them, and in moments they were coupled together, forgetting everything but one another and the passion which drove them. It was a most relaxing way to spend an hour. It cleared Ardenai's mind, leaving him invigorated and well exercised. Io, who always enjoyed sex, found it the most delightful one of her duties as Firstwife, and told him so.

"Amazing," he whispered, looking up at her where she sat astride his hips. "The child I knew seems another life altogether, and I am blessed by the woman she has become. Thank you so much."

They were lounging in the expansive hot pools which overlooked the city, bathing one another and laughing about small things, when Gideon returned to the royal apartments, bringing Criollo and Ah'brianne up the stairs onto the entresol level with him, and carrying Lionel tucked under one arm. "Ah, the children of the keep nave," Ardenai smiled. "We shall be well represented tonight. Ah'rane and Krush should be here soon. Have you bathed? Would you care to join us?"

"I, for one, would love a bath," Ah'brianne exclaimed, and moved not another step with her companions. She laid aside the evening clothes she was carrying and sat on the stonework flanking the pools to remove her boots. “I’ve been fussing around with Ambassador MalDor the entire afternoon. He couldn’t decide what to wear tonight. Doesn’t have enough fingers and toes, and earlobes, and nostrils and whatever else, to accommodate all the rings he wanted to flash, poor man.” She laughed as she tossed her clothes aside, flipped her hair up and waded into the pool, where she sank with a sigh up to her armpits. “I suppose poor *being*, would be more accurate. I think he’s hominoid only in the most expansive sense of the word. Oh, but he’s nice, don’t get me wrong. He’s just different, you know. Criollo, Gideon, get in here. History major, you smell like ten thousand volumes of ancient lore, and Gideon, you smell like a horse. Not that that’s bad – not as bad as smelling like books. They smell really musty and a little sour. You just smell like horse sweat and leather.”

She looked expectant, and Criollo shed his boots and clothing and slid in beside her, drawing breath in through his teeth as the steamy water passed his crotch. “Oooh, hot, hot, hot,” he grimaced. “Gideon, you coming?”

“Ah...sure,” the Declivian replied. “Let me just set all these good clothes in my room, you know, in case Lionel decides to chew, or take a nap on them. I’ll be right back.” He gathered up the garments and hurried toward his room at the far end of the entresol, leaving his father wondering if he’d actually be back.

The first time Ardenai had asked Gideon if he’d like to bathe with him, the boy had panicked, fearing molestation or outright rape. Ardenai shivered a little, remembering the series of painful conversations they’d had about Gideon’s past, about his mother selling him as a tyke-whore, about the diseases which had ravaged his body, leaving him both sterile and impotent; being shown the terrible, disfiguring brands which the boy bore on his belly and buttocks, marking him as unclean. In the seasons which followed Gideon had grown accustomed to bathing with close friends and family and some weeks ago he’d allowed Pythos to remove the brands. But bathing with Ah’brianne, could be embarrassing for the boy.

He didn’t have a tuckable phallus like an Equi male. He would be truly naked, and for Gideon, who’d been teased more than once for being a prude, getting his naked self into a pool with a beautiful young girl who was also naked – a beautiful young girl he seemed rather sweet on – might be just too much to ask. Ardenai sighed to himself, regretting his offhand invitation. The boy wasn't Equi yet. The boy had issues, and forcing him into awkward situations wasn't going to help at all.

In the same thought Ardenai wondered if Doctor Keats had made any progress on a cure for Gideon's affliction. Perhaps he should check in with the good doctor. See how his incarceration on the Declivian island of Dorset was going, see if he needed anything to help with…

"Are you listening to me?" Io asked, giving him a poke, and he realized he wasn't.

"I...was thinking about dinner," Ardenai smiled. "What's the order again? The welcoming of the Lebonathi, then the riding, then dinner, then dancing, is that it?"

"That's it," Ah'brianne nodded, "MalDor recited it about a dozen times this afternoon. He's thinking the Lebonathi won't eat what we feed them, and that the lights off the alabaster walls of the Great Hall will be so bright they'll refuse to sit in there, and that the whole thing is going to be a diplomatic nightmare and that maybe there are cleomitite deposits on Lebonath Jas or Lebonath Tras, and we'll never be able to get to them."

"I appreciate that about MalDor," Ardenai chuckled. "A personage capable of seeing the entire canvas."

"Sorry I'm late," Gideon said, "Lionel wanted a snack." He was clad only in a robe of creamy white wool, which he dropped casually to one side before entering the hot pools. "Well, Woman," he said to Ah'brianne, "you're the one who says I stink. Are you the one who's going to bathe me?"

"Form a circle," Ah'brianne laughed, "and stop growling like a troglodyte. I'll bathe Criollo, Criollo can bathe you, and you can bathe me. That way we'll get done sooner, and be ready to go when my parents get here, and yours, Criollo."

Gideon's mouth turned down in appraisal, much like his sire, and he nodded, "Acceptable."

Ardenai took a deep, steady breath and smiled down at his wife.

"You said you were talking to me, Fledermaus. What were you saying?"

"Just speculating about the Lebonathi. It can wait," she grinned. "Best be finishing our baths and getting dressed for this evening's revels. If we hurry, we'll have time for a bit of a snack, too."

"I understand the Lebonathi have dressers," Criollo said, splashing scrubsand off Gideon's back. "I met a girl, seemed very nice, by the way, coming up the stairs early the other morning, and she said it was her job, her duty, to dress the young noblewoman they brought with them. They have servants who actually put their clothes on them. Isn't that the strangest thing?"

"In some cultures it's a sign of wealth and power if you don't have to put forth any effort on your own behalf," Ardenai said, wading out of the pool and reaching for a towel.

"Would you like to have a dresser, Firstlord?" Ah'brianne asked, eyes twinkling. "I know a lot of Equi woman who would line up for such a position."

"I have a dresser," he replied with a wink, and bent to kiss the tip of his wife's elfin ear. "We'll see you downstairs for a snack. Ah'brianne, are your parents coming here, as well?"

For a moment there was uncertainty in her deep green eyes. "I asked them to. I hope that's all right."

"Of course it is," Ardenai reassured her. "They're of our keep-nave. As a matter of fact, I want them to walk in with us tonight, and then stay over. I have a task for them."

But it bothered him as he dressed – the look on her face, and the uncertainty in her eyes. She hadn't been sure of their welcome, hadn't been sure they should come to the apartments of the Dragonhorse. They would never have been uncertain of their welcome at Canyon keep, or at Sea keep. What had changed? Everything on the outside. He wondered if things were changing on the inside, as well.

He finished braiding his hair and tucked it up under itself, wishing it would grow back a little faster and wondering why Pythos had thought hair chopped off shoulder length would camouflage him better during his flight through the stars than long hair would have. In either case, it hadn't worked very well. He wiggled the circlet into place, hoping for once it wouldn't give him a headache, adjusted the heavy imperial collar, the bracelets, and, on impulse, he added the forearm knives.

"Are we serving something that has to be carved?" his wife asked, busy with her own mass of unruly curls. "Oh, drat."

"Let me," Ardenai chuckled. He gently pushed her hands away and finished braiding the last of the fresh gold sun flowers like a crown into her wealth of curls. "The season for these is waning fast. I'm glad there were some left for tonight. There. You're beautiful."

"And you're avoiding my question," she smiled, reaching for a purple over-cape.

Ardenai took it, holding it up so she could slip into it, and saying at the same time, "I'm not avoiding your question. I'm just not sure of the answer. Perhaps I am not quite sure of how these people will perceive us if we seem too passive. Of course, I'm not sure how they will perceive us in any case. Have you had any contact with them at all since their arrival?"

"Only briefly, with Naram, their Nuntius d'affaires, checking on any unusual protocols, dietary needs, that sort of thing. I know that Bashkir did that as well, but I wanted to make sure that I understood. That way I could make some requests of my own regarding the dinner and the ceremonies tonight."

"Very wise. Thank you," Ardenai said. He belted her shimmering white under-sheath with a wide gold girdle bearing the seven chevrons of the Firstlord, and straightened her luxurious cape so that it flowed out to either side. "Perfect," he smiled. "I would never in my wildest dreams have imagined that the self-willed little imp who climbed up into the lavage basin and cut her hair off while I thought she was asleep, would turn into the most beautiful woman on planet Equus."

"Whatever you want, we don't have time for it," Io drawled, "but thanks for the compliment." She turned to him with an appraising eye, and ran her hands down his bare arms, over the wide gold armbands imbedded in his flesh, and the beautiful pythons which coiled from shoulders to wrists.

"It seems rather unfair that those armbands have to show any time you're in public. You're going to be cold."

"No colder than the members of the Horse Guard, who will be wearing exactly the same dress uniform I am."

"Sorry. No," she grinned. "They're in long sleeves. The season is turning you know."

Ardenai chuckled, "I do know, and I have – what is it Marion Eletsky says – an ace up my sleeve. I know, I have no sleeves. But I do have," he paused for dramatic effect, "this!" He opened a wooden chest and from it drew a beautiful woolen robe of such deep purple as to be nearly black, which he held up for her inspection. "The sleeves have fasteners, see? They can be unfastened from the shoulder to the elbow, or from the shoulder to the wrist if I'm wearing forearm knives. Yet, if I relax my arms while seated, or fold them, it is designed so that the fullness of the sleeves covers my arms and keeps me warm. Ah'din made it for me as a surprise."

"She does amazing work," Io breathed, stroking first the velvety softness of the robe, then the insignia of the Firstlord, emblazoned in silver across each shoulder. "The seven chevrons of the Firstlord, are woven of," her fingers caressed the material, "horsehair. Silver horsehair. This is truly beautiful, Ardi. A princely gift."

Ardenai put it on, adjusted the sleeves to fit the knives, and gave it a perfunctory shake. "So much for primping," he said, "Let's find some food!" He paused outside their bedchamber and looked toward the now empty pools. "The colts seem to have bathed and exited in a timely manner. Hopefully they're getting dressed."

Io studied his profile in the dim light. "You seem much preoccupied with the young ones today, Dragonhorse. Is something on your mind? Are you missing your creppias?"

"No," he replied, not looking at her. "No, of course not. Come on. I hear my father's laughter, and I wanted to be downstairs to greet them when they came in."

They were all there: Krush and Ah'rane, Timor and Ah'mae, Teal and Ah'din – Jilfan standing awkward and silent with Abeyan and Ah'kra

– and the three youngsters, who looked up as Ardenai and Io came down the stairs. There was a sudden and utter silence. Krush set his wine glass aside and bowed deeply from the waist. "Ardenai Firstlord," he murmured, "Ah'riodin Firstwife. Equus honors us with thy presence."

"Ahimsa, my father," Ardenai said formally, nodding in his foster father's direction. "I wish thee peace. Thee, and those with thee. We are the ones honored, to share our home with thee this night."

One by one they nodded deeply, and Ardenai returned each nod, as did Io, and only she could feel the slight rise in temperature which marked his discomfort. Well, it was something they'd both have to get used to. While the Equi allowed their leaders a good deal of normalcy in their day to day lives, recognition was inevitable on state occasions, especially since this evening, dressed as he was, the Thirteenth Dragonhorse was handsome enough to stop the rotation of the planet. A striking man, and every inch a prince.

Io smiled and gave herself a little hug, the slightest motion of her elbows against her sides. She was married to the man she'd been in love with her entire life. A sidelong glance at her father let her know that he was unforgiving of the match. Unforgiving of something, at least. His eyes were cold in his smiling face, and the look he gave Ardenai, even as he bowed respectfully, smoldered with resentment. Hadn't they resolved this? Io sighed, and Ardenai gave her hand a gentle squeeze as he returned the bow.

There was an echoing chime which announced entry and the huge double doors swung open to admit The SGAS Belesprit's Captain, Marion Eletsky, her protocol officer, Oonah Pongo, Ship's Interim Doctor and head of the Science Wing, Winslow Moonsgold, and her Wing Commander, Ah'ree Kehailan Ardenai.

"You made it!" Ardenai exclaimed, striding to meet them, and Io could see the shading of wonder on their faces. For a moment, she felt sorry for her unassuming husband, who'd caught the look they'd not been able to hide, and sensed the thought they'd telegraphed at the top of their awestruck lungs. Then, as she always did, she thanked the Creator Spirit, the Wisdom Giver, that the kindest, gentlest, most intelligent man on Equus, had been handed the reins of government.

"Thank you for coming. Please, come and have a bite to eat. It could be a long evening," he was saying, and Oonah was giving him a hug, and some back-slapping was going on, and the moment of strangeness had passed. He was Ardenai Friend once again, introducing them to Timor and family, Abeyan and his wife, and urging them to help themselves to refreshments.

It was at that point that Lionel chose to make his appearance, wandering across the expanse of the main floor and wagging himself sleepily down the stairs into the family dining room. Oonah clapped her hands with delight, and her rich laughter filled the space as she hurried to scoop up the tiny dog and cuddle him under her chin. "What a precious baby you are!" she crooned. "Oh, Io, he's perfect! The perfect birthing day present! And I've missed you, yes I have, little one."

"Oh, ah ha!" Ardenai exclaimed. "I might have known it was my wife. How could I have been so silly as to think that just because she no longer looks like a trouble-maker, she isn't one."

Oonah looked from one to the other and made an apologetic face. "Oops," she murmured. "Apparently the tale has yet to be told."

"I must confess, my sister-in-law did not work alone," Ah'din said, drawing herself up to her full six feet and coming to stand beside Io. "I'm the one who suggested it in the first place. Io only agreed with me, and then made the appropriate contacts."

"Precious Equus, we're choosing up teams," Ardenai muttered in an aside to Krush. "Males against the females." Something clicked. "Oonah Pongo, you know this dog?"

"Actually," Kehailan chuckled, "I'll have to go to that side. "Oonah and I actually found the breeder, acquired the puppy, and ultimately handed him off to Criollo."

"And I, exploiting my newfound power, expedited his import papers," Teal grinned.

"Is anyone *not* in on this?" Ardenai asked, looking around. "My sister, my son, and now my brother-in-law?"

"Me," Moonsgold said soberly, standing with his arm around Gideon. "Most definitely not me. Of course I wasn't asked, except to neuter the little bugger, and by then it was a done deal, so to speak. Cute, isn't he? They told me if I did the deed I could come along tonight and eat well, spend time with Pythos, and see these fascinating people from Lebonath Jas. Really I was bribed with three things I can't resist, so it would be unfair to say I was actually a willing part of the dog acquisition team. Where is Pythos, not to change the subject or anything?"

Ardenai was suddenly aware that the old physician was missing, and turned a questioning face to his family. "He's here somewhere," Krush said. "He came ahead of us."

"He said he had a meeting with Ah'krill," Teal nodded. "He'll be there to enter with us."

And so he was, writhing with pleasure at the sight of Winslow Moonsgold and hurrying on his short legs to greet the lanky Declivian. "I am sso pleassed to ssee thee," He whispered in a sibilant hiss. "Perhapss we can ssit together at dinner and behave badly."

"I shall make every effort," Moonsgold grinned. "I have news of our old friend, Doctor Hadrian Keats, to share with you."

The Firstlord's sensitive ears perked up and his head came around in the direction of the two physicians. "You couldn't have mentioned that while we were socializing earlier?"

"Slipped my mind," Moonsgold said apologetically, though his bright gold eyes were dancing with mischief. "I was so alarmed by the looming civil war over that puppy. Really, it's just general news, not anything important, though of course I wish it was."

Ardenai sighed and turned forward again. "Are we ready?" he asked, and without waiting for an answer, gave the slightest hint of a nod to Master Bashkir in the shadows.

There was the sudden thunder of the great Equi drums, which set the very floor vibrating beneath their feet. Io put her hand over his and together they entered the Great Hall of Ceremonies, Kehailan, Gideon and Jilfan immediately behind them and the others a few paces back. Ardenai could feel Jilfan's seething displeasure at being separated from Ah'krill, but he was pleased that the boy was trying to hide it, and that he'd been obedient in coming.

Over the pounding of the drums, another noise became audible, the roar of the galleries, level upon level filled to capacity – ninety thousand voices cheering the Firstlord. Ardenai nodded graciously and tipped his head back to smile up at them, the lights glinting off the gold of his armbands. He paused in the center of the huge floor and turned to bow toward his mother, already seated on the elegantly curving rostrum at her end of the chamber, accompanied by snow white clouds of Eloi which stretched up and away in the fan of silver-green seats behind the High Priestess. Ardenai couldn't help wondering how many of them he was going to be expected to settle. A few, he had no doubt. He gave Jilfan a brief nod of dismissal, but the boy smiled, dropped his eyes and stayed with his step-brothers. Interesting, and it pleased Io, Ardenai could sense it.

He turned and faced forward toward the seven rows of dignitaries in their chairs on the long wall of the chamber, plush seating for five hundred and eighty-eight senators and ambassadors on each side of the room, and every seat was taken. He turned and acknowledged the other half of the audience before proceeding down the length of the floor, feeling like an insect in the vastness of the edifice, with its alabaster vaults and ornate pillars carved from the living stone of the mountain. The flags of Equus and her affined worlds dipped respectfully as he passed, and he was amazed, as he always was, that all this fuss should be for him.

They approached the fan of royal purple chairs over which hung a huge and ancient tapestry – the seal of the Great House of Equus – the seven stacked chevrons of the Firstlord emblazoned against a rich purple background. To one side and slightly lower hung the Corvus Eagle, Fir tree and sea of the Seventh Galactic Alliance, and, on this night, the four-spoked wind-paddle and axle representing Lebonath Jas and Lebonath Tras.

Ardenai stood with Io to his left at the center of the bottom tier, and the others filled in behind them, leaving the five remaining seats beside Ardenai empty, as well as the second row of nine. This evening, those would be filled by the dignitaries of the Lebonathi delegation.

When everyone was in place, Ardenai raised his right hand, and the drums went silent. He made the ancient gesture of greeting, passing his right hand over his left. "Ahimsa, I wish thee peace," he said, not much above a normal tone of voice, and it carried to the farthest seats. "This is a time of joy for us. We are welcoming this night a delegation from the Lebonathi Federation. Not in our recent history have they visited us, and we are honored by their coming." He flicked his left hand palm up, and in an instant, it was pitch black in the Great Hall.

There was a gasp which sounded like wind from the sea, and from the vaulted entry through which they'd just come, a rider entered at a slow canter, carrying a lighted torch. He proceeded to the far end of the hall, used his torch to light the torch which was in an ornate stand to the left of the Eloi, then wheeled his mount and backed into the boulevard-width passage beside the rostrum. Another rider appeared, and lit the torch on the other side of Ah'krill's rostrum, then backed into the shadows of that passage. A third and fourth rider appeared in the same fashion, and the torches were lit on either side of the Firstlord and his retinue. A fifth, sixth and seventh rider appeared and lit the torches on the pillars which framed the daises where sat the dignitaries, so that the whole hall was lit just enough to see. Those horsemen moved to the center of the Great Hall and stood, facing out in opposite directions, their horses' tails nearly touching. The other riders moved from the shadows and assumed like positions, so that they formed a hub. Slowly, the hub of horsemen spun around three times, then the first rider led off, the rubber covers on her horse's shoes beating quiet cadence, and the others followed from the hall into the darkness. There was a roar of appreciation from the galleries, and it made Io smile.

In the silence which followed, Ardenai leaned into his wife and whispered, "You do everything so beautifully," and the sound carried on the updrafts and created a fond chuckle from those in the gallery close by.

"It seems a great lot of fuss for us to go to," MalDor said in an obvious stage whisper from his seat halfway down the hall, "for people who stink, from a miserable wreck of a world who have nothing to offer but trouble, and who have quite probably come to beg."

"We are all guests at the table of our beloved Equus, and all of us will eat and be entertained," came Ardenai's very quiet but firm retort. "No rudeness will be tolerated in this chamber, nor at this gathering. Here, we are all one, welcoming those who have sought our friendship, or perhaps our help. It does not matter for what purpose they have come, they will be heard with courtesy and welcomed with open hearts, for that is the Equi way of doing things. If there are any who do not think they can conform to that code of behavior, they may be excused without prejudice to their chambers or their keeps."

A murmur of approval rustled through the ranks of the Equi, and for the space of thirty seconds or so there was a hiss of whispers in the Great Hall while MalDor glared and studied the rings on his fingers.

Again Ardenai ducked his head ever so slightly toward a figure in the shadows, and the voice of Bashkir, Master of the Great House, filled the Hall. "It is with pleasure that Ah'krill Ardenai Morning Star, Firstlord of Equus, the Thirteenth Dragonhorse, and Abeyan Ah'riodin Ardenai Morning Star, Primuxori of Equus, welcome the Lebonathi delegation to the Great House of Equus."

The drums began to beat a measured cadence, and the musicians of the Great House joined in, playing an extended fanfare written by Master Composer Anseri for this occasion. Ah'brianne reached on either side of her and grabbed the boys' hands, squeezing them and whispering, "I'm so excited! This is so much closer than being in the galleries! Oooh, here they come!"

"We see them," Criollo said patiently.

"I hope MalDor keeps his opinions to himself for the rest of the evening," she went on. "I was so embarrassed. I'm glad Ardenai spoke sharply to him. I just hope the Lebonathi didn't hear. That would get us off on the wrong lead, wouldn't it? They certainly look serious, don't they? I hope all these people aren't scaring them. That ... I think it's a woman ... in the long black and gold robes looks like a person of authority, and she's bald, or her head is shaven! Don't you think that's strange? She looks like a huge pearl in a gold setting, being so pale and all. I wonder why that woman behind her is heavily veiled like that, like a bride in those ancient flickernick tales. It's a wonder she can walk at all in that tight skirt, poor thing. The girl with her isn't all twisted up in cloth like that." Gideon's hand became uncomfortably tight on her arm and she subsided, wiggling from time to time with anticipation as the delegation made its way slowly toward Ardenai, who had stepped down to floor level with Io to greet them.

They came to a halt, and the music with them. MalDor was correct. These people had an unpleasant odor about them – like something dead. Ardenai wondered how the horses would react if any one of the delegation got too close. He made the ancient gesture of greeting, passing right hand over left, and said, "Ahimsa, I wish thee peace. I am Ardenai, and this is my wife, Ah'riodin. We welcome you on behalf of the Equi people."

The two men in front bowed deeply from the waist, their pale eyes glowing red in the light from the torches, and from behind them and slightly to one side a third man stepped, accompanied by the woman in the gold robes. "I am...Naram," he said, and Ardenai recognized him as the man who had threatened him the night before. The Firstlord hid his smirk, Naram his startlement. "I am Nuntius d'affaires for the Autarkhos of the Lebonathi Federation. This is the Lady Samarra, Anchoress of Womankind." The woman nodded and, at a backhanded gesture from Naram, stepped back. Naram paid her no more attention.

"Please allow me to introduce Girsu," he gestured to the man on Ardenai's left, "Secretary of the minority party of the High Council of The Lebonathi," he then gestured to the man on Ardenai's right, "and Halaf, Secretary General of the High Council of The Lebonathi. Together, they advise the Most Wise Lord, Eridu. They wish to speak on behalf of our people and our government."

What an odd combination of terms, Ardenai thought. *How can you be an Autarkhos and a Federation at the same time?*

He stopped his musings, nodded his assent, and the man introduced as Girsu, the minority secretary, took a step forward. He was not tall, but squarely built and rather thick-set, as were most of them. He had eyes that, upon close inspection, were a very pale blue, not colorless, and his hair was blond, not white. He was dressed elegantly in black and white, and he had a pleasant, though slightly guarded smile. "We are pleased to be here," he said. "We wish to thank your mother, High Priestess Ah'krill for her invitation."

Ardenai's expression didn't change, but he saw his wife's shoulders jerk just the slightest bit. Had Ah'krill invited them at this specific time, or had she issued a general invitation to visit anytime, as a gracious guest would do in the home of another? It was a question which bore asking, and as usual, he hadn't thought to do that. He gave himself a mental whack in the middle of the forehead, and said, "Her forethought pleases me, and serves Equus well. You are welcome here. How may we serve you?"

"We do not need anything material from you, nor do we seek your services," he replied, "only your friendship, and your wise council. Too long have we kept to ourselves while affairs swept by us in the outside worlds. We would change that, and no planet is more noteworthy for its incisive assessment of galactic affairs than Equus."

"You honor us," Ardenai murmured.

"You honor yourselves by your service to and friendship with others," Girsu responded. "You have been at peace within your own borders for all of your history. Your planet is pristine, and your people healthy and happy. You are a people of firm moral codes. You honor the Gods, and one another. In the councils of the galaxy no voice is more respected than yours. You are quick to ride to the aid of your friends, and to succor even those who hate you.

"We Lebonathi have been called a suspicious lot. Xenophobic. Some have even called us jingoistic. We choose to think of ourselves as discerning. Long have we watched Equus and how it conducts its affairs. It was you who chose to visit us, and our government felt that you visited us for no other reason than to extend your sincere friendship. It was Equus who reached out to us two years ago, and we would return the gesture."

Halaf stepped impatiently forward at that point, and again nodded to the Firstlord. He was dressed much like his counterpart, but his skin was truly stark white. His eyes were nearly colorless but shading to pink, as was his hair. Almost, Ardenai thought, as if it had wanted to be red early on, but couldn't muster the courage for so bold a statement. He was taller than Girsu, gaunt rather than pudgy, and slightly round shouldered. The penciled set of his mouth said he hadn't been particularly pleased with Girsu's speech, and he stuck out his chin and looked up the length of his long, thin nose at Ardenai.

"The Autarkhos of the Lebonathi Worlds congratulates you on your Rising to Firstlord," he said. His voice was as thin as he, reedy, and to a musician's ear, slightly flat in tone. Not an easy voice to listen to. "We, too, are powerful worlds, ruled by a single, powerful leader and a wise, and widely represented council. We understand the need to bind ourselves fast one to another with ties stronger than mere political affiliation. We know that all the lines written on all the documents ever signed and sealed with good intentions, cannot match the affiliations created by blood, and the giving of flesh gifts."

He took a deep breath, and assessed for a few heartbeats the formidable alien who stood in front of him: the deeply scarred, gold-bound arms with their elegant serpent tattoos, the incongruity of a soft, full mouth paired with dragon's eyes, and the low, resonant voice which rumbled up from deep inside his soul, like the soft, patient growl of some huge beast, awaiting the approach of its prey. A man who knew the extensible strength of his physical, intellectual and political power and was comfortable with it. Most definitely not an imposter, nor a weak man, nor, at first observation, a cruel one. A man sure enough of himself to marry a woman not of his own species, or at least not entirely so. A beauty she was, though, no doubt about it. She radiated intelligence and passion like a small sun, her warmth nearly palpable at this proximity. And the Firstlord adored her. It was obvious from the way he maintained contact with her as he listened, his arm just brushing against hers, his head inclining toward her from time to time as though they were exchanging thoughts.

Halaf reminded himself that they might well be doing exactly that, and it made him uncomfortable. He wondered if they were secretly mocking him, mocking Girsu. He'd spoken too openly, too intimately for a first encounter. They should never have brought the man, but Eridu had insisted on it, as a gesture to the minority party, he'd said. More likely it was because Girsu's ward was a close servant of Princess Eridi. Well, they were paying for his naiveté. Now it was up to Halaf to salvage what of their dignity he could. He realized it was silent, and took up his discourse.

"Knowing that the Firstlord mates with many to forge both bloodlines and alliances, Our Most Wise Lord Eridu, has sent you the most magnanimous of gifts, Firstlord." He turned and extended his hand, and the heavily veiled girl stepped forward, head bowed to stand beside him.

"This," he said, "is the Princess Eridi. She is the eldest living daughter of Our Most Wise Lord Eridu, and since her birth sixteen years ago, she has been prepared as a fleshgift for you. She is trained in the sexual arts for which the Lebonathi are rightly praised, and, having now reached full and regular menses, she is ready to bear you a child, or many children, as you wish. She has not lain with a man, and her maidenhead is for none but you, Ardenai Firstlord. Will you accept her?"

At the mention of her age a buzz had grown in the galleries, and Ardenai made a slight gesture with one hand toward the galleries. It was instantly quiet."Let me see her," He said, and the Anchoress carefully removed the heavy white veil which covered her head and face to reveal the countenance of the young girl Ardenai had found weeping beneath the ancient trees of Equus. She did not look at him, and so did not recognize him. Her eyes remained glued to the floor.

Samarra was reaching for the front of her gown to unfasten the frogs and open it, when Ardenai said, "Not here. Not now. If this is something which protocol requires, we will do it in a more private place, for the sake of the lady." He reached for her hand, and when he took it there was the slightest tingle of pleasure which traveled up his arm and through his body to lodge in his loins. There was an aura about her, a slight smell, that was definitely attractive, and Ardenai wondered if it was being artificially generated. Whatever it was, it was unmistakably sexual in nature.

"Princess Eridi, look at me," he said gently, and when she raised her eyes to his, she blinked a moment, then gasped, and her mouth formed a little O of surprise that made Ardenai smile. "What says the lady in all of this? Is this something to which you agree?"

"I do...agree," she whispered, and again dropped her eyes.

Ardenai wondered, even at that moment, why Kehailan, the Twelfth Dragonhorse, had refused so lavish a gift, and if it would be to the betterment of the Thirteenth Dragonhorse to do likewise. But he did not refuse, because he knew it could cost the girl her life if he did. He brought her palms together, briefly touching just her fingertips with his forehead. He released her immediately and nodded to Halaf and Naram. "Tell Lord Eridu that his gift is precious indeed, and that Equus accepts the Princess Eridi into the Great House."

There was a roar of applause from galleries which Ardenai had momentarily forgotten were there. It made him jump a little, and it made Eridi jump a lot. When the noise had died down, Ardenai said, "It is not within my power nor desire to make a fleshgift of another person's life, and our beautiful horses would soon die on your planet, which is inhospitable to most of the animal life we know. But surely there must be some way in which I can repay such a sacrifice. May I send doctors, educators, engineers, priestesses, historians, musicians? Certainly there is something Equus can offer Lebonath Jas, which will approximate the richness we have gained this day."

"Going home to Lebonath Jas knowing that the princess is pregnant with your child will be riches enough," Halaf said. "And when the child is born, bring the princess to visit her father, so that he may meet his grandson and see his daughter once again."

The request caught Ardenai off guard, and he sensed the sudden concerned undercurrent of the assemblage. The thought of intercourse with a child was repugnant to the Equi, and Eridi, by all Equi standards, was a child. He closed his eyes for a second and sent a single thought to the galleries, *"Trust me."* Then he opened his eyes, smiled, and said aloud, "We do not..." That wouldn't do. "She isn't..." Not any better. He took a breath, and felt the galleries holding theirs. "She will have to be schooled first in our ways. These are all details which can be worked out over dinner, and in further negotiations between us in the days which follow." He was trying not to sound lame and terrified though, despite his preparation, he was both, and all the time he was thinking, *Io, help! I can't just end this so abruptly. What do I say now?*

"As you know," Io said, stepping in front of Eridi and reaching for both her hands, "we are a people whose very existence is interwoven with horses. Now that you are going to be bound to the Equi, you, too, will be intimately associated with horses. We knew that we could not send horses home to your people, but, anticipating the gift of yourself, Princess Eridi, we chose a horse for you. It is with pleasure that we give you the mare, Kantara, for your own while you are here."

The lights rose slightly, and through the main archways came two grooms, leading with twisted cords of maroon velvet, a beautiful golden mare with a snow white mane and tail, a red colt trotting beside her. Io took the girl by her arm and walked through the Lebonathi delegation to meet the animal as it paced toward them, freeing Ardenai from being the center of attention, and drawing the course of events off in another direction. He exhaled sharply with relief, and felt his heart swell with pride in his Primuxori. His beautiful, quick-thinking partner. He wanted to throw his arms around her and make love to her on the spot.

When I said you were a trouble-maker this evening? I didn't mean it. You know I like the puppy. And you know I love you. You're a life saver.

I love it when you grovel, Io replied, *but this really doesn't solve your problem for very long. They do expect you to have intercourse with this little girl, and all of Equus expects you not to. This is not something that can be fixed with the gift of a horse, even one this pretty.*

Pythos' voice cut into their thoughts. *Sorry to eavesdrop. Worry about the diplomatic aspects of this, my darlings, and let others deal with the medical details.*

"Please," Ardenai said, breathing a sigh of relief and turning to the rest of the delegation, "Allow Master Bashkir to seat you. This presentation will take but a few minutes, and then we will be entertained by the Horse Guard of the Great House of Equus."

Bashkir stepped forward and began showing the delegation to their seats, and Girsu stood with Ardenai, watching Io and Eridi petting Kantara. "She will learn to love it here," he said very quietly. "She loves the idea of animals and plants and being out in the open air."

"Of those things, we have plenty," Ardenai smiled.

Gideon appeared at his elbow and bowed formally to both men. "Sire," he said, "if you will excuse me, I must ready my horse for the evening's entertainment."

"Of course," Ardenai nodded. The boy kissed his father's temple and disappeared into the shadows.

"A most handsome young man. He's just about Eridi's age, isn't he?" Girsu asked innocently.

Ardenai turned his head very slowly and met the man's unflinching gaze. "A year older," he replied, "still just a child."

"I understand," Girsu replied, and one corner of his mouth turned up a little.

▲ ▲ ▲ ▲ ▲ ▲ ▲

"She's very bright. Given the opportunity, she's capable of learning a great deal."

You know her well then?" Io asked, observing the duo across the dimly lit table.

"I do," Girsu replied, nodding in the girl's direction. "I've known her since she was a babe-in-arms." He appeared to think a moment, as if he wanted to add something, then abruptly averted his eyes. "You have such a variety of food, and all of it is delicious. This is very good. What do you call this?" He held up the creamy green item in question with his eating sticks, one hand under it to keep it from falling.

"It's called verdanbutter. We spread it on our flatwraps, like butter, hence the name."

"And how do they grow?"

"On trees. You've not had a chance to try them before?"

Girsu looked momentarily unhappy. "Very little grows on trees on my planet, except dates and that sort of thing. As a matter of fact, very little grows on my planet at all, aside from herds of caronai, which provide our main source of sustenance. For less important food sources we are dependent on what can be grown underground or in water under shade, which is adequate in quantity, but limited in variety. We used to import some things from off-world, but it's prohibitively expensive. The Nargawerlders are the only ones we've ever dealt with, and they're neither honest nor reliable. We tried buying fruit and other foodstuffs from them, but half of it was spoiled when it got to us, and the last shipment nearly killed us all off with whatever kind of bacterium was in it. Whether or not it was intentional we never found out, but we learned our lesson and bought no more from them."

"It took us a long time to get back to eating what is in season in our own gardens, and to stop being dependent on imports from other worlds or even other regions. Look over there, she's smiling at last. I think Eridi is beginning to relax with my husband."

Girsu smiled at Io and nodded. "It was very kind of you to give up your seat to her. Halaf is momentarily pleased. He was hoping to marry Eridi to Ardenai tonight and have her pregnant tomorrow. Finding the Firstlord already mated, and madly in love with his wife, is a big disappointment, and not just to him, I might add. How long have you two been married?"

"Not long. A few seasons."

"You seem like such dear old friends. Like you have been together for many years."

"We have been," Io chuckled. "Ardenai and his wife Ah'ree raised me after my mother died. My father was away most of the time, and Ardenai was, for a long time, the only father I knew. He was my first teacher when I was a five-year-old. He taught me to ride, and to think for myself, and to go after what I wanted in life. After his wife died, going after what I wanted, included him."

"And now you have him. It must be hard, sharing his love with so many women."

Io shook her mass of peach-colored curls and sobered a little. "I share his body with other women – the purest get of Equus, as is written of old, and required of all who rise to be Firstlord. But I do not share his love. Of that, I am convinced, and in that, I am comforted." She shot a quick glance at the high priestess.

"The Dragonhorse has not one intention of having...of making love to Eridi, does he?"

The question was abrupt and pointed, and it left Io sputtering for a moment, wondering if Girsu had ulterior motives. If he did, they were well hidden under a layer of concern. "I'm sure he will do his duty by her, if it's what she truly desires and the Great House allows it," she hedged, watching Eridi trying to master her eating sticks under Ardenai's patient, if thoroughly left-handed tutelage. Ardenai had seated the girl between himself and Naram on his left, with Marion and Kehailan down the table, and with Halaf on his right side, Teal beyond him with Ah'din and two other members of the delegation. Next to them, sat Ah'rane and Krush with the Anchoress Samarra. Across from them, Moonsgold and Pythos were laughing and joking, creating a sound barrier so that Io could have an untrammeled discussion with Girsu.

"Just not any time soon?"

Io took a deep breath. "No. Not any time soon." She turned to Gideon, who was on her left next to Oonah Pongo, and pointed toward the platter of intricately shaped alcibus croquettes within his reach. She took one, offered the plate to Girsu, then handed it back to Gideon and spoke again without looking at the Lebonathi. "On Equus, the rape of a child, is one of only two crimes punished by death. You rape a child, you die, period. She's barely a woman even by your standards and a fairly young child by ours. We will keep her, and love her, and teach her Equi ways, even as we learn from her. If, when the time is ripe she desires it, and the Great House endorses it, she will bend under the weight of the Dragonhorse. So, tell me," she said, pointing subtly with her eating sticks, "about the two young men over there who are trying so hard to look disinterested. Criollo has tried to engage them, so has Gideon. Who are they?"

Girsu sighed and looked put-upon. "They are Prince Basra and his older brother, Prince Addur. They are Eridu's sons, and Halaf's nephews.

Halaf's sister, their mother, is a concubine, a subordinate wife to Eridu. Eridu wanted them to come along for the experience. As subjugate sons, they will be expected to serve in the political realm or the priesthood, the flamen, when they are of age. Right now Prince Basra is still in school. Addur has finished and is being groomed as a diplomat."

"I see," said Io, and shoved a bit of food in her mouth to mask her expression. She didn't like their attitude and she didn't trust their motives one little bit. The way they were looking at Ah'brianne made her tremble inside. "And who is the pretty young girl down the table there, next to Criollo? She's unusually dark for a Lebonathi, isn't she?"

"That is Jasreth," Girsu smiled. He cocked an eyebrow and murmured with dramatic emphasis, "She's a near-surface dweller, and as wild as the winds which sweep the ancient city. She is lovely, isn't she?"

"It sounds as if you know her as well as you know Eridi."

"I do. Jasreth is my niece. My wife and I raised her after her parents were killed, much as the Dragonhorse raised you. She and Eridi have been fast friends for years, so Jas wangled the job of being her dresser, and came along for the adventure. It's going to be heart-wrenching when we have to separate them."

"And why do you have to do that?"

Girsu blinked at her. "We're leaving Eridi here. She's a fleshgift."

"I understood that part. That doesn't mean you have to separate them, does it?"

"You mean leave Jasreth? Here?"

"So, when it's your child it's different, is it?" Io asked coolly. "Eridi is the easy sacrifice, because she isn't yours?"

"Lady Io, you are a hothead, aren't you?" Girsu laughed. "My hesitation was merely an indicator of my amazement. To keep Jasreth, to allow her to continue to serve Eridi, and to serve you, is a very generous offer."

Io blushed, then chuckled a little. "If you are to believe the Firstlord, yes, I am a hothead, and I do apologize. The gift of a child whom Eridu wants us to immediately impregnate, has unsettled all of us – none more so than my husband and me. In any case, Jasreth won't be a servant. Children that age are students. They go to school, and they have chores at home, and if they wish, they serve the Great House as pages, but they are not servants. The concept as you understand it is really quite foreign to us. We serve each other, and we serve ourselves, and everybody has a job, *after* everybody is a student. That will include both Jasreth and Eridi. If they choose to stay, they will follow the rules."

"I see. And for how long are children students on your world?" Girsu twinkled, still highly amused. She really was a lovely, passionate woman – small by Equi standards, but formidable. She was taller than most of the Papilli he'd seen in pictures, and slightly less fragile looking. That, must be her Equi blood coming out. She and Jasreth would get along well, he thought.

"School begins for our young when they are five," Io said stiffly, sensing his mirth. "Compulsory education ends when they are twenty-six. At that point they are considered young adults. Most of our children go on to Lycee for another four to ten years, after which they travel, or take up the work they have chosen for themselves. Some marry that young, most do not."

"You live such a long time," Girsu sighed wistfully. "There is such luxury in that lifespan of yours, time to educate oneself, and to travel, and to choose…so many things. And Jasreth, could go to school? A real school, with both boys and girls in it?"

Io gave him a questioning look. "You sound like there are other kinds."

She was baiting him, and he knew it, but to get the truth, one must also be truthful, so he took a deep breath and began. "On my world, yes. These days. Our world was dying, people were starving, desperate to live from day to day. Our population had exploded, our educational system collapsed because of the inability to agree on what should be taught, and because our students had no discipline and no consequences. Because we could no longer educate our young our economy collapsed. We called it the Kaiein – the Burning Time – and it was our faith that got us through it. We gave ourselves and our government over to the Gods and to the white priests, and they saved us. As the flamen repaired things, and our values changed and became more conservative – not that it isn't better this way – it was deemed the will of the Gods that the girls stay home out of the way of temptation...anyway, they're not as well...they don't get...need as much education as boys do. All most of them do is raise young, or become anchoresses. It's good. They're our precious possessions, and well protected. They're happy that way."

"And you believe every word of that, which is why it flows so easily off your tongue," Io drawled.

Girsu just waved his hand as though he had a bug on his nose, and glanced again at Jasreth, then at Eridi and Ardenai. "Who would protect her? Who would take care of Jasreth?"

"Here, she wouldn't need protecting," Io said patiently. "She is Eridi's friend, and so would fall under the same care as she. She would become a fosterling of the Great House. She would go home with us as part of our household, and, as she makes friends, she would go home with them, and learn from them, just as Eridi will most likely do."

Girsu's brow clouded a little and he shook his head. "Don't make too many assumptions about Eridi, Lady Io, and what Eridi will let Jasreth do. You may not be used to servants and being served, but she is. Her family is wealthy and powerful, and even though she has trained hard, and has, in many ways been abused by your standards, she is used to being waited on. She's not like hardy old rules-be-damned Jasreth down there, already finding out from that tall, auburn haired girl what sports are to be played and what adventures are to be had here. Eridi has one purpose in life and one only, to bear a child for the Firstlord of Equus. It has been drummed into her head until she thinks it's God's will for her, her only purpose for living, and she will pursue it single-mindedly to the detriment of herself and everybody else, if need be, even to the ultimate detriment of Equus."

"Her plans may have to change," Io muttered, and the Firstlord caught her attention. To the well trained eye he looked slightly vexed, and Io excused herself and moved around the table. She kissed the top of his head and laid her temple against his dark hair, her arms coming over his shoulders to lock across his breastbone.

Have you thought about what a truly strange gift this is, Io? They have given me a living, breathing child. What in the Ten Tribute Worlds of Equus do I need with a child? And this one has some exceedingly odd ideas.

Having as yet no answer, Io ignored the question. *Did you notice that earlier this evening I could understand you without touching you? Were you suitably impressed?*

Now that you mention it, yes, I was. Mostly I was impressed with your forethought. The gifting of that mare was... he paused and his fingers drummed restlessly on the table as he thought. *It was almost as though you knew, not generally, but very specifically, what was coming, wasn't it, First-wife? Who, exactly, prepared you for that?*

She chuckled and shrugged, but the name had already flashed through her mind, and she was entirely too close to her husband to hide it. *Ah'krill.* Ah'krill had prepared her for a few things this evening, hadn't she?

If Ardenai's good mood had been slipping, it was now gone entirely. He was tired, he was vaguely annoyed by something he couldn't quite put his finger on, and there was an underlying agitation setting in that worried him. Was he coming into heat already? Was this girl with her odd smell and sensuous ways bringing him in? He couldn't afford it. "Gideon," he said, rather more sharply than he meant to, and the boy looked up from his conversation with Girsu across Io's vacated chair. "I would like you to take Princess Eridi..." Where? He needed to be rid of this girl. He was wishing he'd never seen this girl, never heard of her, and he wasn't sure why. She was lovely in her own way, and a pleasant enough conversationalist. "Take the princess ..."

To visit with me? Came the amused suggestion.

"...to visit with the High Priestess," Ardenai said aloud, and sent a brief, grateful nod in his mother's direction. "We have been lax in our duty to her."

"Of course, Sire," Gideon responded, and immediately rose from his seat and came around the table to where Eridi was sitting.

"Eridi," he smiled, "I would like you to meet my grandmother,

Ah'krill. She is the religious leader of our people, and the one who will be responsible for some of your training."

The girl looked up at him. "I need to be trained?" she asked. Her voice was soft, and sweet, and Gideon felt himself prickling a little as though she had rubbed the words on him, like honey on wounded flesh. "I can assure you, I do not."

"Certainly not as a lady, or as a princess," Gideon smiled. "But as an Equi, yes. Just as I am being trained. Come. She awaits us."

"My Lord Ardenai?" she whispered, bowing her head in submission. He gave her a palms-up gesture, and she rose and slipped her arm through Gideon's.

Io took the seat Eridi had vacated, and looked into her husband's troubled face. "What's wrong, Beloved?"

"I don't know," he replied, fingers still drumming the table top. "Something is just...I don't know. I need to know where Senator Konik is. I need him home safe."

Io blinked. "Where did that come from?"

"It's been right here," he growled, tapping his forehead just a little too hard. "Right here in my mind, at the top, in the back, in the corners, but always right here. He didn't disappear, he was kidnapped. I know he was. He's mixed up in this – I know he is. And all the time you were talking to Girsu, Eridi kept looking at you, and she'd say things like, 'I hope she's not jealous of me and my purpose,' which is, of course exactly what she was hoping for from you, and then she'd say these incredibly mature and sexual things to me, and I was both appalled and titillated." He caught his own mood and said nothing more, lapsing into a dark and meditative silence.

Io looked at the Firstlord with something approaching alarm. He seemed almost irrational in a quiet sort of way, certainly not his usual reasoned and good humored self. "These two things are tied together how, exactly?"

Ardenai stared at her for a long, long moment in silence, and then he smiled, and began to chuckle. "I have no idea, my love, but they are. I know it. I can smell Konik on these people's breath somehow. I don't know.

Maybe I'm just scared. I have not a single clue what I'm going to do with that girl, where she's going to live, what her immediate purpose will be. I have my life in order, all planned out, and suddenly I'm Firstlord. I manage, with the help of my companions and my bride, to regroup. I have everything set to go in a certain direction, and Konik disappears. I manage, with the help of my companions and my bride, to regroup and set off again in that same direction, having added Konik's disappearance into my agenda. Now, up pops this princess from a strange world, who..."

He was interrupted by Naram, who bowed beside him and said with a great deal of suppressed annoyance, "The princess Eridi has been in your possession for more than three hours, and you have not yet bled her. Now she is with your son, who is probably sexually active, and beyond arm's reach of your heart. This is not permissible in our faith."

"I do not mean to give offense," Ardenai responded, rising from his chair to face the man. He had the pettish urge to ask Naram if he was supposed to keep the girl tucked under his arm like a saddle, but he refrained. "Please, tell me what is proper among your people, so that you may report back to her father that I am respectful of the princess and the traditions of her culture."

"You must satisfy yourself that she is whole."

"That she has all her fingers and toes? She seems fine to me."

"That she is a virgin," Naram grated.

Ardenai had known this was coming since those first minutes in the Great Hall, and had prepared himself with an answer. "Very well," he said smoothly, "If it is important to you that I am satisfied of her wholeness in that respect, we will remove to a private space where my physician, and High Priestess Ah'krill can do that."

"But you are her master," Naram sputtered, "I expect you to bleed her." Ardenai held up a placating hand.

"You have your rules, Nuntius, I have mine. I am not a free agent. The seed of the Great House of Equus dwells within me, but it does not belong to me. My physician decides when it is to be given, and my mother decides whom it enters. Pythos will determine her ripeness, Ah'krill her worthiness. In that, I have no choice. I will touch her in a sexual manner when I am allowed to do so, and not before."

"Do you not bed your lovely young wife at will? Did she not recently lose the daughter she was carrying for you?"

Ardenai winced with the memory. "My wife, is my wife, and of an acceptable age to be married. Since my rising to be Firstlord, she is the only one I am permitted to set my head against for sexual purposes without the express request of the Great House or one of its representatives." If not a lie, it was an exaggeration, somewhat assuaged in Ardenai's mind by the addition of the last four words. It was Teal who had asked him to set his head against Ah'nora, to put a High Equi son in her belly against his possible demise on the war grounds of Calumet. It had been a wise suggestion, and one Pythos had agreed with. Who better represented the Great House of Equus than those two trusted advisors?

The Lebonathi nodded, though his face was sullen, and the Firstlord breathed a silent sigh of relief. So far, so good. He had no desire to insult these people, though he found the gift of a human being exceedingly backward and odd. He understood the concept of blood alliances, and he understood the Lebonathi's deep desire to establish such an alliance with the Affined Equi Worlds. Only once in every seven hundred or so years could it be done, and, apparently, last time around, no such alliance had been forged. Nonetheless, it seemed a bizarre thing to be happening between two reasoned races, especially with him in the middle of the fray. He realized he'd felt the same way facing first Sarkhan, then Konik, armed only with his wits and a pair of forearm knives. Ah yes, the forearm knives. He unstrapped them and sent a thought to Bashkir, who received them, nodded and disappeared.

Ardenai knew his duty, and his manners, and even though he was appalled on the inside, he was smiling on the outside, and raised his hand to beckon Halaf and Girsu to follow him to the place where Ah'krill was sitting, talking to Gideon and Eridi. "Mother," he said, bowing in her direction, "may I present..."

"Yes, yes, I know who they are," Ah'krill said, waving them aside with an impatient hand. They stopped in their tracks and stood gawping at her, and the room fell silent as the tension made itself felt. “Barbaric thing to be doing with this child, this young priestess, having her inspected like a filly in heat, in order that you may breed her to the stallion of your choice. Does a prize stallion choose his mares? No, he is bred to those who will best serve the bloodline. With Eridi I am thrilled, make no mistake, but with the manner in which she was presented, and to whom, I am not pleased in the least. She should have been presented to me, to be kept by me, as are many of the other young women with whom the Dragonhorse will mate.

“She has been presented to Ardenai Firstlord, and I have no power and no reason to remove her. Eridi finds herself in my son’s tender care, and in that she will be well served, but she is on the time line of the Eloi, and to that, both she and the Dragonhorse must submit, and that is final. Now, we shall retire to a chamber which has been prepared for this, though we have no ceremony for such a purpose. If there is one which you must perform, feel free to do so, but you will not harm or defile this young woman.” She linked her arm through Eridi’s and led her out of the banquet hall in a silence so complete their footfalls could be heard on the alabaster floors. Pythos rose from his chair, excused himself from Moonsgold’s company, and followed the two females.

Ardenai watched his birth mother’s retreating back and resisted the urge to applaud as if he were at a polo match. Brilliantly played. Absolutely brilliant. He offered his wife his arm, then nodded to the dazed Lebonathi delegation, excluded Halaf’s glowering nephews with a warning palm, and followed the High Priestess. He could hear Halaf’s irate whisper behind him. “It is not too late to take our princess from the clutches of these savages and go home, Samarra. Look around you, how the women flaunt themselves. Eridi will become as sinful as they. Please…”

There was a shushing from someone, and they proceeded in silence into the chamber, where Eridi stood waiting with Ah’krill. The Lebonathi formed an awkward line on the far side of the room, and Ardenai and Io joined Pythos next to the girl. The Anchoress moved forward, placing herself on the other side of the princess. “The cleansing ceremony which prepared this woman to be given for her people, has been performed in the bleeding moon," she said in a high-pitched sing-song voice. "The blood which the Firstlord will draw, this woman sheds for her people. The child which this woman brings forth in blood, is the binding gift of the Gods upon the world of the Lebonathi and the world of the Equi. New life is brought forth and is given to the Gods. This is the body which will serve the Gods at the pleasure of the Dragonhorse."

With the last words, the Anchoress began to unfasten the frogs which held the girl's sheath in place, and when it was unfastened all the way to the floor, she stepped behind her and pulled the dress back off her shoulders and down her arms, leaving her naked. She shook the garment gently, and a light, almost imperceptible musk filled the air.

Ardenai heard himself gasp, though he didn't mean to. Eridi was perfect. Her breasts were full, with large, upturned nipples that had hardened with the rush of cooler air against them. Her belly was slightly rounded and soft, as it is on women who do not do vigorous exercise, and her blonde pubic hair was luxuriously thick and curled, and he knew it was fragrant. He could feel himself beginning to tremble slightly, and crossed his arms to hide his hands. His robe and the blessedly strong support of his riding britches hid the erection he didn't even try to control. He knew it was useless. His phallus had already slid from its protective sheath, and he could feel dampness between his thighs as his semen began to flow with the desire to mount. Eridi took the palms of her dimpled white hands and stroked the sides of her breasts, caressing them until beads of liquid welled up from the nipples and balanced there like dew on the lip of a flower, and when his eyes moved again to her thighs, they were trembling, and wetness was rolling in white droplets down her legs.

The Equi mustered every ounce of self-control he had, and resisted the urge to throw everyone else out of the room and bury his mouth against that wealth of pubic hair, to lick those beads of dew off those lovely young breasts, to accept the invitation in her eyes to bury his phallus in her and mix her blood with his semen. He could hear her soft voice, crying out with pleasure, begging him to push harder, and harder. He didn't lick his lips, he didn't squeeze his eyes shut, nor did he open his mouth to say anything, because he knew his teeth would chatter with urgency if he did.

How could he have thought this was a useless and potentially annoying child? How could he bear to wait a year, or a day, or even a minute? All he could think about was the need to lay across her back and feel her neck in his teeth. She turned slowly, and bent over in sexual display. Then she stood up, and turned back forward, her face slightly flushed from having her head lower than her heart. Pythos flicked Ardenai with his long, sympathetic tongue in passing, and stepped up to the girl. She leaned back a little away from him, her eyes registering horror and disgust, but she was well trained, and, like a filly at her first breeding, she stood still for the inspection. She spread her legs slightly, expecting his fingers, and found herself caressed gently by his tongue against the side of her face.

"Sshe iss intact," the old dragon hissed, and stepped back.

Ardenai barely heard him. His vision felt cloudy, as well, and his head was throbbing with every lunge of his heart. He half-heard Ah'krill ask Io to take the girl behind an ornate, horse-hide screen, dress her and then take her back to the banquet.

When Io was behind the screen with Eridi, Ah'krill made a slight beckoning motion to Samarra, and slipped her arm through her son's. "Come," she said, "I have blood for thee to spill." He didn't resist. Images of Eridi were all he could see as he stumbled along, the fragrance of her body as she was disrobed, the way her fingers moved gently over her breasts, with their dripping, erect nipples.

The room to which she led him was an ithyphallic chamber, very dimly lit, pulsing with color, redolent with incense, its walls hung with images of men with women, men with men, women with women. The furnishings, the rugs, the figurines, all invited coitus, stimulating the mind and the libido. There was a priapic bench, its elongated shape and straddling shaft representing the erect male phallus, its height set to make intercourse comfortable for long periods of time with the male standing, as was the traditional Equi way of ceremonial mating.

"You do not need to control yourself," she was saying, unfastening his robe and laying it aside, then his tunic, then, somehow, his boots and britches. There were Eloi helping her, but Ardenai was uncaring. All he could think about was Eridi.

The woman who glided toward him from the steam of the pools was very pale, and her blonde pubic hair was thick and curled up toward her belly and out toward the tops of her shapely thighs. "Come to me," she said in a voice barely above a whisper, and her hands stroked her breasts invitingly as Ardenai went to her, his breath heavy with desire. He was shaking hard with the passion he couldn't seem to get under control, and his awkwardness at that moment, gave him that moment in which to think. How…had this gotten to this point? What…exactly…was happening?

His mother had said he didn't have to control himself. His mother had said...he didn't have to control himself. Why was that? He realized it had been some time since he'd had a cogent thought. He fought the pounding in his head, and the blindness, and the desire, hiding his effort by mopping the sweat from his face with both hands. Instead of touching her, which he knew would be his undoing, he motioned toward the priapic bench, its outline red in the dim light.

She walked to it, positioned herself on hands and knees facing away from him, then dropped to her forearms in the front, leaving her buttocks elevated. She moved sensuously, flexing first one thigh, then the other, until she felt his weight come down on top of her, not all at once, but more carefully, almost gently as he stretched out across her back. His teeth sought her neck, but he had not yet penetrated. She could tell he was being thoughtful and worried that he was already regaining his senses. It was inevitable, of course. Samarra had said the hypnotic properties of the plant esters would last but a short time. Still, with luck, she would be able to capture the essence of a daughter. A tiny priestess for the Great House of Equus.

"I hate to disappoint you," came the dangerous growl in her ear, "but the first daughter belongs to Ah'riodin. You, are much bigger, Priestess Ah'nis. For you, I have a strapping son. But not this night. Tell your bead rattling ilk that I will not be ambushed in this manner."

She snarled with outrage, but he had her in the inferior position and his teeth closed on her neck, leaving a painful bite. He stood up, caught her easily in his arms and carried her, squirming and cursing, to the cold pools, where he waded in to his waist and dunked her, head and all, over and over in the icy water until she cried out for mercy.

He carried her out again and set her on her feet. "Not quite so hot to trot, Priestess Ah'nis?" It was a vulgar question, and even as he said it, he regretted it.

She glared at him and said through her teeth, "I will never bear you a son of my own will, Dragonhorse. You have made mock of me, and my holy duties and I will never forgive you for that."

"Good," he said softly. He unhooked a thick robe from the wall beside them, settled it around her shoulders, and his fingers momentarily caressed her cheek. "You have been made mock of this evening, Priestess. You have been used shamelessly. I just hope you realize, it was not by me."

"No," she said through her teeth. "No."

He wasn't sure what that meant, but she didn't pull away from him, and if it was not respect he saw in her green eyes, there was a healthy dose of fear. Rather a satisfying departure from her traditional haughty gaze, he thought. Another old adversary. Another woman his mother had considered as a wife for him. This one, was still a contender. And yet another after her. Three wives. Awful thought. He squeezed his eyes shut, then forced them open. The pain in his head was nearly unbearable.

"If you have no more use for me?" She practically spat the words at him.

"I do have use for you," he hissed, still breathing hard as he caught her shoulders. "I have a job for you, Ah'nis. Can you hear me or is your anger overriding your reason?"

"I hear you."

"Then listen, please. And keep your voice down." He pulled her close and spoke just above a whisper. "I have reason to think that Eridi's life might be in danger." He had her attention. She raised her eyes to him, looking puzzled. "She seems to think that this offering was made seven hundred years ago, and that the girl who was offered, was killed by her own people when the Twelfth Dragonhorse rejected her. Have you heard this?"

The priestess shook her head. “That sounds insane,” she whispered.

“Yes, it does. But we do not know the hearts of these people. She is afraid, and Io and I are afraid for her.”

“What would you have me do?”

“Until we can get her settled – not that kind of settled – settled at home, wherever that may be, I want you to stay with her every minute as her protector. Can you do that? I know you can. Will you do that?”

“From this moment on, I will make her my charge,” Ah’nis nodded. “May I go?”

“Yes. Thank you,” Ardenai said, and nodded deeply as she walked away into the shadows.

With her departure he bent forward, hands on his knees and took a shuddering breath. His legs were shaking, his teeth chattering, his still foggy head was pounding mercilessly, and for a cold, queasy moment, he wasn’t really sure what had taken place. Would he have raped that woman? It was a thought that brought a wave of panic, and a wave of nausea. Had he raped that woman? No. Probably not. No. He hadn’t.

The passion he’d felt turned suddenly to a seething anger and he spun around and peered into the dim interior of the chamber. “Ah’krill,” he said through his teeth. He knew she was there, somewhere. This had her smell all over it – maneuvering, and maneuvering – but hadn’t he walked in here with her? Ambushed again. Outmaneuvered again. And she had his clothes.

“Ah’krill,” he said again, clutched at his head and groaned – ashamed of what he had almost done and embarrassed to find himself, on an important State occasion, naked in an ithyphallic chamber when he should have been dancing with his wife. Another wave of nausea hit, this one stronger, and Ardenai let go of his temples and clutched at his middle instead. “This just gets better and better,” he muttered, and gagged. He staggered over to the priapic bench and sat heavily, bracing himself on either side with his hands.

He was looking around for another robe – anything to cover himself – when something uncoiled from the shadows and toddled his direction, hissing with displeasure. “Thee jussssst doess not lissten, doess thee?”

"Pythos?" Ardenai wiped the cold sweat out of his eyes and blinked hard. "What…how…long have you been there?"

"I told thee thy High Priesstesss mother wass up to no good, and yet, here *you* are, and aren't *you* a fine, fine messs?"

"I'm freezing. You know that."

"Yess," the doctor said, and Ardenai could tell by the inflection that he was highly amused, even as he rattled his scales in annoyance. "That iss what happenss when thee takess an iccce cold bath."

"I needed one. And what was I supposed to do, throw her?"

"Yess," Pythos said, bobbing most of his long body in affirmation. "If thee had impregnated her, THEN it iss appropriate for thee to enter the water with her. Ssince thee was punishing her, ssimply throwing her would have been adequate." He produced a thick robe and wrapped it around the Firstlord, who was beginning to shiver.

"Thank you. At least you're going to warm me up while you lecture me. She is a priestess of the Great House," Ardenai said, trying to control his chattering teeth enough to make himself sound firm. "As such, and because she is alive, she deserves respect. At least some respect. Throwing her would have been too much. Too much."

"Really? For thiss transsgresssion? Thee iss indeed a kindly fool."

Ardenai didn't rise to the bait. "I ask you again, Sir Pent, how long have you been here?"

"All along. I knew at oncce they had drugged thee, but then thee knew that as well."

Ardenai chose not to admit he'd known nothing of the kind. "So, you rescued me?"

"And how would I have done that, exactly?"

"I don't know. But those drugs wore off long before they should have, or I miss my guess."

"Yesss" the serpent nodded.

"So, you caused that?"

"No."

"Why not?" By now Ardenai was pacing, trying to warm up after his icy plunge. He wasn't having much success. He still wanted to vomit, and his head hurt like he'd been hit with a polo mallet. He just wanted to throw something. Hard.

"Becausse, thee got thysself into thiss. I only came along out of cold-blooded curiosssity, to ssee if thee could exsstricate thysself." Suddenly the old doctor's manner changed, and he was once again Ardenai's gentle and loving friend. "Beloved," he hissed, "Beloved. I had to know if thee could ssave thysself. If thee hadn't, what would the conssequencces have been?"

"I would have raped that woman."

"In that, you are missstaken," Pythos said. "Sshe, would have raped thee. Taken thy precious ssseed. Not sso bad until you look at it in thosse termss."

"Pythos," Ardenai sighed, and thought about what he wanted to say next. He was still more or less naked, he was freezing cold, he felt like a fool, he had a blazing, sick headache, and he was supposed to be upstairs somewhere at a State dinner that he was supposedly giving. "Do you think we could..." and out of the shadows trotted Gideon, fresh clothing clutched in his hands.

"We can't let you out of our sight for a minute, can we?" he laughed, proffering a dry tunic and britches. "El'Shadai, you're blue. Let me help you. They're looking for you upstairs."

The old sea dragon watched in silence for some minutes, then flicked the struggling Firstlord with his long, gentle tongue. The pain and the nausea subsided. Ardenai gasped with relief and glared up at Pythos. "Took you long enough," he breathed, pulling on his boots.

The serpent just shrugged as one does who has no shoulders. "Now, I have resscued thee. Did sshe ssay sshe would help thee?"

"Me, probably not," Ardenai replied, shaking himself into a semblance of order, "but the girl, yes."

"Are we talking about Princess Eridi?" Gideon asked as they started back. "Being around her gives me a headache – I mean physically, actually gives me a headache."

"So, it's not just me," Ardenai said, almost to himself. But there was no time to pursue it. They had arrived in the banquet hall through the same door Ardenai had exited earlier. The ballroom doors beyond had been thrown open, the music engulfing them as they entered.

The torchlight off the sparkling white walls made the huge room flicker – the floors flickered with the sweep of gowns and firelight – and Ardenai reached for a cool drink to steady himself. What, exactly, did one do for a drug hangover? Wine was probably not the answer. And where were the people he sought? Head raised, a slight sniff of the air told him where Princess Eridi was. Turning that direction he was in time to see Ah'nis arrive from another direction, her hair slicked back under a turban, seeming not much the worse for use. She went immediately to Eridi's side, and Ardenai noted that she was quickly joined by Ah'krill and Samarra, both wearing looks that were questioning and joyful. They didn't know? They didn't know. An interesting turn of events. And unnerving, because it was unexpected.

Priestess Ah'nis, I assumed they were watching.

She turned her head and found him with little effort. He was taller than most, and she knew the direction from which he must have come.

So did I. If they discover you have spurned me, I will lose my standing amongst the Eloi.

The Firstlord squeezed his eyes shut for a moment, thinking hard. *Tell them I passed out on you, that the...whatever it was, had a very adverse effect on me. See what they say. And tell my mother the priestess that we will be having words shortly.*

Ah'nis gave only the briefest nod and turned her attention to the two women who flanked her. Ardenai's interest in that particular conversation was interrupted by the warmth and smile of his wife, who slipped her arm through his and asked softly, "How was it?"

Ardenai just stared at her. "What?"

"What do you mean, what?" she asked with some annoyance. "Ah'krill told me that you were mating with Ah'nis tonight at the behest of the Great House."

Ardenai took Io by one elbow and propelled her into a more secluded spot, where he could stare down into her face and look as puzzled and annoyed as he felt without others noticing. "When did she tell you this?"

"Today. Early this morning. What is the matter with you? Are you angry because I didn't attend you? I wanted to, and Ah'krill told me I couldn't." Io studied him a little more closely in the dim light. "You look a little blue about the ears. Are you feeling well?"

Ardenai puffed out his cheeks instead of following his first inclination, which was to grab his hair in both hands and scream at the top of his lungs. "So, you knew?"

"I just said I did."

"Well, I didn't," he growled. "She didn't tell me."

There was a pause of several seconds before Io said, "So…did you?"

"No!" Ardenai responded, setting aside his drink. "I did not."

Io slid her arms around his waist and looked up into his face, smiling as she laid her head against his chest. "I thought, after the way you reacted to that girl, you would have..."

"…Jumped at the chance?" he finished. "I very nearly did. Even Gideon said that girl gives him a headache and I have a feeling that we are in deep trouble."

Io caught his arm and led him toward the dancing. "Let us dance, and mingle, and test the air," she said, and laughed as Ardenai swept her into his arms and spun her out onto the floor.

"The Firstlord and his lady," announced Bashkir, and for a time they danced alone, lost in each other.

Then Io reached out and pulled her father into the dance, Ardenai his foster mother, and as dancers once again filled the floor Ardenai looked around for Ah'krill. When he sighted her more or less alone he excused himself from Ah'rane and made his way through the crowd, smiling at Gideon, who was dancing with Ah'brianne. He also made note of the fact that Criollo was close by, showing Jasreth the steps of the dance, and that the four of them were laughing. As it should be.

And what was to become of poor Eridi? Poor poisoness Eridi.

What sort of effect was she having on the other men in this room? Precious Equus the havoc she could wreak on a keep – old men, young men. Did he dare take this child home? Did he dare not? And had Ah'nis come only at the behest of the Great House, not knowing that he had not been informed in advance? Had he perhaps treated a perfectly innocent person, one who was only doing her duty, in so shameful a manner?

By that time he had reached the edge of the floor and the chair where his mother sat. He had also decided upon a tack to take with this. Telling her that he'd have her killed or kill her himself if she ever tried such a thing again, was hardly the image he wanted to present. Then again, he didn't want to leave himself open for another using, either. He nodded to her without speaking, extended a hand, and led her out onto the dance floor. Catching her close he said, very quietly, "Pray tell, good Priestess, what were you thinking?"

"That I could save you the catastrophe of raping a child," she murmured, swaying easily in his arms. She was tall, and a superb dancer. "I had no idea that Eridi's pherine would make you ill."

"You will excuse me if I don't believe a word of that," he growled. "Regardless, I do not mate with anyone, anywhere, unless I am attended by my wife. You were wrong to put me in that position, and you will not do it again."

"Of course not," she said soothingly. "Please forgive me, Dragonhorse. I want only to serve the best interests of the Great House."

CHAPTER 3

And you believed her?" Pythos smacked down a particularly succulent morsel of ice cold sugar melon and leaned back in his chair to contemplate the Firstlord. "Sshe iss playing thee, Beloved, and sshe'ss jusst acquired an amazing new insstrument."

"I really don't know who to believe, or what to believe. I will say that if it was a plot, it was a disturbingly brilliant one. We have learned some things. I know, from Ah'nis not veiling her thoughts very well, that Priestess Samarra was the one who had the potions, not Ah'krill, but if Ah'nis was party to this, then so was the high priestess. Soon we will have enough conniving priestesses for a polo team."

"How cassual thee iss about thiss" Pythos hissed. "How like a heedless colt thee walked into danger without a moment'ss contemplation. Did thee go into that room with Eridi exsspecting to lose thysself? Exsspecting to be drugged? Exsspecting to impregnate Ah'niss just to be rid of the imagess in your mind of a ssixteen-year-old child?"

Ardenai set down his coffee cup and adjusted his seat to get the first rays of sunshine touching the balcony out of his eyes. "No, I did not. Admittedly, that part disturbs me. How did those drugs, or whatever they were, kick in so fast?" He shifted again, this time with annoyance. "I admit, more than one aspect of this troubles me. Where is Moonsgold? He was supposed to be here by now. I suppose the Terrenes and the Declivians have tried to catch a couple hours sleep, which seems unwise to me. They should have stayed up. It's easier on the body."

"They tried to rape thee," the serpent hissed, "and thee doessn't even recognize it. It iss only the merccy of the Wissdom Giver that the drugss did not affect thee to a greater degree. What ssayss thy wife about lasst night'ss...deviation?"

"She was worried," Ardenai sighed, pinching the bridge of his nose in an attempt to ease the pain in his head. "But she chose to protect Eridi, assuming I could take care of myself. What is the worst that could have happened? I would have impregnated Ah'nis and gotten it over with – a coupling I know has been sanctioned by the Great House and the High Priestess. Using the word, rape, is an overstatement, old friend."

"And wass the ssituation hard to ressisst? Wass thee at all tempted?"

"Of course, to both. I was drugged, I know that now. I was caught unshod. Who knows, maybe Ah'krill was trying to make it easier on me. She knows I can't stand Ah'nis, and that Ah'nis can't stand me, either. And now I feel like I need to apologize to Ah'nis."

"No."

"Well, Ah'krill's explanation to me afterward was very well played. When she was on Lebonath Jas, Anchoress Samarra told her in confidence about the plant pheromones they use to stimulate libido. It makes me wonder if I was the only male in the room to fall under Eridi's spell last night. I do know it won't happen again," he looked pointedly at the old physician, "BECAUSE of information received in confidence from the High Priestess."

"After sshe had failed to get what sshe wisshed of thee. It makess a convenient sstory with Ssamarra as the villainesss – jusst trying to get her little Eridi impregnated with the seed of the Thirteenth Dragonhorse. Almosst, I could believe it mysself. And yet, to thy credit, thee uses the term, played."

The Firstlord shrugged and slid his hands inside the sleeves of his robe to chase the morning chill. The season was changing rapidly. His fingertips were cold against his elbows. "Samarra also told Ah'krill this concoction," he went on, "was used in marriage ceremonies. Since this was ideally to be a marriage, or at least a mating, Ah'krill assumed they'd use it here, as well. Since she knew Ah'nis was in heat, and that I was dreading such a coupling, and since she knew that, at the very least, the Lebonathi would want to know I was potent, she set this up as a possible scenario. Admittedly, Ah'krill didn't tell me, though she did tell my wife beforehand. If she's trying to drive a wedge between us, she's going at it from a multiplicity of levels. Anger my wife by not letting her attend me – make me feel powerless. Again, well played."

"At lasst," the old physician sighed, "the light beginss to dawn in thy tiny mammalian brain."

Their discussion was mercifully interrupted by the arrival of a sleepy-eyed Winslow Moonsgold, wrapped in his robe, clutching a steaming cup. "Morning," he yawned, shuffling into a chair and blinking his bright gold eyes against the light on the pavers. "I hope I'm not supposed to do anything protocol-ish here, like bow or something, because I will fall over. It's freezing out here, and the sun's barely up. Lovely reception by the way, though sleeping in would have been a pleasant touch. Why are we here?"

Ardenai hiked his brows and grinned at the doctor. "Fewer well-meaning ears out here at this hour and at this temperature. Those tests you ran on Konik, Sarkhan and the others. You're absolutely sure of the results?"

"Unfortunately, yes. Absolutely. And I was not the only one who tested them, and mine was not the only facility used, though I was present every single time and I never let the evidence out of my sight. Those people were and are one hundred percent Equi back many thousands of years. Even Konik, who now lives on Anguine II, is it? Even he is pure as rain. Especially him. Old royalty."

Ardenai squeezed his eyes shut a moment and concentrated as best he could – trying to swirl that information into something that made sense. It didn't. It hadn't, and probably wouldn't. No point in pursuing it further at this point in time. He puffed his lips gently in frustration and looked back at Moonsgold. "What word from Doctor Keats, or is he going by Dennis Strathmore these days?"

Moonsgold shook his head and adjusted his hands around his cup for warmth. "Hadrian Keats. He says he's been Keats for too much of his life to change now. He's done some checking, and Keats' old man is dead – had a sister, and she's dead, as well. Apparently there's no other family to care if he keeps the name. Besides, he says if he decided to unincarnate himself back into Denny Strathmore, he'd have to have his towels re-monogrammed."

The Declivian yawned hugely, rotating his long, slender feet at the ankles until they popped like corn in his slippers. "He's doing all right, I think. Gotten used to his so-called incarceration. It was kind of you Ardenai, not to tell the other researchers that he's a prisoner. They were delighted to have a fresh insight, you know, and the fact that they have someone on their team who has access to all kinds of medical supplies and equipment, has made Hadrian Keats more popular than he's ever been in his life. Hell, he may not want to come back."

"I'm pleased to have improved his social status," the Firstlord said, reaching for the carafe on the table, "but I hope he hasn't forgotten why I sent him there. Is that Demetrian white coffee you have?"

"Oh, he remembers, all right," the doctor snorted, nodding and extending the cup. "But...thanks, that's plenty...Declivis is so riddled with venereal disease, so many kinds of sexually transmitted bugs and shit, it's no wonder they've had a whole research team on it for years without much success. You know why, don't you? Declivis is the place everybody stops to go a'whoring. We've got insectum copulatum from all over the galaxy. It lives in its host, or hostess, for a good while, and then it mutates and goes on its merry way to the next person or species, where it mutates again, and so on.

"According to the numbers code that was tattooed onto Gideon's belly and butt, he had three different diseases, all at the same time. Hadrian was able to get hold of the hospital records from the boy's stay, and he's thinking that the erectile dysfunction may have been caused as much by the curing, as by the disease. He's thinking there might be nerve damage, and that Pythos might check the boy for same, though how you'd be able to do that without starting a war, I'm not sure. I visited with him awhile last night, and I think Gideon's made up his mind that he's impotent for life. He's resigned himself to it. He's not going to be anxious to step out of that comfortable footprint, you know. Lot less responsibility when you don't have to be accountable for a sex life."

Ardenai poured himself more coffee, gathered his heavy woolen robe a little more closely about him and cast a weather eye to the west, out across the straits of Viridia, gleaming momentarily serene in the early morning sunshine. Something in the air told him the first storm of the season might be blowing in, and if it did, he wanted his parents and his sister at Canyon keep. But he wanted to talk to them first. He wondered if they'd have time to have a leisurely meeting with him and still outrun the storm if it came. Wouldn't do to have the first storm hit with an incomplete harvest. He set that thought aside for the time being, and turned his attention back to Moonsgold. "I suppose until the impotency problem is solved, there's not much point in wondering whether he could actually be generative or not."

Moonsgold cocked his head. "That, Hadrian says, the team itself has been working on for some time – long before he got there. Apparently, though nothing is in concrete, there's a way of taking a functioning reproductive system from a donor, like from a man who has died in an accident or a man who has no more use for his, or doesn't want offspring, whatever, holding it in stasis and infusing it with DNA from the man who is to be the new host, until the sperm being produced are actually his, and then implanting it. It's more or less found technology from way back when and who knows where, but with new techniques, it's pretty promising. Finding a compatible donor is always a problem, though the fact that Gideon is a mix of so many races may be helpful in that respect. Of course not many men want to donate their reproductive systems to research, so the ones they're getting are pretty well used up, or eaten up, you know."

"What do you mean, so many races?" Ardenai asked. "I thought the boy was Coronian and Declivian."

Moonsgold shook his head. "Oh no. He'd look a lot more like me if he was, and that would be a shame, now wouldn't it? He's got those dominant gold Declivian eyes and that tiny cleft in his chin, but that's about it for actual Declivian blood. He's pretty much equal parts of four different races. He's Declivian and Coronian, that's on his mother's side. He's also got Terren blood, and he's at least a quarter Equi on his father's side."

Ardenai rocked back in surprise. "This is just now coming out because…?"

"I assumed you knew. It really doesn't make a lot of difference, except in maybe finding a donor. I do apologize for not mentioning it sooner."

The look Moonsgold gave Pythos told Ardenai that the ancient dragon knew this, and had known it all along. Why hadn't he said anything? The Equi database could trace the boy's blood to his father. Ardenai caught his own thought and smiled. Gideon had a father. Gideon had Ardenai.

There was a rushing click of claws on pavers and Lionel sprinted by, ears flying behind him, to disappear up the steps to the top of the hill. "A man with a mission," Ardenai chuckled. "If Lionel is awake, Gideon is probably awake also. We should wrap this up."

"One more thing," Moonsgold said, and dropped his voice as he looked around. "Hadrian says to tell you that a couple weeks after he got Gideon's records from the hospital on Declivis, he was contacted by a woman who says she's Gideon's mother. She says he ran away from home, and she was wondering if Hadrian might be able to tell her where the boy is, being as he was accessing her beloved son's records."

Ardenai's greengold eyes narrowed, and as the light hit them, the ophidian pupils stood out in ominous contrast. "And what did Doctor Keats tell the good woman?"

"That he was a member of a research team, and that Gideon's case was an unusual one. Says he didn't tell her more than that. Why, are you concerned?"

The Firstlord shook his head. "I don't know. I don't suppose I should be. For all intents and purposes Gideon is nearly grown by Declivian standards, and can go and do as he pleases." He studied the dregs of his cup, and then looked back out to sea. "I do wonder if contacting her would bring about some healing for that part of his life."

"Don't even think about it," the Declivian advised. "The second she found out that Gideon has been adopted by the most powerful prince in the known galaxy, you'd have the kind of trouble that hasn't been seen since Adam ran into Eve."

"You're undoubtedly right," Ardenai said.

Privately he figured she probably already had at least an inkling, given the wealth of cosmoscope projections that seemed always to be floating around. He decided a little record-checking – a little snooping around in general, would be a good idea. He knew someone who would do that quickly and efficiently. He smiled, and was preparing to stand up just as Lionel sprinted back in their direction. The pup launched himself at a dead run and landed in Ardenai's arms, kissing him under the chin and burrowing into the sleeve of his dressing gown before the Firstlord had time to defend himself. "Precious Equus, he's quick, and his little feet are like ice!" Ardenai gasped. "I do think he's hinting that it's cool out here and that we should go in, forthwith. You, too, Winnie, I'd like to meet with all of you over breakfast, and I see they're laying it now."

"I'll be there in ten minutes," the doctor said, turning toward the balcony door of Kehailan's apartments, "I try never to breakfast with beautiful women until I've brushed my hair and put my pants on, or back on. I'll round up the others and be right back."

He was as good as his word, and a few minutes found sixteen of them seated around the table in the Firstlord's dining room. No Abeyan, no Ah'kra, no Jilfan. Sad though it was, it was just as well, Ardenai thought.

Some of them looked sleepier than others, some were still in evening dress, and some were in their dressing gowns; some were more thoroughly brushed than others, but they all looked expectantly at Ardenai. "I have called you all here this morning to have a palaver," he said gravely, "but I have also called you here to eat, and I think we should start with the most important thing first, don't you? Sire, please pass the lacey cakes. So, what were the impressions you received from our guests last night?"

"That they smell really, really rancid," Marion chuckled, sliding crepes stuffed with fresh fruit and ammon cream cheese onto his plate. "And that they are very sheltered. At least the girls are. I sat next to Jasreth for some of the evening. She's a little doll, by the way, smart as a whip, and she kept looking at my hands, and then at my face, you know, and I could tell she was dying to ask me something, so I said, 'what would you like to ask me?' and she said, 'May I touch your skin?' So I said of course she could, and she took her fingers and rubbed me, very gently across the back of my hand, and then she looked at her fingers. Then she moistened the corner of her napkin in her water glass and rubbed again, and looked again, and then she looked at me with those big eyes and said, 'What have you done to yourself, you and that pretty lady over there, to make the light go out of your skin?' She'd never seen anyone with black skin before. She asked me if I dyed my skin as a cultural decoration, and when I asked her why she thought that, she said it was because the palms of my hands still had light coming through them, so all of me must have been like that at some point." He turned them over and contemplated them, chuckling softly. "When I told her I'd been born with dark brown skin, and that Oonah had been born with black skin, she was absolutely amazed. Gideon and Winslow's gold eyes amazed her. The fact that Equi have pupils like dragons amazed her. Either their textbooks don't have pictures, or..."

"Or they don't have textbooks," Ah'brianne blurted with annoyed disbelief. "Can you believe that? They don't have textbooks, she told me so. Oh, the boys do, but the girls don't. They have cookbooks, and The Book of Virtuous Comportment, but no texts, not a one. The girls are home-schooled, which means they hide themselves in some hole and study how to be subservient whether it's smart or not. They learn to cook, and clean, and take care of babies and pray, and that's just about it! I mean... oh, I interrupted you, didn't I Captain Eletsky. Please, do go on with what you were saying...it's just that any creppia nonage tot knows that education is the right of every citizen, and that no one has the legal clout to subjugate that to any personal, religious or political agenda. Why, our constitution says that! I asked her if she'd like to go with me today to meet the horses in the Great Stables, and the very thought of it scared her to death. She said Eridi snuck out the other night to go for a walk, and Samarra nearly shook her teeth out of her head. Jasreth said if Eridi hadn't had to be blemish-free for the Firstlord, Samarra would have beaten her within an inch of her life."

"A notion which appeals to me just now," Timor drawled, giving his daughter a smile across the table. "I remember the first notes that ever came home from school with you. 'Ah'brianne has an amazingly quick mind, and a mouth to match.' Do you remember those, Ardenai teacher?"

"Very well," Ardenai chuckled. "She was a challenge. Of course so was Criollo, and so was my wife, for that matter. They all seem to be doing fine."

Ah'mae flashed a smile and gave her husband a gentle punch on the shoulder. "See, there's hope for her. But you did interrupt, Ah'brianne, and you must learn not to do that."

"And soon, hopefully," her father sighed, patting his wife's hand. "Captain Eletsky, you were telling us about your encounter with Jasreth?"

"That's about it. I shared her with Ah'brianne, and I think we've about covered it, haven't we?"

Ah'brianne nodded, and Kehailan took up the conversation. "I sat next to the Lebonathi Standard Bearer. Brak, is his name. And I can tell you it's not only the women who seem uninformed about other cultures. He got one look at Ambassador MalDor and nearly had a heart attack. Admittedly, MalDor takes some getting used to, but in such a civilized setting as this he shouldn't be viewed with fear. I found that a little disturbing. That, and I too must admit, the smell. I don't think they bathe at all."

"They were afraid of Pythos, also," Oonah added. "Apparently on their homeworld serpents are extremely poisonous and prone to strike the unsuspecting. And, it's the most poisonous snakes that have eyes just like yours, Ardenai. That was grounds for deep concern."

"And they couldn't tell the difference between a wild, lower order snake and an extremely gentle and intelligent being with serpentine ancestry?" Ah'mae asked with a frown. "That doesn't bode well for their intellectual capacity, does it?"

"It doesn't bode well for the way they've been taught to think, that's for sure," said the Firstlord. "I got very much the same reaction from Eridi. She was terrified of Pythos, and wondered if he had been possessed by a demon of some kind and changed into a serpent for his transgressions."

"Actually, I've wondered that myself," Krush drawled.

The old serpent writhed, hissing with amusement and nearly choked on a piece of sugar melon in the process. Krush slapped him on the back until Pythos bobbed his flat, hairless head to signal that he was fine, and then Krush turned to his daughter-in-law. "You got to spend some quality time with the one who seems to be the sanest of the bunch. What were your thoughts on Girsu?"

Io smiled at him through the steam from her cider, and rocked her head back and forth slightly in assessment. "Well, I won't say he doesn't have an agenda, but I think it may be different from everyone else's. Jasreth is his niece, you know, and he dotes on her. I find him rather a likeable man, and he's a wonderful dancer. Very quick to learn."

"That's certainly incisive, Captain," Ardenai chuckled. His eyes widened slightly, registering the possibility of a blunder, and he immediately gave her a mollifying little pat under the table. "Sorry, Wife. I assume you're not ready to pass any sort of judgment?"

"No judgments yet," she said, and gave him a sideways look that didn't escape the rest of them. He'd been gone for a good while last night, and Io's demeanor this morning seemed a tad chilly where her husband was concerned. "My biggest puzzle, was how much trouble I had explaining to Eridi that her horse was real."

Ardenai's brows came together. "I'm lost at this point."

Io shrugged, and Criollo said, "I think I can solve that one. From what Jasreth told me last night, they have pets, or what they call pets, but none of their pets are actually alive. They're robotic. She didn't use that term, but I got the idea. Apparently some of them are very realistic, but none are actually alive. As far as she knows, except for caronai, there are no live animals left on Lebonath Jas except snakes, and she described something that sounds like what we would call rats."

"Stranger and stranger," Krush muttered. "I'm beginning to worry about these people."

"Do we need to worry about Girsu?" Ardenai asked, looking at his wife.

"I really don't know yet, but I don't think so. Girsu's going to brave the daylight, and we're going to have a bit of a lookround. Mostly agricultural concerns. From what he said, only one of their continents is livable these days, and we spent a good deal of the evening talking about the problem of feeding a densely packed, water-based population on a world that is mostly desert."

"And what can you show him that will help solve that?" Timor asked curiously. He was an agriculturalist, and interested in such things.

"I'm not sure," Io sighed, "but I can continue the exploration of his heart."

"Something I'm not sure Anchoress Samarra has," Ah'rane said. "On first impression, her mind seems both single and narrow. Even in her faith, which should be the light of her life, there is no light, only duty and punishment. She seems a very frustrated woman, and a very sad and bitter one. The only time I saw her smile, was when she was conversing with Ah'krill, and looking at you, Ardi."

"She certainly seems to have no use for us and our way of life," Ah'din added. She was a soft-spoken woman with a gentle voice, and in her tone was sadness. She shivered a little inside her warm red robe, and smiled as her husband's arm came around the back of her chair. "Oh, her eyes told me what to expect," she said, rubbing Teal's hand on her shoulder. "She held no surprises. She believes that religion should dominate secular life, and that it should intervene to pass judgment quickly and terminally. She can't fathom a faith so ingrained that every thought and action, every smile, every gentle response, every day's hard work, is worship of the Wisdom Giver. Our level of acceptance seems to her a subversion of faith. She assumes, I think, that the only reason we have very little crime, is because we don't care what people do. Population control is unthinkable to her. The familiarity of the Equi people with their Dragonhorse, she views as his weakness and their disrespect for that weakness." She grinned at her brother and gave her shoulders a little shrug. "You told me to listen, Ardi. I did. I guessed that if I struck up an argument with everything she said, we wouldn't get very far."

"And you were right," her brother smiled, "which is why I chose you."

"Samarra has a twin in Halaf," Teal said, passing a platter of fresh fruit to Pythos. "What my dear Ah'din was hearing from Samarra, I was hearing from Halaf. She took a whining tone, and he a swagger, but the end result was the same. He spoke of those who are homophilic with the utmost disrespect – hatred would be a better word – and even though it is his spoken desire to have Eridi mated with the prince of another species, or at least another race, his demeanor speaks against it. He is an apocalyptist in every sense of the word, and those two nephews of his are just as rigid and arrogant as he is. They are the only ones who actually…worry me for some reason I'm not quite ready to state."

"On that we agree." This from Io, who applied herself to her breakfast and said no more.

Moonsgold dropped his eating sticks and threw his hands up in botheration. "Then what the hell do they want? Why are they here? This wasn't exactly a weekend jaunt to the sea for them. They're willing to sacrifice a child of royal blood to you, and yet they think you're – what? Certainly you Equi aren't a dream come true for them, from the way they're reacting. Why give you the girl at all? Why come at all?"

"Very good questions," Ardenai muttered. "Would that we had some answers."

"Perhaps we do, or at least we will," Gideon said. "Sometimes, when you're around somebody who has so much more than you do, who needs so much less than you do, and you really want to ask them for something, you need some elevation. The easiest way to get that is to tear the other guy down a little so you're standing taller by comparison, or make them in some way beholden to you. By giving them another human being, for instance."

Ardenai cocked his head slightly to one side. "And?"

"I just…I can feel an undercurrent of danger here, like a whole hidden agenda that centers on you, Sire. I can't put my finger on it. I do think it has nothing to do with anything they've told us so far. They make me nervous and I wish we could just pack them all up and send them home."

"I think you're right," Criollo agreed, slipping the puppy a bit of seedcake under the table. "What I got from Jasreth while we were dancing last night – not what she said, but from her body language – she's really uneasy about being given any freedom at all, and I think that's going to come to a head if she's torn between your authority, and that of Halaf and Naram. She's afraid for her uncle and I can't figure out why. I know she's scared half to death of Basra and Addur. I just think," he looked directly at Ah'brianne, "you should stay as far away from those two boys as you can. I agree with my cousin. I wish they'd all go home. At least most all of them."

Ardenai just sat there, shaking his head and looking around the table. "The more questions I ask, the more I have about these people. I'd like nothing better than to assign each of you to one of them and have you shadow them until they leave, but I know that's not possible. It feels like a storm blowing in, and I think all of you who keep nave together, should head home."

"And what about your new acquisition?" his father asked, reaching a nonchalant hand for the cider pot. "What is her disposition to be?"

"Their disposition," Io said, and had the attention of the table. "I asked Girsu to leave Jasreth, as well. He hasn't made up his mind yet, but I do think he's leaning that direction."

Criollo and Gideon gave each other a subtle thumbs up and Ah'brianne, she of the expressive face, clapped her hands quietly under the table, leaving no doubt as to their collective delight.

"Ah, yes. The only thing better than one Achernar pony, is two Achernar ponies," Ardenai sighed, but he smiled at his wife when he said it. "I really don't know when we're supposed to take…possession of our new..." again he paused, "... wards, but since I have duties at that end of the hall this morning, I shall make it my business to find out."

There was a rising moan of wind around the edge of the ancient stones, and Krush quickly dropped his napkin. "The wind has reached the coast, and I think we have not much time to be safely in the air out of Falconstones," he said, "so we had best be into the tube and on our way. Who is going with me?"

"We are," Timor nodded, putting aside his coffee cup. "Ah'brianne, you and Criollo need to come home for a bit as well. Ardenai thinks it's time you two went to get the Eldest, and Krush and I agree with him."

They immediately rose, but Gideon looked questioningly across the table. “Eldest?”

Ardenai nodded. “Yes. Even he should be able to see the signs by now. Gideon, I want you to go with them. It will be for just a few days, and I think you will enjoy the adventure. Please get Lionel and prepare to leave. Mother, Ah’din, are you going back to the keep as well?”

Ah’rane nodded, but Ah’din shook her head. “I have business here for a bit.”

“And I am here as well,” Teal added. “I have a dozen new fledglings who need to be matched with a horse before they can start training, so I will be interviewing people and riding horses for the next brace of days.”

“We,” said Captain Eletsky, gesturing at his companions and himself, “are still at the disposal of the Great House, and so at yours, Dragonhorse.”

“Good,” Ardenai responded. “I have need of thee. Get some sleep and meet me back here in time for second lunch.”

Goodbyes were said, hugs exchanged, and people hurried off, though Gideon was obviously reticent. He received an encouraging nod from Ardenai and a strong, steering hug from his grandsire, who propelled him out the door and down the hall, Lionel yapping excitedly in his carrier.

When the doors had shut again, and the officers of Belesprit had gone back to Kehailan’s apartments to sleep, Ardenai was left with Pythos, Teal, Io and Ah’din. “I would much enjoy the company of this few,” he smiled, “but I must be about business which is equally upon my mind at this point.”

“At the far end of the hall?” Teal asked, and the Firstlord nodded. “I will accompany you that far on my way to the stables, Brother Mine. Wife, will I see thee at lunchtime?” She nodded, and received a lingering kiss on the top of her head as the two men departed. The closing of the huge doors echoed in the vast and ancient apartments, making Ah’din shiver and wish for the warm, homely fires of Canyon keep.

“The Dragonhorsse may not be pleassed that we are plotting,” the serpent hissed. “But we sshall, nonethelesss. Moonssgold, we are waiting for thee," he added, slightly louder, and the physician immediately appeared and joined them. They seated themselves on the plush octagonal lounge near the fire, and looked expectantly at Ah'din. "Tell uss what thee needss."

"I need a little piece of everything about that girl," Ah'din said, leaning forward and clasping her hands in her lap. "I don't need much. Blood, saliva, vaginal fluid, tears, feces, sweat, a bit of skin, a bit of hair, even a bit of fingernail if we can figure out how to get it."

"Because?" Moonsgold asked, clearly fascinated.

"You do know Ah'din is a physician," Io said. "She is an herbalist, which is why I went to her last night and told her of my concerns. Oddly enough, she already had the same ones."

"Sspeak," the serpent gestured, and coiled himself gracefully onto the deep, woolen rug beside the fire.

"Ardi was plenty sick last night," Io said. "He made it through the evening with his usual grace, but when we got back here, he spent most of the rest of the wee hours in the lavage with vomiting and scours, and he still has a terrible headache."

"He wass drugged," Pythos hissed, hooding his yellow eyes.

"Or he had an allergic reaction," Ah'din amended. "Neither is good."

"But Gideon also complained of a headache," Io said. She squirmed a little with discomfort and went on. "I saw how Ardenai reacted to that girl last night. He was absolutely beside himself, and he is supposedly the best Equus has to offer in the way of male self-control. All he could think about last night, after he stopped thinking about having sex with her, was that we absolutely cannot take that girl home with us, or to school, or to the stables or anywhere there are males if she is going to have that effect on them. She is a war for dominance, waiting to happen. Whether or not it is intentional is of little or no consequence. Either we need to divest her of her powers, or come up with an antidote for everybody else." Io rose and nodded to the others. "I have said my piece, and I promised Girsu a bit of a tour of our agriculture. If we don't get going we might not get to go at all. Do you need anything else of me?"

Ah'din shook her head. "I think we will be fine."

"I'm sure you will," Io smiled. "Whatever you choose to do, I will back you."

When she had donned riding boots and a warm cloak and departed, Moonsgold looked from Ah'din to Pythos and chuckled. "I'd ask what you two very formidable physicians need me for, but I think I know."

"Pray tell," came the serpent's laconic drawl.

"Well, it seems to me that sweat, spit, hair, would be relatively easy to come by. Vaginal fluid and some of the rest of it, not so easy. Am I on the right track?"

Ah'din nodded. "I hope so."

"To acquire the samples you need, would require a full examination, but if you were to do such an exam, Ah'din, it would arouse immediate suspicion in Samarra, given that you are an herbalist. She would immediately begin a potion-y counter-attack. Pythos has already said the girl is whole, so he can't very well renege and ask for the full poke and prod."

"Thee iss abssolutely ssspectacular in thy devioussnesss!" Pythos hissed. "I am proud to call thee friend and fellow consspirator."

Moonsgold nodded graciously. "To be honored with the title of Spectacularly Devious from one so slithery as yourself, is more than I could ever have hoped for."

"Oh, for goodness sake, you two," Ah'din laughed, "You're ridiculous together. I need this done now. Can we get on with the hows and whys?"

"The why of it should be obvious," Moonsgold sniffed. "Him. That one over there on the rug. A serpent. Quite possibly some sort of cursed being. I think it only fair and right that, given the Lebonathi revulsion for all things snaky, the girl's suitability be ascertained by something that at least has shoulders and hips...and teeth. You know, for the peace of mind of all concerned."

"Brilliant!" Pythos hissed. "Ssstunningly brilliant."

"However brilliant it may be," Ah'din cautioned, "Who is going to authorize this? It makes perfect sense when you say it, but exactly which authority figure came up with the idea? Surely it can't be us three."

Moonsgold had to nod in agreement. He thought a minute, then raised a finger and scratched at one of his long, bony chins. "How about Io? She's Primuxori, and she said we could involve her."

Ah'din looked thoughtful. "All right. Why would she do this?"

"Sshe is angry with me," Pythos said quietly. "I let Ah'krill take her babe'ss esssence from the Dragonhorsse, and he sseemed not to mind. Perhapss sshe wisshes to ssatisfy hersself that sshe and her nexsst unborn child are not in any danger from whatever alien disseasess this girl, this threat, might be carrying. Everyone ssaw how her hussband reacted to Eridi; it sseems a very valid conccern, given her powerss of...perssuassion. The Lebonathi might well take it as a compliment – an inching toward what they want."

"Good enough," Ah'din sighed, and she didn't look very happy. "What has to be done to protect my brother, and the rest of us for that matter, needs to be done quickly. Pythos, can you take Doctor Moonsgold along to Eridi's apartments and summon her to the healer's sanecere for a quick but thorough examination?"

"Yess," he replied uncoiling off the floor and reaching for the emerald green robe he had cast aside earlier. "Thee will possition thysself at the healer'ss so that thee may ssee and hear without being sseen for the moment. Come, Winsslow Moonssgold, time to look officiouss and efficient."

Ah'din stared into the fires for a minute or so after they left, wishing for her warm kitchen, her loom, and thinking about all the alliums that yet needed harvesting before the ground froze. Then she thought of her brother, and quickly went upstairs to the suite she shared with Teal. There she retrieved her medical bag from the table, put on her heavy woolen cloak, flipped up the hood, and made her own way out.

▲ ▲ ▲ ▲ ▲ ▲ ▲

Ardenai let his long stride carry him down the corridors of the Great House, vaguely aware that the sun's passage was no longer high enough in the sky to cast full light into the cavernous space below. He had worn high, horsehide moccasins instead of riding boots this morning and he was glad; he needed no martial cadence to mark his passing. He turned right at the end of the passage, climbed a flight of stairs and walked past the doors which opened into his mother's expansive chambers. They had said their words to one another last night, and he did not pause. Walking another hundred paces or so he once again turned right, and into the darkest part of the Great House. A few moments later he stopped in front of yet another set of double doors. These doors, unlike any others in the Great House, had guards outside. Two Lebonathi Royal Guardsmen stood at attention in their white uniforms, their empty hands twitching for want of the weapons they usually held.

The Firstlord nodded graciously in their direction. "I would speak with Priestess Ah'nis," he said. After a moment's hesitation one of the doors opened enough to let him in. The room was only dimly lit, as he had assumed it would be, but the smell was most unpleasant – the intensity of last night without the pleasure. He looked around to see if there were windows which could be opened, and when he looked back, Anchoress Samarra was standing in front of him. "Anchoress," he said with a gracious nod.

"Dragonhorse," she said, nodding in return. Then she just stood there and stared at him. It put him in mind of going to the home of his late wife's parents for the first time – that intense scrutiny – and the memory of it made him smile, which surprised the anchoress. "Your princess is asleep," she said.

"I have not come to see Eridi," he responded. "I would speak with Priestess Ah'nis."

"You think she is here?"

"I know she is here, Anchoress. Please tell her I wish to see her. Now."

The woman nodded and moved silently away into the deep shadows, her pearlescent orb of a head glowing from time to time as she passed under one of the pale lights. The stench in the apartments was growing more intense, and Ardenai recognized it – dirty bodies and rotting flesh. It made his skin crawl, and every one of his equine strands of DNA urged him to bolt and run.

In less than a minute Priestess Ah'nis appeared, and he was startled by what he saw. She looked ill, and her eyes looked haunted. There was no haughtiness about her when she bowed deeply before him. “Dragonhorse,” she said, and her voice was barely above a whisper.

“I would speak with thee, please,” he said, and she nodded. “Outside. Let us walk for a bit.” He offered her his arm and she took it willingly, allowing him to steer her back out through the doors and into the hallway.

“Please,” she gasped, “I need air!”

He walked her quickly back the way he had come earlier, but instead of turning left he propelled her straight ahead, up a stairway hidden in the shadows and out onto the top of the hill which formed the roof of the ancient palace. The wind was bitter, but she spread out her arms, opened her robes and turned her face up to it, gulping the fresh air as though it were water and she were dying of thirst.

After a minute or so she came back to herself and closed her robes, pulling her arms closer to her body to conserve warmth as she looked up into his face. “For this moment, whatever you may have done to me, I forgive you,” she said, and she almost smiled. “Why did you want to see me?”

“Sit,” he said, gesturing toward a bench. “I would speak with thee.”

“I’d rather walk,” she said. “I’ve been standing beside Eridi’s bed for hours, watching her sleep.”

The Firstlord’s dark eyebrows came together as he frowned. “What? Ah’nis, I didn’t mean for you to stand over her.”

“It wasn’t you. It was them. I was not given a chair, nor was I allowed to sit on her bed. Servants stand. Since you assigned me to care for Eridi, according to Naram I became a servant instead of a priestess.”

Ardenai made a pained noise deep in his throat, took off his heavy cloak to wrap around her, and they began to walk away from the sea, so the wind would be at their backs. “Please, I need to know, tell me what you were told before…what went on last night between you and me.”

Ardenai felt the priestess stiffen, and she walked for a bit in silence, gathering her thoughts. “I was told that I was to be mated to the Dragonhorse. I was told that it might be a difficult mating and that I might need to be…encouraging. Because of our long-standing animosity toward one another, I found nothing strange in the request. I was told it was at the summons of the Great House."

"Nothing more?"

"Only that as part of the presenting ceremony the Lebonathi would use certain sacred herbs and plant esters, and they weren't sure how they would affect you."

"Who do you mean, 'they'?"

"High Priestess Ah'krill and Anchoress Samarra."

"What else did they tell you?"

"Only that as the herbals wore off you might become disoriented, and that I had best have you cover me quickly. And that I might have to control the sex of the child."

"And it didn't strike you as odd that you would have to do that? That you were not worthy of a mating without outside stimulation? That no one was there to attend us, as is proper?"

She waved off his questions and jerked the cloak more tightly around her shoulders. "Everything is all so fuzzy. Now that you mention it, it does seem odd. It didn't bother me at the time. All I could think about was bending under the weight of the Dragonhorse."

Ardenai took her by one shoulder and turned her to look at him, placing his body in front of hers to block the wind. "When they told you all of this, where were you, exactly, and what were you doing?"

Ah'nis scowled, partly in annoyance, partly in thought. "We were having tea, the three of us, in Ah'krill's study."

"Tea," Ardenai groaned. "The catalyst was in the tea. I am so sorry," he whispered, dropping down on one knee in front of her, "Ah'nis, please forgive me. I am so sorry. I acted like an idiot. I thought you were party to this, and you were not. Please forgive my actions last night, I beg you."

"Now I begin to understand several things," she muttered, "They didn't tell you, did they? That's what you meant by an ambush. You are an idiot, Dragonhorse, no act needed, but in this I find you blameless." There was a pause. "Get up from there. You look ridiculous."

He lost a little air through his nose, but he didn't actually laugh. It wouldn't do at all to laugh at a woman so obviously put upon as was this one.

"No, they didn't tell me" he said, brushing leaves off his britches, "but I did have tea with my mother earlier in the day, and I'll bet Samarra gave it to her. Ah'nis, I could have hurt you, badly!"

She turned away from him and began walking again. "That drenching was no nicker and nibble. I have bruises on both my arms where you grabbed me, and a bloody bite on my neck, thanks to you."

"I will make it up to you. I swear to you, Priestess. I take back my words of last night. I will give you a daughter if you want one. You and I will choose the time and the place, Io will attend us, and Pythos if you so choose, and when we go again into the cold pools it will be to settle you with child."

"I will hold you to that," she replied, and for a moment it chilled his good humor. Had she said these things to get him to change his mind? Carefully, with the quiet subtlety of the most ancient dragons, he touched her thoughts. What she had told him was truth as she perceived it. He could ask no more.

"I believe, we should be going back." he said. "I think I will demand my child bride."

"If you do you're a fool," she snapped. "She will rape you and you will welcome it, and your life will be over."

He looked at her, striding along beside him and contemplated her as he considered those familiar words. A tall woman, unusually fair, but rather pretty when she wasn't sticking her lip out. Caustic to a fault, but more intelligent than he'd suspected. He could see why she'd made a good stand-in for Eridi. "Please don't tell me you want to stay in there," he scowled. "You're hungry and thirsty, you're exhausted, and you smell like you've been dead for about a week. That can't be doing you any good."

"I am pleased to note that becoming Firstlord has not made you less an imperceptive ass than you have always been, Dragonhorse. I know I am tired. I know I stink. I am comforted in the fact that your cloak will now smell just like I do."

Ardenai looked at her in wonder for a long moment, and burst out laughing. "Priestess, I have enjoyed getting to know you a little better," he said. "So, have you figured out why they smell as they do?"

"They are flesh eaters to the exclusion of most everything else," she said matter-of-factly, "and the flesh which they brought along to eat has turned altogether, and yet many of them are determined to eat it, because Naram and Halaf and that nephew of his, Addur, have convinced them that our food is suspect, and that eating flesh, even spoiled flesh, carries more status, and more safety, than eating plants. For most of them, this is as close to status as they have ever come, so they have no point of reference. In addition, they do not bathe. Water-based society or not, they do not use or view water as we do, and they are firmly convinced that the bathing pools are some kind of death trap. They splash half a cup of water on their faces and hands, and the rest of them goes untrammeled. Their clothes stink, their breath stinks, their urine and feces stink. And so, I stink. I am a woman, so I am strong. I am a priestess, so I am strong. I do the bidding of the Firstlord, and so I am strong. I will in no way succumb to this small tribulation. Go on about your business and pay me no mind." She dismissed him and his petty concerns with a flip of her hand.

By that time they had reached the stairway going down, and Ardenai lowered his voice. "I have to get you out of there, Priestess. What if we could get Eridi into the hands of the Eloi? I know the High Priestess would be thrilled."

"Patience," she said, and said not another word until they reached the guards at the door.

Ardenai looked at her as she shrugged his cloak off into his hands. *I do not think they are telepathic in any sense of the word, do you?*

No. I am quite sure they are not.

Tell them that I was here inquiring after the princess. They will assume that I am caught between my desire for her and the will of the Great House. Maybe that will keep her safe. And you. I am worried about you.

Ah'nis rolled an eye at him, and as the doors opened a crack to let her in, the angry voice of Naram came screeching out. "How dare you let them in here! You may not take the princess anywhere! She is the property of the Dragonhorse, and he has said nothing to me about an examination."

"But the Firstwife requests it," came Samarra's voice, followed by the sharp sound of a hand slapping bare skin.

Dragonhorse and priestess exchanged a quick look and stepped into the dimness and the stench. "Good Nuntius," Ardenai said, nodding in his direction. His mouth was smiling but his eyes were hooded ever so slightly and his elegant ears were pinned tight against his head. "What seems to be the matter here?"

"These two, whomever they may be," he said through his teeth, gesturing at Pythos and Moonsgold as though he were throwing a rock at them, "have come to take the princess for, 'an examination' at the request of that… female you're married to. Who does she think she is to give me orders? What gives her the authority to request such a thing? What are they really going to do with our beautiful princess? Tell me that, Dragonhorse!"

Pythos flicked his tongue to get the Firstlord's attention, and Ardenai caught his breath as a morning's worth of planning and plotting slammed into his brain. He managed without effort to turn the sound into one of annoyance, and his eyes became more dangerous. "My wife governs beside, not beneath me. In these matters, and many others, her authority equals mine. In a few cases, it supersedes mine. This is one of those cases. If she has requested that an examination be done by a hominoid as well as a serpent, that examination will be done, and it will be done now."

"We will call back our ship! We will take the princess and go home!" Naram shouted. "And if Eridu chooses to rain war down upon your pathetic dirt-eating, shit-eating heads, let the blame fall on you, Dragonhorse!"

Ardenai's voice was perfectly flat, and cold as the wind outside. "You will take the princess nowhere, Naram. You have no authority to do so. She was presented as a gift to our world, we accepted her and we intend to keep her. If you would like to go home, you may call your ship without further delay, and any of you who wish to leave may do so. If you, Nuntius, would like to go out of here standing up, keep a civil tongue in your head." He turned and nodded to Ah'nis. "Please, Priestess, go and get Eridi. Tell her the Firstlord's personal physicians await her. Bring Jasreth, as well, so Eridi will have familiar company. And have Jasreth bring a few of their things.

They will not be coming back here any time soon."

By this time the entire retinue had gathered in the entresol, all but Girsu, and Ardenai addressed them in that same, flat tone. "You are welcome here, as friends and as guests, not as enemies, or as those who flaunt our customs in favor of your own. It is obvious that your food supplies have spoiled. Food we have, and plenty. We are not the Nargawerlders, we will not poison you nor feed you unwholesome food. Several of you sat at our table last night and ate well. You may do so again. As a matter of fact, it will be habit for all of you to do so from now on; all of you, not just those whom you deem important. To harbor fetid flesh, or flesh of any kind is repugnant to our culture, and you offend us by doing so. You perplex us by holing up like marchlings and feeding on your fears about us rather than venturing out into the open and learning about us."

"And where is Girsu?" Halaf demanded, stepping forward and attempting to look down his nose at someone considerably taller than himself. "He went out this morning and never came back. We have been told of your wiles, Dragonhorse. We know that if we leave the relative safety of place and numbers, we could well be counted amongst the dead or missing. We know. We have heard what happened to the Telenir who dared cross your path. You cut the heart out of one of them, and the others, every one of them on this planet, has gone missing. Is that what you have planned for us?"

Ardenai's expression did not change, nor did his eyes waver. *Again that knife fight comes up, Pythos! Is there not one single soul anywhere in the galaxy who has not heard about that kraaling knife fight? Thanks to this one, I begin to understand why people go insane and kill other people.*

"You have nothing to say?" Halaf sneered – or wanted to. Lucky for him his quavering attempt amused Ardenai.

"I assure you, Halaf, I assure all of you, your fears are totally of your own making. Girsu went with my wife this morning to watch the harvest. They will be back by dinner. As for the rest of it, check historical records if you are curious. They are open to you, and I encourage you to take advantage of them. Hear me. Members of the Great House will be here shortly to help you dispose of what is left of your supplies. They will then assist you in airing out your apartments and getting more comfortable with our laundries and our baths, which I think you will truly enjoy, as they are warm and soothing. Physician Pythos will assist you with protection for your eyes and skin against our sun so that you may be out and about in the city and acquaint yourselves with us as a people. It is my wish that you do so. If you are not comfortable with Pythos, Doctor Moonsgold will be happy to assist you, as will the Equi physicians of the Great House. Does anyone have any questions?"

No one shifted a foot, or coughed, or turned to speak to his neighbor. There was absolute silence, riveted to the words of the Dragonhorse. He let them dangle for a long minute, then released them from his gaze and turned to Eridi, who was making her sleepy way into the room, still swaddled much as she had been the night before. She was clinging to Ah'nis, and Jasreth was close behind, looking very worried. When Eridi was within easy speaking distance, he nodded a greeting and said, "You will be going with Doctor Moonsgold, and Priestess Ah'nis will stay with you. You will do as the doctor tells you. When you are finished, Priestess Ah'nis will take you for a bath, and to the Eloi for the garments of the akolytus, which you will wear while you are in the city. Do you understand?"

She did not look up, but only nodded, and he realized she was thoroughly frightened. They all were. Good. Their mood would improve with the arrival of fresh air and clean food. At Ardenai's gesture Ah'nis led the girl from the apartments, followed by Moonsgold and Pythos. Jasreth stood uncertainly, but with her head up, waiting to see what he wanted of her. "Go with your friend," he said, and gave her a ghost of a smile. She scurried out, and the Firstlord turned to follow her. At the door he turned back. "I will send those who can help you be more comfortable. I expect to see you out and about. Again, I welcome you as friends. Avail yourselves of our table, our city, and our libraries." He bowed very slightly, caught Naram's eyes in his own for a moment, and was gone.

He trotted back up the shadowy stairway, and across the gardens, pulling his tunic off over his head despite the cold wind. When he reached his own apartments he shed the last of his clothes on the balcony, ran through the bedchamber and literally threw himself into the hot pool. Only when he surfaced, blowing water out of his nose, did he realize he was not alone.

"Are you all right?" Marion grinned.

"I'm cold, and I've been with the Lebonathi, and I stink, and I apologize." He made a sound of utter disgust and once again disappeared under the water. When he re-surfaced, Oonah Pongo was waiting with foaming rosemary, peppermint oil and scrubbing sand.

"The good news is, you don't stink," she said, as she began working on him. "The bad news is it's probably lodged in that sensitive nose of yours. Here, snort a little peppermint, my friend, and tell us what you have been up to."

"And have you seen Winslow?" Marion asked. "He disappeared right after the rest of us went back to bed."

"Doctor Moonsgold is with Physician Pythos," Ardenai said by way of introduction, and began explaining the morning's events.

He was pretty well through his account of things when Bashkir, Master of The Great House, strode into the room. If appearance was an indicator, he lived up to his title. He was not only tall, he was broad, powerfully built, and had a close cropped black beard which spoke to his mixed heritage. It was joked around, though fondly, that he could create wind with his voice, which flowed easily from the bottom of his register. He was also a powerful telepath, and a very discreet man – both necessities of his office. Now he flashed a smile at the other two bathers, and focused on Ardenai. "You have need of me."

"I do. Thank you for coming. There is a disgusting mess that needs cleaning up in the dark apartments, and I must beg your indulgence to see that it is done. I will help you, since my inattentiveness may well have caused this. "

"It is not your doing," Bashkir said. "But, apparently, it is done. Your mother and the other priestesses have noticed a certain odor making its appearance from that direction."

"Well today, it stops. We need a crew in there cleaning up – helping the Lebonathi clean up – I don't know how many pounds of fetid meat, then themselves and their belongings. As a matter of fact, let's move them out of there before we start scrubbing." He made a wry face, then looked apologetic. "Where in the ten tribute worlds of Equus did they get all that rotten meat?"

"Have you counted the horses lately?" Marion asked, and the First-lord gave him a look askance.

"Aww, Marion, that's just disgusting, and it makes me want to laugh for some horrible reason I can't even comprehend." He looked back at Bashkir and despite himself, the question stood in his eyes.

Bashkir did laugh. "You have always had a tender heart and a vivid imagination. They are not eating horseflesh, Ardenai. Unless they have managed to corner a Gaknar, they are eating what they brought with them." He sobered, took a deep breath, and a look that was portent of unpleasant things to come settled over his usually cheerful features. "I shall put together a crew at once."

"We will help you," Captain Eletsky said, reaching for a towel and wading out of the pool. "Let us take care of that part of the clean-up while you focus on airing things out and acquainting the Lebonathi with baths and laundry." He looked at Ardenai. "If that's acceptable to you, Dragonhorse, and you, Master Bashkir."

"Unexpected help is the most appreciated of all," said Bashkir, and Ardenai breathed a sigh of relief.

"I did have another assignment for you and your crew," he said, "but I think this takes precedence. Maybe your attendance will help this go a little more smoothly, since you will most likely be perceived as outsiders, just like they are. Too, you are much less homogenous as a group than are we Equi. Some of you have eaten flesh. I think one of your crew – the navigator on the exchange program with the Sixth Galactic Alliance – isn't he a carrion eater?"

Marion nodded and grimaced the slightest bit. "I did have him in mind for the meatier parts of this, yes."

"Good. You have plenty of women on board, a couple of you are both male and female, and you come in some amazing colors. A wondrous diversion for our xenophobic houseguests, to take some of the sting out of the reprimand."

Bashkir nodded, stroking his manicured beard with his left hand and studying his Firstlord with a slight smile. "Perceptive," he said, and it was a vast compliment. "Captain Eletsky, when you have dressed, will you and your beautiful companion please join me in my chambers and we will get organized and get busy. I will have the cooks prepare a wonderful soup for all those who labor in this endeavor today. It contains certain herbs which clear the air and the nasal passages. Dragonhorse, I will send up some tea for you. Pour some of it down your gullet while it is hot, and the rest into your sinuses when it is cool enough." He nodded respectfully and turned to go, then turned back momentarily. "When you feel sufficiently scrubbed and refreshed, your sister has asked that you attend her in the sanecere for a brief examination."

▲ ▲ ▲ ▲ ▲ ▲ ▲

"Not my definition of brief," Ardenai groused, lacing up his high topped moccasins, and his sister gave him a kiss on the top of his head as she bustled around the sunny, plant-filled space that was the outer sanecere.

"No more than what was asked of Eridi," she said, scraping something into yet another tiny jar, "and Jasreth, as well. I want to see if they come by these pherine naturally as a species, or if they are something being introduced into Eridi's system. I also tested Priestess Ah'nis, to see if she had any residual influence – or damage."

Ardenai caught the stressed word and cast a weather eye in his sister's direction. "And what have you found so far?"

"Nothing yet, obviously. Except for the bruises on Ah'nis. You really roughed her up last night, Ardi. That's not like you."

"And for that I have apologized profusely, and allowed her to call me both an idiot, and an ass. I think that's sufficient, don't you?"

"Probably," she laughed, "though if she roughs you in return at mating time, don't take it to heart. Are you anxious to get out of here? You seem fidgety."

"I am anxious to get back upstairs and see how things are going with the clean-up. I must say, Ah'nis gathered an impressive amount of information and insight in a very short period of time."

Ah'din nodded absently and went back to her row of little jars. "I wish we could have tested Gideon, or Criollo." She turned to her brother and there was worry in her eyes. "Do you think they got home in good order?"

"I know they did," he soothed. "Our sire got word to me through Bashkir. May I go?"

"You may," she smiled. A pause hung in the air. "Ardi ..."

"Um?"

"Would you please…at least think about letting Pythos take those whip scars off your poor back? Seeing them just breaks my heart."

The Firstlord snorted with amusement. "The scars on my arms don't bother you, but the ones on my back do? I can assure you, the ones on my arms hurt a kraaling lot worse for a kraaling lot longer."

To his dismay her eyes filled with tears, and her expression said his words had cut. He took the tray of jars from her hands, set them aside, and gathered her in his arms as he spoke, kissing her fragrant hair and rubbing her back in the little circles she liked so much. "I'm sorry. I don't know why I said that. Some of the scars on my back, yes, if it will please thee. The one that curves over my collarbone, no, and I will tell you why. When I was in the mines with Gideon, I was literally dying of thirst, and I couldn't get my balance so I couldn't get up, and Thatcher put the lash to me – no, don't wince. It saved my life, Din. Because I was bleeding in a place I could touch with my lips, I could drink my own blood and survive. Every day that I am responsible for the Equi worlds and the Equi people, I will have a visible reminder that in the worst of circumstances, if we are not too proud, we may be our own salvation." He tipped her chin up and realized that she had big tears rolling down her cheeks.

He brushed them away with the tips of his index fingers and kissed the trails they had left on her face. "You know what I thought about most while I was in there – in the mines, and for all the time I was running toward an uncertain future and an even more uncertain fate? Flatwraps. My baby sister's wonderful flatwraps. And I would sit in the kitchen with you and watch you making them at our huge old cookstove, and smell them as they bubbled up, and everything else just vanished."

She made a little sound in her throat and hugged him so fiercely he could hardly breathe. "I'm so glad you're alive," she whispered, "I'm so glad you're alive. I love you so much."

They held each other for a long minute, relaxing in the warmth and a lifetime of familiarity, and Ardenai finally said, "I'll have Pythos take off the other scars first thing tomorrow. I promise you."

She nodded against his shoulder and he slowly released her to look up at him. "I do need to go," he said. "Tell Sir Pent I owe him one for that not at all brief, and overly intimate exam. I do hope what you gathered from us helps. It's a brilliant idea, by the way, Doctor. Thank you for thinking of it."

"Like most things, it was a group effort, and continues to be." She wiped her eyes on her long apron and made little shooing motions with her hands in his direction. "Run along now, Ardi. I have work to do and so do you. I'll see you at dinner."

Ardenai turned at the door and studied her for a few moments. "You work so hard. Why don't you and Teal do something romantic together while you're in the city? Or perhaps we could all go to a play, or a concert."

"That would be lovely," she murmured, not looking at him, and he figured she hadn't heard a word he'd said.

"We could go down to the beach and kick sand at each other."

"Ah'rane Ardenai Krush," was all she had to get out of her mouth before he was shutting the door and hurrying back upstairs.

There was more light, though it was not overly bright, and there were people – everywhere – not one in a uniform, but all in the everyday dress of the world from which they came. In each group there were Lebonathi, and most of them were smiling; nodding and listening as they went about their chores. In the wide corridor Bashkir had set up tables with tea and other refreshments, and as Ardenai looked around approvingly he saw two familiar adults and a line of small children trotting his way, each child holding a bouquet of flowers. They were laughing and talking amongst themselves and he realized that they were a mix of the primary class from Belesprit, and his own creppia nonage class from Falconstones.

"Ardenai Teacher!" a little voice yelled, and Mahruss broke away from the pack and came at him at a dead run. "Ardenai Teacher!" In a second flowers were scattered everywhere and Ardenai was on his knees trying to hug everybody at once while they swarmed over him, covering him with kisses and laughing for pure joy.

"He was a teacher before he rose to be Dragonhorse," Bashkir said to no one in particular, though his voice did carry. "Those are the little ones from his classroom. They have brought flowers to welcome you."

"And I am sure they will remember them soon," the teacher chuckled. "Right now I need to collect my hug, too. Ardenai was my teacher when I was their age."

Marion Eletsky cast one blue eye at the Lebonathis, who had stopped what they were doing at the shouts of the children and were watching in amazement. He cast the other blue eye in the other direction, to where Naram and Halaf stood glowering. "Gotcha," he said softly.

He then looked toward the second adult who had brought the children, and was rewarded with a fleeting smile. Yup, he thought, giving the man a thumbs up, they could say all they wanted about that broody boy, that sourpuss prince, old storm cloud Kehailan, but quite often Wing Commander Ah'ree Kehailan Ardenai had a very good idea, and this was one of them.

CHAPTER 4

Let me give you an example," Io replied. She lifted the craft to clear a stand of huge Equi pines populating the banks of a wide and fast flowing river, then dropped back down to skim the tops of an orchard that seemed to stretch forever. "My husband's sister, Ah'din, you met her last night – she is a doctor, an herbalist – she raises herbs for medicinal purposes, and for dye, and for cooking. She has a huge garden devoted to alliums, as well as other vegetables and fruits, and because she has a huge garden, she keeps bees. Because bees need a lot of tending, she shares that task with our neighbor, Ah'mae.

"Ah'mae has a huge garden, but she doesn't raise alliums except in the most casual way for day to day use, not for storage. She does raise exotic long-haired sheep, and their wool is highly prized. When she shears her sheep each early Segens, she gives Ah'din fine wool in exchange for the alliums and the various herbs for medicines and dyes she got the Oporens before, and together they harvest the honey from their bees. Does that make sense?"

"Well of course that part does. That's simple barter. How do they decide how many alliums are worth a pound of wool?"

"Now I see your confusion," Io said, setting the little Flyer down next to an astoundingly enormous stone barn where a broad belt powered by a team of draft horses was lifting bale after bale of fragrant hay into the loft. "The amount of alliums you need, is equal to the amount of wool you need. There is no value beyond needing it."

Girsu's face twisted. "What if you make shoes, or sing opera?"

"What's the difference between what you have, and what you do?"

The man's questioning look hardened into a mild glare, and Io realized she'd snapped at him. "Girsu, I was raised to believe that it is a privilege to contribute – first to my family, then to my neighbors, then to my community, then to the Great House. Just like the farmer and the townsfolk we saw harvesting sun flowers earlier, and the community we visited that was pressing cider." She gestured toward the barn and the dozen men operating and unloading trundlers. "This hay will be used here on this keep, then for the stables of the Great House. If Master Pottuck and Master Eider decide there is more than we need, it will be exported to another planet, most likely one of our affined worlds. Back will come something we would like to have, though that is not a requirement. If the hay is needed, it is sent."

"Surely this cannot work for everyone. There has to be a dissenting voice. This just cannot work all the time for everyone," he said. His face twisted with the problem even as his eyes were fixed on the people unloading hay. "Nothing works for everybody all the time."

Io's eyes widened and she snorted with amusement. "Of course it doesn't work for everyone. Girsu, there are vegetables that don't like each other – who they're planted next to – or where they're planted – too much sun, too much shade – or what they are fed. That's just life. All you can do is try to move them around until the majority of them thrive productively where they are planted."

Again Girsu disappeared into his own thoughts and Io braced herself for another hard question. Probably shouldn't have used the plant metaphor. Now he was going to ask if they moved dissenting citizens to some gulag in a far-off orbit. Despite herself, she sighed. She'd been up all night, she was worried about her husband, and she hadn't heard a single word from Ah'din or Pythos or Moonsgold. To top it all off she was hungry and after sampling all that cider, she had to use the lavage in the worst way.

As if in answer to her desires, a voice hailed them from the house, and Io turned to see a woman beckoning them with a wave of her apron. She waved in return and they walked in that direction down a path between some spreading Equi maples, crunching through leaves that three small boys were rather ineffectively trying to rake into piles. Each time a pile got big enough, they were overwhelmed with the desire to jump in it and throw leaves at each other before starting over again. Their laughter filled the crisp air and the fragrance of new mown hay filled Io's senses. She wondered how Girsu was doing with all the new scents and sounds but she refrained from asking, not being in a mood for what he might tell her. She thought momentarily and involuntarily of tiny Ah'leah, whom they had lost, and wondered if she would have enjoyed playing in the leaves.

"I am Ah'lauren," the woman smiled, brushing the palm of her right hand across the back of her left in greeting, "Ahimsa, I wish thee peace. Please come in."

"Thank you," Io smiled, returning the greeting. "I am Io, and this is Girsu. He is visiting us from Lebonath Jas."

"I know you both," she said shyly, "I am honored to have you here."

As was Equi custom they went, not to the main room, but to the kitchen, where baskets were heaped with food for the workers and frosty earthenware jugs sat in a row, full of tea, cider and cold water.

"You are about to set out food for the harvesters," Io exclaimed. "Let me help you with that. But first..."

The woman just grinned, moved her hand that direction, and Io scurried off, leaving Girsu alone with Ah'lauren. "Are you enjoying your visit?" she asked, offering him a chair. "Would you like some tea?"

"Thank you, that would be nice," he said. The time it took her to fix it, gave him time to study her and her surroundings. The house appeared not over-large, but very comfortable, made of plastered stone and Equi Alabaster, like most of the structures he'd seen. The kitchen was a fascinating if cluttered space, with big, deep-silled windows full of plants, and lots of cupboards, some with open shelves, some with doors. The cookstove was a marvel, with ovens below and above and a smooth surface that looked like very heavy metal or slab stone of some kind. It made quiet chuffing and hissing sounds like a steam engine, and there were several pots and kettles sitting on it, some elevated, he assumed to be further from the heat, and there was room to spare. The woman herself, like most Equi he had encountered, seemed timeless. Eternally youthful and energetic and glowing with good health. Her hair was a soft brown and so were her eyes, so she was not… full blooded? Was that how it worked? "Are you from here?" he asked, wondering if he should do so.

"Yes," she smiled, turning toward him with a steaming mug in her hand. "My family and the family of my husband have lived on this keep for many generations. Why do you ask?"

He wasn't sure he wanted to answer that, and it showed. Ah'lauren smiled and turned back to the stove to give him time to collect himself.

"I'm trying to get used to the whole concept of being frozen in time," he said finally. "People here seem to stay put, you know. Put down roots and never move, never travel."

"We do travel. I have brown eyes because my grandmother on my father's side is from Corvus," she said, and he was amazed. That wasn't what he'd said at all, and yet, there was the question he'd wanted to ask, answered. "Most all of us take time to get out and about for a bit before settling down."

"Did you?"

"I did," she said, holding a mug of her own and coming to sit close by. "I served aboard a science vessel with the Seventh Galactic Alliance for a while. I got to travel and meet all sorts of interesting people. As a matter of fact, my husband and I still volunteer with the SGA almost every Chionos and Aellaeno. Those are our stormy seasons, when we're not needed here."

There it was again, that amazingly long life span. That penetrating, illuminating thought that this woman in her simple, homemade moccasins and her peasant's apron, had spent at least twenty-five years in school. And now here she was, seeming happy in a stone cottage in the middle of nowhere. He tried to really think about that, and it escaped him. Here there seemed to be no up or down, no forward or back. No rank. Equal privilege. And yet some had more than others. A lot more. Was there resentment simmering under there somewhere? Somehow it seemed like there had to be. "Ah'lauren, what did you specialize in during your last years of school?"

"I'm a telemetry specialist," she said. "I program and launch deep space probes. What do you do?"

Io returned at that moment and Girsu breathed a mental sigh of relief. Ah'lauren busied herself with a hot drink for Io, wrapped her into a spare apron, and the two of them began stirring pots and talking about getting food on the table for the menfolk. He didn't have to answer the question, but it did interest him. What did he do? What was he? A lawyer, a politician, a perpetual student, maybe. If so, here was a study in like and un-alike. Two women doing womanly things in a traditional woman's role – comfortable in the extreme with one another because what they were doing at the moment was so ingrained. And yet, both of them had had a choice. Ah'lauren was a technician who could have stayed on with the Seventh Galactic Alliance full time, of that he was sure. And Io was a military strategist of the highest order, former Captain of the Horse Guard of the Great House of Equus and married to the most powerful man on the planet, and there she was, stirring a big pot of something, standing on her tiptoes to do so, and asking if Ah'lauren was set up to feed everybody outside or if they ought to come in, given the impending weather.

"We're set up to eat on the ground floor of the barn," she said, and even as she said it the door opened and men's voices poured in, laughing and talking as they entered the kitchen. They grew quiet as introductions were made, but they were not awestruck. Instead the man who had been introduced as Ah'lauren's husband, Rounce, insisted they stay for lunch, picked up one of the big pots and trotted off to the barn with it, the others behind him, carrying pots of pickles and soup, platters of crisp fried vegetable patties, cheese, olives and that wonderful sour, seedy Equi bread, along with the big jugs of drink and a sheet of small, sweet cakes that Girsu carried himself.

As they ate they discussed the weather and the crops, asked questions about agriculture on the Lebonathi worlds, and were politely but obviously taken back when Girsu admitted he didn't know much about it. How could you not know where your food comes from, they wondered aloud, and how it's grown and what nutrients are in the soil, and how it's harvested and stored – how it's handled and tended, and fed and cleaned?

When they were back in the flyer and pushing their speed to stay ahead of the storm, Girsu looked at Io and asked, "Does everybody on Equus know all those things about their food supply, or is it that we are in an agricultural region of the planet?"

"You probably wouldn't have been grilled quite so hard on Andal or Benacus," she chuckled, but it is an integral part of our education to know about food and nutrition, and what food is, exactly, and where it comes from."

"Andal and Benacus. The other major continents?"

"Yes. The rest of our planet consists of islands large and small, given that we are mostly water here. Andal has more industry, and Benacus has the technological support system for the interplanetary satellite systems. But, like Viridia, they have their holds and keeps. We are, above all else, far above all else, an agricultural people. We're going to set down and make a run for the transonic tube back to the city. Are you up for it, or would you rather stay in Pomonar until the storm blows itself out?"

A married woman was asking him if he wanted to stay in a strange city with her. He had spent all day with her, and no one had said a thing about it. She obviously didn't think it odd to be asking him. "Frankly, I don't want to have to explain such an absence to Naram or Halaf, or even Samarra," he said aloud. "I think we should try to get back if we can."

The wind was a relentless shriek by the time they left, and the scenes which had seemed so pastoral on the way out, were now black and windblown, streaked with such lightning as Girsu had never seen. No wonder everything was made of stone! The tube stuttered and slowed a time or two, but glide into Thura it did, and they rushed for the Great House in winds so strong Girsu was amazed that Io didn't blow away. As a matter of fact, he was a little afraid that he would, as well. Luckily there was a service tunnel not far on the surface from the station and they ducked inside. From there it was an easy walk to the main kitchen.

Entering that bastion of Equi cuisine – the heartbeat of the Great House – assailed every one of Girsu's senses. While most of their food tasted good, it did not smell particularly good in large amounts. It had a sharp, strong smell, like the soil it grew in, and that raw, unprocessed tang that was disturbing to his more refined nose. In addition to a hundred different aromas, not all of them pleasant, the lights were blinding even with his protective contact lenses and the languages and laughter were a cacophony. The entire place was orchestrated chaos. There was the biggest stove he had ever seen in his life – not that he'd seen that many – but this one was longer than six men standing fingertip to fingertip, and flanked by stone wall ovens big enough to hold half a full grown caron. This stove was making the same noises Ah'lauren's had made, but on a much larger scale, like a full-sized train idling impatiently in the station. Powered by heat from hot springs, from volcanic activity beneath the surface, Ah'lauren had said. He wondered uneasily for a moment if they ever blew up. This one could take a city block with it.

And the people – the beings, he corrected himself – some of them were definitely not hominoid, were everywhere. There were two or three dozen children of both sexes darting around to no one's dismay. There was a small being of some kind in one of the windowsills gathering herbs, probably, and it was chittering away to – what was his name – Bashkir, who was wrapped in an apron, chopping up something, and making eyes at that woman who had no light in her skin, and she was making eyes right back at him as they worked together. He counted six cooks at the stove, six more preparing bread, or rolls of some kind to go in the ovens, and to top it all off a cook knocked on one of the far oven doors, open it came, and out slithered that immense and terrifying serpent from last night's banquet. Call him anything you wanted, he was hideous beyond anything Girsu had ever had to deal with in his most frenzied dreams.

In a shadowed corner sat, of all people, Princess Eridi, dressed in Equi clothing, her hair piled on top of her head in the fashion of Equi priestesses, observing and conversing with that formidable priestess who had become her guardian. And where was Jasreth? Another few moments of looking located her slicing chunks off a huge wheel of...cheese? Cheese, apparently, and placing it into a pot at one end of the stove under the tutelage of a young man who was much too close to her. And that knife looked much too sharp.

"Wild, isn't it?" said a voice at his elbow, and he jumped noticeably.

"Sorry. I didn't realize you were – the term we use is, out walking."

Girsu looked over, then up, past a powerful body into a face the Equi considered handsome. He had met this man last night. "I didn't mean to startle," he smiled, "I'm tired, and I didn't hear you come up. Master of Horse Teal, isn't it?"

"Just Teal," the man smiled. Beautiful white teeth. Large, like everything else about him. "You wouldn't have heard me coming if I'd been riding a horse with iron shoes. But, forgive me, you do look tired. I'm assuming Ah'riodin ran your legs off all day?"

"I'm beginning to feel a little overworked and overstimulated, yes."

"Here, come sit with Eridi and Ah'nis and I will get you something hot to drink."

Too tired to wonder at the servitude of one so powerful, Girsu thanked him, and lowered himself into a chair a little distance from the priestess. Sitting unbidden beside Eridi would have been improper. They nodded to him, but were in the middle of a conversation of their own, and he was allowed simply to sit, and observe. Eridi's head was up, not down. She was not tightly bound, nor was she revealingly dressed, but she could move freely and she looked…comfortable. Even as she spoke with the priestess she was smiling. Jasreth was dressed in the same sort of tunic and trousers Io had been wearing – slim, but not suggestive – an acceptable if unusual costume. Her hair was braided down her back, and she was laughing; he could hear her. A very pleasant sound. And Teal, who was obviously a person of importance, was handing him a mug of something that had steam rising from it.

"Try this," he said. "I enjoy it when I'm tired. We call it hot mulled cider. Io told me you went to see some of the pome orchards today, and this is one of the end products." It was good. Sweet and spicy, with a pleasant aroma.

As though Teal sensed that Girsu was exhausted he nodded to him, placed a hand momentarily on his shoulder, and was off in a series of long, unhurried strides that carried him with amazing speed across the huge kitchen and out the doors leading to the main part of the palace.

Because Girsu had been gone all day he was not prepared for the summons to dinner that included all of them, Equi and Lebonathi – all the Lebonathi, not just the delegates – and many of the Equi from the Great House, including High Priestess Ah'krill and the Dragonhorse himself, plus some of the SGA crew members from last night, and several more as well. And all those children, tiny boys and girls together, all tangled up at a shorter table with two or three adults in charge. Quite the assemblage, with everyone talking to everyone else as though they were old friends.

He was about to ask if it was a special occasion when Halaf plopped down beside him in a huff and said, "So this is what it comes to. We are summoned like Caronai to the slaughter, to be fed Caronai feed and interrogated by our captors."

Girsu responded with raised eyebrows.

"They didn't tell you? Oh yes, the Dragonhorse stormed in this morning and took Princess Eridi away. Then he had a hoard of people descend on us and remove us from our apartments. They took our only source of protein and threw it away as though it was garbage, and then proceeded to scrub us, our clothes and our apartments as though we were sewage. I feared they'd drown the lot of us with all that water. Princess Eridi was gone for hours and came back looking like," he jerked his chin, "that. Now they tell me she is to be moved to other accommodations to 'begin her training'. And where were you while we were being harassed and humiliated, and she was being defiled in such a manner?"

Girsu resisted the urge to laugh. He'd wondered how long the Equi would put up with the smell of that rotting meat and Naram's truculence. So, he'd run afoul of the Thirteenth Dragonhorse, had he? He and Halaf with him. Splendid turn of events. Girsu was glad he'd not been around, though being a fly on the wall would have been worthwhile. "I was with Firstwife Io, looking at sun flowers, vineyards and pomes, and an amazing haying operation, sampling cider with a community and eating well at the house of complete, but completely charming strangers, and in general having a wonderful time. Perhaps she will take you tomorrow, if the weather clears."

"You are not in the least concerned, are you?" Halaf grated. "You have done what you wanted to do, Girsu. You have escaped from Lebonath

Jas and brought Jasreth with you. Well, I hope you like it here, because we are prisoners of that," he flipped a bony forefinger in Ardenai's direction, "that snake-eyed savage."

"Uncle Girsu!" said an excited voice at his left elbow, and Jasreth put a tureen on the table and then sat beside him, her face flushed with pleasure and the heat from the kitchen. "I made this myself! I had help, but I made it myself! Please try it. It's called cheese and allium soup. There are lots of soups here tonight, but I made this one!"

He'd never seen the girl so excited. She was ladling him soup almost before he'd said yes, and she studied him intently as he picked up his spoon and took a tentative sip. "Jasreth, this is amazing," he said, and her smile nearly split her face. She was happy. Nothing had happened here today to frighten her. Obviously nothing had happened to frighten Princess Eridi; she seemed to be almost in another world. Gone were the overtly sexual, sultry, or terrified looks and in their place a curious, and curiously serene girl sat between the high priestess of Equus and Priestess Ah'nis, having a lucid conversation with Anchoress Samarra, who was sitting across the table. Safely, across the table.

As for the snake-eyed savage, he was laughing with his wife, and looked up in time to catch Girsu looking his way. "Did you have a good time today?" he asked, and the table quieted a little. Unassuming as he was, there was certainly no lack of respect, and even with so many at table, his voice was unmistakable.

"I did, Firstlord. I came away with more questions than answers, but I did have a very good time today though that lightning storm on the way back scared me nearly out of my wits."

"And now you know why tampering with the fulmentactus computators carries the death penalty," Ardenai laughed. "What question is uppermost in your mind?"

"I'm not sure," Girsu smiled. "I'm torn between asking about how you control the lightning, and what farmers do in the winter."

"Depends on the farmer," Ardenai replied, leaning back in his chair. He was holding his wine glass in both hands and Girsu realized that he had the Firstlord's complete and undivided attention. The realization made him a little giddy.

"Farmers like we met today, for instance; Ah'lauren and Rounce."

"I can answer that one!" Eletsky chortled, rubbing his hands with exaggerated delight. "They are coming aboard Belesprit! Three full rotations I've applied for them, and I finally got them. Couldn't be because friends in high places pulled strings, could it?" He grinned and looked over his spectacles at Ardenai, who immediately gave a negative shake of his head.

"I did not interfere in any way. You probably got them either because you were annoyingly persistent, or because you have the newest science vessel in the fleet." Ardenai turned his attention back to Girsu and said, "Ah'lauren is an absolutely top-shelf scientist with the Seventh Galactic Alliance, and Rounce is an experienced documentary historian. After their part of the keep is secured for the cold weather, they and their twin sons will join Captain Eletsky. When it is time to plant crops, they will go back to being farmers."

Girsu looked slightly puzzled. "I thought your wife said she didn't know them."

"She didn't. I do. I've been around longer. A lot longer," he chuckled. "You may hold the floor for one more question."

"Please tell me how you control your weather! If we could do that, maybe we could reinvent our agricultural system."

The Firstlord shook his head and set aside his glass. "Alas, we cannot actually control the weather. We do have a priceless quadrium of ancient computators that keep the worst of the lightning off the planet's surface. They draw their energy from the same source as the transonic tube in which you rode today. On a usual day the trains – the tubes – generate enough energy by their passage to run themselves and generate much of our city's power as well. When the weather is rough, they draw from another source, the super-heated steam of which our planet has plenty, being volcanically very active. When the computators need more energy to protect the planet, they take it from the trains and other technologies, and ultimately, if a storm is bad enough, they take all the energy that is not reserved for emergencies.

The city runs on lamplight, we get around on foot, and are grateful that our steam-operated cook stoves are part of the emergency system."

"And then we sleep in our nest and tell scary stories," Mahruss said knowingly. "Are we going to sleep in a nest tonight, Ardenai Teacher? Because I am positive we will not be seeing Falconstones and our own beds."

Despite his adult observation the thought must have scared him a little because he left his own table and climbed into Ardenai's lap. Ardenai hugged him close, kissed his hair and said, "Don't you remember? You and your class are going to entertain the primary class from Belesprit in the Great House tonight, and tomorrow night they're going to entertain you aboard Captain Eletsky's science vessel. You're going to do experiments and everything."

"Yah," he said, but not happily, and hid his face against Ardenai's chest.

"I think you need to be tickled. Do you think you need to be tickled?"

Mahruss wiggled and giggled and shook his head. "No."

"What would you like to do instead?"

"I would like to sing," he said, and sat up straight. "I think we should all sing."

"I think that is a wonderful idea," Ardenai said. "Right after we finish our dinner we will all go into the other room and sing and play instruments and maybe play some games. How's that?"

"Acceptable," the little boy said, gave Ardenai a jaunty salute, and marched back to his table.

If Girsu had been fascinated by the Equi, he was now becoming enchanted. True to his word, the Dragonhorse gathered them all into the huge room next door, which was full of comfortable cushions, intimate corners in which to talk, board games, and musical instruments of every description large and small, simple to complicated, and people just naturally gravitated to them. Ardenai chose a rather large wooden instrument with many strings and a back-angled head, and when he strummed it, the room filled with music. Teal picked up another stringed instrument, smaller, that tucked under his chin and was played with a long bow. High Priestess Ah'krill chose a long wooden flute. Bashkir sat at a set of horsehide drums, and so on until nearly everyone was playing something. Even the children had small instruments of their own, and they sat with whichever adult had the bigger instrument they wanted to learn to play.

"The Ballad of Wielkopolski's Battle!" someone shouted.

"As you wish," the Firstlord nodded, and pointed to Bashkir. "And you, Sir, will you sing lead, being as you are the deepest bass in the House?" Bashkir nodded, laughing, and in a moment the room was filled with the most amazing sound Girsu had ever heard. There was no practice. There was no tuning. It was just – there. Fine musicians, excellent singers, everyone together. It was like paradise. Everyone sang.

Ardenai, Teal, Marion Eletsky – what an interesting looking fellow he was, with his blue eyes and his burnt toast skin and those odd spectacles he wore on his face – and Bashkir, sang a jolly song in four part harmony about a man choosing a wife based on how pretty her horse was, and there was some instructional time – all of it very informal where the children sat in laps and played instruments, and they sang a song they'd learned in school, apparently from Ardenai, and that was when Girsu actually realized that before he had risen to be Dragonhorse, the man had taught five-year-olds. Astounding. Few men on Lebonath Jas with any means at all would stoop to such employment as that.

The lights grew even dimmer, and there began a droning of some ancient instrument. "It is time," came the solemn pronouncement, and Ardenai nodded, crimping a grin that brought out his dimples.

"Come closer," he said in a conspirative and mysterious tone, "and learn of The Wind Warriors."

The entire room shivered with delight as the children gathered at his feet and Ardenai began the intricate fingerings of the introduction. When he actually began to sing – just his voice in the room – it was like a bell across a valley on a clear day. Barely could Girsu focus on the words for the beauty of the voice. Barely was he aware of Jasreth, clinging to his arm and humming along. Surely this must have been planned. Surely this must be staged.

Nothing so beautiful could be impromptu. He felt himself bogging down in the internal argument and losing the moment. He shook himself.

The last notes of the ancient song died away and Ardenai leaned forward, asking the little boy who had sat on his lap at dinner, what he wanted most to sing.

"The Naming Song," he smiled.

"Mahruss has requested the Naming Song," Ardenai said. "Females, lead or follow?"

"We will lead," said Io, and came to stand with her hands on the Firstlord's shoulders.

This time, there were no instruments at all. The room was absolutely silent, and then Io's clear soprano began the song. In a moment all the women had joined her, and they split the melody into harmony. The music rose, and Girsu felt like he was floating. When the men joined in, singing what the women began and again splitting into harmony, it was a round like nothing he had ever heard in his life. He basked in the beauty of the sound for a time, and then he began to hear the words. The Naming Song, was all the names for God in the known universe. It was worship, as natural as breathing, and suddenly, it all made sense. Of course the Equi way of doing things worked, why wouldn't it?

Girsu closed his eyes and let his head fall back and vowed silently to himself that Jasreth was never going to set foot on Lebonath Jas again. Truth be told, he wasn't planning on going back, either, because he was falling deeply in love with a man he knew he couldn't have, but whom he didn't think he could live without – and he knew, that if his government or this delegation got so much as a sniff of his feelings, he would be a dead man.

▲ ▲ ▲ ▲ ▲ ▲ ▲

"You won't have a great deal of time between storms," Timor was saying, "though you should have a few days of clear weather. If another storm blows in, hunker down and wait for it to pass before you try returning." He tightened the cinch down on the packhorse and turned to look at the three young people. "Any questions?" Ah'brianne and Criollo shook their heads.

Gideon had several. It wasn't particularly light yet, it was cold, and there were any number of trundlers and Equi flyers sitting around just begging to go on a trip into the Viridian solitude. Why were they taking horses? Why were they going to be gone a week when they could be gone half a day? Why did Lionel have to be left at home? Who were they going after, exactly, and why did it have to be done on horseback on the edge of winter?

Ah'brianne leaned into him and whispered, "I'll explain all this to you later. We'll have plenty of time while we're riding." The thought of her endless yakking didn't do much for his state of mind, and he thought he caught Criollo rolling his eyes at the prospect.

Actually, it had kind of been explained to him already, last evening over supper with his grandparents. The eldest, no name apparent, had no use for mechanized vehicles. If he heard one coming he would disappear and there was no telling what would happen to him over the cold, miserable seasons of Chionos and Aellaeno. He had to be brought back to the keep where he could be tended and kept warm until Latter Omphas rolled around again. Gideon hadn't even been able to figure out if this was man, or beast. Were they fetching home an old man, or an old horse? They'd said, "Him," so at least the possibility of an old woman was no longer in the equation. He stomped his feet in his boots to warm himself, because even with the heavy woolen socks Ah'rane had knit for him, he was a little chilly. Tolbeth rubbed her head companionably against his shoulder and chuckled softly either to him or at him, he wasn't sure which, but it lightened his mood.

Krush, who had ridden over to Lea keep with Gideon and Criollo, added his warning to be careful. "Watch the weather, and watch out especially for protopeds – they're kraaling quick. Shake out your caves before you sleep or explore. Kels are slow this time of year, but they can be proddy if you wake them up, and cerastapers are always a concern in the solitude."

Criollo patted the crossbow in its case under his left leg and said, "We will remember what you have taught us, Grandsire. If we should be attacked the Lebonathi will have fresh meat."

"That's disgusting," Ah'brianne said, wrinkling her nose, and Krush shook his head, even though he crimped a grin.

"Don't let your uncle hear you say that. I'm pretty sure he's had his fill of the Lebonathi and their eating habits," Krush said, and Criollo did his best to look contrite.

Gideon wished Krush were coming with them, just in case. But he and Ah'rane had decided to close up their house at Sea keep and move to Canyon keep, "At least for the snows," Krush had said, but there was a certain sadness and finality in his tone. The babe they had raised was now Firstlord of Equus, their daughter married to one of his closest advisers. Ah'din's time, as well as that of her husband, might well be split between keep and capital. There were just not enough people to keep two huge, multi-generational homes running. There weren't enough of them to fill even one of those houses. The thought had saddened Gideon, and had torn him once again between his sire and his grandsire. He was careful to keep those thoughts very quiet and very deep, as he knew both of them wanted only the best for him. It was like Krush and Ah'rane, loving and giving, to move themselves, when they could have asked everyone else to move in with them, and by tradition, it would have been done. Now, two Equi sunbursts would stand silent along the banks of the Little Sister.

When they had said their goodbyes and were moving out at a smart jog with the packhorse in tow, Gideon ventured, "Why," he began, "can't we take a horse trundler part way and then ride the rest of the distance? How good is his hearing, anyway?"

"Not up for an adventure?" Criollo grinned.

"No," Gideon replied shortly, "And I'm surprised that you are. My father needs me, and my grandfather needs me even more right now. I'm sure our Granddam could use both of us about now, don't you think?"

Criollo nodded and gave his cousin a gentle smile. "I know you're worried," he said. "Please remember that Canyon keep is as much home to our grandparents as is Sea keep. Not much will change. Perhaps not even for them."

Ah'brianne said nothing, being busy with the lead rope on the packhorse, and they rode for some time in silence, dropping off the prairie to follow the river bottom of the Little Sister south, the sun rising warm over their left shoulders, bringing up steam from the river and the meadows, and causing the birds to sing their songs of welcome after yesterday's storm. It was a beautiful ride through the golden grasses, knee high to the horses in some places, cropped shorter by wildlife in others. The leaves from the maples and oaks crunched underfoot, and fleeters looked up to watch them pass, following them with their large brown eyes, but showing no signs of fear as they chewed the last leaves off the wild azure berry bushes.

"I hope they leave some of the berries for us," Ah'brianne said, "They'd taste good with breakfast tomorrow morning."

"If we make good time to the caves at the river fork there should be daylight left for picking," Criollo said, then turned to Gideon, who was pacing along beside him. "That is where we'll stay tonight. We will be two-thirds of the way to the south edge of Lea keep, close to where the Middle Sister empties in. Tomorrow we'll cross the river and head southwest, past the borders of Upland keep, following the river into the true solitudes."

"And when do you suppose we'll catch up with this mythological creature?" Gideon asked. "Why all the secrecy?"

"He's not so much a secret as an enigma," Ah'brianne said from just behind him, and he saw Grendith's black nose come even with his stirrup iron. "No one knows for sure who he really is, or where he came from. Your father was just a boy when he found The Eldest for the first time, and he seemed to be an old man then. He was injured, and Ardenai brought him back to Sea keep for his mother to nurse back to health. When he was better they gave him a little cottage of his own, off in the rocks a bit from the others, and when Omphas and final thaw came he asked to go back to his solitudes, so Ardenai took him."

"And how do you know he's opposed to anything mechanical?"

"Experience," Criollo said. "He's terrified of the flyers or the trundlers. When Ardenai tried to find him once, early in Chionos, he took a trundler partway in and then rode, and when he got The Eldest back that far, the old man panicked, clouted Ardenai in the head with a rock, and disappeared for nearly two weeks before he was found again and taken to safety."

Gideon sighed. Suddenly this pleasant little jaunt wasn't so carefree. "And we're supposed to persuade him to go with us, how?"

"As always, we will speak softly and hope for the best," Criollo muttered.

"But don't worry," Ah'brianne said brightly, "He's almost impossible to find, and he may be dead by now, so all we will have to do is gather up his horses and bring them back. Unless we find his body. Then we will have to bury him, or cremate him, unless we are very lucky and the kels or the cerastapers or the protopeds have eaten him down to a few bones. Those we can just toss in the river."

Gideon's eyes were huge and his mouth was half open and Criollo couldn't stand it any longer and burst out laughing. "She's teasing you! Please, don't fall off your horse! We always have to face the possibility that we will find him dead, or that we won't find him at all, but it does not relieve us of our obligation to try. He is among the most ancient of our people, and a national treasure known to but a few. Someone from one or the other of our keeps has been making this trip for over eighty years, and we are not going to be the ones to break with tradition. Until we know there is no longer a need, we will continue to come."

They shambled along at a good pace for the rest of the morning, stopping once to water the horses and have a bite to eat from their saddlebags before continuing. Near midday Gideon's sharp eyes caught a movement on the side of the canyon, and he pointed without speaking.

"Gaknar!" Ah'brianne said quietly, excitement evident in her voice. "I'd heard they were moving north. It's very rare to see them."

They moved quickly into the branch dappled shade of some myrianotus trees, dismounted, and crept forward for a better view of the huge animals. They were cropping grass on a bench part way down the side of the canyon wall, and as they moved in their grazing they became more visible. The youngsters counted a dozen animals – six cows, five with calves, and a bull with jet black horns and a shaggy mane covering his short, powerful neck and sloping shoulders.

"I wonder where the other calf is," Gideon whispered.

"Protopeds, probably," Criollo replied. "Kels are too slow, and cerastapers are vicious, but compared to Gaknars, they're pretty tiny. They probably wouldn't try anything."

"So…nobody hunts anything here, right?" Gideon whispered, trying not to sound concerned. He, too, had a crossbow on his saddle and a slingshot on his belt, as did Ah'brianne, but he was pretty sure he didn't want to find himself in a position where he had to use them. He was better than he had been, but a long way from proficient, and he'd suddenly realized they were three colts out in the middle of nowhere, surrounded by a plethora of big, hairy animals with teeth and claws and razor sharp hooves. Tolbeth was fast. Gideon wondered for how far.

"Not unless an animal starts picking off people," Ah'brianne whispered, "or domestic stock. Because we leave all the animals alone and don't hunt any one of them, they keep each other pretty well sorted out. Look, they're moving down the bench! I wonder if they're coming to the river to drink."

"Not in the middle of the day," Criollo replied. "More likely they're going to find some sheltered spot and lie down."

"Not the sheltered spot we're in, I hope," Gideon said, and realized he was coming across as a coward. His father would be embarrassed for him. No, Gideon thought, he would not. He would understand. His father knew how brave he could be. He had saved Ardenai's life. Gideon took a deep breath, and let the knot in his middle loosen up.

"I hope you're right," Ah'brianne grinned. "This is a rare opportunity, but I am a little scared right now."

Gideon smiled and nodded. Was she reading his thoughts and saying that to make him feel better? Maybe. In any case it was a kind thing to do, and he gave her hand a little squeeze.

The animals continued down the slope and onto the river bottom, passing two furlongs or so from the watchers and meandering into the evergreen trees on their far right nearest the river. As quietly as they could they mounted up and moved left, closer to the side of the canyon wall before proceeding south. If the Gaknars made note of their passage they were not disturbed, and the three did not speak again until a half mile or so separated them from the herd.

"That was really exciting!" Ah'brianne laughed. "We'll have something to share with our classmates when we head back to school."

"Well, excitement makes me hungry," Criollo stated, and it was not long after that they settled themselves along the river bank to eat lunch. Because they had seen the gaknars, and assumed that where there were gaknars there might also be protopeds, they did not turn the horses loose, but eased their cinches and set them out on long lead ropes to graze. There was no need to dig into the larger cantle bags to find lunch. Ah'mae had packed traveling food into the pommel-bags that each of them carried in front of their saddles. They chased down thick flatwraps of nut butter and jam with cold water from the river, then laid in the sun awhile, heads propped against a half-rotten log, munching vegetable sticks, sun flower seeds and dried fruit.

"Too bad the water's gotten so cold," Ah'brianne sighed. "I would love to go for a swim. Maybe I could try it."

"We don't have time for you to indulge yourself in a swim right now," Criollo said, picking himself up on one elbow. "If we get moving there will be time to soak for a bit in the hot pools at the cave, and there will be time to pick some azure berries for breakfast."

"Oh fine," the girl muttered, and rose to her feet, brushing the sand off her britches and peering around in the bright sun to see where she'd parked her boots.

Criollo leaned toward Gideon and whispered, "She didn't really want to get wet, or, trust me, we'd have been waiting while Herself went swimming."

"I heard that!" she snapped, and the boys sprinted, laughing, for the horses with Ah'brianne close behind them.

It remained warm for most of the afternoon, and as the going got rougher and the boulders bigger, the climb steeper, they found themselves grateful for the shade of the huge rocks, even though it forced them to go single file. The sun glared off the white granite, creating deep, moving shadows that caused the horses to shy, and once they heard a sound like a baby crying in the distance. "Protoped," Criollo observed, and Gideon pulled his arms a little closer to his body and reached to pat Tolbeth's sweaty neck.

The canyon walls to their left began to diminish, and when they stopped to let the horses blow, Gideon could see that the oaks and maples were turning to pines and upland shrubs along the up side of their trail. The river was far below them now, faster and angrier, and he thought longingly of the peaceful beach beside the quiet river where they'd had lunch a few short hours ago. He didn't ask questions. He had sense enough to know that the river would be back, and be fordable, because not Teal, nor Ardenai, certainly not Timor, would have allowed them to come if it were all that dangerous. At least really, really dangerous.

When they got close enough to the top they turned off the rocky trail, leaned far forward over their horses' necks, and scrambled for the plateau above them, the horses lunging and panting with the effort. On the level they immediately dismounted and let the horses catch their breath while they did the same. From there, it was easier riding, and the views were spectacular. Gideon had expected rolling hills, fresh from the harvest of alcibus and einkorn, not the sharp nearly impassable profile of boulders, huge trees and precipitous slopes which greeted them on both sides in the distance.

"Tomorrow," Ah'brianne said. "Today we will ride the crest to the convergence of the rivers, and we are nearly there."

Nearly, was another hour and a half, but there was a breeze up here, and the views went on forever. Ah'brianne and Criollo pointed out landmarks which told Gideon they were familiar with where they were, and as they rode they told him about some of the history of the four keeps which adjoined one another to form their keep nave, and which had belonged to Krush and his family for well over forty statute generations. When Gideon did the math, it boggled his mind. On Declivis, a generation was twenty years; on Equus, it was fifty. Most Equi had their first child when they were in their fifties or sixties – hard for Gideon to even imagine. His mother had given birth to him when she was seventeen. Forty statute generations on Equus, was two thousand years. Gideon couldn't even conceive of two thousand years, and yet it was only eight Equi lifetimes. But not for him, he reminded himself. Equi though he was in his heart and by decree, by blood and bone and hope for life, he was Declivian. He would be dead and buried while the people he rode with this day were still having children, and adventures, and remembering him from a fleeting past.

"Does that mean you don't want it?" Ah'brianne asked sharply, and Gideon came back to the present conversation.

"Sorry," he said. "I was doing math in my head instead of listening to what you were asking me. Please, again?"

She made a small, exasperated noise. "Kehailan isn't going to want any of the keeps, we know that. My family only leases ours, so we can be asked to leave. Canyon keep belongs to Ardenai and Io. That leaves Sea keep, Upland keep, and Lea keep. Are you going to want one of them?"

"You mean, am I going to be a keeplord like my grandsire?"

"Oh precious Equus, Gideon, can't you just answer a simple question?" she snapped.

"I could, if it were a simple question," he sighed. "For me, it's not."

"Why not?"

Criollo shook his head and looked disapproving. "Don't pry, Bree. I'm sure my cousin has his reasons."

"Like what?" she insisted, and Criollo dropped his reins and threw up his hands in annoyance.

"You are the most persistent thing ever, Woman. Gideon, I apologize for her."

"Don't," he said. "It's all right. I've had a lot of time to think today, and I've realized that, as much as I want to be like you, I'm not like you and I never will be. I can live with you, and love you, and inherit my father's lands, but there are things I can't do, and marrying is one of them. The keeps should go to Criollo, or to the sons that my father and his wife – wives, I guess it will be – have together, not me."

"Not to me, either," Criollo said, guiding his big paint around a protruding root. It was getting toward dusk, and the trail was less visible than it had been when the sun was higher on the horizon. "My father lives where he does instead of keeping with his parents, because he travels with the cavalry and he wanted my dam to be close to Krush and our granddam. Shortly after Teal married Mother they moved to Canyon keep so my mother could make a home for both him and Ardenai. Even when your father married Ah'ree my parents didn't move. Of course, Ah'ree was never very strong, and Mother knew she was needed. Everyone is still so busy, it seems only logical for them to stay there forever. But as for inheritance, I will inherit – pardon, my father, then I – will inherit River keep, my grandparents' vineyard between Pomonar and Falconstones. My sire is an only child, so it's my job to provide little winemakers to take over the business."

"It seems like everybody is always at Canyon keep," Gideon said, "but I've yet to see your sire's parents there. Why is that?"

Criollo shook his head and sobered a little in the eyes. "Gidran is ambassador to Taraxia, and of course Ah'clare is with him. She's the Director of Education for one of the schools there. We haven't seen them since they were home for Ah'ree's funeral. Their vineyards are leased out. It has left an empty spot in my father's heart, I can tell you. He still supervises the winemaking most of the time, but it's not the same."

"Why can't you get married?" Ah'brianne persisted, cutting into the conversation.

Gideon had known she would, of course. He'd decided that it was time to get it all over with so they could make appropriate adjustments. Did that mean he cared for her? Sassy, impudent, annoying, blabbering thing that she was? He wasn't sure. He just knew that on some level or other he was lying to his friends, and that sooner or later it was going to rise up and bite him, as old Captain Josephus would say. But how to tell them. How had he muddled through it the first time? He looked away from the conversation and let his mind go back to the time when he and Ardenai had been acquaintances, racing through Alliance airspace luring Sarkhan toward Calumet. They'd been talking…about what? Like many memories there were only fragments left, and the shock of revelation – the shock on Ardenai's face as he realized what Gideon was going to tell him – the pounding fear in Gideon's throat, wondering if that revelation was going to ruin their friendship, wondering if Ardenai would ever be able to look at him again, knowing what he had been. He took a deep breath and felt Ardenai's arms around him, felt the gentle, rocking comfort, felt the shame and the relief of stepping out of his trousers to show Ardenai the brands on his belly and buttocks – the brands which marked him as unclean – saw Ardenai's tears, heard his words, and knew beyond any doubt, that what he had been, no longer mattered. Who he was becoming, that was what mattered.

"Don't answer that," Criollo grumbled, and Gideon returned to the present conversation.

"I need to," he said. "I can't get married because I can't give my wife any children."

"Well, that's just plain silly!" the girl scoffed. "You could raise children for the Great House, and they'd be just like your own. You should know that better than anybody."

Gideon gritted his teeth and soldiered on. "And I can't give her a sex life. I don't...function, for lack of a better word, and I never will. You know my mother was not a nice person; that's no secret. But what you probably don't know is that when I was two years old, she started selling me to the men who came to our house. For the next ten years I was raped almost every day of my life at least once a day, sometimes more, and the upshot of it is, I got some really, really nasty diseases with some seriously long-term side-effects, including sterility and impotence. The diseases are gone, but not the side-effects. So, now do you understand why it's not a simple question?"

There was utter silence, broken only by the soft clopping of horses' hooves in the duff, and their gentle blowing, the jingle of the bits, squeaking of good leather. After a minute or so Gideon stole a look at Ah'brianne out of the corner of his right eye, and realized she was crying.

"I didn't mean to lie to you all this time," he said apologetically, thinking she was angry or in some way disappointed, or disgusted. The thought of it made his heart hurt and feel heavy in his chest.

Ah'brianne sniffed and wiped her eyes with her sleeve before she answered him. "You know I am terribly, horribly sorry that those things happened to you, I am. But what really pisses me off," she grated, "is that somebody has convinced you that your sole worth is in your phallus, and that if you can't offer that to the person you love, and who loves you, that you have nothing to offer. That's about the dumbest, male, phallus-induced nonsense I've heard in all my life. If you're afraid of relationships, just say so, so that you can get some help – but do not assume that everybody else values you the same way you value yourself, Ardenai Gideon Morning Star, because they don't!" She dug her heels into her gelding's sides and trotted away from them up the trail, dragging the packhorse and leaving Criollo and Gideon looking first after her departing backside, then at each other.

"Well, I get it," Criollo said finally.

"Sea keep," Gideon said, and his heart felt as light as trail dust.

They took their time in order to let her cool off, and when they dropped the short distance back down to the river and arrived at the meadows near the cave, her horses were already turned out to graze, and Ah'brianne was picking berries near a large waterfall. She glanced up at them, unsmiling, then looked away and went back to what she was doing.

"That's her 'Don't speak to me if you value your life' look," Criollo said warily. "She's already got the perimeter stakes up for the horses." He thought a moment. "After we unsaddle we can go shake out the cave and start getting supper ready – maybe fluff up the beds."

"That bad, huh?"

"Oh yes."

The cave held nothing more ominous than some small, sleepy bats in the far back, and the boys had laid out towels, scrub sand, and the supplies to start supper cooking when Ah'brianne stuck her head in and said, "Gideon, come and look at this," and disappeared again.

"She's not luring me out there to kill me, is she?" he asked, but even as he said it he was heading outside. The sun had gone behind the hills, and the air had a nip to it, but also a fragrance that Gideon found new and pleasing. "Where are you?" he called, and saw her wave from the river edge of the meadow.

"Over here," she answered. "Come and look!"

He hurried over and at the cautionary motion of her hand, slowed his pace and knelt beside her.

"There," she said, pointing, and Gideon studied the various shades of green until a tiny plant became obvious. It had miniscule pink and white flowers, and hairy little tendrils that spread through the larger plants around it. When Ah'brianne picked a sprig and crushed it between thumb and index finger, that same, heady aroma filled the evening.

Gideon closed his eyes and breathed deeply. "That, is wonderful!" he sighed. "What is it?"

"Evangeline's Carpet. It's very rare, and a powerful healing herb used by physicians like Ah'din."

"Can we dig some of it up and take it to her?"

Ah'brianne shook her head. "All herbalists know it grows where it grows and nowhere else. But," she smiled, "we can harvest some and set it to dry in the cave until we come back this way, and we can mark on our map exactly where we found it, so Ah'din can come to this spot and maybe find some again."

"She has given so much to me. I would love to have something to give her," Gideon smiled. "This is a very good idea."

"Who knows, you may get her name in the holiday draw." Gideon gave her a blank look. "You know, the high holidays of Aellaeno. Our Celebration of Storms." His face did not change. "Start picking," she sighed, "very carefully. Trace each little tendril back to the plant and pinch it off about an inch from the base of the mother. There, like that. Here, we'll lay them on my scarf so we can find them."

The picking occupied their time until it was too dark to see, and by then the good smells of supper emanating from the cave brought them inside, shivering a little with the evening chill. Criollo had done a laudable job of fixing the food Ah'mae had sent along – a hot vegetable stew with crispy mazea crackers, pungent pickled redroot, and peppers stuffed with quinoa and mushrooms, which Criollo had baked at the side of the fire until their skins blackened and curled, exposing rivulets of melted sheep cheese. The beds were laid out close together with the fire between them and the mouth of the cave, and on each bed was a thick towel, inviting them to bathe after supper.

Before they indulged themselves in a bath, they took care of the horses, unclipping the unit on their halters which kept them within the perimeter stakes, giving them each a measure of grain, and then tying them to a picket line in the shelter of some Viridian sychamores near the mouth of the cave, "So we can hear them if anything stirs them up," Criollo said.

The steam rising white from the rocks against the dark sky told Gideon where the hot pool was, but in that one Criollo had heated the stew, so they opted for the cooler one further down, closer to the waterfall, under the canopy of stars. Having determined that their fingers could take the heat they stripped off their clothes, dabbled their feet, and slid into the water with much hissing and "hothothot!" before settling down for a soak. The stars seemed huge against the black velvet sky, and for a time they stared upward in silence, marveling, and Gideon again realized that he must be the most blessed person ever born to be sharing this time, in this place, with these… friends. He had friends. For the first time in his life. He felt tears start in his eyes, and splashed a little water to hide them. Not that he was ashamed. If he could speak as he had spoken this afternoon, he felt he could never be ashamed again of what he had been, because it was not what he was, or was becoming. Ardenai had taught him that. But he didn't want to do any more explaining, either, and so he watched and listened and learned as Ah'brianne and Criollo pointed out the different constellations and spoke of the worlds circling them.

"That one, Gideon, the farthest north star in Demeter, your birthworld circles that one," Criollo said, pointing with a dripping finger to a constellation just spinning into view above the hills.

"And to the south and east, is the parasectra of Kohath Zadok– in Mydrus, the constellation that looks like the top of a fern frond – there are five planets there, and that's where dear Ambassador MalDor hails from," Ah'brianne chuckled. "He was not happy that I needed to be gone for a week or so. The Lebonathi may have dressers, but MalDor needs a jewelry putter-onner, taker-offer, and that's usually me. He says I'm the only one who knows exactly where to put things."

"Spinning over there, just setting, our friends the Lebonathi," Criollo said. "I wonder if we're making any progress at all with them."

"You mean, are you making any progress with Jasreth?" Ah'brianne smiled, then hastily said, "I'm just teasing, please don't throw water. I don't want to go to bed with wet hair. It's too cold."

"She is pretty," Criollo said in a tone close to a sigh. "Much prettier than Princess Eridi."

"At least she has some color," Gideon agreed. "I think she said it was because she had lived closer to the surface, if that makes any sense. And from her tone, I'm not sure it's the real reason she's darker than the others – that being relative in the spectrum of pale."

"I suggested to her that she let Pythos add some pigment to her skin," Criollo said, "so she can be out and about a bit more, and some darker sun lenses, too."

"It sounded like they had some trouble at the Great House," Gideon said. "My sire told us last night that they had found hundreds of pounds of spoiled meat in the Lebonathi quarters, and that Captain Eletsky and his crew had been most gracious in helping with the clean-up."

"According to my father's friend, the rotten meat wasn't all that got sorted out," Ah'brianne said. "I guess your sire had some serious words with Halaf and Naram. I cannot imagine how scary he must be when he's angry."

"Very," Gideon muttered. "So, tell me about this Celebration of Storms. What do you mean, when you say I might get Ah'din's name in the draw?"

"Thank you for changing the subject," Criollo said. "Aellaeno is the season which most resembles the Declivian..." he gave it some thought, "...Wintus? Anyway, as it begins and we celebrate the turning of the year, we celebrate the storms which bring us water and life, and the quiet times of snow, and the challenges of the cold as the earth rests."

"We have big dances and plays and concerts and festivals and for two weeks we celebrate life indoors," Ah'brianne added. "There are polo matches, and horseback games, and showcases for the talents of horses and riders, and in addition to the feasting and playing, we give gifts to one another. It's supposed to be something we've made ourselves."

"She's confusing you, I can see it," Criollo said. "Turn around, let me wash your back. We draw names within the family, and for the person you draw, you make something special just for them. We usually give small gifts to everybody, but to that one person, we give a special gift. Does that make sense?"

"Oh, I understand," Gideon said, feeling a little desperate. "Ah'bri-anne, get over here, let me wash your back. But what if, like me, you don't know how to make anything yet? I know how to break rocks in a cleomitite mine, and I know how to clean and polish tack, but I don't know how to make anything."

"Remember, it's something to suit the person," Ah'brianne said, turning the circle tighter so she could wash Criollo's back. "If you got Ah'din's name, you could gather all kinds of herbs for her – I would help you with that. If you got your father, you could make a journal of your travels together and put pictures in it ..."

"And if you got my father you could let him use you as a punching bag for a year," Criollo laughed. "He's still miffed that you dumped him off his horse that first night on Calumet."

"You know your family and you love your family, and whatever you choose to do, it will be perfect," Ah'brianne said, "because that's the kind of person you are. There, you're all finished, Criollo. I'm going to go have some hot challa and sweet cakes and go to bed."

Fortunately for Gideon, both Ah'brianne and Criollo knew exactly what they were doing. By the time the sun had cleared the horizon they had filled their bellies with hot mazea cakes and azure berries, rolled up their bedrolls, put them on the pack horse, washed the dishes, and broken camp. For as comfortable as they had been, the tidy-up was lightning quick. "The higher the sun, the faster the river," Criollo explained. "We want to ford while it's still frozen above us to the south."

Just before they rode away, Gideon carefully laid out the harvest of Evangeline's Carpet on one of the waxcloth wrappers his lunch had come in the day before, and he placed it on a narrow shelf just inside the mouth of the cave with a swift, silent prayer to El'Shadai to keep it safe.

They rode up again to the rim of the canyon, which at this point was only as high as the waterfall, and once again headed south. In half an hour's jog they reached the place where Criollo and Ah'brianne said they could safely cross the river. "It's a little wider here," Ah'brianne said, "but the bottom is sandy for the most part, so it's less likely that the horses will stumble and dunk us. The water will most likely just touch the bottom of your stirrups, and Tolbeth shouldn't have to swim. Keep her head slightly up river and keep her moving. You'll be fine."

Criollo led off on his tall black and white paint, Bimini, with the pack horse in tow, followed by Ah'brianne on old black Grendith. "It's just you and me," Gideon said, patting his little bay, and they waded in. Because Tolbeth was more intent on catching up with the others than in being afraid of the water, their crossing was quick and without incident. As Ah'brianne had said, the water came barely to his irons, and both Criollo and Ah'brianne, who were on taller horses, touched no water at all.

"Let's hope it holds until we get back," Criollo said, and lined them out with the sun once again over their left shoulders, but angling more sharply behind them. "The river we're following now is the Middle Sister," he said. "Today will see us clear the southern boundary of Upland keep and get pretty well to the southwest. There's another set of caves we can stay in tonight, and tomorrow will begin the hunt for The Eldest."

"He couldn't just know to meet us someplace this time of year?" Gideon asked, trying not to sound whiney.

"Usually, he doesn't want to be found," Criollo said blandly. "The only way we ever find him is if our horses find his horses."

"Will someone please explain this to me? I mean REALLY explain it?" Gideon exclaimed. "This makes no sense. He doesn't come to us, we go find him, but he doesn't want to be found, but we make him go with us anyway. I am truly befuddled."

"He's kind of..." Criollo began, and his eyes said he was searching for just the right words.

"Stuck in time?" Ah'brianne offered.

Criollo nodded. "Yes. Stuck in time. He can't remember from year to year that this is what happens, so it's always new."

"We try as much as possible to go, Criollo and me, because The Eldest remembers Ardenai as a colt – a young person, like we are now."

"He comes around after a while, and either he remembers, or he's persuaded to try something new, but it takes some doing sometimes."

Gideon thought about that a bit while they jogged along. "I know the Equi put a very high value on personal freedom," he said at last, "but isn't there a time when keeping someone safe, even if they don't want to be kept safe, is the best thing to do?"

"A man of his years, no," Criollo replied. "He is not endangering others. He loves the freedom of the solitudes, and he has earned that freedom. If we find him dead, so be it, but to 'keep him safe,'" he made little quote marks with his fingers, "would be tantamount to imprisonment. We might as well just kill him and have done with it."

"So, no disrespect meant, why don't we leave him alone to live out his life?"

"Because he is magical," Ah'brianne said. "He knows the solitudes, and the animals, and the hidden places, and he tells wonderful stories about ancient cities and draws odd maps in the dirt."

Criollo turned and fixed them both with a deadly stare. "And your father, my uncle, Ah'krill Ardenai Morning Star, The Thirteenth Dragonhorse, Head of the AEW and the Seventh Galactic Alliance, absolute ruler of Equus and her ten affined planets, the Arms of Eladeus, the most powerful man in the known galaxy, has instructed us to GO and find him."

"Well, when you put it like that, I'm in," Gideon chuckled. "I would do almost anything to please my father."

"Hopefully you won't have to," Criollo muttered, and clucked Bimini into a slow, ground-eating canter.

It was late in the afternoon of the third day of hard riding when they finally heard horses whinnying back and forth and calling to their stock. Their horses set up a reply, and after half an hour or so of searching they found them in a small box canyon near the river. Caves dotted the granite faced sides, and trees and shrubs clung at odd angles where there was enough soil to support them. In front of them and to their left was a sandy bowl in front of a larger cave, and there, squatting beside a fire, was The Eldest. It had to be. His hair was snow white and hung nearly to the ground as he hunkered near the flame. He was dressed in garments of ancient design, and when he looked up, his face was so deeply lined they could hardly see his features.

He looked startled, but Criollo immediately called, "Ahimsa, Grandsire. We wish thee peace. May we share your fire for a bit?"

The ancient being stared at them for what seemed a long minute, then made a beckoning gesture. "You may share my fire," he said, and his voice was strong and resonant – a startling voice in one who looked so frail. "Your horses look tired. Share some supper and spend the night – let them rest."

"Thank you," Criollo said, and they dismounted. "That was easy," he whispered under his horse's neck, and Ah'brianne whispered,

"Well don't relax just yet."

They took their time unsaddling and wiping down the horses, who were anxious to spend time with those of The Eldest, and danced around restlessly despite efforts to quiet them down.

"The bay mare is in heat," the old man observed, watching her toss her head and nicker. "She wants to be with my stallion, and he wants to return the favor of her company."

"What?" Gideon gasped, but it was too late. His grip was loose on her halter, and in a flash she had pulled away and was gone. In another second they were both gone, pounding down the canyon, kicking and biting in the proverbial cloud of dust. "Well, shit," he said, almost to himself. The mistake was almost more than he could comprehend. So much for being the grandson of a bloodlines specialist.

"Never fear," the old man said. "The colt will be beautiful." He turned and studied the tall youth with the bright gold eyes and the blond hair. "You are beautiful as well, young prince, and different from the others. What is your name?"

"I am Gideon," he said.

"Just Gideon?"

"I am Ardenai Gideon Morning Star," the boy amended. "Who are you?"

"I am Chirion," the old man said, and his face became a work of art as he smiled. "Bring Ah'brianne and Criollo and come sit by my fire, Ardenai Gideon Morningstar. I have been waiting for you for a very, very long time."

CHAPTER 5

"You're sure there's no danger for them?" Ardenai asked for the third time in the course of a five minute conversation, and Tarpan tried his best neither to laugh, nor to register the resentment he was beginning to feel. True, he was young, but he was thorough. Ardenai should know that by now. He sensed the Firstlord's nervousness, and let it go by.

"I am as sure as I can be, Dragonhorse. We have done absolutely everything we can do to assure that those among the Wind Warriors who did not lift their hand against the Equi government are safe now, and will be in the future. Their crops are harvested, their homes stand ready to receive them. We have members of your personal guard in every household to protect them should the more violent members of the Telenir faction show themselves. Since the man most responsible for this whole uprising is no longer…with us, as it were, their reappearance seems unlikely. What else would you have us do?"

"Take them home," Ardenai smiled. "All but Taki. Please ask him if he will stay for one more day and speak with me regarding his knowledge of the Telenir and the legends which have grown up around them as the Wind Warriors."

Tarpan nodded. "I will ask, but if he has truly given Io and me all the information he has about the Telenir in general or Konik specifically, there will be precious little to it."

The Firstlord sighed and sat looking at the ancient portcullis which spanned the distance in front of the double doors to the entrance of Mountain hold. On the outside the hold was rocky, mossy and hoary with age – thousands upon thousands of years old. No one actually knew for sure when it had first been built, but it had assumed its present shape roughly twelve thousand years ago when it had gone from being a fortified castle to being the training ground for each of the thirteen Dragonhorses and their earliest predecessors. It looked cold and uninviting, and the Firstlord was prepared to continue his shivering. The weather was holding on Viridia for the moment, but in the high reaches of Andal it was snowing, and had been. They exited the Equi flyer into knee deep drifts. "Let the man go," Ardenai said at last. "He has been in our tender care long enough. He must be aching for hearth and home. I will have more than enough here to keep me busy over the next quarter season or so."

They stopped in front of the portcullis and Ardenai said, "I am Ah'krill Ardenai Morningstar, and I am the Thirteenth Dragonhorse." There was a pause, then a hiss and a creak and the mechanism lifted upward as the doors swung in to admit them.

He needn't have worried that the Telenir here for safekeeping were cold and uncomfortable. Inside, the walls were Viridian alabaster, just like his home at Canyon keep and the Great House in Thura. The floors were heated and the halls were bright from some hidden source he couldn't immediately discern. Someone was there to take their traveling cloaks, and Ardenai found that the gently moving air was pleasantly warm and fragrant. He looked at Tarpan, and just shook his head as he began to chuckle. "The questions you don't think to ask," he said.

Tarpan cocked his head and smiled back at the man who had been his teacher. "Meaning?" he said, and gestured with his right hand down the wide hallway.

"The Telenir have been our guests here for how long? And I have never once thought to ask you or my wife about the condition of this place. I just assumed that if anything was wrong you'd have let me know right away."

"I would have. You've had much on your mind. The last few days have been especially busy, so I have asked the kitchen to lay an early dinner for you. Then, since you are here, all of us must depart. This time is for you to be alone here, and then with your family." There was a pause. "I know you didn't want to do this until the Lebonathi delegation had gone home, but we will entertain them for you."

The Firstlord smiled and nodded. "Thanks. Will you join me for dinner before you go?"

Tarpan shook his head. "I must gather our guests and get them safely home to their sundry venues. If you go down this hall and turn left, you will find your chambers. From what I understand, your training will begin in the morning."

Ardenai placed a hand on the young man's shoulder and gave him a gentle shake. "Very well done, Tarpan. Thank you."

"I am ever at your service," he replied, gave the Firstlord a brief smile, turned on his heel and walked quickly back the way they had come. Within a few moments Ardenai could hear a drum, beating out the rhythm which called people to assemble.

He meandered on down the long corridor, looking this way and that through the massive archways into different rooms. There was a gymnasium, a conference room with a long table of Calumet Mahogany, a sitting room, and several rooms which had closed doors. He rounded the corner in the direction he had been instructed and found himself in a more dimly lit corridor, and one which seemed older than the previous spaces. He had gone a few paces, still checking the air and his surroundings when there was a piercing screech and something landed on him, biting, scratching and pummeling – shrieking all the while like a demon from a nightmare.

For a split second Ardenai's reflexes told him to fling the creature, but in the same second he realized it was human, so he shook himself instead. As the assailant lost his balance, the Firstlord reached back, caught him by the neck of his tunic, and pulled him over his right shoulder. His humanity got him a sharp slap and some deep scratches on one cheek before he managed to elevate the man, for a man it was, to his tiptoes and hold him at arm's length to see who he was.

"You killed my son!" the man shrieked, still kicking and thrashing and trying to scratch Ardenai's face. "You murdering filth! You killed my son! You killed him and took what was rightfully his!" Then, Ardenai recognized him. It was Sarkhan's father.

"Sir," Ardenai began, but in his mind he was calling, *Tarpan! Come quickly! The corridor by my chambers!* "I deeply regret what transpired between your son and me, but you need to calm down. Your heart is going to stop from anger, and then your wife will have neither son, nor husband. Please, try to calm down."

"You murdered him, and now you're SORRY?" he snarled through gritted teeth, eyes crazed, still hissing and spitting. His breath was coming in shorter gasps and the thrashing lessened, most likely from exhaustion rather than being asked to do so, but he became easier to control, and the Firstlord steered him, still at arm's length by the scruff of the neck, into a small easy chair beside a table. From the angle of the chair, Ardenai assumed it was the one the old man had hidden behind. He was trembling now, and sobbing, and Ardenai let go of his neck and went down on one knee beside him, holding both the man's hands firmly in one of his own and keeping a weather eye out for getting kicked.

By now even Ardenai had seen the cosmoscope documentation of the event. Primitive, hand-cranked cameras aside, it was obvious what had happened, and who had done what to whom. Surely this man must know that he was not speaking fact. "You misunderstand, Sir. I do not regret my actions. I regret the circumstances which compelled my actions," he said quietly.

"You cut his heart out!" the man sobbed. "You cut his heart out!"

Again, not quite true. Ardenai had thrown a knife an impossible distance hard enough to cut his heart in half as it went through him. The thought of it still made him shudder. "He…died like a warrior," Ardenai said. "You should be proud." It was a bald-faced lie, but the man's grief was nearly unbearable and the Firstlord was truly afraid that this frail old lunatic was going to die right here on the spot – his first day at Mountain hold for what was supposed to be learning and meditation, and he was going to be instrumental in the death of yet another of the Telenir.

By then Ardenai could hear running feet and a woman's voice crying, "Saremanno!" She came to a breathless stop next to the man's chair and threw her arms around him. She turned, prepared to say something sharp to Ardenai, then saw the blood on his face and was immediately contrite. "What have you done?" she whispered. "Firstlord, Dragonhorse, please! I am so sorry for my father's actions."

"Do not concern yourself," he said gently, and released the old man's hands. "This has been a terrible time for him. Please take him home and see that he rests in a familiar place."

"You're injured," she began, and Ardenai waved it away with a sour chuckle.

"My sister's lithoped has done worse. Not that your father isn't still formidable," he hastened to add, more for the old man's sake than hers. "Are you in a position to care for him?"

"I am," she said, and gave him a ghost of a smile. Unique face with large, equine features, and accented by hair the deepest shade of mahogany red Ardenai could remember seeing. "I am Ah'cora, and I am in your debt."

"You are not," Ardenai said, standing up and blotting at the scratches on his cheek with the sleeve of his tunic. "It is I who am in your debt for coming when you did. I was afraid his heart was going to stop or his brain was going to explode."

"Let me help you with him," said a voice, and Ardenai realized Tarpan's had been the second set of footfalls. The young captain raised one eyebrow ever so slightly and asked, "Will there be repercussions, Dragonhorse?"

"No. Anger has had repercussions enough. Please get everyone home before the storm gets worse."

Again he was alone, and after the departing gong had sounded, truly alone except for the few who tended the needs of the hold itself. His chambers were adequate if a little austere, but that did not dismay him. The bed was long enough for his six foot six inch frame, and wide enough to accommodate both himself and his diminutive wife, who usually slept curled tightly against him, back to chest. He missed her as he wandered the corridors, familiarizing himself with his surroundings. It was not grand, nor even remarkable but for its age and condition – until he found the library, and stood transfixed. It was an immense decagon of alabaster and burnished Calumet mahogany and rose, level after level, row on row of papyrus scrolls, leather folios, paper paged books, cosmoscope documents, maps on leather, maps on paper, maps on parchment – historic documents under glass, some thousands of years old. "Precious Equus," he breathed at last, and began a slow circumnavigation of the room, craning his neck, mouth half open in wonder, touching with reverent fingers the words which had shaped his world.

How long he had been there, exploring and reading, he didn't know, but a woman in grey livery with a snow white apron over top appeared from the far end of the library and told him his supper was getting cold. She turned silently and he followed her in a church-like hush to the kitchen, where she gestured him into a chair near the big cookstove and set a plate of breads and cheeses and a large bowl of soup in front of him. He thanked her, was rewarded with a slight, smiling nod, and as silently as she had come, she departed, leaving him alone in the kitchen with his supper.

"Interesting," he said aloud. But the soup was good, and he was hungry. Since no one was around he helped himself to a second bowl, found what he needed to make a pot of tea, and relaxed with bread and cheese and his feet to the fire. When he was ready to leave, he took the soup pot off the stove so it wouldn't scorch, washed his dishes, took the teapot and his cup with him, and wandered back in the general direction of his room, realizing he was very tired. "Tomorrow," he said, "I will begin to do that library some justice." His voice echoed in the hall and he felt a little silly, talking to himself. He realized he was used to some noise, and people around him, and the smell of horses, and the sound of laughter. Here, there was none of that, and he suddenly felt very alone. He took a quick bath and crawled into bed, uneasy in the silence even as he drifted off to sleep.

When he awoke he could only assume it was morning, and when his bare feet hit the floor, it was cold. "Light," he said, and nothing happened. He found the lavage mostly by remembering where it had been the night before, and groped his way back into the bed chamber. Two choices, he decided. Find some light and get dressed, or get back into bed where it was warm, and wait for rescue. Since Tarpan had said he would be alone, and Tarpan usually knew whereof he spoke, Ardenai opted for the former and began feeling his way along the walls for a curtained window. There was none apparent and he made a little sound of exasperation, realizing he'd not paid nearly enough attention last night to where he would find himself this morning. Well, perhaps this was part of some test. In any case he'd left a very busy schedule behind in order to study this place and the documents it held, and he wasn't about to waste that time fumbling around in the dark. Where had he seen windows – a window? None came to mind. If he could find the kitchen, chances were he could find some light – where there was heat, there was light. The simple science of incandescence.

He assumed with a self-deprecating little chuckle that if he'd not had the sense to bring any clean clothes to a place twelve thousand years old, nobody else had brought him any, either. There surely wasn't going to be a refabricator in here. His fingers told him right side out and front part before, and he dressed quickly, socks first, feeling the cold. He put on his boots, wishing he'd brought high, wool lined moccasins, felt around for his traveling cloak, and realized that whomever had taken it as he entered last afternoon, had put it somewhere unknown. He felt his way out the door and began moving in the right direction down the hall, humming The Naming Song as he went.

The portcullis had responded to his voice yesterday. "Light," he said again. Nothing. He sighed and went back to humming. At least he wasn't out in the snow. His nose led him finally to the kitchen, following the spoor of cold soup, and at last to a crack of light coming from under a heavy curtain over the sink. When he pulled the curtain, light flooded in and he reveled momentarily in the blessing of small miracles. "Thank you," he said aloud.

The stove held residual warmth, and that, too, was a blessing, as he was getting very cold. In the dim light he found the valve which allowed hot steam from the fundus chamber into the cookstove, opened it, and the hiss of steam told him that this room, at least, would soon be warm. The window was of good size. Why wasn't there more light coming in? Snow. Completely covered with snow. He hoped all the Telenir and their escorts had gotten home safely, and he wondered if Sarkhan's father had come to his senses. Could be madness ran in the family, though Ah'cora had seemed sane enough.

There had to be alternate lighting in here. Even city folk in the most modern of dwellings had alternate lighting. Surely, logically, this old castle had lamps, or lanterns, or torches or candles or light jars somewhere. The kitchen was a good place to start, he thought. He put the kettle on for something hot to drink and began the task of rummaging through a huge, darkened kitchen he was not familiar with. He found Demetrian white coffee. Good. Wonderful, as a matter of fact. He found sacks and jars of grains and nuts, and strings of dried fruit hanging in one pantry, a huge wheel of cheese and a honeypot in another. In a third, lined neatly on a shelf, he found six friction lanterns that had no charge, and a dozen waterfuel lamps, their chimneys blackened and dusty. When he shook them, they contained liquid, so while he was cooking some cereal and sipping a cup of shockingly strong coffee that he managed to boil, he found a fire shaver and tested one of the lamps. It lit briefly, then sputtered and died. He found a scissors used for tying the string which bound peringrass together for cooking, and used it to trim the wick on the lamp, washed the glass chimney, and tried again to light it. This time it worked, and he again said, "Thank you!"

He hated to leave the warmth of the kitchen, but the thought of bringing precious documents in here where they might get soiled was unacceptable, so he picked up his lantern and a spare that he'd cleaned up after breakfast, and trudged off toward the library.

Despite his desire to start reading, he stopped off in the gymnasium and, having established where things were that he might bump into, he blew out the lamp to save precious fuel and spent some time stretching and limbering up. It helped get his blood flowing. He knew he'd need it. He turned to the spot where the sun would rise and raised his hands and said his morning prayers, adding one for the safety of the Telenir, one for the understanding of the Lebonathi, and a special thanks for having found such a strong advocate for Eridi in the unexpected person of Ah'nis. He ended with, "Open my eyes and my heart, Creator, that I might find here what will help me best lead my people wisely in the paths of peace and prosperity." Then he lit his lamp, and set off again for the library, humming The Naming Song.

"Where to start, where to start," he said aloud. Surely someone maintained these documents. There must be a whole host of people caring for this most precious of strongholds. A desk. If he could find a desk perhaps he could find some kind of information about the filing system. But even if he found it, where would he start? What, exactly, was he supposed to know? Pythos had said a hundred times over the last seasons, "*In your studies at Mountain hold, you'll learn about...*" whatever. Here he was. Why didn't any of those conversations pop into his usually quick mind? "You're asking yourself too many questions at once," he said aloud. "Find the desk. You must have seen one. Where was it?"

He found the desk and the window pretty much at the same moment, and because he was focused on the window, he found the desk chair with his left shin. "Precious Equus," he muttered, rubbing the abused part for a moment before opening the draperies. This window was bigger. This window had more light! "Thank you!" he said. Now he could use the lantern to find what he wanted, bring it back to the desk, and blow out the lantern. But what was it he wanted? He sat down at the desk and found the chair very comfortable – almost familiar. He blew out the lantern and set it to one side, then began studying the top of the desk. It was very large and appeared to be made from Calumet mahogany, like the table in the conference room and the shelves in here. It had a blotter on it, for scribing in inks or oils. It had three drawers on each side and one in the middle. He hesitated momentarily before opening the center drawer – feeling as though he were a child, snooping through his parent's things. The thought made him chuckle. He was the most powerful ruler in the galaxy. That ridiculous notion made him laugh out loud. "If only I'd brought a cup of coffee with me," he said to the ceiling, and opened the center drawer. In it was an envelope, and on the envelope it said,

To my son, The Thirteenth Dragonhorse

He sat there staring at it for a long while, trying to comprehend how long ago this had been written, and by whom. Had he sat here in this very spot to write it? Why was it hand written? Easy. Technology fails. Handwriting spoke to a man's character and his soul. When he finally slid a finger under the flap and eased it open to read it, the first line said,

On the outside chance you're sitting here in the dark, you'll appreciate this. They didn't leave any instructions for me, either. I went three days and nearly froze before I figured out how to turn on the house and the staff.

Ardenai burst out laughing. His father had been just a man, like him. A man with a sense of humor, apparently. Turn on the house and the staff? Now the woman in the grey livery made sense; she was Androtech! What a clever way to maintain a house meant only for people who lived hundreds of years apart. He continued reading the short note.

There is a small room behind you and to your left, behind the books on Viridian Agriculture. The main controls for the house and staff are in there. Once you identify yourself and introduce a personal code, the house will come to life for you. When the house is activated, everything and everybody else will be activated as well. I hope this helps.

Your Loving Sire,
Kehailan

Hardly the note Ardenai had been expecting, but one he was grateful for to the point of feeling giddy. He rolled back the desk chair, swiveled around, and looked behind him at the tomes until he found the set labeled, A Detailed and Extensively Annotated Study of the Agricultural Practices of the Viridians. He had to poke around a little before he found the concealed release for the door – a good idea in times past, or present, for that matter, in case someone actually managed to break in. The door swung willingly open, and a work light came on overhead. The panels were unfamiliar, but being a Computator Design Engineer, he was soon saying, "I am Ah'krill Ardenai Morningstar, The Thirteenth Dragonhorse."

"Acknowledged," said a cool male voice. "Please enter a code which will identify you."

He thought through a few that were obvious – his mother, his father, his sons, his wives, then he smiled and entered, L I O N E L - "Lionel."

"Mountain hold recognizes The Thirteenth Dragonhorse," the male voice said. "Long have we awaited you, and we rejoice in your presence. We, and this house, are yours. Ahimsa, we wish thee peace, Dragonhorse."

"Thank you," he said again, and when he stepped out, the house was alive. The lights were on, he could hear footsteps in the corridor, the air was once again fragrant and moving, and he could hear hot water surging through the walls and floors.

"So," he said to the room, "You'll work for Io and Tarpan and the Telenir, but you won't work for me until I go through some identification ritual? Why is that? I can hardly wait until my sweet wife gets here to explain this to me."

But, it was working, which was enough. He sat back at the desk, made a gesture with both hands as though he were opening a book, and a list of documents appeared in front of him in the order he was to read them. He did no more than look around when a light shone onto the document he wanted. He got it, reseated himself at the desk, and was deep in study when someone appeared at his elbow with hot tea and sweet cakes. "Not as good as your sister's I'm afraid," the woman said as she put them down, "But they should fill that hollow spot one gets about this time of day, especially if they've had only hot cereal for breakfast."

Ardenai started slightly and looked up into her laughing eyes. It was the woman from the night before, and she was very much alive.

"Thank you," he said, and studied her more closely for a moment. "Do you have a name?"

"Of course I do," she replied. "I am Lark."

"Not, Ah'lark?"

She shook her head. "In here, just Lark."

"May I?" he asked, reaching tentatively for her arm, and she nodded. She was warm and fully fleshed. "Are you…I mean, are you…?" he began, and the look on his face made her laugh.

"Alive? Yes," she replied, still chuckling. "I am a highly sophisticated and fully sentient andro-organism, like the rest of your visible staff. Treat me as you would any other Equi, because that is exactly what I am. Do you need anything else?"

"No, thank you," he replied, still obviously bemused, and she turned from him with another small laugh.

"Harrier says to thank you for doing your own dishes last night," she said in parting. "I will come and get you when your lunch is ready."

By the time she returned for him, he had fewer questions about his duties as Dragonhorse, and more questions about the house and its staff. Most of what he'd read so far about his position, he'd figured out for himself already. Apparently there was much to be said for training in motion. He walked beside her, marveling at how lifelike she was as she pointed out the different rooms and their function and told him a bit about the history of the place. He further marveled when she told him she was many thousands of years old.

"Don't look so surprised," she smiled. "The staff is contiguous. We are out and about in the world, and we care for this place, whether or not one of you is in office. We serve Equus and her people, just like you. We adapt from time to time in order to conform to your mode of dress and definition of beauty. Our hair may change a little, or the way we shape our eyebrows, and of course we're continually improving ourselves and learning new things, but our memories of the past stay intact."

"And where do you go for your various updates?"

"I'll bet if you think about it, you know the answer to that."

He did think about it, and after a minute or so he nodded. "Achernar."

"Very good. Actually, they come to us. As the overlords of Mountain hold they are here often, and it is they who make many of the most important decisions regarding us, our particular charges, and what our charges are to accomplish during their reign."

"I see," Ardenai mused. While it was news, it didn't really surprise him. For all Pythos' talk of allowing the indigenous population to develop on its own, he'd been pretty sure the ancient dragons of Achernar still had their ferny fingers in the mix. They were good, and wise. The thought of them as beneficent keepers did not disturb him in the least. If anything, it was comforting. "Speaking of very good," he said, shaking himself into the present, "how did you know your sweet cakes wouldn't be as good as my sister's?"

"Many of us have associated with you for your entire life," she said, "and everything we discovered about you was programmed into this house. We are some of your oldest and closest friends."

"I am…honored," he smiled, finding it a better choice than 'alarmed,' which is what he was thinking. Lark glanced at him out of the corner of her eye, controlled a smile, and ushered him into the dining room, where a substantial lunch was laid out for him.

"I ate in the kitchen last night," he said.

"True. The Firstlord's first meal is always taken in the kitchen, and it is always the same thing, soup, bread and cheese. Comfort food. They're usually in a lot of pain, and a little more stunned and exhausted than you are – probably because you did not come here on schedule."

"And do they have as much trouble as I did figuring how to turn things on?"

"Because they almost always have their serpent physicians with them, they usually don't have any trouble at all." she smiled. "Your royal father was a rare exception, as are you."

"And because my administration is already in motion, my physician had business elsewhere. Pressing business. He could not see his way clear to come with me right away."

"Quite probably," Lark replied.

"Or he wanted to get even with me for something or other which escapes me at the moment."

Lark just continued passing him dishes and chuckled under her breath.

He took a bite of food, nodded his approval, and motioned for her to sit down. "I would speak further with thee," he said, and she acquiesced with a gracious nod. "So the serpent physicians know how to operate the house?"

"They do."

He reached to spear a fragrant, crisply baked tuber. "The Andalese kartfels are exceptional this year," he said, preparing the tuber with sun flower butter and a good sprinkling of fresh pepper while he composed his question. He did not want to give offense, if that was possible, or get the conversation going off in the wrong direction. "Then it was Pythos who activated the house so that the Telenir who petitioned for peace could be safely kept here?"

She looked momentarily puzzled. Then her face cleared and she smiled. She really was charming, and very pretty. "The house was already activated." She noted his expression and said, "Now I have really confused you. When your father, Kehailan, activated the house, it remained activated until your arrival. At the last hour of your first night, the house deactivated to await reactivation as your house."

"Because it's one of the tests."

There followed a slight, smiling shrug. "More of a tradition, but useful."

"And if I hadn't been able to figure out how to turn the house back on, or if I had been killed before I got here? Could Sarkhan have activated the household?"

She just smiled, and turned her hands palms-up, encouraging him with her expression.

"Your actions do not depend upon mine," he said at last, and any vestige of his own importance in all of this, slipped into the background as she shook her head.

"Will you be comfortable on your own for a space?" she asked. "I have something I need to do."

"Of course," he smiled. "One more question, and you may answer on the fly, as long as you can hear me. How much of this place did the Telenir have access to?"

"Only the places they could see," was the enigmatic reply, and she was gone.

Ardenai was pleasantly full and a little drowsy, just finishing a third cup of tea and an especially nice anise pizzelle, when a man with light brown hair and a sharp, aristocratic face entered the room carrying a small bottle and a bit of cloth. "I am Kestrel," he said, and it was the voice from the house activation system. "I just want to look at those scratches on your face." He sat down in the chair next to Ardenai, cupped the Firstlord's chin in one hand and studied him with bright green eyes. "Wouldn't do to get an infection."

"They don't seem serious," Ardenai said, and Kestrel gave a slight tip of his head and downturn of mouth in agreement.

"Still," he said, "Saremanno was an odd old man with odd old habits. Not sure what might be under his fingernails. This might sting just a bit." It did, but after the comment about odd habits and fingernails, Ardenai didn't object. "Did he get you anyplace else?"

"I didn't notice," Ardenai replied, "but then again, I haven't looked."

"Better look. Take off your tunic." Ardenai set his teacup aside, stood up, and did as he was told. He could feel Kestrel's fingers lightly on his back, and around the back of his neck. The man dabbed a place or two, gave one spot a little extra attention, and ended by running his finger the length of the whip scar on Ardenai's shoulder. "Nice keepsake," he said, "but if you'd gotten here when you were supposed to, I'd have had better luck with the scars on your arms, and with less pain."

Ardenai glanced down at his arms. They really were deeply disfigured where the armbands had been poured in place. "They're fine as they are," he said, trying to head off anything physically unpleasant, and Kestrel just sniffed as he handed Ardenai his tunic.

"Later," he said, and left.

Ardenai spent the afternoon in study – a very pleasant time. Several people moved quietly about in the space, and from time to time one of the long, slender ladders slid silently on its tracks to another spot to be inspected along the walls of books. They did not introduce themselves, and Ardenai was too engrossed in what he was doing to stop and visit. Another time, he promised himself, as the care of old books was of particular interest to him. *Criollo is going to love this place,* he thought, and the idea of family – of showing this to his family – was both exciting and relaxing. He was where he was supposed to be. Finally, he was doing what he was supposed to be doing as Dragonhorse. That notion made him laugh out loud.

As the light began to slant more sharply through the window Lark again set a tray down beside him, and again he jumped a little. She was so quiet and he had been drowsing just a bit. "Sorry," she said softly. "I didn't realize you were out walking." She poured him a cup of fragrant hot cider, set kurbis winterbread to the right of him, which meant she knew he was left handed, and departed without breaking his train of thought.

When she came to tell him dinner was ready, he said, "I'm going to put bells on you so you can't sneak up on me."

"I'll wear riding boots next time," she replied, and it put Ardenai in mind of the fact that boots, and one set of clothing, was all he had. In a day or so that would become all too apparent. When he mentioned it at dinner she just shook her head and said, "You haven't explored your room thoroughly. Everything you need is there."

And it was. When he saw his closet he knew for sure Pythos had either made the choices or been there ahead of him. He selected clean clothes, most of them green, which was the color Pythos favored. Even the briefcloth was pale green, which made Ardenai chuckle. He tossed everything on his bed and went off to the bathing pools. These, were especially delightful, with a wide, sandy beach and some large boulders creating private coves in the corners for intimacy while bathing, something not usual in Equi pools. There were smooth stones for sitting at various heights in the water, the usual waterfalls for rinsing off, and in a separate section a place for swimming against a current, which could be adjusted for temperature, ability and stamina.

Before entering the water he walked around behind the boulders at the back and found the shadowed, downward spiral of ramp he had been expecting. It opened onto a dim room much like the one he'd found himself in with Ah'nis not long ago. There was a priapic bench and cold pools, a low chair where a woman could sit astride a man flatfooted, and various levels where both could adjust for height if they chose to copulate standing up. There was a discreet place for observers, if that was the protocol, and a series of large cushions strewn about on the floor to be gathered into any configuration the lovers chose. The walls were decorated with scenes of couples in various sexual positions – men with women, women with women, men with men – all in full coitus and so real they almost seemed to move. Ardenai found himself staring at the images and realizing just how much he missed his uninhibited little Papilli wife. She knew variations on at least one of those positions that never failed to take his breath away, despite their difference in height.

He realized again that he was alone, at least for the time being, that he was in a room where the temperature was adjusted for people getting some serious exercise and that he had an erection he needed to do something with or he wasn't going to sleep. He went back to the hot pool and lowered himself into the water, sitting on a low stone and leaning against another as he stretched his long legs.

"May I join you?" someone asked, and Ardenai looked up to see an exceptionally tall, radiantly beautiful woman just sliding off her robe. "The question was rhetorical," she smiled, wading into the water. "I am Wren, and I am your hetaera, sanctioned by the Great House, as has been custom for many thousands of years, and I am trained to pleasure you in the ways you most desire."

To her mild surprise, Ardenai looked apprehensive and a little sullen. "The last time I heard that, I had a headache for three days," he said. "I am married. I have a wife whom I adore, and who pleases me very much."

"I am happy for thee," she said in a voice that was rich, soothing and just slightly growly. She had stopped a few paces from him, sensing his reluctance. As a rule the Dragonhorse still had that potion rolling around in his system from his initial mating with a priestess. This one didn't, though he was obviously aroused and exceptionally handsome. "I am to care for thee when thy wife is not here, which she is not, and you are warm."

Ardenai had to admit she was incredible, even as Equi women went. She was nearly as tall as he was. Shapely. Athletic. Her mouth was soft and kissable. As a matter of fact several things looked soft and kissable. She had jet black hair which hung loose to her waist and her legs were long and well-muscled. He realized she had stopped where the water was just past her knees so that he could get the full effect of her beauty, and it was not lost on him. He struggled to keep his breathing steady as he wrestled with his thoughts.

"Dragonhorse," she said softly, "Pythos says to tell you there is a difference between being faithful, and being a prude, and you're not seeing it. I am sanctioned by the Great House as a hetaera, and if you were still Ardenai Teacher, or Ambassador Ardenai, and far from home, you would not hesitate to avail yourself of my expertise. You have much studying to do, and many physical tests you must accomplish, and you cannot do that if you are sexually distracted."

"No," he said quietly, "I cannot. "Tell me some things first."

"Of course."

"Are you currently channeling Sir Pent, by any chance?"

"I am not," she laughed, flashing a perfect set of white teeth. "But he did tell me what to expect."

"My second question," he said. "Are you Androtech?"

"If that is your choice of terms. I prefer to think of myself as mechanically inclined," she chuckled. "I am a sentient being, just like you, capable of great strength and stamina, and I will not speak to anyone but Pythos about the details of what goes on between us. But, I am also highly sophisticated, and more than capable of getting cold if I stand too long naked in the open air, even in a bathing pool."

"Best come here then," the Firstlord breathed, and as she settled herself facing him, he took his hands and swept her hair up, flipping it expertly into a knot on top of her head. "Some men like wet hair. I don't." He closed his eyes and let his head drop back against the smooth stone behind him, groaning with pleasure.

When he pried his eyes open the next morning Kestrel was standing at the foot of the bed. "Wakie-wakie Dragonhorse. Time to see what you're made of."

"Oh, Precious Equus, what does that mean?" Ardenai scowled, tasting at his mouth and wishing he'd not spent half the night playing nicker and nibble with a delightfully funny, very real...machine. How was that even possible? "Tell me what that means," he said again.

"You'll see. Riding tights and your hair well back. Bare feet, no shirt, bladder and bowels empty, morning prayers said. Meet me in the gymnasium in half an hour." No smile. No explanation. Just...gone.

"Fine."

Ardenai was where he was supposed to be in the given time, prayers said, tunic tossed over a chair, high topped moccasins beside the door. "I'm here," he said, and in the next second Kestrel had launched himself at the man. Ardenai responded by flinging him halfway across the room onto his back and snapping, "My brother-in-law has been trying that with me since we were six! I haven't had breakfast, so tell me what you want or I'll put you in the repair shop!"

"You can try," Kestrel responded, and for twenty minutes they brawled like drunken Nargas, until both were panting, spitting blood onto the mats and wiping bloody noses on their sweat-slick arms. Kestrel managed to get Ardenai by his braid and jerked his head back until his neck cracked. Ardenai in turn, hoping the man was fully functional, brought his heel up into Kestrel's groin. He was functional, and as he buckled Ardenai brought an elbow back into his midsection, jerked an arm up to make him let go of his hair, spun around and landed a hard left on Kestrel's jaw. The man went down, grabbing the Firstlord behind the ankle as he did so, and jerking him off his feet to land sprawling on his back. In a second, Kestrel was on top of him. "Sloppy, very sloppy," he said. "Never assume you've landed the final punch in a fight."

Suddenly, Ardenai's legs were under Kestrel's armpits and up around his neck, feet locked at the ankles, and Kestrel was being bent in half backwards. "Did I mention that I'm limber?" Ardenai grated, and Kestrel finally slapped the floor twice, signaling capitulation.

"Not bad," Kestrel said, sitting up and rubbing at his throat. "Let's see how limber you really are, Dragonhorse."

For the next quarter hour Ardenai made one single fluid movement. Starting with his legs straight, palms flat on the floor in front of him, he went up on his toes, and without bending his knees, elevated himself very slowly until his legs and pointed toes were straight overhead, then slowly, slowly on over his head until his heels rested on the floor just in front of his fingertips. A perfect, tight backbend.

Kestrel was amazed. With each Dragonhorse they grew stronger, more beautiful, more intelligent. The first real Dragonhorse had been a soldier, strong but not limber, rugged, but not handsome, wily, but not overly intelligent. The second, a farm machinery engineer. Under them, planets had been added to the Tribute Worlds, but the population had skyrocketed and the cities had become large and smoky. The third had been a senator – smart, but not particularly physical. Politics had its heyday under that one. The Fourth Dragonhorse had been intelligent, strong and kind, the captain of a great stellar ship. Under him, science had made great strides and Equus had begun to take on its present shape. The Fifth Dragonhorse had been a farmer, had seen less need for conquest and more need for stewardship. He had been a delightful man, a lover of wholesome food and good company; brilliant, but the pudgiest of the bunch. With his reign had come cleaner skies and bigger crops, and a recognizable Equus.

The Sixth Dragonhorse, had fallen to the Wind Warriors, or so the story went. He and his husband had not made it to Mountain hold the first time before they were shot out of the air and the priestesses had taken up the reins of government again without even a hiccup in the history books. The seventh, like the fourth, had been a spacefaring man, and new planets had again been added to the Affined Equi Worlds. Under him they had proposed and formed the Seventh Galactic Alliance, and Terren had become an Affined World. Vanner's only fault had been a very bad temper, which had caused certain planets in the Fifth Galactic Alliance to bear a lasting grudge against the Equi.

Balearic, the Eighth Dragonhorse, had been a TimeWhip Engineer, and generally a good man, but he had been gravely wounded and his family killed by usurpers at the very outset, and though he had moved Equus forward on many fronts, and had done his best, he had never fully regained his strength physically, and had grieved for his parents, his wife, and his little sons to the end of his days.

The ninth, had been a bloodlines specialist, and Kestrel's least favorite. As a matter of fact, he'd roundly hated the man, and had plenty of company in the hating. Kabardin had considered himself above all testing, above all questioning and though he occasionally complied, it was always with a sneer. Kabardin had reminded Kestrel of Sarkhan in many ways, and under his reign had come what the history books referred to as "The Time of Calamity." If not for his high priestess mother and her allies being able to outwit him and ultimately do away with him, Equus might well have been lost. As it was they chose to eliminate his bloodline from the gene pool, and had spent some time marrying off most of his unsuspecting heirs to a series of Androtech partners with whom they'd been ecstatically happy.

Number ten had been a beautiful young man like this one, and like this one, his name was Ardenai. Kestrel was pretty sure that in him they'd finally gotten the bucks out of the formula for the perfect Dragonhorse. Since then, they'd only gotten better, stronger – smarter in the case of Asturian, and in the case of Kehailan, funnier – The Laughing Dragon they had called him, because he also had a quick and fiery temper. It seemed his son had all those traits as well, plus an incredible, flexible athleticism and probably the strongest sense of what it meant to be truly kind, truly merciful – reports from the field and day-before-yesterday's encounter being prime examples. No apparent weaknesses aside from a certain initial aversion to unnecessary pain. That was healthy. Obviously clever and inventive – smart enough to surround himself with smart people, and outsmart yet another imposter to the title. And this one taught creppia nonage. Interesting.

By now Ardenai had reversed his direction and was two thirds of the way back to his starting position – still perfectly in control of his body – no shaking arms, so tension in the jaw, just liquid motion.

"Acceptable," Kestrel said, allowing himself a smile he knew the Dragonhorse couldn't see. "When you're through you can go and have breakfast. Study until I come for you again."

"Thank you," came the calm voice. Kestrel, had his hearing been less acute, would have missed the soft chuckle which followed.

Having gotten a whiff of himself, Ardenai opted for a quick, stand-up soaping under the waterfall before dressing in trousers and tunic and presenting himself in the dining room. Lark was nowhere to be seen, so he stuck his head in the wide arch of the kitchen door. "I am sorry to be late," he said, and the man at the stove turned and smiled. He appeared more mature than Kestrel, and a bit softer, with a happy face and kind, deep-set eyes that were more gold than green.

"Ahimsa, Dragonhorse, I wish thee peace," he said, brushing his right hand, which happened to be holding a long wooden spoon, over his left in greeting. "I am Harrier. Kestrel said you'd be late, if you showed up at all, but we had faith in you. Here, sit. I've started an early lunch for you. I'll have something ready in just a minute. Tea?"

"Absolutely," Ardenai said, and the dimples in his cheeks made the man ask,

"Something is tickling your funny bone. What is it?"

Ardenai shook his head and allowed himself to chuckle. "Kestrel. Yesterday he showed up at breakfast with medications for something that didn't amount to more than a couple of scratches, and today he tried to break every bone in my body, bloodied my nose," he poked at a corner of his mouth with his tongue, "cut the inside of my cheek, and didn't offer to spit on it to make it better. I think that's funny."

"It wouldn't be if you'd been around that old man," the cook muttered. "He's as crazy as ever his son was, and probably the reason. If he'd stuck a knife in your back none of us would have been a bit surprised, which is why we made sure he didn't have access to knives."

"What did he have access to?" Ardenai asked casually, stirring cream and honey into his tea. He made sure not to look the man in the eye to make it seem like a challenge.

"His quarters. The indoor gardens. The game and music room. The small library. Same as the others in the so-called Telenir delegation. No access to any sensitive places."

Ardenai pricked up his ears. "So-called? You don't think they're who they say they are?"

The cook shrugged. "I've been around a long time, Dragonhorse, and I've seen some pretty deluded people. I think, they think, they are who they say they are, especially the older ones. The younger ones, not so much. If I were you, I'd talk to Ah'cora. She's a lovely woman with the patience of a stone. Both her mother and stepfather went barking mad and she left the Eloi to take care of them. Now, she's trapped in this whole Wind Warriors nonsense that's been going on for the last couple thousand years because of some fanciful ballad by a cloud gathering poet that happened to have a rhyme that lent itself well to music. Verdanbutter and tomato sandwiches?"

"Um? Yes, please. You think the Wind Warriors are a figment of someone's imagination?"

"Of course they are, and from your tone you know it as well as I do. Soup? It's black phaselus. Would you like fresh sheep cheese on your sandwiches?"

"Yes, please, and no, thank you. They seem to have appeared in history from time to time, have they not?"

Harrier set a crockery bowl of soup in front of him and a plate of sandwiches on bread still warm from the oven. "If 'seem' is the operative word they have, but have they really? Nobody had ever heard of them until the song came along and suddenly, there they were, storming out of the clouds, trailing death. At that time in history we were about the only ones doing that, as I recall. Maybe we're the Wind Warriors. Maybe the poem was written to honor our own conquests. You'll notice that the Sixth Dragonhorse 'fell to the Wind Warriors', though the song didn't appear until the Ninth Dragonhorse. Ask yourself who would benefit most by such a retrofit. Who would benefit at all? "

Ardenai busied himself with food for a few minutes while he sorted through a lifetime of songs, poems, sightings, portents and reports. The thought that he'd gone chasing across six sectors after something that never existed made him feel foolish, but the fact that something which didn't exist had turned up in the same place and tried to kill him, perplexed him a great deal and made perfect sense all at the same time.

"People everywhere," he said at last, wiping the corner of his mouth with his napkin, and rubbing gingerly at the cut in his cheek with the tip of his tongue – the tomatoes were good, but they stung – "have a tendency to sanctify, or vilify legends. People also tend to enjoy being frightened until it becomes too real. That's why children love ghost stories. If I wanted to get people to believe I was some legendary character they'd never seen and had no real knowledge about, I could probably do it with a minimum of trappings and fuss, given enough time."

By now he was speaking more to himself than to Harrier, but the man nodded and turned from the counter where he was working. "My point exactly. What better way to instantly create fear than to claim to be the dreaded warriors from beyond the clouds? I think these so-called Telenir are about as much Wind Warriors as you and I are. Less likely to be, as a matter of fact. I think they've been brainwashed for a few generations until they actually believe it. When you get a few glasses of wine or hard cider in them and then ask them what the plan was, they don't have a clue. There was no plan. Sarkhan was the barking mad son of barking mad parents. Konik knew that, tried to control the situation, and that's why he is no longer with us."

"You think he's been killed?" The thought made Ardenai's heart speed up.

"No. Probably not. At least not yet. He was taken, I think, not killed. You must admit, he looks and acts the part of a Telenir Lord – deeply intelligent, dashingly handsome. Who would benefit by that, is the question. If I were you, Dragonhorse, I'd be careful. Can I get you anything else?"

"Yes," Ardenai said with a sigh. "What do you have for a headache?"

By the morning of the third full day, Ardenai was getting worried. Another storm was sweeping across Viridia, and he'd not heard whether the children were safe at home. He was sitting in the library, half studying a book on the process of conquest and citizenship when yet another stranger walked into the room – or rather, appeared in the room – because he came from behind Ardenai, and there was no door to the rear of the alcove where he was seated except that small one with the panels for activating the hold and staff. He looked up, smiling, and then his head turned very slowly until his left ear was nearly resting on his shoulder. The man was Ah'jin Kehailan Morning Star, The Twelfth Dragonhorse.

"Precious Equus, they're drugging my tea," he said. He squeezed his eyes shut and pinched the bridge of his nose for a few moments. When he opened them, the man was seated across from him at the desk. "You're still there. Are you real?"

Kehailan brought his hand down with a resounding slap on the desk. "Define real, Dragonhorse."

Ardenai put his elbows on the desk, his chin in his hands and just stared at his ancestor – not a single cogent thought presenting. He was, literally, stunned. Finally he managed, "Uhhhhh..."

"Exactly! When my father did this to me I thought for sure I was going drooling naked crazy," Kehailan said, crossing his legs and resting one elbow on the desktop. "Now you're going to ask if I'm Androtech like the others. No. I'm more of a corporeal program. They're much more sophisticated than this – some of them extremely so, as you'll find out. I'll only be around for a while, as sort of an introduction to the role of Dragonhorse. Of course you've already had a crash course, thanks to Sarkhan and his ilk. You did come out well, my son. Your mother would be beaming for joy. Your actual mother. You do know your mother is not your mother?"

"You mean Ah'krill," Ardenai managed, pleased to have found his tongue and a subject simple enough to discuss. "Well, no, I don't…I mean, I know she isn't, either. Your wife, or whomever she was, is my mother. I was carried forward by Pythos, implanted into Ah'krill as an embryo and given to Ah'rane and Krush as a newborn."

"Good! You have made progress. I assume you managed to squeeze some information out of Pythos?"

Ardenai's eyes widened. "You knew Pythos? Yes, of course you had to have known him, since he was both mother and father to me for a few hundred years."

"I did, yes," Kehailan chuckled. "I knew your fine young physician, just as you will know your son's – probably all too briefly, but you'll at least get to meet her before you go."

"As in, die?"

"If you choose to call it that. Ninety-nine percent of you will move on with your physician to new heights of exploration and joy, and one percent of you will stay behind to have this little chat with your boy – and you will sit here and be amazed at the man he has grown into. Good, I see you can smile. I was afraid you were a sourpuss like your eldest son."

"That would be Kehailan," Ardenai said. "I don't think he's sour so much as that he always has a lot on his mind."

"He's with the Seventh Galactic Alliance, on the good ship Belesprit, yes? Don't forget that when the hold accepted your rising, it downloaded everything about you and your family. That included filling my informational circuitry as well. I've had the chance to sort it all out and reach some conclusions."

"Then we don't have much to talk about," Ardenai said, "Or is this to be instructional time? I would welcome that most of all."

"We have much to talk about!" Kehailan exclaimed. "You are my family, too. How is your sister?"

"Ah'din is well. She's a medicinal herbalist and a master weaver.

She's married to Teal, who is my..."

"Not your niece, your sister. How is Ah'rane?"

Ardenai gasped like he'd been punched in the gut. "What? Gideon was right?"

"Oh, sorry," Kehailan grimaced. "I assumed, since you knew the whole business with Ah'krill, and you being implanted as an embryo, that you knew Pythos had carried Ah'rane forward, as well. I did not mean to startle you further, and I can see that I have done so. I know you're not that dense, but you do seem to be resistant to things you don't particularly want to know."

Ardenai stood up abruptly and strode over to stare out the window. *Creator, my world is falling apart! Please, I just want to go to school and come home to my wife and my horses and my gardens. Please. Please let this be a dream.* But he knew it wasn't. No prayer, no matter how fervent, would change that. "She is well," he said at last, puffing his cheeks with resignation. "She is kind and beautiful and married to a wonderful man in whose shadow I will stand the best day I ever live. She is a Friction Analysis Engineer."

"You know it's foolish to be even a little shocked," Kehailan said, not unkindly, "You look just like her, which, of course, was the plan. It was the perfect safe place to hide you, and in fact it's the way it's always been done. Either the mother is a sister or the father is a brother. She's still your mother. No fact can change that truth. According to Pythos, Gideon has known all along, since the first day he saw you two together, and he's mentioned it on more than one occasion to you."

Ardenai continued staring out the window, though it was white with snow. "Yes, well Gideon sees much that I do not see, and yes, I probably should have listened to him. I wish I knew that he was safely home at Sea keep with my parents."

"He is safely at home at Canyon keep with your parents," Kehailan amended. "They have closed Sea keep for the time being." Another jerk of Ardenai's shoulders as that little shock registered – too many little shocks at once for this youngest son of the Twelfth Dragonhorse. Why hadn't he come here immediately, as he was supposed to do? That answer was obvious. Kehailan sighed and gave the man a chance to catch his breath before proceeding in his brightest tone. "Next week they will be here – all of them – Teal and Ah'din, Ah'rane and Krush, Gideon, Kehailan, Criollo, and, of course, the lovely Ah'riodin and her son, Jilfan. Here, each of them will learn his or her place in the wondrous order of things. Pythos may come as well, if he finds a safe place to leave Eridi and Ah'nis. I should go. My signal needs boosting and Kestrel has need of thee before lunch."

Ardenai turned slowly from the window to contemplate his ancestor. "Good," he said slowly, "I'm in the mood to break something. Tell me, since you seem to have information I do not – did they find The Eldest?"

"They did."

"And did they get him and his horses to safety?"

"They did. Now you tell me something. Why do you bother with that crazy old man? He gave you a concussion and still you crawled after him and have continued to go after him year after year. And not just you," Kehailan added before Ardenai could respond, "Now you send others on this particular errand. If you care so much for him, you could at least go yourself."

"He remembers me as a youth. That is his place in time. He seems to respond better to the children than to me. As to me not going myself, this is the first year I have not gone, but I'm sure my father or Timor did. Sometimes two or three of us go and make a bit of a holiday of it. We stay at a distance and allow our children the adventure in problem solving, but we also stay close enough that if there is real trouble, we can get to them. This is something they do not know, and I would prefer that they did not find out, thank you very much."

"You distrust me," Kehailan said, and even as his mouth turned down his eyes twinkled.

"You do seem to have a penchant for blurting."

"You did not answer my question, Dragonhorse. Why do you bother with that crazy old man?"

"Because he draws breath. The fact that he does not think the way

I do, does not lessen his value. The Creator Spirit gives each of us both blessings and challenges; to question them when they become apparent, is to question the Creator."

"I see," Kehailan said. "Kestrel is coming for you." and he abruptly vanished.

Kestrel didn't need Ardenai for boxing or wrestling, or brawling or gymnastics. "We have to get some work done on those scars," he said. "They are unsightly and they make you look like a savage."

"They don't bother me in the least," Ardenai replied. "They are an insignificant matter in the bigger picture, don't you think?"

"I do not," the man replied. "And this is not a debate. You must look sophisticated and finished in order to properly represent our worlds and your position in them. You do not."

To his considerable consternation Ardenai found himself once again strapped tightly into a device much like the one he'd been strapped into that first day, when they had put forms on his upper arms and poured molten metal into them. He could feel his flesh searing away, smell it burning, hear himself screaming before he passed out.

"I just need you to be very still and get your heart rate down," Kestrel said soothingly. "I'm going to put some injections into your arms to make them numb. After that, you shouldn't feel much at all."

"Don't wreck my pythons."

Kestrel made an exasperated little cluck and muttered, "I swear, you're going to set us back ten thousand years. Hold still."

The injections stung, but that was all, and Ardenai could feel pressure as Kestrel worked, but very little pain. "Better than the first time?" the man asked, and Ardenai nodded as best he could. "These must have hurt for a very long time left untreated as they were."

"They were not untreated," Ardenai said, glancing down at what Kestrel was doing. He could see raw flesh and what looked like muscle, and looked quickly away again. "Pythos did…something to them before he put fresh skin over top. They did hurt," he admitted, "but I was able to function and get on about my business."

"The business of luring Sarkhan across six sectors to Calumet?"

"Um hm."

"And everything that could go wrong did go wrong, and yet here you are. You are an amazingly lucky man."

"I am more than lucky," Ardenai chuckled, "I am blessed."

"And now, because of your visit and your blessing, a woman on Calumet grows heavy with your child. A beautiful woman whom you care for very much. She would make you a good second wife, I think. You will have to have one, you know, and one after that. Those are the rules. Three wives. Better get at it."

The Firstlord couldn't jump, but he did squeak with dismay and flex his fingers, which Kestrel promptly slapped into submission. "How do you know about Ah'nora?"

"I believe we already told you that, but let me put it into simpler words. We have been with you since the day you were born, Dragonhorse – in the form of Pythos, and others. Everything, EVERYTHING comes through us, or back to us, because we are your historians, your knowledge bank, your friends, your allies, your physicians your advisers, your companions, occasionally your judges – we are the sum of what you are, and ultimately what history knows of you, will be what comes from us."

"I see," Ardenai said, but he was suddenly feeling a little woozy, and his brain was thick and stupid, and he didn't see at all...at all. He tried to shake his head to clear it, but it was fastened tight, and when the cold sweat started running down his face, he couldn't wipe it off. "I am sorry," he managed through numb lips, "but I think I'm going to pass out."

"I think you are, too," Kestrel muttered, and began calling for someone…or something…but it was lost on Ardenai.

He woke up in his room under warm blankets, propped up with pillows, Kestrel beside him proffering a cup of something steamy and fragrant. "Can you hold this?" he asked. "If you can drink it you will feel better."

"I think so," he breathed, taking the cup and swallowing at the bile in his throat. "I am very sorry. I don't know why I did that." He let his head fall back momentarily and took a good, deep breath to steady himself. He felt very foolish, and his skin prickled with embarrassment.

"I believe you were losing too much blood," Kestrel replied. "The scars are much easier to repair when they're fresh. Still, I think, other than some dermabrasion, that you are done."

Think what you will, Ardenai thought. *It was probably the chair, and, of course, the fact that you know all about Ah'nora, Oh, and my biological father, who has been dead for a few hundred years popped in on me this morning to tell me my mother is my sister, and my sister is my niece.* "I feel like someone is inflating an alabaster balloon in my head. And not that soft, Terren alabaster that can be carved into interesting shapes. Hard, eternal Viridian alabaster."

"We'll leave the bandages on for the rest of today and take a look tomorrow. Right now I think you should get some sleep before dinner."

Ardenai thought about that for a few seconds. "Dinner? Didn't I pass out before lunch?"

"Are you hungry?"

"No, but that's not the point. I've had wives, lovers, friends and children pass out on me and they've always wakened after a minute or two. And yet, here I am, sleeping until supper. How long was I out, and what did you do during that time, if I may ask?"

"Well, first I gave you a bit of a general anesthetic and finished working on your arms – that took another two hours or so thanks to your gallivanting, and the fact that I had to get you out of that chair and onto your back to stabilize your blood pressure. Then I measured the length of your muscles, put a tracking device in your brain, stole your sperm to create an army to overthrow the galaxy and uploaded your brainwave patterns so I could get to work on your evil clone."

"Because you'll need him to command the army."

"Yes. You can't be trusted not to pass out at the sight of your own blood. Now go to sleep or you'll get naught but gruel again tonight."

"No, no, not naught but gruel," Ardenai chuckled, and realized he was, indeed, very ready for a nice nap. He set the cup on his bedside table, tossed one of the pillows to the other side of the bed, and was quickly asleep.

He awoke from a dream where he was running in a public place that went on forever, looking for the lavage, but there was none. He was slogging through water up to his ankles, his knees, his waist – and then his feet were over the side of the bed and he was hurrying into the next room. With the most urgent of his needs met, he realized he was hungry. No. He was ravenous. He looked in the mirror for his usual desultory pat-down, and was not impressed. His eyes were squinty, his hair was wild, he had a bruise on his chin and scratches on his left cheekbone, his mouth tasted rotten – he couldn't see that part, but knowing it was there didn't help his overall inspection any. And his arms were bandaged above and below the golden armbands which marked him as the king of the universe, or whatever he was supposed to be. Bandages. Did that mean he couldn't take a shower before dinner? How did one raise an alarm around here? So far there had been no need, but this evening, he needed a ruling before he stepped foot into any kind of public space populated by Androtech folk or not. He looked back into the mirror, and saw Lark's reflection in the doorway.

"Good morning," she smiled. "You had a nice long sleep. You look better."

Better? Really? What did I look like before? "I need… morning?"

"Yes. What do you need?"

"A bath. Desperately. I'm wondering if I can get these bandages wet."

"Kestrel says to tell you that you may have a waterfall, and then,"

"Oh please, tell him I need food."

"And then, breakfast," she smiled. "Today will be a lighter day, Firstlord."

Standing under that waterfall felt so good. He could remember being chained to the ore carts in the cleomitite mines on Calumet, day after day after day of being filthy and thirsty, and as he was remembering he was letting clear, clean water pour down on him, rinsing the foaming rosemary out of his hair and sending its clean fragrance over every inch of his body. Calumet. Ah'nora had smelled of rosemary and the sweat of desire as he had lain across her back and penetrated her, stroking the damp tendrils off her forehead with one hand, wanting to touch her breasts with the other as she began to cry out and surge around him – but it was a formal coupling with Io in attendance, and he had known that even though Ah'nora would have welcomed his touch, Io would not have been pleased, and it would not have been proper.

He waded onto the smooth, porous stone of the beach, took a towel from the stack which filled a basket nearby and dried himself carefully. His arms were exquisitely tender, and he dabbed slowly, thoughts more on Calumet and Ah'nora than what he was doing. That first night after he had killed Sarkhan, and Io had been so terribly wounded, and he had endured the pain of absorbing their infant daughter's essence. That night, Pythos had instructed him to make love to Ah'nora, and he had not. Why was that? She had been willing. Even as he lay exhausted in bed she would have opened her blouse and raised her skirts and sat astride him, allowing him to stroke and suckle – and he had not. Because all he could think about at the moment was his precious Io, lying so near death. And now he regretted not having made love to Ah'nora in private, where they could touch one another and say intimate things. Because…he had…at some point, in some way…fallen in love with her sweet face and gentle spirit.

Precious Equus. He was in love with Ah'nora! When had that happened? How had that happened? Had Kestrel done this along with the rest of it? Ardenai found himself sitting on the edge of his bed, damp hair dripping down his back, hands over his mouth, eyes to the floor, feeling like he'd been hit with a polo mallet. He could feel his heart pounding in his chest. He loved his wife. He adored his wife! How could this have happened? Amazing as it seemed, he could, in fact, feel worse about himself and his emergent personality than he already did.

"It is not the end of civility as you know it. You knew you had to take a second wife, and a third," Wren said, finishing the braid in Ardenai's hair, and Harrier nodded from the stove where he was fixing ammon and cinnamon crepes.

"She's right," he said, flipping one expertly onto a plate, rolling it up with fresh azure berries and dusting it with powdered sugar before setting it in front of Ardenai. "The Lady Io is a beauty, but she's not high Equi. If she were, you could maybe argue the case for one wife, but she's not, so you don't have a leg to stand on, Dragonhorse. By the law you embody, you have to be married to at least one High Equi. Your father had the requisite three wives, and they all seemed to love one another very much. You're a product of one of them. I can see her in you. And Ah'rane is the product of another. This woman already grows heavy with your son. And by your own admission you love her. How much better could it get?"

"It's complicated," Ardenai sighed.

"Io would get used to it," Kestrel said, walking into the kitchen and the conversation. He was carrying an open box that contained a jar of copper integument, rolls of gauze and a scissors, which he set aside as he took a seat across from Ardenai. "She's a legendary hothead, but she is also the Captain of the Horse Guard and your Primuxori. Nobody knows the law better than she does, and by the time she leaves here, she'll know its every nuance. She does have to give up the Horse Guard, by the way, but you know that."

"Already done," Ardenai said, cutting into the crepe and allowing a steaming stream of bright blue butter to trickle onto his plate. "Teal has taken her place for the time being. The problem isn't Io, at least at this point it isn't. It's Ah'nora. Her home is on Calumet. Her son and her husband are buried on Calumet. Her entire family is on Calumet and has been for many generations. I put that baby in her belly in case Sarkhan managed to kill me instead of the other way 'round, but also to honor Calumet, and Ah'nora, with the raising of a prince of the Great House. If I ask her to marry me and come to live in Thura, she will say yes. I know that. She is a creature of duty. And in saying yes to me she will lose home, family, continuity and honor to become the second wife of a man whose duties keep him too often away from the home and the wife he already has. Ah'nora deserves her own home, her own family, and a man devoted to none but her. That, my friends, is not me."

"You make a compelling argument, at least from your point of view," Wren said, and she reached to pat his hand. "We know this is a hard decision, but it is one that needs to be made."

"And I have to choose someone of whom my mother, as in Ah'krill, High Priestess of Equus, approves. So far I've been married to a woman whom I adored who was not High Equi and who bore me a single son that nearly killed her, and then she died of a wasting illness long before her time. After that, I married a woman my wife and I had raised since babyhood, also not High Equi. I think her father, who used to be one of my best friends, still wants to kill me, or at least cut my phallus off – maybe both and not in that order. I've been presented with a sixteen-year-old alien child with unnatural sexual desires who I am supposed to marry and immediately impregnate, even though I'd probably kill her in the process, and in all of this I've apparently missed the woman I should actually have married. Honestly, I don't think I'm anybody's best chance for lasting happiness." Ardenai exhaled sharply and applied himself to his crepe, avoiding the eyes he felt boring into him. This whole thing just was not getting any less complicated.

"Your mother the high priestess does not have to approve, by the way," said Kestrel. "We do. She is going to find that out soon enough, and I don't think she's going to be particularly happy."

"Which means nobody else is going to be happy," Ardenai said around the last bite of crepe. He sat back, picked up his tea cup and contemplated the four people with him. Machines. Thinking machines thousands of years old, who knew his past and quite possibly controlled his future.

CHAPTER 6

Ardenai spent the afternoon exploring one corner of the immense underground gardens – breathing deep of the same fragrant air which kissed the rest of the huge old castle – stretching his hands to touch ancient trees, tipping his head to catch the song of rare birds, walking in a light muslin tunic even as the snow continued to fall outside. There were flowers and vegetables, fruiting trees and medicinal herbs, quiet walkways and trickling water to soothe an agitated soul. He was stopping here and there to examine a plant, crush a leaf between thumb and forefinger to sniff its aroma, nibble at a stem of something or other. But even though they were his gardens, and he cupped the fruit in his hand in passing, he did not pick it – a fact which did not go unnoticed by those who observed his progress.

"It has crossed his mind that Harrier may have plans for that fruit," Kestrel said. "I don't know whether to admire him for that, or to admonish him for not grabbing his birthright with both hands."

"If it were something he could eat out of hand, and if he were hungry, he would pick it," Harrier said. "He's not hungry, and he doesn't take what he does not need; it's not in him. Finally."

"And is conquest in his soul, do you think?" Kestrel asked.

"For the right reasons, yes," Lark said. "I think he's an extremely powerful individual who effortlessly controls himself because he is also deeply spiritual, and deeply kind. I think if he felt that conquest was in order for the good of the people, he would do it."

Wren shook her head. "I have to disagree. I think he would debate until the knell of eternity the question of whether or not it is ever moral to take another's freedom, or their culture, or their right to choose their own government. True, he is thoughtful and kind, but he is too little impressed with his own value and his own power, and far too concerned about decorum. He loves privacy, simplicity and anonymity, and I do not think he will ever develop enough ego, or enough sense of himself as a demi-god, to be insuperable in the galactic spotlight. I'm not sure that's a bad thing, but I'm not sure it's good, either."

Kestrel eyed her, then the Firstlord, who was on one knee examining a tiny plant. "You're saying he's too introspective? Too weak to be Dragonhorse?"

Wren shrugged. "Weak? Not at all. I am saying that at his very roots, he's a prudish man."

"Nonsense," Harrier drawled. "You're miffed because he didn't wet himself the second he saw you."

"I am not that vain," she snapped, but after a moment's contemplation she wiggled one hand side to side just a bit and grinned. "Maybe. This I do know – when he loves someone, it is with all his heart. When he loses someone, he bears that wound forever. While he views many things with more sophistication than I've seen in any Dragonhorse so far, when it comes to loyalty, he is rudimentary in the extreme, and I think it's going to impede his thinking about certain people and situations. We may have to step into that arena and…push him a little."

"Are we at all surprised that, unlike his father, he chose to keep the Lebonathi girl because he feared more for her life than his kingdom?" Lark asked.

"No," said Harrier. "He could afford to do what his father could not. Ardenai was raised by a stronger foster sire and dam than we've seen so far, cultivated stronger relationships than Kehailan did. He fell back on those for advice, which was very wise. My esteemed colleagues, I think he is exactly the man he was bred to be, able to accomplish the tasks chosen for him long years ago on a timeline far exceeding our predictions. I think he will go beyond anything we have yet seen in a Dragonhorse, and accomplish far more, forge more alliances, than we could ever hope for."

"But is he ready for his second and last Imperial Dragonhorse cycle?" Kestrel asked, "Because it is nearly upon him, and if he can't control that, he can't control anything else, even-tempered or not."

"Oh yes," Wren nodded. "Tentative though he may yet be in a few areas, he is very athletic. Very strong."

"Then I think we should bring him in," Kestrel said.

"Bring him in?" Wren scowled, "as in, force him into heat? No. Absolutely not. There's no need to do that to him. He's close enough now that a few more days…"

Kestrel rolled his eyes and mouthed what she'd just said before continuing with his thought. "If we can monitor every aspect of his heat cycle for three full days, we can end them for him once and for all – or at least I think we can, and I'd like to get that particular bit of misery well over with before his family gets here – most especially that wife of his. Why he married that woman I do not know, but she is going to be trouble, and I do not think she will look kindly upon those who hurt her beloved husband. I so wish he'd just come here instead of luring Sarkhan away. Now we are behind his needs, not in front of them. I thought yesterday he was going to die of shock."

"Never," Lark said, "I think of all the Dragonhorses so far, he's the best able to deal with his own needs, control his own desires, and examine his own weaknesses. If we have to be behind in the training of one, we couldn't do better than Ardenai."

"I hope you're right," Kestrel replied. "Let's get ready. Wren, I know you have feelings for him, but do not fall in love with that man and do not…"

"…tell him. Don't worry. I won't say anything," she sighed, turned on her heel, and walked back into the depths of the old fortress.

Ardenai came in from the gardens much refreshed. He returned to his studies with the intensity he usually brought to things, and though his mind wandered once or twice to the concerns of home, and of the Great House – and to how good it would be to see his wife and family – he used the rest of the day to delve into the deeper workings of the Eloi – the ancient sisterhood of priestesses. There was a puzzle locked in a mystery, and he wanted to start solving it before his high priestess mother got the best of him on yet another front. Who were they? Where and when had they come into being? They were there in documents so old he almost feared to touch them – in songs and legends and teaching chants that predated writing. They were the solid rock upon which Equus had been built. If Ardenai had not already had knowledge of the serpent people of Achernar – the old dragons – he would have thought the Eloi had been there at the beginning of all things. And they were all women, always. In many ancient cultures gender neutral or gender reversed men joined the priesthood or became medicine men, or were revered as seers. Not so with the Eloi of Equus. Why was that?

He murmured a thank you when Lark set orange mulled wine beside him, and sipped at it while he read, nibbling absently at bits of cheese from time to time. Half of it was left when she came to get him for supper. He'd abandoned the dining room days before, preferring to visit with Harrier, Wren, Lark or Kestrel while he ate. This was his time to learn as much as he could; he was loathe to spend it in a sterile setting.

Tonight he looked around at the nooks and crannies in the ancient kitchen, wishing he had his paints to work with. There were so many colors and textures, interesting shapes and the play of light on the walls, reflecting off the pots which hung there. While he ate he talked to Harrier about painting, and about his sister, Ah'din, who did wonderful things with fabric, and Harrier said, "She sounds very much like Ah'nora. Perhaps together they could become the force behind the keeplord, as Io is the power behind the king."

Ardenai cocked a thoughtful eyebrow in Harrier's direction and nodded. So many, many things had to be accepted. Maybe Ah'nora would be happy at Canyon keep with Ah'din and Ah'rane. Or not. He couldn't bring himself even to contemplate what Io would say, or what he would say to Ah'nora. "There's something interesting in the vegetables tonight," he said, by way of changing the subject. "There's a flavor in here that seems vaguely familiar, but I can't quite place it."

Harrier winced a little inside, but he nodded and spoke of his herb garden. He hoped Ah'din would enjoy exploring it when she got here. He was looking forward most of all to meeting her.

An hour later Ardenai's blood began to heat up and his head began to fill with images like those in the ithyphallic chamber. Everything began to smell like women in heat. He could taste it in the very air he was breathing. He pushed himself away from the floor harp he'd been playing, excused himself from Kestrel and Lark, and said he had business to tend to. When he got to his chambers and looked in the mirror, the whites of his eyes were amber. In the next minute his head was throbbing and his intromittent organ had rolled from its sheath and begun to pulse like the heartbeat of a running horse. He was trying to catch his breath and figure out where he was, when Wren put her arms around him, and her head against his. "Come to me," she said quietly. "I have a place to cool your heat."

He stood there, swaying slowly back and forth in her arms, eyes closed, and it took her a a minute to realize his grip on her was growing more and more painful. "Dragonhorse..." she began.

"Shhhhh," he whispered, dropping his forehead to the side of her neck.

"Let me help you..." she began again. Again he hushed her, and she became aware too late of a growing pressure as he worked his jaw, like a slowly closing steel trap, into the side of her neck where her main nerve cord connected brain to body. "You're hurting me," she said.

"Really?" came the oily smooth voice. "Good. Why did you drug me?"

"You're imagining things," she whispered, hands against his chest. He had her locked up tight. There was nothing she could do, and she was beginning to get small shocks in front of her eyes. "You know I'll die if you continue with that pressure." She began to go limp in his arms, and felt his teeth on her neck.

"If you try that, I will bite through to your primary cord. You will be in the repair shop until my grandson is Dragonhorse." He was breathing hard and slick with sweat, but if he was feeling any weakness Wren couldn't detect it. Again the soft, menacing voice asked, "Why did you drug me?"

"So we could get you through a heat cycle and make adjustments in your primary sexual receptors so you won't have to go through the pain and disruption of another Imperial Dragonhorse cycle. Please, Dragonhorse. You're killing me."

"Good. You've discovered my greatest weakness. I don't deal well with betrayal."

"We did not intend...to betray you," she managed. "We gave you only…what the priestesses gave…you that first…day. Please..."

Now, Ardenai could taste it, and he began to growl, deep in his throat, with more anger than he had ever felt in his life – more than he knew he could conjure. It was only with a supreme effort that Wren was not already dead.

"We were trying to do what is best for you," came Kestrel's quietly annoyed voice from the doorway. "You are the master of this house, and we love you. It is not in our destiny to cause you harm. Pain, yes. Harm, no. She is your lifelong friend. Please, Ardenai, let her go."

He straightened up and fixed a malevolent gaze on Kestrel as Wren sagged in place against him. "I have a good mind to kill all of you," he said flatly, and Kestrel was truly afraid of a Dragonhorse for the first time. "I think it may be time for Equi to befriend and defend this place, and for all of you to be deactivated and put back in your boxes."

"We are your history. We are your advisers!"

"And are you also the Telenir?" Ardenai snarled, and as he said it he picked Wren up over his head and threw her into Kestrel as though she weighed nothing. They went down in a heap, and when they managed to untangle themselves and get up again, Ardenai was sitting on the edge of the bed, gasping for air and staring at them like a cornered protoped.

Kestrel, for the first time in nearly six thousand Equi lifetimes, got down on his knees and put his forehead on the floor in complete subservience. "No, my Lord," he said quietly, "We are not the Telenir. We are your friends and your advisers. So before you kill us, or banish us from our destiny, which we cherish, please, speak to your friend the serpent, who instructed us to do to you exactly what we are doing, in exactly the same order." There was silence, and when he dared to look up, those dragon's eyes were still fixed on him, but the expression on the face had changed a little – The Dragonhorse was thinking. "We are not the Telenir."

"Then don't act like them," Ardenai said, not loudly, but with such deep and ferocious anger that Kestrel shook and Wren leaned against the wall in the corridor and cringed. "You have not treated me as a friend. Does one do something to a friend without explaining why he is doing it? Does one embarrass a friend who is already uncomfortable in a strange place? Do I strike you as such a dull and mannerless lout that you would do so personal a thing as bringing me into heat without telling me what you were going to do and why, regardless of what Pythos may have given you to do? If you're not any more intuitive than that, you are machines indeed."

Kestrel just shook his head slowly from side to side. "You are brilliant and beautiful beyond all our hopes," he said, "and I can only say that what we have done, has followed the instructions given to us by your personal physician. Always has it been accomplished in this manner, that we may observe how the Dragonhorse reacts to new situations. The fact that you have been Dragonhorse for many seasons before coming to us, has made the rules and our designated tasks with you…hazier."

"Then you should have had sense enough to discuss them with me and change them accordingly, shouldn't you?" Ardenai said, and he was beginning to sound more tired than angry – certainly saner. "Now, I am going to go take a bath and swim in the cold jets for a bit – and when I am through, and dressed, I'm going to sit down with a nice cup of willow bark tea for this headache and you're going to tell me exactly what you are hoping to accomplish by bringing me into heat. Are we of an understanding?" Kestrel nodded. "We will not speak of this again," Ardenai said, stripping off his shirt, "and you will never do anything like this to me or to any member of my family again." He turned and glared at Wren. "And you, Machine… pretending to be my friend, pretending to be real…your place will be on the priapic bench so that I don't have to look at your face."

Wren nodded mutely and turned away. Even in anger he looked so much like his great-grandfather. It made her heart ache to feel such hatred coming off him – this precious memory returned in the flesh. She knew that he was going to rape her savagely the second he got the chance, and she prepared herself for it. She told herself she had it coming for allowing herself to be part of such an antiquated and uncaring cycle of discovery, valuable though it might be.

As they sat at the table in the kitchen and Kestrel explained to the Firstlord what they were going to do and what he could expect, Wren watched his face, but he didn't look at her. He was civil, but his laughing eyes were cold, and his jaw was clenched. Except for the whites of his eyes, which were getting redder and redder and beginning to swirl with full heat, there was no sign that he was in distress.

"We will test blood, saliva, ejaculate, and brain tissue," Kestrel said.

"I understand that it will be painful, but to my ultimate benefit," Ardenai winced. "More than at any time in my life I wish Pythos were here to advise me. I did not realize until this moment how much I have depended on him and how much I love him." Again the eyes grew cold as they looked at Kestrel. "I only wish I trusted you, Kestrel, to do what you have promised to do and nothing more."

Kestrel turned his palms up and looked at Ardenai. "Not trusting me, is foolish for you and painful for me. No less than Pythos, I have had you in my care since the day you were born. You and a dozen others before you, and even before them, Dragonhorse. I would not have had things go this way, but they have."

"I promise you I will come with him," Harrier said, dropping a hand on Kestrel's shoulder. "But I can also promise you that he will do you no harm, Ardenai. None of us will bring lasting harm to you in any way. Kestrel just has that terrible personality that makes him seem like he would. If you'd like, I will help you put him out of commission, and I will take care of you myself."

"With what, a spoon?" Kestrel snapped, and despite himself, Ardenai chuckled.

"I'm dreading this, so can we please get on with it?"

They rose, and with a finality that felt like execution, they walked the long corridor to the ithyphallic chamber, stripped the Firstlord of his clothing, and Harrier and Kestrel stepped into the shadows, leaving Ardenai with Wren. She took off her robe and sandals and set them aside without meeting his eyes. “What would you have me do?”

He said nothing, made a gesture, and she assumed her position on the priapic bench, adjusted herself, and presented up to him. He was not long in covering her, and groaned with relief as he penetrated. As his body came across hers he said quietly, “You must tell me if I hurt you.”

She nodded, wondering if he was taunting her. “Tell me one thing, please,” she said, and she could feel him nod against her neck.

“What?” he managed.

“I am not the only one who planned this for you – I am not the one at all – why is your hatred directed at me, Dragonhorse?”

He raised his chest up off her back, and when he had recovered himself momentarily he said, “I think – no, I am sure – that it is because you represent that which troubles me most about myself – the inability to separate love from passion. Remember, you must tell me if I am hurting you.”

▲ ▲ ▲ ▲ ▲ ▲ ▲

They locked up in coitus for hour upon hour, Kestrel and Harrier present to take swabs or samples, with no sense on their part that the Dragonhorse even knew they were there. He lay heavily across Wren, jerking spasmodically from time to time and gasping, but not really seeming to be conscious. When Kestrel reached tentatively to tip up his chin, Ardenai’s eyes were completely black.

“He’s full in,” he said quietly. “We need to take a small sample of brain matter.”

“I will do that,” came the soft hiss, and they realized to their vast relief that the Firstlord’s personal physician had arrived and entered the chamber. “I can make thiss much lesss painful for him,” he said. He leaned close over the Firstlord, put an arm across his bare and sweating shoulder, and touched him deep in the ear with his sensitive tongue.

"Pythos," Ardenai managed, and for a moment his whole body relaxed. "Thank you."

"Thee iss welcome, Beloved," the old serpent hissed, and made a fluid curve in the direction he wanted the watchers to go, leaving the Dragonhorse and his hetaera on their own.

"He sseems a little more sstresssed than I exsspected," Pythos said when they were clear. "Lark tellss me thiss hass been lesss than ssmooth from time to time?"

"Whatever would give her that idea?" Kestrel muttered.

"Well, we sshall have time to talk thiss to a conclussion whilssst we gather herbss for the firsst of the corrective decoctionss which will end thiss for him oncce and for all," Pythos said, toddling on his short legs but with good speed toward the stairs which led down to the gardens, and again visions of being put in a box to rot flashed through Kestrel's head.

It was nearly nightfall again when Pythos caught Ardenai by the convenient handle of his braid and handed him a small earthenware tumbler, saying, "Drink this."

"Mmmmm?"

"Thee hearss me. Drink thiss. Now."

Ardenai managed to take the tumbler, downed it in a single gulp, and flung it with a soft snarl to shatter against the far wall.

"Charming," Pythos murmured reprovingly, but he retreated, and in an hour he was back with the same request.

Again Ardenai drank what was in the tumbler. Again he flung it, this time to be caught by Harrier, who was none too happy about losing medicinal tumblers five thousand years old. "Maybe he does have his father's temper," he muttered.

When Pythos returned a third time he found them on the cushions with Wren on top and Ardenai beneath. Good. She could control him to some extent. When the serpent peered over Wren's shoulder he could see that the Firstlord's eyes were losing some of their color – moving from black to red. "Resst a minute and drink thiss," he said.

Ardenai nodded and raised himself onto one elbow. He drank the mixture a little more slowly, and handed back the tumbler. His eyes closed and he dropped back onto the cushions. "More to go?" he mumbled. "Making me sick."

"Not for a while, my hatchling," Pythos said tenderly. "Resst a little and let your partner do the work." Ardenai nodded without opening his eyes, and Pythos dipped his head to Wren before departing. "Soon," he mouthed, and she nodded in return.

The fourth time Pythos came back, the drink was warm. He found them again at the bench in the traditional position, and when he said Ardenai's name, the Firstlord turned his head and looked at him with bright red eyes, but he was responsive, and when Pythos said "Drink thiss, pleasse," Ardenai did so, grimacing at the taste as he handed back the tumbler.

"Not getting any better, is it?" he said, and it sounded as if his lips were numb.

"The medicssine, or your condition?" Pythos asked. "Hold sstill a minute, my child." When Ardenai stopped moving, Pythos again caressed him in both ears with his tongue.

"Oh…Eww," Ardenai groused, sounding pretty much his old self.

"Better than the way Kesstrel would have ssampled thy brain had I not been here," he admonished gently. "Now lissten to me. Thingss are going to get rough for a bit – a few hourss – Just like they did when thee went through thiss on Calumet, doesst thee remember? Thee musst trusst thy partner, and me, and thee musst let go of thy ego and let thy body what it musst. Doesst thee undersstand?"

"Sounds ominous," he sighed, moving just a little – his body still anxious to get back to the act of copulation. What had happened on Calumet had been…what? He couldn't remember. He couldn't even remember being on Calumet. Didn't care.

"Doesst thee undersstand?" Pythos insisted.

"I do," he said. "And I'm sure Wren does as well."

"That I do," she said quietly.

Pythos touched his shoulder briefly and left. Ardenai had built up some urgency during the pause, and he squeezed his eyes shut and pushed hard, panting with relief as his semen flowed again. That was all his body wanted to do – copulate, and copulate some more. It filled his brain and his being with the need for it. Empty the ancillary testicles, empty the primary testes, watch as the black semen turned to pale blue motile sperm – the purest get of Equus.

After a few minutes he placed his hands on Wren's back and pushed himself up off her. His stomach was beginning to churn and he did it as much for air as to give himself a more direct entry. "That last drink isn't sitting very well," he grimaced, and a second later he was spewing over the side of the priapic bench. "I'm so sorry!" he exclaimed. "I..." he vomited again, and his knees began to turn to water. "Bad reaction," he managed, and Wren shook her head.

"No, good reaction. If you want to switch positions this would be the time."

"What? Oh, Eladeus…no," he groaned, and lost control of his bowels.

"Too late," she said. "Put your weight on me and just ride it out."

"Oh no," he groaned, "Oh no…I am so sorry." He collapsed onto her back, still overwhelmed with the urge to ejaculate, and as he did he vomited again, this time down the side of his partner, and the stink of feces filled the chamber as his bowels exploded. And even with all that, they remained firmly locked in coitus – he couldn't withdraw, though he would have given anything, anything at all, to be able to do so. If anything, the urge to copulate grew more intense, and he fought with every ounce of strength he had left not to pound Wren to a pulp.

"Just relax," she urged. "If Ah'riodin could take this, you know I can. You won't hurt me, and resisting may be hurting you more. Put your weight on me and ride it out."

At the end of the next hour, when he was standing in his own excrement, and his partner was coated on both sides with the slime of vomit, Pythos appeared with a tumbler and said in a perfectly normal tone of voice, "Drink thiss."

Ardenai raised his head from the side of Wren's neck, where he was sure he'd been breathing his fetid breath into her face, and looked with blank eyes at the old physician. "Drink thiss. It will make thee feel better, I promisse."

He took the cup in shaking hands and drank, losing his grip on it and pouring the last of its contents onto Wren's reddened back. "I'm sorry," he said again. When had he said that before? To Ah'nis – down on one knee asking her to forgive him. How would she react in this situation? Almost, he could let his mind wander to that scenario.

"Good," Pythos said. He took a bucket of warm water, fragrant with herbs, and sloshed it over Wren, then another bucket went over Ardenai's backside and onto the floor, then a third across the floor itself and into the drain. "You sshould be empty ssoon" the old physician said matter-of-factly. "Dry your partner as besst you can." He tossed Ardenai a towel, and picking up the buckets, he toddled out of the room.

Ardenai did as he was told, drying her gently with long strokes on her back and sides, and when he reached under her to dry her belly, his hands paused to caress her breasts, which brought on another emission, more vomiting, more feces. With the pleasure, it seemed, came the shame and the pain and the realization that one could copulate, regurgitate, and defecate all at the same time. *If I ever begin to puff up with my own magnificence, I will need only remember this,* he thought.

He'd put the towel over her back to protect her from the worst of it, and now it was just slime and bile, his bowels just water, but it stank, and he was hurting all over, shaking with exhaustion, and trying to bear his own weight so as not to breathe in her face. When he did collapse momentarily, he held his breath as best he could, though when one is panting it is hard to do that. Even then, as he lay across her back, he was cramping and jerking and ejaculating, over and over with no space in between.

He was putting her through this, and she was letting him – this woman he had picked up and thrown as though she were a bundle of rags. Stressed as he was, he felt the shame. What could he say to apologize for something so…uncharacteristic? How could he apologize for the actions of someone he didn't even know? Suddenly there was a blinding flash of light.

"Did you see that?" he gasped.

"There's nothing there," Wren said gently. "Put your weight on me and ride it out."

There was another blinding flash and then the screaming started. Screams, and crying, and voices pleading, and the voices of men and women raping and being raped, and children screaming, and in those voices he could hear Gideon's little voice crying, "Mommy, Mommy, please, please don't let him do this to me. Mommy it hurts!" and he was screaming and crying and Ardenai could smell the blood as the little boy's flesh tore, and to his horror it was he who was doing it, forcing himself into a tiny child – and into Eridi – and she was screaming and pushing herself onto him as hard as she could, begging for a baby, and though she was a child he was pushing back, biting savagely at her neck, and Gideon was begging for him to stop because it hurt, and he was sobbing and crying, and there was fire and Ah'ree was trying to give birth to a baby that didn't exist, and she was screaming, and Io was screaming, trying to give birth to a baby that was monstrous, and Pythos wasn't there to help, and in the blackness around the edges of his shattered thoughts a voice kept saying, *control yourself, control yourself, control yourself....* Behind that voice, dimly another voice saying, "Ardi, put your weight on me and ride it out. It's only a passing effect of the decoctions. Ardenai, Beloved, put your weight on me and ride it out." At last, that dim voice was all he heard, and he sagged fully onto her, sobbing and making hoarse screams deep in his throat which left him raw and streaked the last of his vomit with the pale blue of high Equi blood.

There came another sloshing of warm water and blessedly fragrant herbs. "Drink thiss," Pythos said, and when Ardenai didn't respond or raise his head from Wren's back, Pythos jerked him upright by his hair until he was off her, and poured another concoction down his throat, most of which he swallowed, some of which he choked on and spit up. "Look at me," Pythos demanded, staring into the tear streaked face and trying not to cry himself. "Hatchling, open thosse eyess and look at me." Slowly the Firstlord's eyes came open, and Pythos nodded. Amber. "Good," he said. "Can thee move yet?" Ardenai responded by groaning and sagging back to his original position.

"I think we can," Wren said, and began slowly picking herself up with her hands until Ardenai tilted backwards a little, and Pythos pulled him up into a standing position. "Put him on his back," she said, indicating the priapic bench, and she straddled him with one foot on either side. "He's not going to vomit any more, is he? Because if he does I'm afraid he'll choke if we lock up again."

Pythos flicked him gently with his tongue in a place or two and said, "You won't. He'ss empty, poor hatchling. Hiss eyes are nearly clear now. If we can get them completely clear, he won't ccycle beyond his usual dessir-ess, which sseem pronouncced enough to me." He turned from the Firstlord and gave Wren's face a little flick as well, which made her smile and nod. "I know how tired thee musst be, Daughter. Thee hass been mosst kind. We appreciate thee."

"Thank you," she said, and leaned forward to press herself against Ardenai's chest. Though his eyes opened only momentarily he smiled; his hands reached to caress her, and she whispered, "That feels good. Let's make love, and when you waken, all of this will be just a dream, that you can choose to remember, or choose to forget. Touch me again – just like that," She licked her lips with pleasure, and joined him with cries of delight and the sweet sense of victory.

Ardenai's nose told him first, and he breathed in the familiar perfume of the small person snuggled under his chin. Foaming rosemary, leather, very faintly the smell of horses. He opened his eyes, but it was dark in the room and he had no sense of what time it might be. Vaguely, but only vaguely he could remember Wren and terrible dreams, and intense desires – and Pythos – and a warm bath and a long, long cool drink of something soothing and nourishing. Was it over? Had it happened?

"Ardi, you're pulling my hair," Io mumbled.

"It is you," he whispered, adjusting his cheek where it pinched her hair against his arm and kissing the top of one of her beautiful, butterfly wing ears.

"It is me," she whispered, "and it's the middle of the night." But he could hear the smile in her voice. "Have you missed me, Dragonhorse?"

"More than you will ever know," he said, catching her in his arms and rolling until he was on top of her. "Would you like me to show you how much?"

"Um hm," she giggled, and he kissed her deeply, and caressed her, and used his legs to spread hers and made love to her until Lark knocked on the wall from a discreet distance and told them it was time to rise for breakfast.

"You got here early," he said as they bathed.

"No. We're right on time," she replied, scrubbing at a spot on his back. "It looks like somebody bit you right here." She scrubbed a little more. "Your arms seem to be healing up nicely for the second time. What's this?" She traced a ring of small, pinprick bruises on his forearm, almost hidden by the python tattoos. "You have them on both arms. Have you been in Jacerei bands?"

"I don't think so," he said, but when he urinated a few minutes later it stung a little, and there was just a touch of blood. He stood in front of the reflector, braiding his hair down from the crown of his head and trying to recapture time. "Wren," he said aloud, and his wife gave him a questioning look.

"Wren...what?" she asked.

"Wren," he said in laughing reply, tucking his braid up under itself and fastening it in place with a clasp, "is who will know about the marks on my arms."

"And she is?"

"My hetaera. As a matter of fact, she has been the hetaera for most of the Dragonhorses." He finished his hair, and glanced at his wife in the mirror. She was sitting on the bed, snickering softly. "What? She looks just fine. She's Androtech. Apparently they don't age. What?"

Io laughed harder, which made Ardenai laugh, and he snatched her off the bed and swung her around as he set her feet on the floor. "Tell me or

I'll tickle you until you wet. You know I can do it."

She wiped her eyes and tried to pull a straight face. "It is a learning curve," she responded, not meeting his eyes. "I thought I was a sex machine until I met you. Now you, apparently, have met a real sex machine." She burst out laughing again and waved her hands to fend him off. "I don't know why that's so funny to me, I really don't. It's just that I have the immediate urge to compete with her, which is ludicrous."

"You're a better kisser," Ardenai said. Their eyes met and they lost themselves in gales of laughter. They were still laughing like children when they entered the dining room and the embrace of family.

Again, Ardenai sighed, the worst of it was over. And, with an inkling of implanted memory, he remembered that Pythos was here, and that Pythos would know. He returned hugs and made the usual small overtures as they sat down, but he also reached out to his physician.

Pythos?

I am here.

I choose to remember.

Are you sure? That may not be such a good idea. You will remember everything clearly – both Imperial Dragonhorse cycles.

I am sure.

As you wish.

Ardenai snapped back in his chair with a gasp of remembered pain, dropping from his shaking hands the platter his father caught. He swallowed hard and sat panting, eyes squeezed shut, then opened a little too wide for a few moments until he had himself under control. He realized Krush was holding the platter and looking into his face, and that the table was completely silent. "Careful what you wish for," he muttered, and managed a sour chuckle. "Sorry about the platter, Sire. Nice catch by the way."

Ah'rane gave him a no-nonsense-from-you-young-man look from across the table and he gave her a nod and smile. "Really, Mother, I'm fine. I just asked Pythos to help me remember something, and he has a way of ... hurling things into my much slower brain. I'll sort through it later. Where is he, by the way?"

"Jusst coming in," that entity hissed, toddling to his place at the table. He coiled onto his special bench and looked around, flicking his tongue with pleasure. "How lovely to ssee all of my family here at the ssame time." And they were – Teal and Ah'din, Ah'rane and Krush, Io and Ardenai, and all four sons – Kehailan, Gideon, Criollo and Jilfan. "Lovely," he said again. "After breakfasst we will all have a chancce to explore. But right now, in honor of uss all being together, and becausse of the date, Krussh and I have deccided it iss time to draw namess for the Ccelebration of Sstormss!" He rang a glass with an eating stick borrowed from Gideon, and Lark appeared with a crockery bowl. "Ussual ruless. If thee getss thine own name, put it back. Krussh?"

He reached into the bowl Lark handed him, laughed, put the name back and drew again, stirring the pot as he did so. He passed the bowl to Ardenai, who drew out a name, smiled and said, "This year I'm eating mine so nobody gets wiser before the day." He didn't. He slid it under his plate and passed the bowl to Io.

Gideon had his fingers crossed, his toes crossed – he so wanted to get Ah'din's name. He had brought home the Evangeline's Carpet, and more. On the way Chirion had showed all of them plants, leaves, bark, grasses, even clay and stones which, when powdered had healing elements. All of these, and the notes he had made about them, he had stashed in his room hidden from curious eyes and the relentless teeth of a growing puppy, who was, at the moment, gnawing on the side of Gideon's moccasin. He pushed him a little with his foot to make him quit, and watched the progression of the pot. Io to Kehailan, to Jilfan – to him. He whispered a quick prayer amounting to, *Oh please oh please,* and reached in. He felt around a bit, pulled out a paper and after a moment brought himself to look at it. Ah'din. Amazing! He laughed with relief and passed the bowl to Teal.

"Well somebody got who somebody wanted," Ah'rane chuckled. "I'll bet there's a nice surprise planned for someone."

"Speaking of which," Ardenai said, reaching for a platter, "I have a surprise for you, Mother, and I hope you'll like it. There's someone I want you to meet, who very much wants to meet you, but there's something you probably need to know first."

"Which is?" she twinkled, and Ardenai suddenly felt a bit of a chill go up his spine. What if she reacted as he had, with shock and disbelief?

"Well…I'm not the only one who's fostered, for one thing," he hedged, and Krush burst out laughing.

"And this is where you tell us that you and Ah'rane really are related, right?" Ardenai just looked at him, and Krush pulled him close with one arm and kissed his temple. "Sweet Boy, we have known for a hundred years, since the first day we got you, who you would grow up to be. You looked exactly like your mother – maybe a little too much. We had been told to pretend that she was pregnant so that everyone would think you were actually ours. That just isn't done with a usual fostering. It wasn't done with your mother when she was fostered. We did some simple math, and we knew we had The Thirteenth Dragonhorse. It didn't make us love you one bit more, or one bit less. Gideon figured it out the first day. I'm surprised he hasn't brought it up to you."

"Oh, I did," Gideon said around a mouthful of food.

"And I didn't want to hear it," Ardenai admitted. "Why it was such a shock to me, I'll never know, but it was."

Krush gave him a pat on the forearm and a wink. "It's fine, Ardi, we know how you are. The only question now is, what is the relationship? Gideon thinks she's your sister."

"Half-sister," Ardenai chuckled. "The Twelfth Dragonhorse is sire to both of us, and it is he, who would like to meet you, Mother."

Krush gave him a dubious look. "Really? What kind of shape is he in by now?"

"We have not finisshed," Pythos interjected. "Hass everyone gotten a name from the pot?" They nodded, looking from one to another and smiling secret smiles. "Very well then," he said, and slapped the table four times. "We have drawn, and all iss well."

The rest of them slapped the table four times and responded, "And who we got we'll never tell."

"The oath is sspoken," Pythos said solemnly. "Who wants to ssee what this morning?"

"I would love to see the gardens," said Ah'din, and Harrier immediately appeared from the kitchen to take her arm. Pythos excused himself and followed them.

Teal opted for the wine cellars with Kestrel, Io and Jilfan went off together to explore the older parts of the castle, and the rest of them headed for the library. "I have someone I want you to meet, too," Gideon said quietly to Ardenai as they walked.

"You don't have a second puppy in that crate, do you?" His father asked warily.

"No. I…El Shadai…look at this room!" Gideon stood staring up with the others, almost afraid to breathe for fear it might vanish. Wonder of wonders – the Great Library of The Dragonhorses. He'd heard tales of it even when he was on Demeter – heard it was just a legend – and now he stood within it. For a moment he thought he was going to cry. *My world just gets bigger and more wonderful every day,* he thought, and smiled at his father's warm hug.

None better to share a wonder with than thee, my friend.

The puppy began to whimper and Wren appeared beside Gideon, offering a hand to take the little crate. "I have a place where he can run and play without getting into anything," she said, and Gideon reluctantly handed over the dog.

"Will you be able to hear him if he cries? Will you let me know?"

"I have no intention of leaving him," she grinned. "I want to play with him myself. You go on and enjoy your explorations. I'll take good care of Lionel for you." With that she held up the crate to wiggle her fingers at the puppy, and in a few moments they had vanished around the corner into the corridor. Gideon could hear her talking to him. In the next second one of the librarians appeared, beckoned to Criollo, and asked him if he would like to help with the manuscript they were cleaning. The boy nodded, mouth completely ajar, and was led away.

"I'm sure there will be a place for each of you to begin when your instruction starts, but for now, just wander and be amazed," Ardenai smiled.

"That's what I do."

"Before the rest of you wander," said a familiar voice, and The Twelfth Dragonhorse had appeared in the room. He took three long strides and was beside them – handsome and smiling, and obviously Ardenai's father in both looks and build. "Allow me the honor of visiting with you for a bit. I'm sure The Dragonhorse has told you who I am."

"I have," Ardenai smiled, "And this is your daughter, Ah'rane."

Kehailan looked at her and every line of his face spoke to the emotion he was feeling. "You're beautiful," he breathed. "I can see your mother in you. She was such a glorious woman both inside and out, and she was the love of my life. Please, sit and talk with me here for a bit. And you," he said, turning to Krush and grasping his shoulders, "thank you so much, Keeplord Krush, for your wonderful care of my son and my daughter. What a brilliant job you did with Ardenai." He turned then to Kehailan and grinned mischievously. "And you are my namesake, though your father didn't realize it at the time. Are you as much trouble as you look to be?"

"I try," Kehailan chuckled, "but I'm not very good at it."

"Oh, I think you are," he said, shaking an index finger. "You are smart and intuitive. A command is in your near future, I think. Your children will be raised on great stellar ships and see more of the universe than anyone thought possible. But you need to learn to love your father without suspicion or jealousy, do you hear me? He trusts your judgment, and he needs both your council and your love in equal measure."

Kehailan nodded deeply and murmured, "Yes, Grandsire. I hear thee. I will do my best."

"See that you do," he said, and turned to Gideon. He looked at the boy for a long minute, pleased that he didn't look away, nor did he take it as a challenge. He simply stood and allowed himself to be evaluated. "The young man who saved The Thirteenth Dragonhorse. Much do I owe thee, Ardenai Gideon Morning Star." The boy nodded and smiled, but he didn't puff up when praised. "Where do you fit in to this, do you suppose?"

"For the future, I do not know," Gideon replied. "Every possibility I look at is more exciting than the last. For now, it is my job to get an education and learn about everything I can, because I'm off to a slow start. Mostly, I'd like to think my job is to love my family, and serve my father, because that's my favorite thing to do."

"You're already the stuff of legend you know."

"I'm the stuff of speculation," he chuckled. "Ardenai is the stuff of legend."

"Well said," The Twelfth Dragonhorse responded, dipping his head graciously in Gideon's direction. "I understand that you have a mare that you love very much, and that in five and a half seasons, she will be having a foal."

"Yes," Gideon responded, rolling a leery eye in Ardenai's direction. "But with all due respect, I think I should discuss it with my father before it becomes any more public knowledge than it already is."

"Of course," Kehailan said. "See where that light is shining on the wall yonder? Go get that book and begin to study it. It deals with the bloodlines of that foal your mare is settled with. That is where your lessons will begin." Gideon moved off in the direction of the light, Krush beside him, and with a nod and a wink in Ardenai's direction, the Twelfth Dragonhorse took Ah'rane's arm and walked with her toward a group of easy chairs near the window.

"If you will excuse me," Kehailan said to his father, "I need to check in with Marion. That's where we stashed Ah'nis and Eridi – aboard Belesprit."

"Good choice," Ardenai smiled, and Kehailan left him by himself. He was grateful. As much as he wanted to ask about this new foal and its bloodlines, and how that had happened, he wanted time to assess what Pythos had sent him, and he needed quiet introspection to do that.

He found a comfortable chair in a quiet corner where there was room enough to stretch his legs, and leaned back to close his eyes. With the initial effort to recall, came a shock behind his eyes that made his whole body jerk, and the first thing he remembered was the pain – but not here, in this place – the pain beside the little lake on Calumet – the pain neither he nor Io was ready for – the veiled black eyes, the vomiting, the running bowels – the monumental struggle not to kill her. He had thought he remembered those days, but he had not, not really. Now he did – every sickening detail. *I did this to my wife? I did this to Io? She endured this filth pouring out of me?* For about a minute he thought he was going to vomit again. Eladeus, how could she have forgiven him? More than that, with all the arguments, all the fights they'd had, large and small – she had never brought it up, even once. He took a deep breath and opened his eyes for a few minutes. The images receded. It was time to change the law. It was time to say, one wife. The one he had. The one who had gone through this with him.

He closed them again. Now, he was in the ithyphallic chamber with Wren – after he had cursed her, thrown her, she had still come to him, and that was the part which caused him shame, not the rest of it. She was a machine – she had been through an Imperial Dragonhorse many times. *Put your weight on me and ride it out* – a lesson never to be forgotten, an offer to be graciously made, and if need be, graciously accepted. *Let's make love.... You can choose to remember, or you can choose to forget.* And then…finally…everything was empty. He had no more, could do no more. Didn't want to. Wren had gotten up off him, and after letting him breathe for a bit, she'd offered him a hand up off the bench. Like being pulled out of mud up to his neck. Somehow, he'd found himself standing, and they had kept each other that way for the time it took them to get to the bathing pools. He had been so dizzy, and so disoriented, and so very tired.

"Thee still hass decoctions in thy ssystem," Pythos had said as he bathed him. "At thiss moment thy brain and thy body have nothing to build with."

"What would you have me do?" he had asked, vaguely hoping that on some level he would understand what he was being told.

"I musst assk thee to trusst me again."

Ardenai had groaned, and Pythos had been quick with a comforting flick of his tongue. "Thee musst ssleep. I would like to use endodermal jacerei to nourish thee until thy sstomach feelss better, and a catheter sso that I can move fluidss quickly through thee. Can thee bear to let me do that? If we have been ssucccesssful, thee will not ssuffer like thiss again."

Ardenai had nodded, trying so hard not to let everything go black.

Pythos hadn't asked him to stand again. As he had done so many times before, he had carried the Firstlord – his precious hatchling – someplace dim, where a waterfall provided gentle company and Ardenai could hear birds in the distance. Whatever he had been placed on had been impossibly comfortable and cool, and aside from their initial, unpleasant bite as they pierced his skin, the jacerei bands had not bothered him. They had nourished him, as though he were drinking long and deep from a spring in a green Viridian canyon, or drinking some of Teal's good wine, and he had slept, and though he could not remember most of them now, his dreams and conversations had been pleasant. There had been a little girl – a little brat of a girl, who did what she pleased, who cut her hair off when he wasn't looking, who challenged norms every chance she got – who somehow grew up into a beautiful woman with masses of golden roan curls and huge blue eyes, and she adored him, and gave herself to him…and he had awakened with her as his beloved wife in her accustomed place under his chin.

Again he opened his eyes, and wondered if he'd dozed off. Ah'rane was gone, Krush and Gideon were at a table with a small stack of books, and note pads into which they were feverishly transferring information, and The Twelfth Dragonhorse was sitting in the chair across from him, watching.

"Are you sorry you asked?" he said gently. "I think, in some ways, I was."

Ardenai thought for a minute. "No. I am not. I don't always like what I've done, but I never cease to be amazed by the things others have done for me, or in spite of me."

"I went through just one Imperial Dragonhorse cycle – with your mother. And though Ah'rane's mother was the love of my life, I chose Ah'vel to help me make you, because she had helped me get through the ordeal. She and Wren."

"I can't believe my wife has never said one single word about what happened at that lake. I'm surprised she can even stand the sight of me after what I did."

"She is amazing," Kehailan agreed, "and incredibly beautiful. Your first wife did a good job of preparing her for you. I think she knew what was coming."

Ardenai thought about that, didn't have a clue how to respond to it, and let it go by for the moment. "Ah'ree, brought me great joy," he said at last.

"And yet you do not say she was the love of your life. That's good."

Ardenai studied him for a few moments, wondering if he should ask. "So, did they completely stop the Imperial Dragonhorse in your life?"

He nodded. "For the most part they did, all praise to the Wisdom Giver, and I think they've managed it for you, as well. They get worse every time, you know. They figured that out when the first Dragonhorse they tried to create actually died a cycle or two into the process. They lost two or three that way. They didn't start numbering us until they figured out how to control the heat a little better, at least enough to keep us alive.

"One of the things I pushed for when I was Dragonhorse was to breed the heat cycles out of Equi males – all of them – not just us. Vanner, the Seventh Dragonhorse, killed a hetaera during an Imperial heat, though he didn't mean to. So did Kabardin, the Ninth Dragonhorse, which is where that rule came from about not using hetaeras once one became Dragonhorse. Kabardin killed one of his own wives, as well. It was hushed up, but it happened, nonetheless. Of course he was a mean, nasty piece of work." He slapped his thighs and stood up. "Enough of this for now. Your golden-eyed son has much to tell you, and I think your sire would very much like some time alone to make love to his beautiful wife."

"Again, blurting," Ardenai said, amused, but slightly vexed and embarrassed as well.

Kehailan looked down at him and just shook his head. "You do realize, don't you, that even though this should be your last heat cycle, you're still in heat. Much reduced, admittedly, but a hot cycle, nonetheless, and any Equi who comes under this roof with you will also immediately go into heat."

Ardenai looked back up at him, and his eyes closed, very slowly. "No." He sighed. He thought about it. "Yes. I should have, anyway. I forgot what it was like on Calumet. They…I would not have brought this on my family. How do these things happen?"

"Boy, you have got to learn to think a little faster and a little more clearly," Kehailan said with some annoyance. "Why do you think they're trying to get this out of you? Why do you think they summon all of you into one place at the beginning of this entire adventure when your system is flooded with those decoctions the priestesses cook up? A summons which, I might add, you chose to flaunt to the detriment of half the population of Calumet? Do you have any idea how many women are pregnant there right now? Do you? If you were in Thura today, the whole kraaling city would be an orgiastic bacchanal, and you'd be smack in the middle of it. Five hundred thousand people would be on the same schedule of heat cycles for years – the city would just declare itself a fucking pleasure palace every hundred and twenty days and shut down for a week."

Ardenai slumped a little lower into his chair. "I know this is a stupid question, but is there anything I can do?"

"Absolutely, Ardenai. You can stop squirming and pouting and apologizing and wringing your already bloodstained little hands, and just accept what's happening. In order to do that, you are going to have to embrace who and what you are and stop being ashamed. Your family and your friends are trying to do that, and you keep pulling back. You are The Thirteenth Dragonhorse. Why do you think they call those intense seventh heat cycles a dragonhorse? You are the epitome of a sexual being. For right now, you are a family of sexual beings. Accept it. Enjoy it. Have sex as a group and compare notes."

"Easy to say if you are one of the three loving couples involved," Ardenai scowled, "but we are not the only ones here, are we? Criollo is here..."

"Lark will be doing some training with him. Kestrel has his eye on that beautiful eldest son of yours, and we both know Gideon isn't going to factor in for a while yet."

"Oh, Precious Equus, you've got this all worked out, haven't you? Why in the ten tribute worlds can't I get ahead of any of this? Why am I ALWAYS behind, going, 'Oh yes, that's what I should have done'? And what do you mean, FOR A WHILE YET?"

His voice rang in the perfect accoustics of the library, and both Krush and Gideon looked up from what they were doing. "Who are you talking to?" Krush asked.

Ardenai's head snapped around. "The Twelfth Dragonhorse. I thought."

Gideon just looked at him and laughed. "No you weren't. You were sound asleep until about five seconds ago. Come here and see what we've found."

Ardenai jacked himself out of the chair and walked their direction, still looking furtively from side to side, wondering if The Twelfth Dragonhorse could just pop into his brain. He stopped suddenly, looked ceilingward with outspread hands and said, "Of course you can! You are a program created for a telepathic people. That's why Lark, and Wren, and Kestrel seem to appear out of nowhere, just after we realize we need something. You're telepaths, just like we are." He laughed and then looked apologetically at the two people who were looking back at him with some amusement and a little concern. "Slowly but surely. Or in my case, slowly but slowly. Gideon, you have a story to tell me." Then, he decided to take a chance and test a theory. "Sire, I'm sure Gideon and I can keep ourselves entertained if you would like to spend some time with your beautiful wife."

Krush looked up and crimped a grin. "Reading minds these days are you?"

"No, but I do know what's been going on here for the last few days, and I'm assuming there's plenty to share."

Gideon gave him a look of comic disgust. "Is what happened on Calumet going to happen here?" Despite Kehailan's lecture, despite his vow to take it to heart, Ardenai felt himself blushing blue as a schoolgirl, and Gideon stood up and gave him a lingering hug. "I'm going to go check on Lionel and I'll be back in about five minutes. Meantime, you can explain this to your father, just in case he decides to say some things that will sear my tender ears." He nodded respectfully to Krush and trotted out of the library, turning in the same direction he'd seen Wren take his puppy.

"So, what happened on Calumet?" Krush asked innocently, and Ardenai did what he'd been wanting to do for weeks and seasons. He grabbed his hair in both hands and screamed something really vulgar in most of the languages he knew. He exhaled sharply and dropped his head.

"Better?"

"Much," he chuckled, sliding into Gideon's vacated chair. "When I'm in heat I bring everybody else in as well – both males and females, which should be a plus. I've been through another Imperial Dragonhorse cycle since I've been here, but this time they forced me in, and forced me out – most of the way out, apparently – and they're thinking I won't cycle again. They did the same thing for the Twelfth Dragonhorse, and he says it worked, so I'm hoping for the best. Sire, I am s..."

"Stop," his father said, holding up a hand. "You need to ease up on yourself and ride with a looser rein. You and Gideon enjoy your day. I'm going to go find your mother."

"You might want to find Teal while you're at it."

But Teal, had already been found. He'd finished his tour of the wine cellars and was prowling the gardens looking for his wife when she appeared from behind a rohanth hedge and pulled him, laughing, into the shadows of an ancient archway. "Well, hello there," he breathed as her arms encircled his neck. He caught her around the waist and returned what had become a very passionate kiss. "I wondered when you'd show up."

"There's something about this place," she murmured, lips close to his as she nuzzled his cheek.

"Um hm," he replied. "And I know what it is."

She pulled back a little and gave him a questioning but largely disinterested look. "Oh. Is it Ardi?"

"Um hm," he said again, and by now he was having definite thoughts of his own. He set his teeth carefully against her neck and pulled her closer. She could feel his breath, and the swell of him in his loose fitting trousers. "Do you have plans for the rest of the day?" he asked, pushing her buttocks toward him.

"I do now," she giggled. She didn't giggle very often, and it made

Teal love her until he ached inside. How could this soft and beautiful soul belong to him? "Husband, I've been thinking about babies, how about you?"

"Mmmmm, me too," he replied, still nuzzling. "Boy, or girl this time?"

"One of each," she said, and the whisper was becoming more of an urgent gasp. "Now!"

"Oh…Oops. That was quick," he said, gently controlling her hands. "Din, Love, are you in there at all at this point?"

"Mmmmm," she responded, sinking her teeth a little too hard into his throat where it met his collarbone. "Now!"

Blood of the Dragonhorse in this one. He gave her a tiny shake and her eyes snapped open. To his amused surprise, she slapped him hard across the face and bit him again as her hands began fumbling with the frogs on his tunic. "Have it your way," he chuckled, scooping her into his arms and walking in the direction of their chambers, "but since an exchange of fluids today will mean a birth precisely in the middle of High Harvest next year, I think I'll just make sure you're able to choose wisely before I put a baby in you, Little Mistress."

She bit him a third time, and this time he bit her back, carefully, but thoroughly as he placed her on their bed. "There better be some skins around here close," he growled, "I'm going to need some, right about… now."

▲ ▲ ▲ ▲ ▲ ▲ ▲

Ardenai was pouring over the open book and the notes, whistling softly from time to time, eyes wide with excitement. He saw movement and looked up to see Gideon, and with him, The Eldest, approaching the table on moccasined feet. By the time he was up from his chair and around the table the man was reaching to embrace him, saying, "Ardenai, Beloved, I am Chirion."

Ardenai grasped him by the upper arms and held him at arm's length to study him. "And you are of this place, yes?"

"Yes," he smiled, and embraced him again. "I have waited so long to hold you like this and speak to you as myself. I rejoice that you have come into your own."

"And I rejoice that you are safe, though I see now that you were never in danger."

"No," he said, smiling as he sat at the table and beckoned Ardenai into the chair beside him. "What we wanted to know, is if you would care for someone who seemed to have no value, and you did. Year after year, no matter what I did or said, you gave me my freedom and provided for my safety. And when I seemed to respond better to younger people, you allowed that, as well, though it would have been easy at that point to just let me go. Even with the pain and the stress of being Dragonhorse, you, and those whom you love and influence, remembered an old man in the solitudes."

Gideon had been listening and now he ventured, "You spent eighty years in the wilderness waiting to see if Ardenai would come and get you every year?"

Chirion laughed and shook his head. "No, Young Prince. I have been many places, and been many people in your father's life. We all have. He sees us a hundred times a year, in a hundred guises." The boy looked puzzled, and Chirion took one of his hands, then one of Ardenai's. "Gideon, I am ten thousand years old. I am a highly sophisticated, sentient, and as your father has discovered, telepathic Androtech being. When I am not Chirion, I am other people in other places on other worlds – some nice, some not so nice – but always one of those who interacts with the Dragonhorse. It has always been so. By this method we are able to judge in advance how each will react when absolute power is placed in his hands. In some we have rejoiced, in others, we have not."

"And in my sire?" Gideon asked quietly.

"In your sire," Chirion said, "we have found…a simple man."

"Simple?" Gideon echoed, but Ardenai sighed hugely and nodded, relief flooding through him as he smiled at Chirion.

"Thank you," he said softly. "You could pay me no higher compliment."

Chirion took Ardenai's face in his hands and kissed him lingeringly on the forehead. "You," he said, "are exactly who we hoped you would be."

CHAPTER 7

We're not going to be able to talk about a lot of what went on with The Eldest," Ah'brianne said, "but we still have the gaknars."

"Yes," Criollo nodded patiently. "We have the gaknars."

"You've been very tight-lipped since you got back from Mountain hold," she observed as they stepped off the lift onto the floor which housed the royal apartments. "Was it awful? Did they torture you or something? After what they did to the Dragonhorse, pouring that molten metal onto his bare arms." she shuddered graphically. "Well?"

Criollo sucked on the insides of his cheeks so he could pull a straight face and murmured, "I've never been through anything like that before." And that much was true. Most of what had gone on he couldn't remember at all, but his first heat cycle – that, he remembered. His time with Lark had been new, and amazing. He was now years ahead of the other boys his age, and since Lark had started his training, she would continue his training, as was traditional. His heat had passed, and so had the desire, but the memory lingered, unfocused and fading rapidly, but sweet. She had been so gentle with him, and though they had not got past the touching it had opened a whole new world of emotion and responsibility that he felt more than ready to accept. That much he could still remember. That, every detail of the library, and whose name he'd gotten in the draw. That was it. The rest of the experience was just… gone.

The doors to the Firstlord's apartments swung open and they stepped inside just as Ardenai and Teal stepped out. "In your fondest dreams, perhaps," Ardenai was saying, then, "Good morning, children," and as they cleared the door they were gone down the hall at a dead run with Teal calling back, "Criollo, get to school!"

"They talk about us," Criollo observed, but it was good to have his father home. He turned back into the entresol, raised his voice and called, "Gideon, time to go." It echoed.

"Coming." Presently he appeared from the top of the stairs looking less than delighted, but compliant nonetheless.

"You look very student-ish," Ah'brianne said, noting the usual school garb and accoutrements.

"I ought to," he scowled. "You picked everything out for me."

"Because you were nervous," she said. "I won't do it again. Come on. We don't want to be late."

They didn't have to do much more than return to the ground floor and walk to one end of the Great House, where a long corridor attached the main building to the school. "Just sit in with us," Criollo suggested, "we can get you sorted out later if need be."

"We have another new student," said Master Breton, nodding and smiling in acknowledgement of their arrival. "Gideon, welcome."

"Thank you," he said, and Ah'brianne hissed,

"Another? Who else is new?"

Criollo elbowed her and pointed with his chin just as Master Breton said, "Addur and Basra are joining us to observe, though they have said they are in more advanced classes on their home planet."

Those two had their heads together and had apparently been discussing the new arrivals when Master Breton's voice cut into their conversation. "Prince Addur and Prince Basra," said Addur, "If it pleases you."

"It does not," Master Breton said, not unkindly. "If I refer to you as princes, I must refer to Criollo as prince, and Gideon as prince, and Ah'win and Ah'dria and Ah'brianne as princesses, and so on. Can you see how cumbersome that would become in conversation?" That answer came in the form of a glare from the two in question. "Here there are no titles," he said quietly, "except for mine, and I have earned it over this last hundred and seventy-five years of teaching in the Great House."

"I am more than happy to be just plain me," Gideon said quietly, taking the chair Ah'brianne gestured him into. "It makes me feel less like I'm disappointing a whole planet."

"Also a good point," Master Breton smiled. "I understand the three of you saw some interesting things while you were out and about in the solitudes recently?"

"We did!" Ah'brianne exclaimed. "We were out helping to find a friend of..."

"A friend's horses," Criollo added hastily, just as Gideon said,

"My father's."

"I see," the old schoolmaster chuckled. "Is this the same friend who put our Dragonhorse in the sanecere wards long ago? The one who cracked his head open with a rock?"

Criollo nodded. "Fortunately, that was not our fate this time around."

Not to be put off, Ah'brianne continued with, "We saw some amazing things. Our first day we saw a small herd of gaknars. Our first evening we found some Evangeline's Carpet, and the stars were really clear because the moons weren't up yet, and the second night we heard protopeds so we brought the horses into the cave with us. And on the way back we learned about plants and bark and leaves..."

"The Eldest was talkative." Criollo said with a firm look from under his brows at the girl.

"It sounds like the three of you had a really good time," said a sweet faced girl with raven black hair and eyes of deep forest green. "Gideon, was this your first trip to the solitudes?"

"It was," he said shyly. "It was beautiful. Ah'brianne and Criollo were very good company."

"Well, next time we all want to come along," said a squarely built boy with sable brown hair and brilliant foxy eyes. He brushed his right hand across his left as he flashed an infectious and slightly mischievous grin. "I'm Plevin, Gideon. Ahimsa, I wish thee peace. My father is your father's friend, Landais, the Master Farrier."

"Of course, forgive me," said Master Breton. "I made the assumption that you had met everyone, when you've been gone more than you've been here."

"Some I do know," Gideon smiled. "Ah'brianne is my neighbor and good friend, and my cousin Criollo, who stuck a puppy under my blankets on my birthing day, and I met Addur and Basra at the banquet my father held for the Lebonathi delegation."

Those two gave him a cool look and went back without acknowledgement to their private discussion which apparently involved Ah'brianne, as they kept casting furtive glances in her direction. Gideon took note, but no offense, as he'd heard about the sorting out his father had given Naram and Halaf, and he was sure some hard feelings remained. He nodded pleasantly despite their snub, and turned back to Master Breton who was indicating the girl who had spoken earlier and saying, "Not everyone is back from harvest yet, but Ah'win is the daughter of Saddle Master Maremmano, Ah'dria the daughter of Keeplord Leedes, who has the vineyards next to Criollo's grandparents in Falconstones. Andalin is the son of Scoter, our Master Orchardist, and Faroe is the son of Master of Drums, Jomud. If he's drumming his fingers on the table he's probably trying to tell you something."

"And lastly we have someone for whom the whole concept of school is very new, so be gentle," said a familiar voice, and they all looked up to see Io in the doorway with Jasreth, who had frozen at the sight of Addur and Basra.

"Ah'riodin Firstwife," Master Breton said with a respectful nod, and she returned it along with one of her dazzling smiles.

"Master Breton, the honor is mine. This is Jasreth, and she would like to join your class, if that is acceptable."

"It is most certainly not acceptable to me," said Addur rising from his chair with his lip curled, pink eyes glinting red with anger. "Having to sit with aliens who shamelessly allow their females to parade their sexuality in the streets, to straddle animals as whores straddle men, to educate themselves as men do, in the ways of men rather than in the ways of women, as God intended, who cheapen themselves by traveling with and sleeping with men unattended, and chatter mindlessly like poingeodes is travail enough. Having to sit in such a space with one of our own kind who knows she is beneath our station and who knows better than to flaunt herself in such a manner, is completely beyond the pale of decency." He glared first at Ah'brianne, then at Jasreth, who cringed and would have turned and run, but as she stepped back, she connected with the third person in the doorway, and his hand stayed her.

"Dragonhorse," said Master Breton, and by then all the students were standing respectfully.

"As you were, please," he said. My kinsman and I were just out for our morning run and I thought I would come by and see how everything is going this fine and frosty day." At his inviting smile every head in the room turned to look at Addur, still lounging in his chair, and at Basra, who had risen with the others. "That well, hm?"

Ardenai leaned forward with one hand on his thigh so that he was close to Jasreth's ear and whispered, "What you do in the next few moments will either alter the course of your planet's history, or it will epitomize that which you hate most. You can either go over and sit next to Criollo, or you can turn around, and I will take my hand off your shoulder and let you go, taking with you the hopes and prayers of every female on your planet. What's it going to be?"

He could feel her trembling like a marchling, but she didn't move. She looked at Basra and Addur, then at the class of young people, then back to Basra and Addur. Criollo pulled out a chair and Ah'win gave the seat a pat. "We would love to have you join us," she said. "We've heard so much about your people and your planet. Sit with us and tell us more, please."

"Thank you," Jasreth managed, though her teeth were chattering. She took a deep breath, dropped her eyes to the floor, and walked away from Ardenai's hand, straight-backed, to the proffered chair.

Ah'brianne looked at Addur, then back to her classmates, most particularly Gideon and Criollo. "I don't chatter like a poingeode, do I? What exactly is a poingeode, anyway?"

In the explosion of laughter Ardenai crooked a finger at the two Lebonathis and stepped aside to allow them to pass him into the hall. "Uh oh," Ah'dria hissed. "The A.A.G. I remember it well."

Gideon gave her a quizzical look.

"Attitude Adjustment Gesture," Ah'brianne and Criollo whispered together, crooking their fingers to demonstrate.

"Prince Basra and Prince Addur are going to be very angry with me," Jasreth whispered. "I shouldn't have let…I shouldn't have come. I didn't know they would be here."

"Of course you should have come," Plevin said aloud. "We've all been anxious to meet you and learn about your people, and they sure weren't going to tell us anything. But first, what would you most like to learn about us that would make you more comfortable? I'm Plevin, by the way…."

With Basra and Addur in the hall, Ardenai stepped away from the conversation coming through the classroom doorway and asked politely, "Why are you here?"

"To observe," Basra said earnestly. "Are we in a place we are not allowed to be?"

"Not at all. You are most welcome in this space, but I do not see that you are observing."

Addur looked up into the Firstlord's face and resisted the urge to claw out those dragon's eyes, to scream publicly about the spectacle of a world leader who stood in a school room in a shirt so soaked with sweat that every muscle, every nuance showed – who invited young girls to intercourse with the slight heaving of his chest – whose so-called son, and his nephew spent nights in the wilderness with a loud-mouthed harlot. And then this – predator – preached to them about how immoral it would be for him to have sexual relations with Eridi. "We are trying to be tolerant," Addur grated. "We are trying to observe as you have commanded us to do."

"It has been my experience," Ardenai said in that same, soothing tone, "that observation is best accomplished when the eyes, the ears and the mind are open, and the mouth is shut. That particular formula seems to be eluding you, Addur."

"We are not your slaves to bend to your way of doing things, though we are treated as such," he retorted. "Fed in a common dining room on peasant slop, walking abroad and finding no respect, but only people jostling us, grinning at us as though we are as common as they, and yet all of you preach to us of your vast and glittering accomplishments and your magnanimous attributes – your history and your technology and your lack of want."

"I am sorry you are uncomfortable," Ardenai said, folding his arms closer to his body. His sweat was drying rapidly, and he was getting cold. Teal was still waiting to finish their run – lounging in an archway at a distance, but within easy earshot. "You must understand that what we eat, is what we all eat, peasant and prince alike. We mean no disrespect by feeding you what we love most. Instead we include you within the larger family. You came to learn about us, which is why we tell you of our history and technology and what we have managed to do in the larger arena of worlds."

Look at Basra.

Ardenai flicked his eyes at Teal, then at the youngster, who was inclining his head toward the doorway of the school room, trying to hear what was being said. The Firstlord nodded slowly. "I think that a good deal of what is bothering you is how women are regarded in our society. I realize that sending you out with a woman to learn of women's roles would be offensive enough to you that you probably wouldn't learn anything, so this afternoon, I will take you. Be ready to leave right after lunch."

He glanced into the classroom and his wife was still there, appearing to be engaged in an animated discussion about climate and obviously prepared to stay if need be. "Until then you may return to school to observe and contribute in a positive manner, or you may return to your chambers."

Basra nodded and would have returned to the discussion, but Addur poked him and jerked his head sharply to one side. They left as a pair, neither of them acknowledging their departure from the Firstlord's presence. Ardenai stuck his head back in the classroom and gave the old teacher a deep, respectful nod. "Thank you for your patience, Master Breton. I apologize for any disruption."

"Such things are to be expected when we explore new ideas," Breton smiled. "Enjoy the rest of your run, Dragonhorse."

Ardenai nodded his way out of the room, jogged over to Teal and the two of them trotted together back down the long corridor to the spot where a tunnel the width of a boulevard opened to the stables of the Great House. There they picked up speed, stretching their legs into a ground eating run but staying to one side so as not to collide with people, people with carts, or people with horses. "You do realize you have a final meeting this afternoon with MalDor before he leaves for Calumet," Teal said.

"I do. But MalDor will listen to you or my wife. Those boys would not."

"Those boys will not listen to any of us anyway, and I think you know that."

"When the mother is wild, more training must go into the colt."

"Ardi, you have done as many things as you can do to influence the Lebonathi. Eridi is firmly ensconced with the Eloi, tightly tucked under the wing of Priestess Ah'nis, and seems not to know that anything or anybody else exists anymore. Jasreth is in a separate apartment with her uncle. Samarra has been moved to chambers within the apartments of the High Priestess, as befits her station – Ah'krill's words, not mine – what's left? The others contribute nothing but enmity. I think you may be worrying too much about doing what's right, and perhaps not enough about doing what's smart."

"I would like – excuse me, Mistress – I would like to try to at least reach Basra. And where there is Basra there is Addur. We'd better slow down before we have a wreck." They dropped back to a jog, and by that time they were in the great stables.

Master Farrier Landais looked up from the horse he was shoeing and shouted, "It's the Rumpus Brothers! Are you two going to be here to practice tonight?"

As one they gave him a wave, hollered that, yes, they would, made a wide turn at a run through the stables and headed back up the avenue toward the Great House, dropping again to a slow jog as they cooled down. "Can I ask you something?" Ardenai asked, giving Teal a quick glance.

"As my sovereign lord, or as my best friend?" A momentary discomfort crossed Ardenai's features and it made Teal chuckle. "Of course you can," he replied, "What do you want to know?"

"It has to do with heat cycles. Still willing to answer?"

"Probably. You're still welcome to ask, at least." They dodged around a cartload of bright blue barrels filled with the syrup used to make sweet grain for the horses, nearly ran into another, and realized it had gotten late enough for commerce to be in full swing. They slowed their pace a little more and began nodding at the greetings they received from merchants, citizens, and other runners. "Well?" Teal said at last.

"I'm thinking." Ardenai said. "So…heat cycles…and by the way, since you and Ah'din choose to go somewhere away from the rest of us, does my sister always beat you up as badly as she did at Mountain hold?"

"Doesn't seem the type, does she?" Teal grinned. "What else did you want to ask me?"

"I was very busy with my own affairs when we were on Calumet. I did get the sense, or so Ah'krill told me, that everybody went into heat because I did. Did you?" He took an extra breath and hastily added, "Because if you did, it wasn't obvious."

"I did. I did at Mountain hold, as well, if that's your next question."

"No, not exactly. Well yes, kind of. The reason I ask is because the Twelfth Dragonhorse said that he'd really pushed the medical science community to breed the heat cycles out of us. Not just the Dragonhorse cycles, but all of them, and you seemed so in control of yourself. Even at Mountain hold you seemed…."

"Unaffected?"

Ardenai bobbed his head in affirmation.

"You are correct. As opposed to my wife, my heat cycles don't elevate me much, they never have. The dragonhorse cycle can be a little intense, but in a good way. Maybe the medical science community is making progress."

Ardenai glanced at him again. "I am sorry that Criollo is now ahead of his classmates in more ways than one."

"Me too," Teal said. "I wish he'd been left out of this for another while. He'll have to learn a lot more self-control if he's going to continue his present relationship with Ah'brianne. They've always been best friends. He could ruin that if he's not careful." He sighed, smiled and slowed to a walk, dropping an arm around his brother-in-law's shoulder. "You did not choose to be who you are, Ardi. You did not choose the time, or the place, or the things which had to happen because you are the Thirteenth Dragonhorse and we are your family. Mountain hold was one of the most amazing and enlightening times of my life. No matter how it seems, I can guarantee you that more was gained than lost, by all of us. I know we will return many times, and that each time we will come back richer than the time before."

"I hope you're right," the Firstlord said, and his eyes were a little sad – they were sad so much these days. "I do have something else I need to talk to you about, but we can do that over dinner, since I'd like to include our wives as well. Is Ah'din back in the city?"

"Um hm. Still getting the last wrinkles out of her magic formula for indifference, though you – we – may not need it if Eridi remains sequestered. That is such a strange thing to me. It somehow feels almost suspicious."

"Not to me," Ardenai said, gesturing Teal ahead of him into the lift. "She is with women, as she has always been, only these women are superbly educated and open minded. She is safe, she is warm, she is well fed and comfortably dressed. Nobody is shaking her, or teaching her how to seduce a man. No one is introducing drugs into her system. For the first time in what could be her whole life, she is just a child, in a safe place, able to ask any question she wishes and study anything she chooses to her heart's content. The awe of that may never wear off."

"I hope you're right," Teal sighed, "It would be one less thing to worry about."

After a quick communal scrubbing and a hasty second breakfast Teal went one way to work with a new crop of young horses and their prospective riders while Ardenai went to his study to reschedule his meeting with Mal-Dor, confirm a meeting with the committee that reconsidered ambassadorial assignments, and look over his notes from his readings at Mountain hold and his chats with Harrier regarding the Wind Warriors. After an equally hasty lunch he gathered up Basra and Addur for an afternoon of activities geared to help them better understand and appreciate the role of women in Equi society.

"But you were right. You were absolutely right," he groused at dinner, and held out his glass for a refill of Teal's latest cleomitite medal vintage. "Addur has no interest in learning anything beyond his own pre-formed opinions, and Basra is so wrapped around Addur's fingers, or so terrified of him, that I don't think he learned anything either. We met teachers, doctors, writers, historians, engineers, chemists, computator technicians. I showed them a dozen things women have invented that have made this planet what it is today – took them for a chat with Ah'krill, who is the most powerful woman on the planet, and – nothing. Zilch. Scratch. Naught. Not a particle, not a blessed thing. The understanding we left with is exactly the understanding we came back with."

"Did you leave knowing what you wanted to accomplish?" Io asked, passing a steaming bowl of summer squash. "Sometimes what we learn in the course of a day isn't exactly quantifiable, Ardenai Teacher."

"Quantifiable? This wasn't even recognizable."

"For you as a teacher," Ah'din said, coming to the table with some of her homemade flatwraps. "But a teacher is also a learner, or so my big brother always says. If you didn't teach them anything, what did you learn from them?" She sat down beside her husband and passed the flatwraps across the table to Ardenai. "I made that jam yesterday before I came to the city. I hope you like it."

"I love anything you make," her brother smiled, taking a flatwrap and tearing it in half. "What did I learn from them? Good question. Unfortunately, I learned that I trust them less and less with every passing day, and that Teal may be right in suggesting that we send most of the delegation home."

"Most, but not all?" Io asked, taking a flatwrap and reaching for the jam pot. "I think that's a great idea. We can keep Girsu as an ambassador, since that should logically be our choice, which means Jasreth would stay. She absolutely loved school today, Ardi. Thank you so much for intervening when you did. And of course we have to keep Samarra, because she's more or less in charge of Eridi, and you're supposed to be marrying Eridi, along with a couple of other women, I suppose." her tone had changed subtly and involuntarily, and Ardenai put an arm around her shoulder and pulled her close to kiss her temple and her left ear.

"And this is what I wanted to talk to everybody about," he said, kissing her again and keeping one of her hands in both of his. "When I was at Mountain hold, and I realized, truly, fully realized, what you had gone through with me on Calumet, during that initial Imperial Dragonhorse cycle, I made up my mind that I was going to fight tooth and claw to change the rules about multiple wives – Eridi or no Eridi. I will never marry her, and all of you have known that. I will never touch her in a sexual manner if she lives a hundred years. I will try to keep her safe until she can make some wise choices of her own, but only in the sense of intellectual property will she ever be a fleshgift. The very sound of that gives me the shivers."

Io had turned in her chair to look at her husband, and when she saw the set of his jaw her heart swelled almost to bursting. He did love her and want only her. What she had been saying to herself and telling others these seasons past, was true. "I will agree wholeheartedly with you about Eridi," she managed, trying not to throw her arms around him and make love to him in the middle of the table, "but there are so many fights to be fought and wars to be won, are you sure you want to go to war over the ancient rule of three wives? I have learned from the Eloi that there's a good reason for it. The first wife, is the one you bring to your office, who may or may not be high Equi. A second wife for the forming of alliances, and a third wife who is high Equi, with whom you pass on your dragonhorse genes." She saw his ears pin back a little and just shook her head. "Beloved, that law came in with the first named Dragonhorse, ten thousand years ago. There must be a way we can figure this out to everybody's mutual satisfaction."

Teal's surprise at her words was obvious, though he caught himself quickly. "I have to agree with Io," he said, casting a weather eye in her direction. "What about Ah'nora? She's a lovely woman. She would be a blessing to Ah'rane, and Ah'din and to the keep nave itself. That's a woman who would leave you and Io alone to run the government while she produces a strong son and daughter to give Krush his crop of keeplords."

"And whom, exactly, are you channeling, Lark, Wren, Harrier or Kestrel?" Ardenai scowled, draining his wine glass.

"No more wine for you," Teal said firmly. "We're playing polo tonight and I don't want to be scraping your ass up off the field. And I'm not channeling anyone. I know Ah'nora. I think she's amazing and I think you'd be lucky to have her. Any man would be lucky to have her."

"Really?" Ah'din asked quietly, and Teal spun around in his chair and seized her, making her squeal and laugh as she tried to push him away.

"Any man but me," he laughed, kissing her throat where it touched her collarbone, "because I have you."

"And Ardi has Io. He doesn't need another woman any man would be lucky to have. No, I think – Teal, stop. I think Ardi should marry Ah'nis. It would make Ah'krill giddy with joy, so she'd leave him alone, and Ah'nis hates his guts, so she'd leave him alone. It's perfect."

"Precious Equus," Ardenai murmured, staring at his sister. "Have you always been evil, or is it just now coming out in you? Was it that whole thing at Mountain hold? Not that I could have done anything about it, because I was indisposed in the extreme when they sent for all of you. But I really am sorry. All of you. I am sorry."

"Now I know you've had too much wine," Teal growled. "We're not only going to lose tonight, you're going to get dumped at least once and maybe hurt yourself, and then we'll lose during High Harvest when it counts and be behind at the Storm Games, and Tarpan and his team are going to have bragging rights for the whole kraaling year."

"I think you've both had too much wine," Io said. "I think talking about the Lebonathis over dinner makes all of us want to drink too much wine. By the way, just so you know, I do vote for three wives. Remind me from time to time that I said that, Teal. And I do vote for Ah'nora. I trust Ah'nora, and I know she loves my husband. Ah'nis, not so much. The boys are home. I hear the front door. Time to change the subject."

"Unfortunately, we cannot altogether do that," Ardenai smiled. "Gentlemen, how was your time with Seglawi? Crossbow practice, I assume?"

"Slingshot," Criollo said, swinging his leg over a chair and reaching for a platter of teosinte pones all in one motion. "For me at least." He caught his mother's look and gave her a ghost of a smile. "I apologize for my manners," he murmured, already forking food onto his plate.

"I, on the other hand, am trying to learn that thing that Teal did to me when I jumped him on Calumet that first night," Gideon said, "that move with the fingers and wrists to the temples? Much trickier than you made it look, Uncle Mine."

"It takes practice," Teal smiled. "Mostly you have to be careful not to kill a person you're only trying to subdue. Luckily your father had said you were to be kept alive, because I could cheerfully have done you in that night." He passed the flatwraps to Gideon, who managed a laugh, however tenuous. Teal was no one to trifle with, no matter how merry he might appear on the surface. "Are either of you planning on coming to the polo match tonight?"

"I have asked Jasreth if she would like to go, and she said yes," Criollo answered. "I hope that's acceptable."

"Why wouldn't it be?" his father asked, and was immediately sorry. Things had happened too quickly. "Criollo, there is no need to change your life just yet. You and I will talk before you have need of the information, I promise."

"Since you have already asked Jasreth, could I impose upon you to include her uncle?" Ardenai asked, pushing back from the table with his coffee cup. "I was going to ask you to do this anyway, and since you're already halfway there..."

"You want me to have a chaperone, Dragonhorse?"

"I do not," Ardenai said. He didn't appreciate the challenging tone, and there was an edge to his voice. "Know this, you have my absolute trust in these matters, and until you prove to me that you cannot be trusted, you will continue to have my trust. I spent all afternoon with Addur and Basra, and got nowhere. Maybe bringing the Lebonathi to a polo match – they like violent games – maybe that will loosen them up a bit." He paused a moment and turned his gaze on Gideon, who was busy ladling a thick, spicy stew onto his plate.

The boy looked up. "Oh, and this is where I come in, isn't it? You're both playing, and the Lebonathi hate your wife over that whole thing that ended up getting Eridi moved, so I get to escort the men?"

"Very good," Ardenai said smoothly. "Will you do it?"

"Do I have a choice?" The second it was out of his mouth he realized his father was tired and a little irked already, and in the next second he was saying, "Of course I will. I did ask Ah'brianne if she wanted to come, and I think Plevin and Ah'win are coming..." again he looked at Ardenai's face, "so she can sit with them."

"Thank you," Ardenai responded, and made himself smile. "I will make this up to you."

▲ ▲ ▲ ▲ ▲ ▲ ▲

Despite being an immense space, it was not unlimited, and the foul-weather polo played indoors in the Great Stables was by necessity a tighter game on a somewhat smaller field, which was created by joining the parade grounds with the training rings and raking the sand smooth. The smaller playing area combined with the shorter turn at each end made it a rougher, dirtier game. But the Equi loved their polo, and though it was just a practice match the stands at the polo grounds were far from empty.

Girsu had been more than happy to accompany Jasreth, and Criollo thought the man looked healthier than he had at first. He had more color in his face, and he seemed more casual in dress, less guarded in his demeanor. He graciously refused the seats reserved for him and the rest of the Lebonathi delegation and chose to sit with Rounce and Ah'lauren, who had hailed him from down the row of bench seats, and greeted him with hugs and animated conversation as they introduced him to those around them. That left Criollo free to sit with Jasreth, and they went with Girsu's cheerful permission to join Ah'win and Plevin.

Gideon was having one of those evenings when being the son of the Thirteenth Dragonhorse was not as desirable as it might sound to outside ears. Brak had been more than willing to come, Halaf and Naram grudgingly so. Addur had told him point blank that he and Basra had been subjected to enough by Gideon's imperious and high-handed sire, and that being summoned yet again to one of his performances was more than they could stomach. At that point Halaf had stepped in and said that it was polite to go when invited, and that their behavior was a blot on the Lebonathi's otherwise shining example of acceptance of a more primitive culture, and so they had come, smoldering along at the back of the pack making rude comments and snickering about the smell of hay and horse shit. When Ah'brianne had joined Gideon from the stands and volunteered to help explain the rules of the game, the silence had become deafening.

Showing them to their reserved seats with as much courtesy as he could muster, Gideon turned to the girl and gave her an apologetic smile.

Oh, they don't want me here, she said, though her lips did not move, and Gideon was relieved beyond belief that they did not have to have an open conversation.

I'm sorry, Ah'brianne. This is something the Dragonhorse asked me to do, and believe me, I wish I didn't have to. I could use your expertise, and I'd enjoy your company, but this evening it's not my choice.

Your first responsibility is to your father, but I may still be able to help you out, she said, and with a polite nod to Halaf and Naram she went to join the other young people. A few minutes later seats were traded and Gideon found himself with Plevin beside him, then Criollo, and the girls at the far end. Faroe settled in just above him and greeted Addur and Basra with a friendly nod and a few words which were flippantly returned, then disregarded.

Further conversation was truncated by the appearance of two strings of polo ponies each with eye and head guards in place, and heavily shielded legs. "They'll play four chukkas ten minutes long tonight," Plevin said to no one in particular but in a slightly louder than conversational tone. "That's because it's just practice. At the High Harvest Games they'll play six chukkas nine minutes long."

"Be prepared for flying dust," Faroe remarked. "Our outdoor polo fields are grass, but in here we don't have that luxury. We tried laying out turf, but it bunched up when the horses slid so that idea was abandoned long ago."

"There are four players on each team," Gideon said to Halaf, and Naram looked over with more interest than he'd shown so far. "Each player will change horses frequently during every chukka. This will be a night when they'll try out horses that maybe don't have a lot of experience. Here they come!"

There was a roar from the assemblage as eight riders appeared, mallets in their right hands, helmets under their right arms. Four men rode to the left, four to the right, and just for a chilling moment Gideon flashed back to that scene on the parade grounds of Calumet – Equi to one side, Telenir to the other. He caught his breath, and Plevin gave him a questioning look. Gideon shook his head. "Old nightmare," he said.

Bashkir's voice quieted the crowd somewhat. "On the Black team in order of the positions they will play this evening we have Landais, Ardenai, Teal and Maremmano. On the Red team this evening in order of the positions they will play we have Jomud, Seglawi, Tarpan and Daleth."

"Young studs against the seasoned," Teal said in an aside to Landais, and the farrier laughed.

"They may have youth, but we have craft," he said, then yelled, "Come on, Tarpan, show us what you've got!"

"Gladly!" he yelled back.

"Helmets!" Bashkir shouted over the crowd. "Mallets up, sides taken!" When the horsemen were in position he threw out a willow bark ball and shouted, "PULU!"

There was a charge and a cloud of dust and the game was under way. Within the first minute of play Teal's young horse lost her head and ran backwards into Seglawi's horse, who stumbled and went down on her knees. Both those riders opted for steadier mounts and the game was once again underway when there was another collision, and fouls were called, one on Tarpan, one on Ardenai, who retaliated with a ride-off and got the black team the first goal of the game. There was a breather and some drills in which all eight participated without competing, and when the second chukka started, that's when the game really got rolling and Gideon lost track of who was where.

He later admitted that he'd gotten too involved in the action, and despite his father's assurances to the contrary he blamed himself for much of the turmoil which ensued in the coming weeks and seasons because of what he considered his initial inattention. His classmates were cheering on their fathers, he was cheering his on as well, and he did not notice when Ah'win, Ah'brianne and Jasreth went to refresh themselves, nor did he notice when Addur and Basra slid quietly from their seats and followed.

He became aware that something was terribly wrong when Teal, who had gone pounding down the field after the ball, flung his mallet aside, leaned out of his saddle, scooped up the ball and, with a shout lost in the noise of the crowd, overhanded it hard in the direction of the archway framing the opening to the parade ground. Bashkir yelled, "Foul!" and in the same second Gideon and most of the crowd spun around to follow the trajectory of the ball, heard it hit the pavers short of the corner with a resounding crack, and saw Ah'win shielding Jasreth and Ah'brianne punching Basra hard enough in the mouth to knock him halfway down. He rocked back onto his feet and was going for her with his doubled up fist when the closest onlooker grabbed his arm. A few seconds later Ardenai's polo pony sat on his haunches, slid to a stop, and Ardenai vaulted off into the fray. By then, of course, Gideon had realized he was a failure as a chaperone, and he and Criollo were running to observe what their inattention had caused.

The one thing Gideon did notice as he careened into the middle of things, was that Addur was smiling – a nasty, secret little smile as he stood to one side, watching what transpired between the Dragonhorse and his brother. Gideon stopped next to Ah'brianne who was rubbing her knuckles and snarling, "I swear, if you EVER lay hands on another female where I can get to you, it will be your last act."

"It's her fault!" Basra retorted, blotting angrily at the blood on his lip and literally spitting at Jasreth. "The whore! And you're a whore just like her! All your women are whores!"

"Stop! Now!" Ardenai said sharply, taking off his helmet and wiping his forehead with the back of his wrist, leaving a muddy smear where dust met sweat. "Tell me what happened."

Ah'brianne and Basra both started talking at the same time, and Ardenai held up a hand to hush them. "Ah'win, if you please."

"Yes, Ardenai Firstlord," she said, though she still had a protective arm around Jasreth, who was shaking with fear for the second time that day. "The three of us girls went to use the lavage and get some juice, and when we came out, there was Basra, and he said that if Jasreth was going to behave like a…that word he just said …then he was going to use her like one. We tried just to walk away, but he cut us off, and when we told him to leave us alone he made a grab for Jasreth, and that's when Master Teal saw what was happening and threw that ball so everybody would look and come help us."

"Luckily someone was looking out for you," Ardenai said quietly, and the glance he gave Criollo and Gideon was all the punishment they needed.

By now Maremmano had arrived, sliding off his pony to stand beside Ah'win, and Girsu was coming up beside Jasreth on the other side. Teal was there looking like Diabolus on horseback, and Naram and Halaf came puffing up full of bluster demanding to know what was going on to upset the two princes. Brak held back and stood next to Addur, who was still smiling quietly to himself. Teal swung off his horse, and only Ardenai's firm hand on his chest kept him from getting to the younger prince.

"I should let him have you," Ardenai said quietly. "I really should."

"It is the fault of the woman and her uncle!" Halaf exclaimed. "She has done nothing but flaunt herself since the second she left the delegation's quarters with Eridi and that priestess, and now she and her uncle have their own apartments, where they can plot against our government and our sacred way of life at their leisure? I think not. Both of you are under arrest – you, Girsu, and you, Jasreth, for plotting against the will of the Gods and the Lebonathi government."

The Firstlord stared at him for a few moments, looking like he might burst out laughing. "You are joking, aren't you?" he asked, still obviously amused. "You have no authority here."

Naram flung an overly dramatic arm at Girsu and Jasreth. "Those two..."

"...are not what this is about, Naram. This is about Halaf's nephews," Ardenai said. "If Basra attempted to inflict rape on Jasreth, the penalty is death."

"What?" Halaf gasped. "It was a harmless scuffle."

"It was not harmless, and you haven't been paying attention," Ardenai said, still calm, though his jaw muscles rippled with anger. "Our children are safe here. They do not need to be escorted. They do not need to be afraid to be alone. They do not need to be afraid anywhere, anytime, ever. Your nephew has chosen to break one of the two rules which will get him killed on this planet. Now, Basra is a child himself, and I have every reason to think somebody put him up to this so I'm not going to kill him on the spot, though I could and I'm tempted. Your nephews are now your sole responsibility, Halaf. I am putting a guard on your door, and if Basra or Addur step foot outside between now and the time you leave, which will be soon, they will die. Do I make myself clear?"

Halaf nodded and dropped his eyes, fists going limp at his sides. "I understand," he hissed.

"You will be sorry for this, Dragonhorse," Naram grated. "What a fine king you are, covered in dirt like an animal, sheltering a criminal who should already be dead, threatening us, shaming us in front of this mob of shit eaters. You will be sorry."

"I'm already sorry," Ardenai sighed. "For the safety of Girsu and Jasreth, they will make their home amongst us from now on. Jasreth is under the same protection as Eridi. Girsu can continue to serve the Lebonathis by teaching us about your people and your world. We offered you our friendship and you spurned it. We would have helped your world and may yet, but not under these circumstances. All of you, return to your apartments and stay there until we can arrange for your transport back to your planet. Master Bashkir, please see that they do so. I'd send Teal but he still wants to kill somebody. Tarpan, please post guards."

Two members of the Horse Guard immediately stepped up, and the Lebonathis, except for Girsu and Jasreth, were herded up the avenue leading to the Great House. Teal held out his arms to Ah'brianne, and she came to him with a whuffle of pent up frustration and buried her face against his chest, pounding her fists gently against his shoulders and mumbling something under her breath that made him chuckle despite himself.

Ardenai turned to the silent crowd, sensing their anger and frustration. They had heard most of the conversation, Equi ears and excellent acoustics being what they were, and the Firstlord thought a moment or two about what to say to them. He mounted his horse to be better seen and just sat there for a bit. "Well, we tried," he said at last. "And now we have horses to be groomed and put away, and baths to take, and business to attend in the morning. If Teal will replace the ball he cost us tonight, we will resume this contest two nights from now. Go home, hug your spouses and your children and realize how lucky we all are to be here, and keep the women and children of the Lebonathi Federation in your prayers tonight."

There was a roar of approval from the assembled Equi, and they began leaving, discussing the evening's events and calling their goodnights to one another. Among others Rounce and Ah'lauren stopped to encourage Girsu, and give Jasreth a warm hug before going on their way, and Gideon approached his father with penitent tears standing in his bright gold eyes.

"I am so sorry," he said, looking first at Ardenai, then at Teal and Ah'brianne. "I am so sorry."

"Good," Ardenai said, and put his arms around Gideon, pulling him close and kissing the top of his head. "You should be sorry, and so should I. We sat at breakfast that first morning and every single person at the table told me that these people were truly alien and truly dangerous, and I did not listen like I should have. And tonight I assumed that simply by having the eyes of two boys on a large alien delegation, things would not get out of hand. In that I was at fault, not you. Fortunately my kinsman was more alert than I."

"The crowd was noisy and you were having trouble with Pavil, who, by the way, is a lost cause as a polo pony," Teal said. "I just happened to ride clear of the dust and saw what was happening. Ah'brianne, are you hurt?

Let me see your knuckles." She stepped back and dutifully held out her hands for him to inspect. "Nothing broken. Good for you." He took both her hands in his and held them against his chest for a long minute with his head down, then took a deep breath and looked into her face. "I want you to get some things from your room in the Pages' Quarters and come stay with us for a bit – until this blows over or blows up."

She shook her head and looked up at him laughing. "I think I proved I could handle myself," she said. "I'm not afraid."

"Well I am," Teal interjected. "Just to make sure, I will go with you to your quarters and get your things."

"I could go with her," Criollo ventured, and for the first time Teal's eyes fell on him. The look was not pleasant.

"I think not." he said.

Let him go with her.

Is that an order, Liege Lord?

No. It is a boon I beg of someone stronger far than I, whom I love like a brother. You have trusted me when I did not deserve it. Surely you can do the same for your son.

"At least not alone," Teal added. "If Gideon will accompany, then I will allow it. Not because I do not trust you, but because I do not trust them."

Gideon immediately stepped up beside his cousin, and beside them stepped Faroe and Plevin. "We will all go," Plevin said, and Faroe folded his lanky arms in agreement.

Ardenai looked at Gideon, who was looking at Faroe and Plevin with a mingling of wonder and puzzlement. "This is what it means to have friends your own age," the Firstlord said, and Gideon smiled slowly and nodded.

When the children had gone and Landais and Maremmano had insisted on putting all the horses away, Ardenai turned to Girsu, who was still standing with an arm around Jasreth, looking for all the world like a man in a dream. "This has been a hard night for you," Ardenai said quietly, "Are you going to survive?"

"It's rather amusing actually," Girsu said with a self-deprecating smile. "I had vowed that Jasreth and I would never set foot on Lebonathi soil again, and now that it has happened I am feeling very lost and afraid."

"I don't blame you," Teal said. "I'm a little afraid for you myself. For both of you. I know we have a guard on the delegates' door, but I'm going to put someone on your door, as well."

"A wise precaution," Ardenai said. "By all means feel free to be out and about, but avail yourself of company when you do so. Jasreth, are you all right?"

"This is all my fault," she said quietly.

"No. You are a catalyst for change," Ardenai smiled. "Take pride in it. Someone will come in the morning to escort you to school. When the delegation has gone, you will be truly free."

Tired as he was, dirty as he was, Ardenai went first to his study and requested that a Lebonathi ship be summoned to take the delegation home, then sought a bath, his bed, and the arms of his wife.

The first person Ardenai searched out the next morning was his sister, who was in the sanecere, dabbling with bits of plants and various compounds in jars and beakers. She looked up and smiled at him and he came to kiss the top of her head and look over her shoulder as she worked. "How goes the Elixir of Indifference?" he asked. "I need to go talk to Eridi today and I may need some."

"I think it's about finished," she said. "It has the unfortunate side effect of turning your teeth green and making hair sprout out your nose, but it will definitely counteract whatever they're dosing that poor girl with."

"Luckily that's all that matters," her brother laughed. He slid one hip onto a tall stool by the window and looked at Ah'din. "Do you think they're still dosing her?"

"I don't know. I have no logical reason to access the girl to find that out. I do know her body naturally produces some of the pherine, but they're giving her something, or gave her something, to concentrate and enhance it."

"And by 'they' you mean Samarra?"

"Again, I assume so. I don't know who else would have a reason to do so, do you?"

"I'm not sure," Ardenai said, rubbing thoughtfully at his chin. Krush did that, and it made Ah'din smile. In many ways Ardenai and Krush were very much alike. She found that comforting, and came to stand beside her brother, folding her hands across his shoulder as he spoke. "I do think they have, by necessity, changed their tack. Whatever they're up to, I'm betting it's not good," he said.

"Well, no matter how valuable they say Eridi is, you can bet she isn't. As a woman in their society she has no value."

"Except as a pawn."

"Or a tool," Ah'din amended, "a delivery system for something. But what? If you had gotten inside her, which is obviously what they had in mind, what would you have come away with?"

"A settled child," Ardenai said, pursing his lips. He could almost feel that, at last, they were getting somewhere with this. In the behavior of the Princes, in the receding of the princess, were more answers than questions.

"A settled child who was settled with your child, don't forget that. Let's think about what they said that night before your blood started pounding so loudly in your ears that you couldn't hear anymore. Let's start at the beginning."

Ardenai set his mind to thinking back. "Here is a flesh gift. A peace offering, trained in the sexual pleasures for which the Lebonathi are famous, whatever that means."

Ah'din nodded. "Coupled with the potions, you came frighteningly close to finding out. What else?"

"I know she had it in her head that she was going to replace Io in my affections. That she was going to bear my child – to be settled before the delegation ever left." Ardenai looked searchingly into his sister's face. "Does that mean that if I'd set my head against her that first night they'd have left immediately?"

"Maybe. Probably."

"So why did they stay?"

"Because Eridi is not settled?"

Ardenai just shook his head and grunted with frustration. "Why would the pregnancy have made the difference? What did they not get, that they think they might still get?"

"Are you thinking Eridi might know? Is that why you're after my magic elixir?"

"And your company, if I may. I'd like you to observe the girl."

"Of course," Ah'din smiled, turning back to her work. "Do you want to arrange for a meeting?"

"No," Ardenai responded thoughtfully. "I think we'll just trot over. Less time to drug her up with something, though I'll bet Ah'nis is keeping a very close eye on what's going into that little girl."

"A good idea," Ah'din said. She was busy for a minute, and then walked over to him with a double ended swab, something green coloring each end. "Hold still, Ardi. I'm just going to run this around inside each of your nostrils…like this…and like this. Now sniff it up into your nose. Good." She handed him a tiny cup with the same green stuff in it, though it seemed more diluted. "Go over to the sink, swish this around in your mouth, gargle it down your throat and spit it out. Don't swallow it, and don't rinse your mouth out afterward."

He did as he was told. "Eww," he complained, making a slight face and tasting at his mouth. "Not one of your husband's better vintages, I must say. This must be your magic elixir."

"Let us hope so for your sake," she said, and took off her apron. "We should go. I don't know how long the effects of this will last."

Like the rest of the Great House, the floor belonging to the Eloi was a work of art, and like the rest of the Great House, it was massive. Five hundred thousand square feet of apartments, chapels, dining rooms and conference rooms – spaces for music, and meditation, education and governance. Within that cloistered setting dwelt the most ancient heartbeat of the Equi people, and Ardenai always entered their presence with reverence. There was such a sense of peace here, and purpose, untrammeled by the concerns of the everyday world. Though the priestesses went out to teach, to govern, to explore and to raise families, to contribute in every imaginable way to the richness of Equus, it was to this place that they, and any woman who chose to do so, retreated to rejuvenate mind and spirit.

Ardenai and Ah'din nodded respectfully at the huge doors, and after a few moments they opened into the entresol, which was slightly smoky from incense. Today, Ardenai noticed, it had no fragrance. "My sister and I would speak with Priestess Ah'nis and Princess Eridi," he said, and one priestess went one way to fetch those in question while another showed them into a quiet antechamber nearby. Within a few minutes Ah'nis arrived, dressed in white and silver-green, her hair swept up on top of her head. She gave the Firstlord a smile that was slightly less cool than in the past and gestured back with a deep nod to welcome Eridi.

The change in the child was nothing short of dramatic. She, too, was in pale green, no white apparent, as she was not a priestess, but her hair was swept up onto the top of her head, and her face was serene and smiling. She nodded to the Firstlord, making eye contact as she gestured for him to re-seat himself. "Dragonhorse, Ah'din physician," she said, and her voice was confident and unafraid. "How may I serve you?"

"I haven't checked in on you for a while. I wanted to see if you are happy."

"I am happier than I have ever been in my life, thanks to you and Priestess Ah'nis," she responded. "Why are you here really?"

It tickled Ardenai, and he laughed his gentle, contagious laugh. Ah'nis in, Ah'nis out. "I really did want to see if you are happy, Princess. I also wanted to see if you are well, and I can see that you are. Are you in contact with any of your delegation?"

The girl shook her head. "No."

"Your choice?"

She gave a slight shrug. "I am Equi now, and my life here is full as I never imagined it could be. I know that I have purpose beyond bondage. I know that I have a right to an education and to speak my mind. For those things, Firstlord, I am thine forever."

"You honor me," he said quietly. "I am relieved that you realize to whom you belong – and that is to you."

If her eyes and her breath are any indicator, she is not being drugged in any way, Ah'din observed.

You can smell her breath? I can't smell anything.

Exactly.

So," he said, realizing Eridi was quite herself, and resisting the urge to laugh at his sister, "None of them have come to see you? Not Jasreth? Samarra hasn't brought any tea or treats from your homeland?"

"Jasreth is in another world altogether now," Eridi said. "And if that witch Samarra tries to drug me again she will go out of here in a shroud, make no mistake. She is as evil as most of the rest of that delegation."

The Firstlord's startlement registered on his face, and in that moment he caught the gleam in Ah'nis's eye. No wonder this child felt safe. He gave the priestess a slow smile and a nod. "Though I knew you to be a formidable foe, I could never have imagined you could be so indomitable a friend. Thank you." *Anytime you want that little priestess I promised you, I am at your service, you know that.*

For those words he received a slight turn of the head that was almost, not quite, a nod of acceptance. *Thank you, Dragonhorse, you have already given me my little priestess. For now, I am happy with things as they are.*

Ardenai nodded and picked up the conversation. "I am having trouble with your half-brothers, Eridi, and things just seem to be escalating. Instead of learning more about us, they seem to be growing more resistant. Can you shed any light on that?"

Eridi shook her head, though she looked thoughtful. "I cannot. I hardly know them, and what I do know, especially of Addur, I don't like. If you are asking me what the larger motives within the upper echelons of the delegation might be, I have no idea. I was kept absolutely isolated – pure, was their word for it. Looking back on it, I'm sure they knew the Equi are telepaths, and they were trying to keep me from gaining any information that you might retrieve from my thoughts. Do remember this as best you are able to even comprehend it, Dragonhorse. Very few males on Lebonath Jas either confide in or value females beyond their reproductive capabilities. As a matter of fact, I didn't know a single one who did."

"One more question, Princess, and I will let you return to your day. What did your father tell you your job was – your mission – your fate? Whatever they chose to call it."

She thought about that for a long time, cocking her head first one way, then the other in recall, her large, pink eyes looking deep into her memory. "I was a peace offering. I was to bear you children who would cement relations between our two worlds." She sighed. "My father was really looking forward to those grandchildren, and I suppose I would have liked showing them to him, and of course to my mother. There really isn't much a woman can do other than that to contribute on Lebonath Jas."

"I have no doubt in my mind that you will contribute much to your homeworld," Ardenai said, "and it won't involve handing over," he chose the next word carefully, "your children to be dandled on their grandsire's knee."

She smiled at him. "I am happy here and content to stay, as is Jasreth. You know, she was probably privy to more conversation than I was, just because she got to move around more freely. You might ask her what she knows."

"I will do that," Ardenai said, rising to take his leave. "Is there anything you need from me? You know if there is, you have only to ask."

"I know that," she said. "If you will excuse us, Firstlord, I have a horseback riding lesson to attend and I need to change. Please tell your wife that I thank her with all my heart for Kantara. She's beautiful."

When they were back out in the hall Ardenai turned to Ah'din and just shook his head in wonder. "Now that," he murmured, "is a turnaround."

"Yes," Ah'din nodded. "I thought I could see it that first night after you took her away from them, and now I'm sure of it. Did the magic elixir do its job?"

"Did I need it?"

"If you have to ask, it worked," she grinned. "Hopefully it will wear off after a bit, because until it does you will not smell anything and you will not taste anything. We will check you out at lunch." She glanced up at him and then away. "And then, I'm going home. I'm sorry, Ardi, I'm just not an apartment dweller. Teal and I are used to being apart, and he's not nearly as far from me as he usually is. Ah'rane and Krush are all alone in that big house. I'm a country girl. I miss my loom and my gardens and my inherited ducks."

"By all means," he said, pulling her close as they walked, "go... home."

"You wanted to say something else," she smiled, "what was it?"

He took a deep breath and blew it out through his lips like a horse. It was his usual action before broaching a difficult subject, so Ah'din prepared herself. "It's about...no, wait, let me start over." They walked a bit in silence. "If, just as a for instance, you lived here, and your family had lived here for a very long time, and you had a beloved husband and son buried here – say Teal and Criollo, horrible though that thought is to both of us – and someone you thought you might be able to love, who was powerful and busy and who you knew you wouldn't see all that much, asked you to be his second wife and move far away from everything you knew and loved, would you do it?"

"No," she said emphatically, "I would not. But since I wasn't going to see much of you – this person – anyway, I would offer to marry him and stay where I was, thereby fulfilling his obligation to have multiple wives without leaving my home. I would ask that when he was here with me, he be exactly that, not here with another wife, or with other business, but here with me, and at the times when I was giving birth, I would expect him to be here with me. I might also volunteer to spend some time with him on his world each year – a season or so if my schedule permitted it, but that's a maybe. That's what I would do."

"Oh," Ardenai said, and was thoroughly preoccupied all the way back to the sanecere, which made Ah'din want to laugh her head off, but she refrained. He was a male of the species and couldn't really be expected to switch perspectives that quickly.

"I'll see you at lunch," she said, giving him a gentle kiss, and he nodded and smiled and turned away, still deep in thought.

His next stop was the school room, though he hated to interrupt. Jasreth had been terrorized the night before and he wanted to make sure she had come, and would continue to do so. At least today he was in the high black boots, black britches and dark grey-green winter tunic of the horse guard, not dripping sweat and spreading dissention. He consoled himself with that and stepped quietly to the doorway where Master Breton's final form class was meeting.

"Dragonhorse," Master Breton smiled, and another man of advancing middle-age smiled at him as well. He was silver haired, but straight of stature, and his face, while still youthful, had seen much of the outdoors. "This is Master Darley."

"Ahimsa, I wish thee peace," Ardenai said with a respectful nod and the usual gesture.

"Ahimsa, I wish thee peace, Dragonhorse," came the reply, and Ardenai knew at once who it was. The face had changed, but the voice had not. "It has come to our attention that some extra tutoring is needed to help Jasreth and Gideon catch up without having to leave the class in which they belong. I have been assigned to do that. I will also be helping Master Breton teach from time to time."

"Thank you," Ardenai smiled. "I assume you are indefatigable, as you will need to be."

"Completely," Darley smiled.

"Darley, as in Darley Arabian?"

"Again, you are correct," the man smiled, and Ardenai caught the barest edge in his voice. Best not tread further onto thin ice. "But you have come on business, and we are distracting you."

"Quite the opposite," Ardenai replied, glancing toward Gideon to see if any recognition glimmered in his golden eyes. If he knew who this was, he was hiding it. So were Criollo and Ah'brianne. Good. "There was some defugalty last night, and I was just checking to see if the principals had got back on track this morning. I see that they are all in their places and ready to learn, so I shall take my leave. Master Darley, welcome to the Great House. I look forward to visiting with you from time to time." He turned and gave his old master his usual, respectful nod. "Master Breton, with your permission, I shall take my leave."

"You may go," he said with a wry smile, and Ardenai nodded himself into the hall. "I truly don't think he sees the irony of that," Master Breton said, and his eyes twinkled fondly.

"An amazing young man indeed," said Master Darley, and turned back to the class and the introductions.

Looks like they're going to keep an eye on the lot of us, Ardenai said to himself, and turned in the direction of Girsu's apartments. He was not at home and the Firstlord put out a quick feeler. *Girsu?*

In the main library, came Bashkir's reply.

At least it was in the direction Ardenai wanted to go for lunch. He'd had no second breakfast and he was hungry. He went down a flight of stairs and turned left toward one of the most public corners of the building, the Library of the Great House. Ardenai had never seen its like until he'd seen his library at Mountain hold. This one was a close second. He walked in and tuned his nose – realized his nose would do him no good this particular day, and began looking for blond heads instead. It was Catrio whom he spotted first, and Catrio pointed with his chin toward a dark, quiet corner behind a section of writings on re-establishing fertility in desert soils. There Ardenai found Girsu. "May I join you for a few moments?" he asked.

Girsu looked up and smiled. Seeing that handsome face, hearing that gentle voice always made him smile – and ache a little inside for what he knew he couldn't have. "Of course," he said, and moved an old book out of the chair next to his.

Ardenai knew full well the effect he had on Girsu – where Girsu's passions lay – and had been tempted a time or two to offer him a trainer so that he would know how to approach fellow homophiles. He'd always thought better of it, and this morning was no exception. He did notice that the always intuitive Tarpan had put Catrio in charge of accompanying Girsu. That had possibilities. His eyes met Catrio's for a moment and he wondered if he could ask such a favor. Girsu, for all his open kindness, was an alien with who-knew-what under those trousers.

I'd like to find out, came Catrio's amused response to the unasked question.

Big transition for him. He is from a very repressed culture. It will be difficult.

If you will trust me with him, I will do my best not to frighten him or hurt him.

Thank you, have fun, Ardenai smiled, and sat down beside Girsu. "How are you feeling by now?"

"I'm fine," he replied, looking from Catrio to Ardenai as if knowing something had transpired between them. "What are you two talking about amongst yourselves if I may ask?"

"Sex," Ardenai smiled. "But just as an aside. I came to ask how Jasreth is this morning."

Girsu just shook his head. "You know, she cried all night, and when she did get a little sleep she had nightmares, and this morning she got up and went to school. Amazing young woman."

"Good for her," Ardenai said. "She looked tired this morning, but determined, as well."

"You looked in on them?"

"I did. I wanted to make sure everybody was ready to get on with things. I got to meet the new tutor that the Great House is providing for Jasreth and Gideon. He will help bring them up to speed so they can stay with children who appear to be their own age."

"But are not," Girsu said. "That's a hard concept for me – the fact that Equi children are so much older than they seem." He looked again from Catrio to Ardenai. "What about sex?"

"I will let Catrio explain it to you later. Tell me first what you knew about your actual mission here. What was the goal?"

"To give you Eridi," Girsu said in a puzzled tone. "And you didn't want her."

"Oh, make no mistake, I did want her, very much. The fact is, we do not have sex with children. Any combination of consenting adults is fine, but not children. I did go see her this morning, and you wouldn't know her. Taken off the drugs Samarra was giving her, she's a very different, very self-assured young lady."

Ardenai had been watching for a reaction, and he got one.

"Drugs?" Girsu gasped, "She was being drugged?"

"Um hm, but no more. What was supposed to happen when you got here with her – what was the entire scenario, start to finish?"

"You were supposed to have sex with her and get her pregnant. She was supposed to have the baby and take it home to show her father. She was supposed to spend the rest of her life here on Equus, I guess, except for your trips to Lebonath Jas to show her father the children."

Ardenai noted the phrasing and nodded. "So, if I had gotten her pregnant that first night, how long would your delegation have stayed?"

Girsu thought about that. "I really don't know," he said at last. "I talked Eridu into letting me come along because I wanted to get away from there – that's not what I told him, of course, but I needed to get away, and get Jasreth away with me, so I convinced him that the Equi would appreciate seeing both parties represented, not just the majority. Jasreth and Eridi were friends. That helped."

"Why were you so anxious to get away?"

"I'm…after my wife was killed, I…I started to feel like my…" he tried, but he just couldn't bring himself to say it. He caught his breath, tried once more and gave up. Finally he said, "I really felt like there was a war brewing. I still think there's a war brewing, and I do not want to be there when it happens. He's not mouthing off publicly yet, but he's planning something. Eridu thinks he's invincible. He thinks he has the Gods and some insuperable, secret allies on his side. I think he's crazy."

Ardenai nodded. "This helps. Are you hungry? It's time for first lunch."

Girsu laughed and shook his head. "You people eat all the time. I had breakfast not that long ago, but thanks for asking." Ardenai rose to go and Girsu looked up at him. "Thanks for caring about Jasreth. If anything should ever happen to me..."

"I'll raise her like my own. But nothing is going to happen to you, I promise. You and Catrio enjoy your afternoon."

Girsu watched Ardenai's receding back. His hair wasn't braided this morning, but pulled back from his face and held with a clip, while the rest flowed past his shoulders like a thick wave of shining black silk. He caught himself and looked at the comely young man leaning against the book shelf.

"It's the mouth," Catrio said, still watching the Firstlord. "For me it's that soft, gentle mouth of his. The voice helps, and the graceful way his neck meets his shoulder. Absolutely, stunningly beautiful man. I had a huge crush on him when I was in his Lycee classes."

Ardenai disappeared around the corner and Girsu slowly looked back at Catrio, feeling his heart starting to speed up, wondering if this was a trap. "What did he mean by that last comment?"

Catrio smiled and came to sit beside Girsu. "Our Firstlord thought you might enjoy some training in the art of lovemaking."

Girsu jumped noticeably and his face colored. "I was married..."

"Not male on female, Girsu. Male on male. Perfectly acceptable, recreational sex between two people who trust one another."

"Like?" he made a back and forth gesture.

"You and me, yes. Ardenai is heterophilic, I am homophilic. Once you have some experience you can make some decisions about how you want to proceed, now that you are on a world where whomever you love is the one you can be with." He held up a finger and chuckled, "as long as it's not a relative or an animal, of course." He stood up to give Girsu some room, saying casually. "If you decide it's what you want to do, just let me know. I will be more than happy to teach you, and to enjoy your company as we learn from each other."

"Thank you," Girsu said, and more fear dropped away than he knew he yet harbored.

CHAPTER 8

"I would keep you here with me forever if I could, you know that," Marion was saying, and Kehailan spun around and strode back across the room, flipping his hands palms up like his father did when he couldn't figure something out.

"I did not ask for a command," he said again.

Captain Eletsky just sighed and shook his head. "Nobody would think less of you if you did," he said with some annoyance. "Kee, you are one of the best tactical wing commanders in the Seventh Galactic Alliance. The fact that your father is now Dragonhorse probably has little or nothing to do with it. You are a battle tactician. Your place is in the command chair of a tactical cruiser, not manning the popguns on a science vessel. I love you, and I will miss you with all my heart, but if you're being reassigned it's for good reason, and I want you to go."

"But a brand new ship? An Imperial Stormclass Tactical Cruiser, fresh from the great shipyards of Andal? There must be a hundred, a thousand captains waiting for a command like that, and who gets it? Somebody who is third in command on a science vessel. No, there's nothing that smacks of nepotism here."

"Have you asked your father if he had anything to do with this?" Kehailan just glared from across the conference room, where he'd taken up pacing back and forth in front of the observation window. "Well, have you?" Marion persisted.

After a pause and a bit of a pout Kehailan responded, "No." and then he chuckled. "Why would I do anything as rational as that?"

"You are such an ass," Marion sighed. "Go ahead. Ask him. Right now. Right here. I want to hear what he has to say."

"Fine," Kehailan snapped, and strode over to the communications display. In a few moments the Great House responded, and Bashkir's face appeared with the main communications center behind him. In response to his request to speak with his father Kehailan got a somewhat tenuous reply, which was unlike Bashkir.

"He is, or was, with the Lebonathi delegation. I'm not sure where he is at the moment."

"I'm here," Ardenai responded, and materialized in one of the somewhat convolving images which said he was abroad somewhere in the ancient building. "Good morning, Son. Hello, Marion."

Kehailan gave him a smile. The image wasn't steady, but his sire looked slightly more sober than he usually did. "Trouble with the Lebonathis?"

"Mmmmm," Ardenai grunted, and began walking again, which further distorted the image and made him look like he was walking underwater. "I have just informed them that their ship is four days out, and that they will be boarding the second she arrives."

"What kind of trouble?" Marion asked.

"It's a long story, and I'd like both of you here when I tell it, so please finish up what you're doing and head this way. Kee, you need to come here to pick up your ship anyway, and I need to talk to Marion. I'd like you to get here as soon as possible so you can get trained."

Kehailan looked at Marion and flipped his palms up one more time. "And that answers that, doesn't it?" he said with exaggerated cheerfulness.

"Answers what?" Ardenai queried, and by that point he was walking down the main corridor of the royal apartments, the sound of his boot heels apparent in the silence which seemed perpetually to reign there.

"How I came to have an Imperial Stormclass Tactical Cruiser, though I've never commanded so much as a shipyard tender."

Ardenai ignored the tone and opened the door to his apartments before continuing the conversation. "Just a minute," he said, bounded up the stairs three at a time, and ducked into his study. "Remember when you had that tactical array panel collapse on you while you were installing it? Broke your pelvis, punctured a lung and scared your mother and me half to death? While you were recovering, you spent a lot of time designing the perfect ship – a very fast ship that could deploy astricting and wave cannon platforms, and control them from a central firing station aboard ship. You asked me to help you with the computations for it. It had all manner of scientific and military innovations on it – a true hybrid."

"I remember," Kehailan said quietly. Just thinking about those seasons of pain made him wince.

"Well, the ship you're picking up is the ship you designed, Kehailan."

Ardenai made a motion in the air with his hand and a sleek craft appeared, turning slowly as the schematics above and below changed with the rotation – a beautiful, powerful piece of machinery, white as snow, bearing the seven silver chevrons of the Firstlord, and the image of a running horse. "I finished up the computator specifications and handed her over to engineering about four years ago. If a prototype is designed by an active SGA line-officer, that's who it goes to for the first five years of operation. Those are the rules. And that, my son, and not nepotism, is why you have an Imperial Stormclass Tactical Cruiser, even though you've never commanded so much as a shipyard tender. Any questions?"

There was absolute silence – not a twitch, not a peep. "Good. She carries two flags, Seventh Galactic Alliance and The Great House of Equus. Like Belesprit is Marion's to command, and yet mine, so this ship is yours to command, and yet mine as well. I think we may be about to get embroiled in a conflict, and I need a topnotch ship and a crack officer to command her. That's her, and that is you."

There was another long silence, then, for want of anything more intelligent to say, Kehailan ventured, "Does this ship have a name?"

"Yes," Ardenai said, and gave a wry chuckle. "She had a name three years ago when they started building her. She is…Dragonhorse."

"Why of course she is," Kehailan said, and burst out laughing.

"We will be there as soon as we can," Marion said, and Ardenai nodded and severed the connection before Eletsky could start yelling at his third in command.

▲▲▲▲▲▲▲

"We have failed," Halaf said for the second time in what had become an angry and somewhat desperate discussion. "The flamen did not want this mission in the first place, and this is exactly why."

Naram turned on him and spat, "We failed because we brought along too many fools – your nephews chief among them. That's what brought this whole mess to a head. And we brought that weakling, Girsu, and his whore of a niece. The Gods only know what they've been saying behind our backs."

"Blame anyone you care to," Brak said, "but the truth is, all of us underestimated the Dragonhorse. First, with the single sling of a knife, he killed Sarkhan, who was our connection to the Telenir with no strings attached. Now Ardenai will not show up in due time with his wife and babe, the Telenir who say they will side with us if we produce the man, will not side with us, and the plan to take enough fertile territory to grow food SO WE CAN EAT, has passed us by. Our people are starving, and here we sit, surrounded by more than plenty. The Dragonhorse has said a hundred times that the Equi will help us. Why don't we just ask?"

"Help us what?" Naram sneered, "Become peasants? Dirt eaters like they are? I'm sure that's exactly what Eridu has in mind, don't you? I'm sure the flamen would just love the idea of eating soup and bread in a common kitchen every night. *Your* people may be starving, Brak, but Eridu and the flamen are not, and they are the ones who make the decisions. I don't think asking these shit eaters to do anything except surrender was part of the plan, and it's a plan we're responsible for. I've seen what Eridu does to people who fail, or who go against his wishes, and I do not care to be one of them."

"Firstlord Sarkhan was wrong to tell us these were primitive people," Basra ventured, and was rewarded with a communal glare. He took a deep breath and continued. "These people may be simple, but they are not primitive. Just because they don't use a lot of technology, doesn't mean they don't have any. They have far more than we do, and we are ignoring that at our peril. Because they value their women there are more of them than there are of us – at least more of them who are allowed to think."

At that point Addur's hand came hard across Basra's mouth, and he snarled, "Go to your room and wait for me. We are going to talk." When the boy had crept away, Addur looked from Naram to Halaf and said, "We still have one option left, and it has always been an option. Perhaps if the Dragonhorse will not take my precious sister home to her father to show off her babe, he will take her home out of duty to someone who was given to him, and who tragically died. He is a man of honor, at least in their version. He would take her beautiful corpse and lay it at the feet of Eridu with all sincere apologies, would he not? You must admit, it's a lot quicker than waiting months for a brat to be born."

The three older men looked from one to another and slowly nodded their agreement, though it was obvious the suggestion didn't have much appeal. "Yes, we still have that option," Naram said, and he was the one who smiled. He snapped his fingers and one of the servants whom they had brought along stepped from the shadows into the dim light of the room. "Go get Samarra," he ordered, "and when you get back, undress and get in my bed – I always think better when I'm relaxed and empty."

She nodded and left through the huge doors. "They have guards posted out there," Addur said, "I wonder how many?"

"I'll ask Akadia while I'm taking my pleasure on her," Naram laughed. Manipulating power always aroused him. He licked his lips and sat staring at nothing, trying to figure out exactly how this might work. Halaf and Brak looked at him with varying shades of disgust, and left the room to have a discussion of their own.

With Naram's comment towards Akadia heating his blood, Addur let himself into the chamber he shared with Basra and found him already naked, stretched face down on the bed. "You're such an obedient little piece of shit," he said, pulling the boy by the ankles to the edge of the bed. He pushed his own trousers down and massaged himself until his erection was hard, then spread Basra's buttocks and pushed himself in, groaning with pleasure as he began to move. "You are lucky to have me, you know," he said, putting his hands under Basra's thighs and lifting up. "Get your knees under you," he demanded and withdrew until it was accomplished. He reinserted himself. "I'd better get a response this time, or you won't be able to piss for a week. You do like having me do this, don't you?"

"I like it very much," Basra said. "You know I do. I always have."

"And you know I don't care whether you do or not," Addur snickered. "You're just practice, Little Brother. Before we go I have someone I need to say a proper goodbye to. But first, I have to figure out how to get us out of here."

▲ ▲ ▲ ▲ ▲ ▲ ▲

Since the Lebonathi ship was still four days out and polo practice had been moved once again because Landais had smashed his thumb with a hammer, Ardenai's suggestion that they all go home for week's end had been received with a communal nod of approval. The six of them with Lionel in his little carrier had run for the afternoon tube, their breaths white in the late season chill, steadying one another against slipping on the icy pavers as the first snowflakes began to drift lazily off the ocean. The outbound train had not been crowded. Most of the goods and produce were safely in the stores of the Great House against the coming of the storms, and Teal was grateful for the opportunity to check the ancient stone barns which he used as wine cellars at Canyon keep, to make sure this year's vintage was safely stored as well.

"I do miss my sire," he said as acre upon acre of bare rhax vines flashed by on the viewing screen. "I know that my first duty is to you, Dragonhorse, and to the Great House, and I wouldn't have it any other way. But with Gidran on Taraxia I am thinking I will lease out the whole operation and let another try his or her hand at making next year's wine. I just don't have the time to do the family label justice. Maybe I'll brew a little wine in the cellar for our household use and call it good."

"None of us have time to do anything justice anymore," Io said, patting Teal's hand on one side of her armrest and Ardenai's on the other. "I am hoping that once this whole episode with the Lebonathi is behind us we'll be able to relax a bit more. I do think that since you are now Captain of the Horse Guard, someone else should take up the reins as Master of Horse. I'm sorry. I know that is where your heart lies."

"It does," Teal sighed, leaning his chair back, "but things by necessity change. One full-time job is enough, and advising your husband makes two. Ah'din and I want another baby, and once she is settled, I am going to want more time at home with her, and then with them."

Both Ardenai and Io looked first to see where the three young people were, then turned their gaze on their brother-in-law. "Are you telling me," Ardenai chuckled, "that you escaped that time at Mountain hold without getting your wife pregnant? I assumed she was already settled and that you just hadn't announced yet."

Teal's unamused eyebrow prefaced his comment. "Wouldn't it be wonderful to be in the midst of High Harvest with hundreds of pounds of vegetables and fruit to put up, and jams and pickles to make, grain to look after, herbs to dry and bees to be cared for and honey to be harvested and garden beds to be mulched and covered, livestock to be doctored and – oh yes – a quick trip to the birthing stool between chores? My wife would love that, and I'm sure her mother would, as well."

"She seemed pretty set on getting pregnant," Ardenai said. "What my sister wants, she usually gets."

"From you maybe," Teal drawled. "She was in no condition to make an informed choice, and I chose not to make that choice for her. You want a High Harvest baby settle your own wife." He stopped, sucked in his breath and a look of physical pain crossed his handsome face. "I'm sorry, I'm sorry. I don't know what made me say that. Io, Beloved, I am so sorry."

Io picked up his hand where it draped over the armrest, held it against her cheek for a moment, and put it back down in her lap. "I'm actually very glad you managed to forget, even briefly, what happened on Calumet, Teal. Truth be told, Ardi and I have decided to put off trying to have another baby for a while yet. Not that there's anything wrong, so don't feel worse than you already do. It seems like we need each other so much right now."

"What my dear friend and wife is trying to say without demeaning her husband, is that I'm not sure yet whether I've seen the last of the Imperial Dragonhorse, and until we're sure that has leveled off we don't want anybody in the way..."

"...in case he needs me," Io finished. "Do you think we could talk about something besides sex and babies and Lebonathis?"

"Absolutely," Ardenai smiled. Teal took his hand back, and they turned their attention to the snow falling outside.

"Early this year," Teal observed. "But we are a very cool planet, so it's to be expected from time to time."

"High Harvest is going to feel more like the Celebration of Storms," Io agreed. "I wonder if they got the kelp harvest in from Old Reefs and Anchor before the seas got rough."

"What did the riding boot say to the horseman?" Ardenai chimed in.

"And these are the kinds of conversations normal people have?" Io giggled.

Ardenai wagged a forefinger. "That's not what it said."

"And this is not a normal conversation," Teal said, stifling a yawn. "I know I sleep. Why don't I feel like I sleep? Maybe I just think I'm sleeping at night."

"And nobody cares about Mahruss's joke," Ardenai said sadly. "He was so proud of it."

"Fine," Io said. "For Mahruss's sake. What did the riding boot say to the horseman?"

"It said, 'You go on horseback, I'll go on foot.'" Ardenai looked at their faces and burst out laughing. "This is what normal people do," he gasped, wiping his eyes. "They laugh."

The side of the train opened up and they stepped out, still laughing, into the terminal at Pomonar. They were close to the center of the continent now, higher in elevation, and the wind had an icy bite which pierced their hastily grabbed cloaks and left them wishing they'd thought a little farther ahead than the warmth of the tube. People coming into the platform area were shaking snow off their clothing, and Ardenai pulled Io over in front of him, wrapping his cloak around both of them as they waited for the Local which would take them to Falconstones. Criollo and Ah'brianne seemed little affected by the weather, but Gideon was looking up at the huge, lazily drifting flakes in amazement.

"Have you never seen it snow before?" Ardenai asked.

"Only for a few seconds as we transitioned from the clipper to Mountain hold," the boy responded. "But that was a blizzard and nobody, least of all me, was looking up. These flakes are so big. They look like white paper, cut into shapes and thrown from a high window. They're beautiful."

He looked up again, snow catching in his blond hair and reflecting in his golden eyes, and Ardenai loved him until he ached inside. How much this one young man had changed his perspective of the world. How grateful he was to have Gideon's guileless acceptance to balance Kehailan's acerbic suspicion. Two brilliant sons, both being tested, and growing in their own way.

"Tube," Gideon said, and Ardenai set aside his reverie and boarded, grateful for the warmth, and the gift of his children. He laughed to himself, remembering Gideon's first ride on the ancient technology – the gut sloshing takeoff followed by no sense of movement at all, no sense of stopping. A singularly odd machine, but very effective. In an hour they could be halfway across the continent.

He thought about what Io had said to Teal. As usual, it was half a story. It wasn't just that Io was concerned that the care of a baby, or a heavy pregnancy would keep her from servicing the Firstlord. Her fallopian tubes were tied shut until she had completely healed from the crossbow bolt she had taken on the wargrounds of Calumet. Having them tied, meant he didn't have to pay any attention to what he was doing – no need to look for a skin before intercourse, no need to think about a male or female fetus – no need to think. His need for sexual release had become so intense, and so frequent, that both of them had pretty well figured out that he wasn't going to be able to control himself all the time, and now that he was Dragonhorse, he was generative all the time. No nibble and nicker, no ejaculating just semen as recreational sex was supposed to be. It was now his business to impregnate the women selected for him – all those women he didn't love – and because of that the one woman he truly loved, might have to go childless, or be pregnant all the time, which was not the example they wanted to set for their people. Like most other families, they planned no more than two settlings together.

"Ardi," that one was saying softly, "Beloved, are you all right?"

"Of course," he smiled, making himself stop staring into space. He leaned in his seat to kiss her ear. "Just thinking about us."

"Well, we're good, so if you're thinking about us, think only of how happy I am to be with you, and how proud I am to be sharing your life and helping you hold the reins of this beautiful and ancient government. I thought giving up being Captain of the Horse Guard would be so hard, that I would feel such emptiness, and I don't. Every day is full of challenges and the joy of learning new things. When you asked me to marry you – the first time you made love to me – I thought that was the best day of my life. Now, every day is the best day."

"Which makes the rest of this nonsense, just that," he sighed, and for a moment he looked infinitely old. "Io, I am so desperate to sit in our own kitchen at our own beat-up old table and laugh while we eat and then crawl into my own bed until time to get up and feed the horses."

"You're about to get your chance," she laughed. "Falconstones appears through the flurries, and you should be home in time to help with the feeding tonight. Double the fun!"

Apparently word had gone ahead that they were coming, because the bigger of their two flyers was backed out of its space and rotated for takeoff when they got to it. With a shout and a wave of thanks they were off down the coast, then up the canyon toward home. They set down long enough to drop off Ah'brianne, and another five minutes found the flyer in its space at Canyon keep and its recent occupants hurrying into the warmth of the huge kitchen.

"Oh, you're home!" Ah'rane exclaimed, trying to hug all of them at once, and Ardenai's heart filled with the knowledge of how hard all of this had to have been on those who deserved it least and who loved him most. When all of them were in Thura, Ah'rane and Krush were alone here. They had told him half a dozen times that they hadn't minded moving across the river to Canyon keep – it was nearly identical to Sea keep anyway. On most levels he believed them. The same people who had always lived on the keep with them still lived here. There were still women to visit with, men to help Krush, a baby or two under foot from time to time. It was still home. But....

"There you go again," Io said, and Ardenai realized she had slid his traveling cloak off his shoulders and was holding it as she looked up at him. She was so little, it always made him want to laugh and nibble at her as though she was a sugary treat. Fortunately he was wise enough to know that this particular sugary treat could make his life miserable if he crossed her by saying the wrong thing.

"I came here because I really needed some think time," he said, brushing her cheek with the back of his hand, "I don't mean to go off walking in the middle of a conversation."

"Well, you're home," she said, folding both cloaks and turning toward the main warming closet with them. "This is your time and your space and I want you to do absolutely anything you want to do for a couple of days to let yourself rest and work through things. I'm going to help Ah'rane and Ah'din with dinner. Krush is already in the barns, so if you're going to head that way, change out of your good clothes, please."

She sounded just like his beloved Ah'ree. "Yes, Mistress," he said, and trotted across the huge central hub to their wing of the house to get his work clothes. He remembered what the Twelfth Dragonhorse had said about Ah'ree preparing Io for him – that she'd known what was coming. He wondered if he was right about that. The man had known about Kehailan getting a ship of his own; of course that wasn't exactly a deep dark secret. Ardenai's work on that ship – those ships – he corrected himself, had been more or less public knowledge in the scientific and engineering community for several years. There was more than one ship. Not something he'd told Kehailan. Truth be told, there were thirteen of them. That would come out when Marion got here with Belesprit. He tossed his Firstlord clothes on the bed, good boots in the wardrobe, put on old woolen trousers, a heavy tunic and the well-used work boots he'd worn as Mr. Grayson, threw on a fleece-lined waterproof jacket and trotted off to the horse barns.

He found Krush and Gideon admiring the six horses occupying stalls on the north side of the biggest barn, and cruised up beside them to receive a one-armed hug and a kiss on the temple from his sire. "Glad you're home," Krush said, ending the hug with a gentle slap on the shoulder. "How do you like the looks of the new bloodline?"

Ardenai leaned on the nearest stall door and studied the dappled gray stallion – the tiny ears which pointed toward the top of his head, the dished-out face, big eyes, flaring nostrils – and his mouth formed a soft "Ohh" of admiration, tinged with wonder. They'd been gathering that man out of the solitudes for years. Ardenai would swear these were not the horses they'd been gathering with him. Not at all. "Are they really who Chirion says they are?" he breathed.

"That they are," Krush affirmed, reaching out to pat the stallion, who had come over in response to the stranger at his door. "Not that I'm a doubting man, mind you, but these bloodlines I definitely wanted to check. I drew some blood and ran some tests. This stud is a direct descendent of Darley Arabian – as a matter of fact, he's a son. Two of the mares are by Byerley Turk, two are Godolphin daughters. The black mare is a Darley Arabian like the stud."

Ardenai's already big eyes turned to stare at his father.

"Don't even ask," Krush responded. "All I can say is that they have one kraaling good stasis program."

"And who is 'they'?" the Firstlord asked, breathing gently into the nose of the inquisitive stallion.

"The great ethereal them, I suppose. Mountain hold coupled with the Achernareans – our most ancient overlords. Whoever they are, whatever their reasons, we are blessed with these magnificent animals. Injected slowly they will rejuvenate our bloodlines, and used all at once, they will revolutionize primitive desert warfare. These are Equus Caballus, the true

Arabian horses of legend, Ardi. Five lumbar vertebrae, not six, seventeen pairs of ribs not eighteen. Unlike Equus Legatum they have no squamate characteristics whatsoever. We are looking at living fossils, ancient beyond all knowing. Ten, fifteen thousand years at the very least."

Ardenai moved slowly into the stall and held out his left hand to the horse, reaching with his right to stroke his neck. "What does Chirion plan to do with these beautiful creatures?"

"He says he has no more use for them," Krush said quietly. "He said they were bred as a gift for the young man who so patiently came for him all those long years, and for that man's golden-eyed son, who he thinks will become one of the most famous and respected bloodlines specialists on Equus. These horses belong to you and Gideon."

Ardenai didn't know whether to laugh or cry and felt like he might do both. He and Gideon shared a past, a present, and now, rich beyond anything he could imagine, a future. He turned to look at his father, and realized that while he might have tears in his eyes, Krush did, too. Gideon was smiling a silly, besotted little smile as he looked at Tolbeth, who was in a stall across the way, and Ardenai realized with a rush of amused emotion that this is what it would be like when all of them stood looking at his first baby with Io, Ah'din and Teal's baby, Gideon's first child. He heard someone laughing and realized it was himself, and he also realized he was having to wipe at his nose and his eyes as he hugged his son and his father.

The stallion was beautiful, the mares no less so. Two were gray like the stallion, one a deep bay that was almost black, one a chestnut and one a true jet black. They all seemed gentle, carefully handled, and curious, as are horses who are well kept and well loved. "And they're all bred," Krush said as they tossed feed into mangers up and down the breezeway, "so whatever you two think you have planned come late Segens, think again."

"We should be over the highest of the chevrons by then," Ardenai said, and lapsed again into one his long and thoughtful silences.

"I will be here," Gideon said, patting his grandfather's shoulder. "I will always be here."

Ardenai managed to put aside his musings long enough to enjoy dinner with his family and hear about how well the wine was doing, how the cold storage bulged with good food, how beautiful the wool on Ah'mae's sheep was this year. "Good wool usually means a hard winter," Ah'rane observed.

"Master Eider says we have more than enough hay to export," Teal said. "Maybe we should send some to the Lebonathi for their Caronai."

"Agriculture is always better than invasion," Krush observed, and Ardenai nodded.

"Yes indeed," he said, almost to himself, "If we use force we will get only hypocrites, not converts. We will need to be careful when we go." He looked up from his stuffed squash and realized they were all looking at him. "What?"

"Just wondering if we're all having the same conversation," Ah'din smiled. "Would you like a nice cup of tea?"

Ardenai's face lit up. "That reminds me, would you come back to Thura long enough to have a nice cup of tea with Ah'krill, preferable hers, not yours?"

"Now I know we're not all having the same conversation," Ah'din sighed, "but, yes. I will. When do we have to leave?"

"Io and I will be leaving very early day after tomorrow, but the rest of you needn't leave until that afternoon. I won't keep you long, I promise, Din. I just need a few more answers – a little more think time and a few more answers."

"Why are you two leaving so early?" Ah'rane asked, "And you didn't answer your sister. Would you like a cup of tea?"

"I'm sorry, yes I would. We are leaving because five of the thirteen new battle cruisers are ready to launch, and since they were built to honor the Rising of the Thirteenth Dragonhorse, I think he ought to be there."

"I assume one of them will be going to their handsome designer," Krush said with grandfatherly pride.

"Um hm,"Ardenai murmured, and Teal reacted with unaccustomed annoyance.

"Precious Equus, he wasn't happy with that, either? I swear, Ardi, you need to drown him and start over!"

Now all eyes were on Teal, and he dropped his head with embarrassment. "I didn't mean that," he muttered. "I probably should have stayed in Thura. I have a lot to do."

"The first thing you have to do is tell us what's wrong," his mother-in-law said, covering his hand with her own. "You are the furthest thing from a hothead we have in this family, and something is bothering you."

Teal just shook his head and looked at his plate with a deep sigh. When nobody took up the conversation he finally capitulated and said, "One of the things we vowed on the train was that we were not going to discuss the Lebonathi, and I've already brought them up once without even meaning to. If I tell you what's bothering me, I'll be bringing them up again."

"Bring them up and get it over with," Gideon advised. "I want to play board games after dinner and I don't want them sitting in." He realized he'd called attention to himself while slipping Lionel a tidbit, and tried to look as casual as possible.

"Yes, please," Ah'din said, flashing Gideon a knowing and displeased eyebrow. "I'm worried about that haunted look in your eye, Husband. It usually means something bad is about to happen."

Teal leaned back with his wine glass and considered his words for a bit before he spoke in his slow, gentle tenor. "They harbor such dark thoughts, those people do. Some of them, Akadia and Hassuna, two of the women they brought to serve them – have never had food security their whole lives. They have families on their homeworld who are hungry, which is why they agreed to come along at all, and now they're being shamefully used. Naram and Addur have thoughts so full of hatred that it's like encountering Diabolus on a dark street. Basra is absolutely terrified of Addur, and I think he's hiding some terrible secret."

Ardenai's expression had been changing slowly as he listened to his kinsman, and now he interjected, very quietly, "Teal, are you saying that you can read their thoughts?"

"I don't know, I've never tried. It seems invasive and inhospitable somehow, though at times I've wished I had. It's enough that they throw their thoughts around like they do. You thought Hadrian Keats was bad? These people are worse – and their thoughts weigh me down like a load of death. I'm sure they bother you no less than they do me."

"Their actions bother me, their thoughts don't bother me in the least. Guess why."

Teal looked a little surprised. "You can't hear them?"

"No. Can anybody else hear them?" He looked around the table. Everyone was either saying no, or shaking their heads that direction. "Well, that explains why you've been so jumpy lately. Why didn't you tell me?"

"I just assumed you could hear them," Teal sighed. He put his wine glass down, elbows on the table, and dropped his head into his hands. "They are planning something terrible, I know they are. I think we're going to welcome in your reign as Dragonhorse with a war. Sorry, but I do."

"You're tired," Ah'din said, rubbing his back as she sat beside him. "You're probably just overreacting."

"No, he's not," Ardenai said in a conversational tone. "If we don't go to them, they're going to come at us, and then we'll have to kill them, which is never a very productive way to reduce a population. As I said, I have a little more thinking to do and I need to get a few more things to fall into place, and then I will share with you my plans, and the plans of Mountain hold, for the next two Tribute Worlds of Equus."

"Well don't get Jasreth hurt," Criollo said, reaching for a flatwrap. "She's sweet and gorgeous and I want to marry her when I grow up, and we'll have funny looking little babies to play with Ardi and Io's funny looking little babies – because you have to know, they're going to be funny looking."

That comment set the table laughing and nothing more was said about the Lebonathi or their dark thoughts, or impending war, or terrible happenings. While the others were still playing board games and trying to decide what to name new horses and funny looking babies, Ah'din excused herself and took her husband with her to their wing of the house. She undressed him, gave him a warm bath, and made her usual sweet and quiet love to him. When he was lying looking up at her with his hands on her thighs, and she was rocking slowly back and forth and smiling at him, hair coming loose and falling about her shoulders, he realized he was going to cry, which was something Teal never did, and though she reached down and wiped his tears away she didn't ask him why he was crying or if he was upset about something, she just stretched out across his chest and laid her head on his shoulder and said, "I love you more than anything else in the world." And that night he actually slept.

Just at dawn when the mist rolled up white from the river into the dark Equi pines Io awoke and realized she was alone in bed. In Thura she often found herself alone in the morning unless Ardenai wanted attention, but he'd said he wanted to go home and sleep, and he wasn't sleeping. She got out of bed, wrapped herself in a woolen robe and opened the doors onto the big terrace, wondering if they'd already gone to feed. She ventured to the edge of the pavers where the path took off for the river, and then she saw him – arms raised to the east – head back, bare chested and unaware of the cold as he spoke with the Wisdom Giver. Immediately she turned and went back inside so as not to become a part of his conscious thought. This was the time he needed. It was to no one's benefit to deprive him of it.

She went to the kitchen and realized she was the first one up, which was also unusual on this busy keep. She turned the valve which pushed steam from the thermal fusion chamber beneath the house into the big old cookstove and set about making coffee, putting water on for tea, and setting a pot of cider on the back of the stove to warm, and while she did that she pretended that this was as far as her life extended, that her husband would come in from his prayers and kiss her and go to feed their horses, and their son and daughter would wake and help their father with his chores, or their mother with the preserving and pickling, or covering the big vegetable beds with leaves and straw so that root vegetables could be left in the ground without freezing. And in the evening they would sit and discuss their day, and play games, and perhaps bring up a cosmoscope image to see what was going on in the way of political intrigue. No, they wouldn't do that. They'd play board games and remain blissfully unaware of the world skimming by outside.

She sliced chilled mazea loaves onto sheets, brushed them with sweetened sunflower oil and set them in a slow oven to crisp for breakfast, put a jug of syrup in a pot of water on the stove to warm, ladled hot cider into an earthenware mug, and with a backward glance to make sure she'd not left a mess, she went to the study she shared with Ardenai and got back to the business of being one of the top military strategists on Equus.

Her current assignment was to find twelve captains – topnotch captains – including one from each planet in the AEW, to take over the Dragonhorse Cruisers. She had many ears, many eyes, and information had been coming in to her from dozens of sources: military records, personal records and observations, anecdotal input – at times more than she wanted to know about an impossible number of people. She had boiled them down as best she could, and now she laid them all out in front of her in hard copy, because that was the way she thought best. She would hand the same list to Teal and Ardi for their input, and perhaps to her father. Maybe Marion Eletsky and Kehailan. But first, she had to come up with an initial list to which names could be added, from which names could be removed.

She sat with her mug warming her hands and stared at the papers in front of her, lists of people from each of the ten affined worlds: Amberia, Anguine Prime, Anguine II, Calumet, Corvus, Demeter, Menorquin, Papillia, Phylla, Terren, and, of course, Equus. Eleven worlds all told. Kehailan already in line for the flagship. That made twelve. One ship in limbo. She wondered privately if her husband planned to keep that one in orbit around one of the Lebonathi worlds – something with big teeth to guard the newest members of the flock. Maybe there would be no incursion. Maybe they'd discover that Eridu was only testing their mettle and it would all go away. Maybe she'd realize she could flap her ears and fly.

Io squirmed in the chair. It was Ardenai's, and too big – too tall, definitely worn in the seat. She'd hidden behind it as a child thirty-some years ago and he persisted in keeping the thing. She stared at the lists of names, most especially the names at the top of each list. A problem kept lunging over the stall door, as Krush would say. At the top of the list from Terren, Marion Eletsky. At the top of the list from Phylla, Bonfire Dannis. Who had designed the ships? Ah'ree Kehailan Ardenai. The top three command officers from Belesprit. The SGA's newest science vessel would be dead in space.

Who was the very best pilot she knew? Ardenai. No contest. Wouldn't do to give the Dragonhorse one more thing to do, would it? Who was at the top of the list from Anguine II and one of the best pilots in the Seventh Galactic Alliance? Ah'ria Konik Nokota. Test pilot extraordinaire. Missing in action, a dying wife at home pleading daily for word of him. Maybe they should reserve a ship for him. He was going to need something to take his mind off things. Back to Equus. Her father was an excellent pilot, but he was head of the Equi Calvary and had worked hard to get there. Teal was probably as brilliant a pilot as Ardenai and Konik – like Konik, a bit to the reckless side – but he was now Captain of the Horse Guard and sworn to protect the Firstlord. He was Ardenai's closest adviser and still Master of Horse on top of everything else, because there was no one even remotely as good at it as he was. He was exhausted. He was out. So far they had exactly one person in a command position. Kehailan. Petulant sack of shit that he could be, he was insuperable as a tactician and cool as ice under fire. One good choice made. Eleven to go. Marion had moved from second in command of a battle cruiser to take command of the old science vessel, SGA Blyth Spirit, before being handed the helm of Belesprit. Would he move back? Should they ask him to move back? Would it be wise to take three close friends and spread them out over three commands of three brand new prototype vessels? Marion, Kehailan and Bonfire. She let those three names roll around in her head for a minute, and moved down the list.

The list from Calumet was the shortest. When you came from a planet where nothing motorized worked, you had to have a whole lot of interest in something you'd never seen and couldn't conceive of to want to move into a position with the Seventh Galactic Alliance. Three men had done that – no women. She put a check mark next to the name, Mecklin. Sterling reputation as someone with quick wits and a good imagination. Strong as a horse, currently Captain of a larger but older battle cruiser. For the moment, just for the moment, she told herself, she put a check mark by Marion Eletsky for Terren and Bonfire Dannis for Phylla. If she reserved a ship for Konik, she already had five top spots filled.

"Are you going to come and eat, Fledermaus?" Sweetest baritone on the planet. She turned and smiled at her husband.

"I'm kind of in the middle of this, Ardi. I'll come and find something later," she said, and went back to staring at the sheets of paper. He looked over her shoulder for a moment, took her empty cup, kissed the top of her unbrushed half-braided mop, and left.

Amberia was easy. They lived for a good fight. They were all either pilots, farmers, soldiers or engineers. Their fleet commander was a man named Ulric Hamar. Amazing pilot. Smart. Nobody to mess with. Amberia would love a new cruiser at the head of their fleet.

If Io got her way, the ship from Corvus would go to Cadence Holofernes. They had served together briefly in the Campaign of the High Plateaus, and if Io thought she could get away with cloning Holofernes enough times to take all the ships, she'd do it and count the SGA well protected. As a bonus, Cadence was married to a woman as brilliant as she was, someone who could plot an entire solar system in her head down to the last errant ball of ice.

Demeter, Demeter, Demeter…she didn't realize she was saying it aloud until her husband's finger came over her shoulder and pointed to Pen Darus's name. "Good man," he said, putting down a hot mug of coffee and a plate of food he'd cut up into bite sized pieces so she could eat it with her fingers. The joys of being married to a creppia nonage teacher. "He's young, Kehailan's age, but I know him fairly well, and what I've seen I like. He captains a science ship for the SGA, and Marion thinks the world of him. As a matter of fact, Josephus knows him and speaks well of him."

"And who do you have in mind for Menorquin?" Io asked, taking a bite of cinnamon roll and licking her fingers.

Ardenai sipped his tea and thought about it as he looked at the list. "Well, since Gallios and Isla are now herding those huge farm ships of theirs…probably…Strea and her husband Devario as a pair."

"Top of the list," Io said.

"They should be."

"Two more to go before I hand this over to Teal. How is he this morning?"

"He seems more rested," Ardenai said. "I wish he'd mentioned earlier that he could hear the, 'you know who.'"

"Don't lose your focus. Papillia? Is there anybody at all?"

"Other than you?"

"Yes," she smiled, "Most definitely other than me."

He thought a bit, and not wanting to be unkind said, "Let's come back to that one. What's left?"

"Anguine Prime. And a second commander from Equus."

"Pochard for Anguine Prime and … Skyros for Equus. There, we're done. Wait, who did you put down for Anguine II?"

She gave him a brief, appraising look. He seemed to be in a good enough mood. "Konik?"

The eyebrows shrugged. "Nik's primarily a test pilot. He could thread a loom with a cruiser like this, but I don't know that he'd want to stay with one." Io's eyes narrowed a little and Ardenai sensed a possible balk. "Nik's a great pilot. We'll just lead his ship around behind us until we find him." Ardenai sipped his tea and stared out the window. "Which, I hope, is soon. Ah'davan is getting very frail. I really don't think she will live to see the turn of the year."

Wasting away – as Ardenai's beloved Ah'ree had done. No explanation, no cure, just death. Io knew a good part of why Ardenai wanted to find Konik was so he could be with his wife when she died, and so Ah'davan would have the comfort of his presence. "Shall we find Teal and run this past him?" she asked brightly, hoping to get her husband's mind off death.

"Yes, let's do that," he said, and crimped a grin as he stood up to offer her his hand. "You haven't forgotten that you're not even remotely dressed, have you?"

Io looked down at her pink fuzzy pajamas, then felt her mass of tangled curls and laughed. "I did. You go find Teal and I will give myself a good currying."

"We're home. A modicum of currying will do," he said as he kissed her.

Ardenai took the scratch list and went behind the kitchen to the big, comfortable baker's pantry where Ah'din stored her preserving equipment, jars, boxes and bottles and where he expected to find Teal sitting at the long work table helping her sort and label garden seeds. He found his sister, but not her husband. "He's in the barns somewhere," Ah'din smiled, setting another tray of carefully selected seeds on the sideboard to dry before storing them for the winter. "How long do I need to stay in the city when I go?"

"Just long enough to determine that Samarra isn't drugging Ah'krill," Ardenai said, pulling a heavy jacket on over his woolen tunic. He gave Ah'din a kiss as she breezed by him, and let himself out the door to head for the barns.

Canyon keep had one disadvantage over Sea keep – the barns at Canyon keep were full of wine. The barns across the river at Sea keep held the horses, and it was a slick and frosty walk this morning. Ardenai wondered if Krush had opened the tunnel yet. It was roughhewn, and being from the earlier times of a shorter population, not particularly high in the middle – easy to bump the head if one wasn't being careful, but it was at least dry, and it wasn't slick. He decided he'd check it out on the way back.

Teal?

With the gentlest ones, came the reply and Ardenai skirted the first barn and went into the second. He never entered these ancient structures without looking around in wonder. Like most rural buildings – homes as well as barns – they were made of solid stone with verdant sod roofs. Thousands of years old, they were impervious to lightning, cool in the heat and snug in the cold, a fact he was especially grateful for this morning, as he was not yet used to the chilly weather.

He found Teal most of the way down on the right hand side, looking at a petite black mare with a tiny star and a single, wide streak of white in her mane. "Little small for you," Ardenai observed, walking up beside him.

"But not for Jasreth," Teal countered. "If she's going to be my daughter-in-law, I suppose she's going to have to have a horse." He laughed and shook his head. "The things young men say in unguarded moments.

Still, the girl is becoming more comfortable in her surroundings, and since she is going to be a permanent resident, she should have a mount."

"I agree," Ardenai said. "I can ask my elfin bride if she'll ride this one out and see what she thinks."

"Thanks. Why were you looking for me?"

"I wanted you to look at this," Ardenai replied, pulling a glove off with his teeth and unfolding the list from his pocket. "Io did most of it. I made a suggestion or two."

Teal skimmed it, then eyed it more closely and gave Ardenai a questioning look. "You think gutting Belesprit for her command crew is going to go over well with the SGA?"

Ardenai grimaced and leaned his elbows on the stall door. "I think my voice will carry some weight."

"I know it does. That's not what I asked you."

"Teal, you and I both know that the Lebonathis are up to something and I'm pretty sure it's a war. You said yourself that they have people in their delegation who have families that don't get enough to eat. The only livable part of their planet is overpopulated – number one reason for war. They're hungry – number two reason for war. Their wealth is unevenly distributed – number three reason for war, though that one is usually civil in nature. They have a repressive religion – number three reason for war outside one's own borders. Mountain hold wants something done, and I have to agree with them."

"You think they're going to come at us?"

"If we don't go to them first, yes, I do, and only the Creator knows with whom they might ally themselves. Can't you just picture a war involving the Nargas or the Turls?" He paused to greet the little mare, who was stretching a curious nose in his direction, then looked back at Teal. "When we go, I want these five ships manned with absolutely the top people the SGA has to offer. If we can scare them we can take them over without firing a shot, occupy them, put an occupational government in place, and be home for the Celebration of Storms. After that, if Marion and Bonfire want to go back to Belesprit, they can do that – so can Kehailan, for that matter. He will have fulfilled…kind of fulfilled…tradition."

He hadn't realized he'd sounded sad until Teal's arm came around his shoulder. "All you can do is keep holding your hand out to him, Ardi. He loves you, I know he does, I've heard him tell you so. He doesn't have any real direction in his life right now. Once he has that, once he can tell you who he is, instead of who he's not, he'll be just fine."

"I hope so," Ardenai sighed. "Any other comments on the list?"

Teal studied it again. "If you want Menorquin to have Strea and Devario, you'll have to wait on that ship. They're in their quadrennial conjoinment phase right now, so they're on leave. There are only five ships available at the moment, so I would say Kehailan and Marion. Mecklin from Calumet. Definitely Ulric Hamar from Amberia. Cadence is brilliant. That will leave Bonfire to Captain Belesprit, and when another ship comes available down the line, you can offer it to her."

"Excellent," Ardenai smiled, taking back the list. He eyed his brother-in-law without seeming to and finally ventured, "I hate to ask, but if you get a chance, would you see if you can get a glimpse into what Halaf and Naram are thinking?"

Teal grimaced and tasted at his mouth with displeasure, but he nodded. "I will try."

"And I will owe you a huge favor," Ardenai responded, "not that I don't already."

"You don't," Teal said, letting himself into the stall with the little mare. "It's my job to keep you alive, Dragonhorse, just don't make it too hard."

"Which reminds me," Ardenai said quietly, "Teal, look at me." He did, questioningly. "I have realized that as Master of Horse and Captain of the Horse Guard, you are now a Master Captain. Even as you work through and delegate those responsibilities, which I want you to do soon, the title of Master Captain will not change. I want the Captain of the Horse Guard to go back to guarding Ah'krill, and I want you to be my closest companion, advisor, and my top military coordinator. You are now, by my order, the highest ranking officer in the military, and I plan to use your talents in that position."

"You do, do you?" Teal responded, raising one eyebrow.

"I do. Your wife said I could."

"Well in that case, so be it," Teal chuckled, obviously unfazed, and went back to the little black mare.

Ardenai sat writing a letter to Ah'nora that evening and wondering if there was anything anymore that wasn't hard. He fooled with the thing for an hour, then two, decided no matter what he said, how he phrased it, he was going to sound egocentric or barking mad, maybe both, so he finally folded it, sealed it, and put it in a packet to send out with the next ship to Calumet. He wondered if he'd do any better face to face, remembered his miserable, unromantic proposal to Io, and decided he probably wouldn't. At least at this distance Ah'nora couldn't take a swing at him or laugh in his face. He had to hope Ah'din's ideas had merit, because he sure didn't have any of his own.

It was well past dark when Marion's face appeared saying they were in orbit. Ardenai said he'd scramble up on the next pass, and in less than an hour he was aboard Belesprit, being hugged by Marion and Oonah, greeted by Moonsgold, and half an hour after that he and Marion were sitting by the friction fires in the royal apartments. Kehailan said he had things to finish up, and that he would be down in the next few hours.

"It's just as well," Ardenai said, uncorking a bottle of wine. "Would you like to start drinking now, or after you've heard what I have to say?"

"Oh crap," Marion groaned. "Better start now. What's up?"

"As you may or may not know," Ardenai prefaced, filling Marion's glass a little more than usual, "There isn't just the one Tactical Cruiser, there will be thirteen when they're finished. Five are available now. I was hoping you could look at this list of five names that Io and Teal and I came up with and tell me if you think they would all be willing to take a ship. Kee doesn't count, of course. He's stuck with one. So, the other four."

Marion looked pleased and a little puzzled. "Sure," he said. He took the list, set it on the table, cleaned his glasses with his breath on the front of his shirt, and picked up the list. "Um hm, um hm, um..." and silence. He put the list down, picked up his wine, picked up the list. Put the list down, finished the wine, and looked over his glasses at Ardenai, who was sitting with his arms behind his head, legs stretched out in front of him – watching.

For a long time they sat there together, old and trusted friends. No motives to suspect. Marion was chasing his own wild ideas around in his head, trying to catch one for a talking point and Ardenai was wearing his patient, you'll-get-this-sooner-or-later teacher's look. Marion drained his glass and poured himself another before he said a word.

"Permanently?" he asked.

"If you want."

"Lots of science stuff on these? I do love the science stuff."

"Lots."

"Why?"

"Bit of a dust-up with the Lebonathis or I miss my guess. After that, whatever's needed."

"Oh. One for each of the AEW?"

"Um hm."

"That's good. Bonfire should be on that list."

"She is. If she wants to be. Her ship's not ready yet."

"What if I don't like it?"

"You can go back to Belesprit, or I will build you whatever you want."

"These are Equi ships, not Seventh Galactic Alliance?"

"Equi on loan as needed to the SGA, but if you take one, you will be working for the Equi government first, the SGA second."

"I'm already doing that."

"Pretty much."

"OK." He stuck out his hand and Ardenai shook it Terren fashion.

"Thank you, Marion. I feel better. What about the rest of the list?"

"I like it."

"Good. I'd like to try to get all five people here by tomorrow at high sun when these ships are dedicated."

"Good luck," Marion snorted.

And that's exactly what they had. Cadence's ship was laying over for some minor telemetry repairs, Ulric was meandering in from SEGaS 7 and said he could turn up the burners a little to be there, and Mecklin was on turnaround to Calumet. He got off as his ship went on, and with the ship went the letter to Ah'nora. It gave Ardenai a cold feeling in the pit of his stomach and he resisted the wild urge to call it back or have Mecklin's First Officer tear it up. He didn't, but just barely.

Kehailan arrived in his father's apartments an hour after dawn and found five people sitting around the dining room table eating first breakfast and more or less waiting for him. "I want all of you to know that I am grateful," Ardenai was saying, "and that this is a temporary assignment. If you like the ship and the ship likes you, she is yours, but if in two seasons – four months – you want to go back to your old assignment or on to a new one, you may do so with the thanks of Equus and the SGA."

"Not likely I'll be looking back," Ulric chuckled. "Amberia is honored."

"As is Corvus," Cadence nodded. "Thank you for thinking of me."

"And your wife," Ardenai smiled, "We're hoping you ladies come as a pair."

"We do," she smiled. "Again, and more so this time, thank you. Merri is pregnant, and we do hate being apart."

"And you, Mecklin?" Ardenai asked.

"Truth be told, I'm happy where I am, but I am also happy to serve, and who knows, I may grow to like the new as well as I like the old, though it is not in the nature of Calumets to do so." He smiled, and gave the Firstlord a deep, respectful nod. "Thank you for including us."

"And that leaves us these two," Ardenai said with a palm up gesture of inclusion. "Marion Eletsky is going to represent Terren for the time being, and Kehailan of Equus is the one who designed the ships you are about to accept."

Kehailan looked a little startled when Marion's name was mentioned, but to his credit and his father's vast relief, he said nothing, smiled and greeted the others, graciously accepting their congratulations and good wishes.

"Dedication is in six hours, so meet me back here in four. The priestesses who just walked in will show you to chambers where you can get a bath, a nap, more to eat, and try on your new uniforms. They're programmed into the refabricators. Black britches, black boots. The tunics should be cut like standard issue SGA dress blues – the ones with the banded collar, but they will be deep purple, with the seven chevrons of the Firstlord sloping on each shoulder and a silver python on the right sleeve. If they don't look like that, call someone – your refabricator's malfunctioning."

Ardenai spent the next two hours explaining his theories on the Lebonathi and the Telenir to Marion and Kehailan, then contacted Bashkir to let him know that the more publicity that went out about this new fighting wing the better. Hopefully the Lebonathi would listening.

"They go home tomorrow," Bashkir said, and breathed a sigh of relief. "They go home tomorrow. Though it is not my usual habit, I plan on getting very drunk."

The appointed time found Ardenai bathed and brushed, and making final adjustments to his new uniform. Though in most ways it fit the description of the other command uniforms, his had fuller sleeves, slightly gathered at the shoulders, cuffed at the wrists, and open down the outsides of the arms – requirement of the office. He looked in the mirror and had to admit that his arms did look very much better than they had before. There was almost no sign of scarring, just those wide, gold bands imbedded deep in his flesh. Oddly enough they never bothered him, though he wasn't sure why. It seemed like they ought to. He added the circlet and bracelets, skipped the heavy gold chevron and the throwing knives, and went downstairs to greet the others. A good looking group of people. One more piece in place.

When he went to get Ah'krill she begged off going, saying she wasn't feeling well, and she looked it. That made him uneasy. He hated asking Ah'din to come to the city, but he'd feel better when she'd looked in on the high priestess.

When they arrived at the appointed place Ah'riodin was there as she'd said she would be and with her, Gideon, Teal and Criollo. The subterranean shipyards were immense and Io reasoned that the boys would enjoy seeing them. Ardenai was pleased. He was grateful to have his beautiful and perceptive wife as well as the formidable new Master Captain to help him with the pleasantries, and he always loved showing Gideon new things. In this case he could show him off a little, as well. He was filling out into a handsome young man, and a very charming one.

The stage set for the dedication was extravagant, with one of the huge cruisers swathed in purple and silver fabric to be revealed at the appropriate time. The ceremony itself was lavish and the place was thronging with dignitaries and military figures. Ardenai realized he had to stay sharp when all he really wanted was a nap. He chided himself for being selfish. These good people had been slaving away unseen for months and years on these ships, and this was their time to celebrate. He was here to help them do that, not the other way around. He found himself smiling and shaking hands in half a dozen different ways, speaking two or three different languages despite the universal translators, and introducing his wife and son, Teal and his son, to what felt like hundreds of different people.

There was beautiful music written by Master Composer Anseri – an overture for what he promised was a suite called The Thirteenth Dragonhorse – and Ardenai felt the compliment to the roots of his soul. Again, as always these days, he felt the weight and the light of his people and his worlds.

At the appropriate time he lined up the captains beside him and said, "This is a special pleasure for me. Years before I knew I was rising to be Firstlord, I watched my talented son as he came up with the design for these ships, and I was honored when it was accepted by the mighty shipyards at Andal to be their celebration project for the Thirteenth Dragonhorse." There was a deafening roar from the crowd, and Ardenai stepped back and applauded with them. Kehailan nodded graciously and smiled, and only those closest to him could see the color which rose in his face. "The SGA and Equi officers beside me have graciously consented to command the first five ships. Ah'calla Mecklin Pentro of Calumet, Ulric Hamar of Amberia, Cadence Holofernes of Corvus, Marion Eletsky of Terren, and Ah'ree Kehailan Ardenai of Equus." Again there was a mighty roar, and this time all the commanders shared the spotlight. "When all the cruisers are on line I am hoping that a pilot will represent each of the affined worlds, because it is our affinity which makes us great. And now, if all is ready to reveal this magnificent vessel, we are more than ready to be awestruck."

There came the thunder of Equi ceremonial drums and the cover raised slowly in thirteen places, revealing a graceful ship with long wings swept up and back, forming the two outside pieces of the elevated tail section. As the cover was removed, the wings began to rise and flare out, like a Sea Falcon taking flight, until they were above the shoulders of the ship – firing position – seven hundred and fifty feet wingtip to wingtip. Ardenai hummed with admiration. In those mock-ups spinning in front of him the ship hadn't looked that big, but it was. It was huge. Eight hundred feet long, two hundred and twenty-five feet tall, two hundred feet across the fuselage. Nearly the size of a battle cruiser, but sleeker, infinitely faster and more maneuverable, and stunningly beautiful. The engineers had tweaked the design just a little, a slimmer nose with the body rising slightly above and slightly below it further back on the ship. Tighter quarters in the tactical wings so they fit closer to the sides for more speed, smaller target.

"Good God, Kehailan, that's a flying wet dream!" Marion breathed, raising a communal chuckle from those closest to him. "Sorry," he whispered. "Nice ship my friend. Well done!"

By the time the tours were over, congratulations extended to one and all, and the dignitaries had begun to leave, the commanders were able to take their leave as well and head up by shuttle to the space port where four of the five ships waited. This last one would be tractored, trundled and tugged up to the surface after everyone had left. Its engines would be started, and it would join the others in space dock.

"Best of luck," Ardenai said, giving each of them a deep nod of respect. "Train fast."

He said no more, and was quiet for the trip to the Great House, content listen to the others discuss the day while Teal flew Dominus. He was tired, and used to getting more sleep than he'd gotten in the last two days. It made him wonder if he was getting a little soft.

It amused him, and comforted him somehow, that when the five of them walked into the royal apartments which had felt so cavernous and echoing not long ago, they now felt like home. Not Canyon keep, of course, but familiar and comfortable. Ah'din had arrived with Ah'brianne, who was going out as they went in.

"I need to go down to Master Breton's room and turn in some work I accidentally left at home last time," she said. "I promised Master Breton I would do that, and he comes in early. I want it to be there when he does." She promised she would be back for dinner, which was just being laid, and trotted off down the hall.

Criollo went to change clothes, Gideon to find Lionel, and Io dropped her cloak over a chair and went to help Ah'din with the table. Ardenai peeled off the jewelry and uniform jacket and was just getting really comfortable on the couch near the fire, Teal pouring them a glass of wine, when the screaming started.

ELADEUS! Help me! Teal, Ardenai, HELP ME, PLEASE!

The wine bottle was dropped and both men were at a dead run before it hit the floor. Thankfully they knew which direction Ah'brianne had gone. They could still hear her screaming in their heads, and then – nothing. They were a hundred feet from the school when Bashkir bolted half-dressed out of a side corridor and flung an arm to his left, toward a seldom used alcove behind the library. "There! She has to be there!"

Ardenai never slowed down. He jerked Addur off Ah'brianne, broke his neck and cast him aside like a rag, all in one swift, terrible motion as his momentum swung him into a one-shouldered collision with the wall. In another single motion he had bounced off and knelt beside Teal and Ah'brianne. Her blouse had been ripped open, her skirt ripped off. She had been bitten until she bled, and her face had been battered by repeated blows. She'd fought for a while before she started screaming for help.

"She's not breathing," Teal groaned, and began to breathe for her. In a few moments she choked and sobbed, and he caught her up in his arms and sprinted for the sanecere, calling frantically in his head for Ah'din.

Ardenai got enough control of himself that he could think over his outrage, and reached for Basra, who was crumpled in a shadowed corner of the small alcove. He seized him by one arm and jerked the boy's head around. His face had been pounded nearly to a pulp. "I tried," he whispered. "He wouldn't stop." He managed to get one eye open and looked without turning his head to where Addur lay, semen turning to urine as his body relaxed in death. "Dead?"

"Very," Ardenai said through his teeth.

"Praise to the Gods," Basra mumbled through bleeding lips and broken teeth. "I have…been alive for one minute when he has not. For one minute…I am free..." and he collapsed onto the floor at the Firstlord's feet.

Bashkir was absolutely motionless over Addur's body, and snarling deep in his throat – as terrifying a sound as ever Ardenai had heard come out of him. For a long minute the Firstlord was so numb he couldn't think. "I am open for suggestions," he managed.

"Time for me to take this trash upstairs and determine how they got out," Bashkir growled. "That one, I think," he jerked his chin at Basra, "needs a fair hearing. Even Ah'brianne couldn't have done that much damage. She needs you, and I'm sure Teal does. You go, take the boy for some help. I will get dressed and take care of this."

Others had come in response to the screams, and someone said she would clean up the blood and the urine, and someone else said they would help with… something. Ardenai just nodded mutely, picked Basra up in his arms, and carried him to the sanecere.

When he got there Ah'brianne was lying unconscious on a bed, face bleeding, hair in a tangle, and Teal was beside her, holding her hand and sobbing – deeply, silently – tears streaming down his face. He looked up as Ardenai came in and though he didn't say it, the thought hammered its way into Ardenai's brain. *This is your fault.*

Ardenai just squeezed his eyes shut and accepted it. He laid Basra on a bed and came to stand on the other side of Ah'brianne. "Where is Ah'din?" he said, trying not to fall apart with his kinsman.

"Right here," she said breathlessly, wiping away tears of her own as she hurried in. "I had to wake Pythos, and he was deep asleep."

And there he was, hissing with dismay, yellow eyes filled with tears. "What hass happened?" he asked quietly. "Who did thiss to our Ah'brianne?"

"Prince Addur," Ardenai said, "and he has paid the price for rape."

"Thee killed him. Good," Pythos hissed, still looking at Ah'brianne. He touched her face with frond-like fingers and gentle tongue, looking at the damage to her hands and arms before turning to the two men. "Out. Now. Quickly! We cannot have a settling from thiss."

Teal groaned and dropped his head into his hands, and Ardenai took him by the shoulder. "We have to go," he said urgently.

Teal wrested his shoulder out of Ardenai's grasp, preceding him into the hallway, and when Ardenai stepped out Teal turned and gave him such a look of pure hatred that Ardenai reared back like he'd been struck. "I know you're upset..." he began, and Teal's hard right fist connected with his face, slamming him into the wall. His head snapped back, hit the alabaster, and he slid down the wall onto his butt, legs drawn up in front of him. In a few moments he shook his head, blotted at the blood oozing out of his nose and mouth with the back of his hand, and looked up into Teal's livid countenance. "As I was saying…I know you're upset, but how is this my fault?"

"Figure it out," Teal snarled, jerked him to his feet and hauled back to hit him again. This time, Ardenai's left hand caught the fist, and his right caught Teal's shoulder.

"No." he said. "No. On the outside chance that this is my fault somehow, I'll give you the first one. But don't hit me again. Shit, I bit my tongue."

"You swore," Teal said, and the anger went out of his face. "I have never heard you swear."

"I've never had someone I love turn on me without an explanation. Please, please…how is this my fault? Teal, I just killed someone over this. I just broke the neck of a young man who had his whole life in front of him."

Teal's hands relaxed, and Ardenai dropped his. Teal took the First-lord's face in his palms and studied it for a few moments, then pulled him into a fierce hug that Ardenai returned. "I killed someone, Teal. Again, I have killed someone," he said quietly, and when Gideon and Criollo found them, they were crying in each other's arms. The boys didn't ask.

The four of them were sitting on the floor outside the sanecere, staring at nothing when Bashkir came down the hall and joined them, folding his legs in front of him and saying quietly, “They caused a commotion inside. When the guards went in to check, they slipped out.”

Teal looked up with exhausted and grief stricken eyes. “What kind of a commotion?”

“They set a bed on fire in their room.” Bashkir replied, turning to include the Firstlord. He squinted, and said, “Do I want to know what happened to your face?”

“I’ll tell you when I find out,” Ardenai sighed. “How did the Lebonathis take Addur’s death?”

“I dropped him at their feet, told them what he had done, and they did not say one word. They just dragged him inside and closed the door. I will check again in the morning if you would like.”

“Did they ask about Basra?” The Firstlord was still shaking his head slightly, trying to get it to clear, and hearing his own voice created a painful vibration. He opened both eyes and Bashkir was looking at him with some concern.

“Are you sure you’re all right?”

“I’m fine, I just need some ice. Basra?”

“They didn’t ask and I didn’t volunteer.”

“Good. If they do ask, don’t answer. I need to decide first what I’m going to do with him.”

“I’m going to go get all of you something warm to drink, and a cloak and some ice for the Firstlord,” Bashkir said, rising to his feet. “Master Captain Teal, why don’t you come and help me, since I would like to speak to you briefly about what we need to do next.”

Teal hesitated, and Ardenai gave him an affirmative nod. “If they call us, I will call you,” he said, and Teal rose and went toward the kitchen with Bashkir.

When they were out of earshot and completely by themselves Bashkir turned and glared at him. “It was you who hit him in the face, wasn’t it? He wouldn’t have taken it from anyone else.”

Teal thought about it for a moment, and nodded. "I did. I blame him for what happened to Ah'brianne. Precious Equus, Bashkir, the girl was dead because Ardenai…"

"I don't care why you hit him!" Bashkir exclaimed. "I don't care whether you blame him for this or not! He is no longer just your best friend, he is your sovereign lord. He could kill you for what you did to him, and instead his heart is breaking because he is a soft and tender soul. You cannot forget that, ever, for even a moment, because he's not going to change. His is the courage of compassion, and when given the choice he is always, always going to be merciful. He did exactly what a diplomat is supposed to do, he used his own best judgment, and it is your job to protect him and support him, regardless. If you can't do that, Teal, it is time for you to resign and go home to your wife and devote your life to wine making. Then, and only then will you simply be Ardi's best friend again."

Teal just stood there trembling like a beaten horse, and Bashkir was quick with an arm around his shoulders. "Teal, this is new for all of us. Ardenai is not who he was, and you can't be, either. He trusts you completely or you wouldn't be the first Master Captain in the history of Equus. Of all the things you cannot do, you cannot cause him to doubt you, and you cannot cause him to doubt himself. Question him, yes, question his decisions. That's your job. Passing judgment, no. Come on, let's go find something hot to drink. None of you got any supper, did you?"

"No," Teal sighed, grateful that Bashkir was giving him time to recover, and they walked a bit in silence. "I…can't remember having ever struck someone in anger, and when I do, it has to be him? Why Ardenai? I would die for him and he knows it. He would die for me. Why him?"

"Because you trusted him. You thought you knew him, and he took your life. He has dragged you from what you knew and loved, to what you do not know and cannot predict. Because he used your love for him to do that, and because you are terrified for his safety, and Ah'brianne's safety, you're a little off your best pace right now. You'll get back on track. I have faith in you. How about some mugs of fresh, hot cream of mushroom soup?"

"Thanks," Teal said, and managed a smile. "Really. Thank you."

"All part of the job," Bashkir chuckled.

We can see her now. I will wait for thee, Brother Mine.

Thank you. I'll be right there. "We can see Ah'brianne."

"Good. You go. I'll bring the soup and the ice. And remember, children are resilient."

That much Teal knew was true. He'd known Ah'brianne her whole life, had stood with Timor while he held Ah'mae on the birthing stool, had held the baby that first day and promised with Ah'din that they would raise her as their own if anything were to happen to Timor and Ah'mae, as Timor and Ah'mae had done for them when Criollo was born.

When he got back he realized the boys had already gone in, and he stood for a moment with Ardenai, steeling himself for whatever he was about to see and hear in there. "Before we go in," he said, looking into his friend's kind and worried eyes, "I want to apologize to you with all my heart and beg your forgiveness, Dragonhorse."

Ardenai just smiled and held him close for a minute. "I accept that you had your own good reasons. Please, don't ever let the Dragonhorse replace Ardenai in your heart, Teal. I know Bashkir chewed your hay for you, I know things around us have changed, but our relationship is perfect the way it is, and that's why I will always want you close to keep me in line. Come on, let's go see our girl, shall we?"

When they walked in Ah'din was to one side and Gideon was sitting beside Ah'brianne holding her hand in both of his, and she was laughing. "Ahimsa, you two, thanks for the rescue," she said, as though they'd headed off some runaway stock. "I want you to know that Basra did what he could to help me, but Addur was really strong. Basra did buy me some time. If he hadn't, Addur would probably have killed me."

Teal let all his air out in a huge whoosh and collapsed into the nearest chair, trying to keep Ah'brianne from seeing how badly he was shaking – trying to keep from screaming at the top of his lungs that Addur *had* killed her – that she had been dead when they got to her. After a moment he got his breath back. The look followed. "Why didn't you yell for help sooner, you crazy thing?"

She shrugged, winced, and laughed again. "I thought I could take him."

Ardenai burst out laughing, but Teal was not particularly amused. "Well, you couldn't, could you, and now you're…hurt."

"I hope you weren't going to say, 'ruined'," she replied, and suddenly she was sober. "Or, 'damaged'. I was raped, and I'm sad about that, and I'm sure it will take me some time to get over it, but I have Gideon, and he was raped every day of his life for years and look at him. If he can go through that year after year and be who he is, I can go through it once and go on being me." She smiled at Gideon and he gave her hand a little pat. Not too hard because her knuckles were bruised.

He had told her. Ardenai was stunned, and amazed, and impressed, as he always was at the things his son was capable of doing. He wanted to take them both in his arms and hold them there forever. Instead he gave Gideon a smile and a wink and went into the next little room, where the light was very dim and Pythos was taking care of Basra. His breathing was even and he appeared to be asleep. "How is he?" the Firstlord asked, just above a whisper.

"Much worse off than Ah'brianne."

"And was she …?"

"Had he impregnated her? No. Which ssaved me a terrible tassk. Thiss boy, hass been raped, time after time for yearss, jusst like Gideon wass, judging from the damage. He hass been beaten, molessted, abussed, ssodomized. All by his older brother, who sshould have been loving him and protecting him and teaching him."

Ardenai turned away and put his knuckles over his mouth, closing his eyes and pushing his thoughts into a semblance of order. The thought of raping a child always made him want to vomit. So, he had saved more than Ah'brianne. He had saved Basra, as well. And who knew who else. For Addur, he would shed no more tears. "I have instructed Bashkir not to give the Lebonathi any information about Basra until I have made a decision regarding him. Before that is final, I will want to talk to Girsu, and I will want you to talk to Girsu, as well."

"And have you any thoughtss on the matter?"

"I think so. I think, life in custody on Equus. It is certain he will not be going back with the rest of the delegation. They'd probably kill him. I need to go back out into the other room. I hear my sweet wife coming in with Timor and Ah'mae." He turned at the door and smiled back at the old physician. "I'm sorry we had to waken you from your sleep, Father. But thank you for staying so close."

"Where elsse would I be but with my hatchlingss?" he replied and shooed Ardenai out the door saying, "All iss well. Have ssome ssoup. Sleep. And put ssome ice on that love tap."

CHAPTER 9

When Ardenai looked in the next morning, Ah'brianne was sitting up in bed doing school work with Ah'win, and his son was speaking quietly with Basra. Ardenai wondered just how much Gideon would tell him about his own experiences, and if he could find it in his heart to befriend the young man to some degree. The rest of the delegation was leaving today and Basra would be left behind, along with Girsu, Jasreth, Samarra and Eridi.

Ardenai didn't do more than give Basra a nod and Ah'brianne a wink and a smile before closing the door and heading for the apartments of the high priestess. There were times he didn't like her very much, didn't really trust her that much, either. But the thought that Samarra might be drugging her, or slowly poisoning her, scared him, and he wanted to see for himself that she was all right.

He nodded to the Akoliti at the door and allowed himself to be gestured respectfully into a chair while he was announced. It was early yet, and he hadn't let her know he was coming. He was doing less and less of that lately – giving people time to plan a strategy before he got there. The thought made him want to chuckle. He became aware, with that keen sixth sense many Equi had, that he was being watched, and glanced over to see Samarra shrink back into the shadows. He wondered what she was thinking. Surely the word was out by now that Prince Basra was in custody and Prince Addur was dead by the Firstlord's hand.

Before he'd gone to his apartments last night, Ardenai had made it a point to go and see Halaf, to extend his regrets that the man had lost a nephew and Eridu a son. Interestingly enough, there hadn't been a lot of grief in the air. Grief was something one could smell. There was anger, certainly, indignation and frustration, but what had struck Ardenai most was the fact that Halaf had ranted about the impropriety of the Equi government sending home a prince in a shroud. "You need to take him home!" Halaf had grated. "You did this. You need to take him home and explain this to his father. You need to face the Mighty Lord Eridu." All very interesting, especially his parting shot. "Poor Princess Eridi will kill herself over the loss of her beloved brother and you will be responsible."

Not kraaling likely, Ardenai had thought, and his last ramble of the night had been to waken Ah'nis for a chat.

"Dragonhorse?" said a young priestess, and showed him into his mother's private audience chambers. She was in her usual spot by the window, where she could both see out, and see back into the room.

He nodded to her, but instead of gesturing him into the chair next to her at the small round table, she stood up and took his chin in her hand in that manner mothers have of examining their children. "What happened here?" she asked.

"Polo mallet," he said.

She studied it a bit longer. "I didn't realize they were making polo mallets with knuckles these days. How is Ah'brianne this morning?"

"I think she is going to be fine," Ardenai smiled, and his mother traced one of the dimples which creased his cheeks.

"You are a beautiful and gentle soul, Ardenai. I am so sorry that you had to kill someone last night. Poisonous creature that he was. He tried to get in here to see Eridi, you know. Of course Ah'nis wouldn't hear of it and neither would any of the rest of us. Still, a life is a life, and it is never easy to take one."

"Thank you," Ardenai said, and settled himself in the chair she indicated.

"What brings you? Though you are always welcome."

"You were feeling ill yesterday. I wanted to make sure you were all right. I do worry about you, you know."

"Tea?" she asked, gesturing toward the young akolyte. The girl came, poured the drinks, and took her place again near the door. "It's some Samarra brought me from Lebonath Tras," Ah'krill said, stirring in sugar and smiling blandly at her son. Alarm registered on Ardenai's face and his mother laughed in spite of herself. "How you ever win at cards is beyond me," she said, still chuckling softly. "I thought perhaps you were here because you are worried about what Samarra may be up to. I can assure you, she is not working her particular magic under my roof, nor yours, though she may think she is. We allow her to think so. It amuses us, and gives her something to do besides cry and beat her breast before her merciless God."

"Mother, you are one of the most perceptive people I know. What is her end game?" He paused and eyed the cup in his hand. "I can…drink this, can't I?"

"Yes, if you are comfortable doing so. If you are not, I will not think less of you. I was rather taken in by Samarra at the beginning of all things, and I can see where trusting me and saying her name at the same time might be difficult for you, especially given what happened to you. For that, I am deeply and eternally sorry."

The Firstlord looked into his cup for a moment, then up at his mother. "I do want you to know that…" he stopped, rethinking what he was about to say. What if telling his mother that he had offered Ah'nis his services would put more pressure on her to use them? She had said she didn't want a baby just now, and hers was the decision that mattered. "That I am grateful to the Eloi and especially to Ah'nis for your loving care of the Princess Eridi. Your attendance upon her has changed her life."

"And you have changed your opinion of Ah'nis in the process?"

Again, the Firstlord paused, sensing boggy footing ahead. "I have certainly come to respect her as the formidable woman she is, and I think Eridi is going to be just like her."

"A valuable commodity to have when you – what would the word be? Invade – the Lebonathi worlds. Probably not invade so much as just take over."

Ardenai just shook his head and laughed. "How do you know that?"

"You asked me what Samarra's end game is," Ah'krill smiled. "Since I know the answer to that, I also know what your response will be. By the way, I did not go yesterday because I want Samarra to think I'm still sipping her tea. If she's dosing me she has to stay close, does she not? It was well covered on the cosmoscope and I was duly impressed with you and my eldest grandson."

"Thank you. Apparently you have the situation well in hand. So tell me, Mother, what is Samarra's end game? Is it hers, is it theirs, and are we out front or trailing behind? What do you see as my part, and what do you see as yours? I've read the reports from the humanitarian junket, including what Sarkhan had to say about his participation. Especially illuminating if one reads between the lines." He studied her for a few heartbeats and was rewarded with a shrug of eyebrows and a slightly apologetic expression. "How best do we fit in?"

"You, have come a long way in the question-asking business since you left the classroom at Falconstones," Ah'krill said. "Let me tell you what I know, and what we are prepared to do."

They spoke for two hours, and for the first time Ardenai could sense that the high priestess was telling him the absolute truth. No hidden agenda. When he left, his mother looked at his teacup and laughed a merry and genuine laugh. He hadn't touched the contents.

He had returned to his study to make some notes and continue laying plans when a familiar voice said, "This is the Imperial Stormclass Tactical Cruiser Dragonhorse Thirteen," and Kehailan's smiling face appeared above Ardenai's desk.

"I always knew you were a quick study," Ardenai responded, returning the smile. Kehailan looked so happy. "How do you like her so far?"

"Marion said it best yesterday," Kehailan chuckled. "She's a flying ...well, you remember. Beautiful ship! Very responsive, very fast. All five of us are already flying maneuvers. We will be ready to go when you are, Sire. I am contacting you to let you know that the Lebonathi ship is an hour away from orbit. Cadence is providing escort."

"Good," Ardenai said, and even as he tried to have a normal conversation his heart was so overflowing with pride in this eldest son, so happy to see him happy, that he felt a little giddy, and hoped it didn't show. "Tell me, how did you determine which TC got which designation? I assume that honor was yours?"

"It was, yes. Mine is the only Dragon Horse," Kehailan said. "Ulric has the Dragon's Teeth, Mecklin has the Dragon's claws, Cadence has the Dragon's Hide, and Marion has the Dragon's Ass." He sat back in his command chair and roared with laughter at the expression which, however briefly, had crossed his father's face. "Gotcha," he said, wiping his eyes. "It's boring, really. Ulric has number one because Amberia is first alphabetically. Mecklin has number four with Calumet, Cadence has number five for Corvus and Marion has number ten for Terren. He has the Dragon's Tail, by the way. I have number thirteen, because my father is the Thirteenth Dragonhorse, and I wanted to honor him."

"You have done much more than that," Ardenai said. "That chair suits you, my boy. Please let me know when the Lebonathi ship arrives, and this afternoon I'd like to go for a gallop, if you have the time for me."

"I will make the time for you," Kehailan smiled, "and bring my little brother. I want to show him my ship."

The joy and the pride in those words buoyed Ardenai up enough to get him through the next difficult hours. *Soon they will be gone. Soon they will be gone.* Ardenai keep that little litany trotting at the back of his brain. Still, when Cadence checked in to say that the Lebonathi ship was in orbit and ready to take on passengers, the Firstlord felt a slight jolt in his stomach. How quickly now would all of this unfold? It wasn't wise to try to look too far ahead in predicting, he knew that. He sent his thoughts to Gideon, who rose with apologies to Master Breton saying, "Please forgive my departure. The Dragonhorse has need of me."

Io rose from a meeting with the governance branch of the Eloi, saying, "My husband needs me for a short conformity. Please continue and I will return."

Together they presented themselves in the uniform of the Dragonhorse to the shunt bay where the big Lebonathi shuttle crouched on its landing pads. They stood respectfully in a line: Bashkir, Teal, Gideon, Io, Ardenai, five members of the Horse Guard on the other side, and watched as four more members of the Horse Guard loaded the coffin containing Addur's remains onto the shuttle, with Akadia and Hassuna weeping loudly if unconvincingly along behind. Next, grim faced, came Halaf and Naram, with Brak behind them, looking none too happy to be leaving, and then the last dozen or so members of the delegation, servants without name or rank. To them, Bashkir nodded and smiled. Not a single word was spoken. The shuttle was rotated into position on the carosello and when the signal was given that it was clear to launch, it moved slowly out of the shunt bay, accelerated, and vanished into the blue Equi sky.

They watched it until it was gone, then Ardenai turned to Bashkir with a sigh of relief and said, "You are now off duty for the next twenty-four hours, or however long you want to be." He raised his voice and added, "Be it known far and wide that the Master of the Great House is not to be disturbed by anyone until day after tomorrow. Maybe longer."

"Well," Bashkir said with a sheepish smile, "I am expecting one person. Her ship is in the middle of a major reassignment, so if anybody sees Oonah Pongo, Please see that she finds me, Please. We have plans."

"Done on the first please," Teal laughed. "Dragonhorse, what are your plans this afternoon?"

"Gideon and I are going joyriding with Kehailan. Would you like to come along?"

"I have joyrides of my own to take this afternoon," he smiled. "Can we meet over dinner, or after dinner?"

"Of course," Ardenai nodded. "Wife?"

"There is a meeting going on without me, and I need to get back. You two have fun."

"Now I feel quite frivolous," Ardenai said, steering Gideon by the shoulder toward Dominus. "Teal and Io are both in meetings of import, and we are going to go play."

"You need to play," Gideon said. "And do tell it straight this time, what happened to your cheekbone? You look like you got kicked by a draft horse."

"Kind of felt like it," Ardenai muttered. They were on board and he had said, "IEC Dominus, requesting permission to launch for rendezvous with Dragonhorse Thirteen," before he turned to Gideon and said, "Before I tell you, you need to know that Teal is Ah'brianne's fostering father. If anything were to happen to Timor and Ah'mae..."

"I know that," Gideon said. "Did he hit you? Nobody else could leave a mark like that."

"Now, don't get upset..."

"IEC Dominus, you are cleared for launch. Vectors programmed. Speed programmed. Destination programmed. Enjoy your flight, Dragonhorse."

"Thank you, Cutter." He bought himself a little more time as they turned and launched, because that part always made Gideon a little sick. When they were underway and clear of traffic Ardenai said, "It's been awhile since we've had time to do any flying together. How about after we leave Kehailan we take some time and do some maneuvering?"

He chanced a look, and Gideon's face had not changed. "Yes, all right, he hit me," Ardenai sighed. "Carefully placed, as it turns out, but I felt it."

"Why in kraa would he do that, Dad?"

"He blames me for what happened to Ah'brianne, and I can't fault him for that, even though I don't agree with him. It's footprints in the sand. Let it go."

"He had no damned right to do that!"

Ardenai spun in his chair and glared at Gideon. "He had every right! Teal and I have been best friends for ninety-five years! If he thought I finally had a punch in the face coming, I'm glad it was him who gave it to me. Now let it go, I mean it."

There was a loaded silence for the space of five minutes, then Gideon said, "I'm sorry. That must have really hurt."

"It did. Do you want to fly maneuvers before supper?"

"I do," the boy smiled. "This thing isn't going to quit on us in flight again, is it, because that scared the hell out of me, and being taken by those giant nomads after we landed was no fun, either."

"Let me show you what I did to get us down in one piece," Ardenai said, and the whys and wherefores of that explanation lasted the time it took them to reach tractoring range of Dragonhorse. Once on board the afternoon sped by in greetings and tours, and speed tests and maneuvering demonstrations that left Ardenai very impressed and Gideon slightly nauseated.

They were running side by side with Dragonhorse Four, discussing capabilities, and possibilities, when Mecklin said, "I would like to be home for my brother's wedding next month. He lost his wife in a flood a few years back, and it has taken him a long time to get back on his feet and fall in love again."

For the second time in a day, Ardenai felt a little punch in his gut. "We'll see that you get there," he smiled. "Is he marrying anyone we would know?"

"You might," Mecklin said. "She lost her husband and son in that same flood. Her family has run the main house for – oh, yes!" he exclaimed, "Of course you do! He's marrying Ah'nora. Surely you know Ah'nora."

To his vast credit and relief, Ardenai didn't do any of the things which immediately occurred to him. "We know her very well," he answered, pleased that, although his voice sounded hollow in his own head, it had about the same pitch as usual. "Captain Mecklin, would you be kind enough to scramble over here so I can talk to you in person for a bit? There are just a few details I'd like to clear up with you."

"Of course," Mecklin said. He was obviously taken back by the abruptness of the request, but he nodded and broke the connection.

Gideon rolled an eye at his father.

Not a word, not a thought. Came the immediate response. *Stay with your brother.*

Ardenai excused himself from the bridge crew and made his way to the conference room, and when Mecklin appeared he found the Firstlord staring out the window.

"Dragonhorse," he said with a respectful nod, "Have I done something?"

"No," Ardenai said quickly. "No, but I have."

Mecklin looked more puzzled. "Firstlord?"

"That letter I sent back to Calumet with your ship? In it, I asked Ah'nora to marry me, which could be awkward, given the circumstances."

Mecklin looked stunned, then his eyes dropped and he said. "I understand. I will contact my brother at once."

"No!" Ardenai exclaimed, waving his hands, "No, no, no! Don't contact your brother, contact the ship. She's still days out from Calumet. We have to get that letter back! Ah'nora cannot get that letter, it would tear her in two."

"You are Firstlord. You are the Thirteenth Dragonhorse," Mecklin said, only beginning to comprehend what was happening. "My brother is a saddlemaker."

"And does he love Ah'nora?"

"With all his heart."

"Does she love him? So far as you can tell, does she love him?"

Mecklin nodded. "I know she does. She lights up when she sees him."

"Well then, they belong together, don't they?" Ardenai huffed. He sat down, folding his arms and looking glum.

"Do you love the lady, Dragonhorse?" The twitch at the corners of the Captain's mouth said he might feel the question impertinent, but his eyes didn't waiver.

"I do. Very much. Which is why I want her to have a home where she is comfortable, and someone who loves her to come home to her at night, who will give her a little daughter to go with the son she carries…" He heard Mecklin suck in his breath, and realized fully for the first time why Teal had found it necessary to pop him a good one. "Probably should have let him hit me again," he muttered under his breath. "I'm sorry. I have no idea why that came out of my mouth – I really don't. I suppose ignoring it is out of the question."

"She's *pregnant*? And you know she's settled because you …?"

Ardenai, despite himself, looked defensive. "It was an honorable mating, Mecklin, and one she agreed to, so don't look at me like that. There was a battle to be fought and a chance I would die without a High Equi son. She was gracious, and brave, and beautiful." he felt his eyes filling with tears and realized that this decision was going to hurt awhile. "And yes, she is carrying my child, and I will want to see him, though… what is your brother's name?"

"Rustem." Mecklin said quietly. "His name is Rustem."

"Like Ah'nora's father," Ardenai said, mostly to himself. "I will want to see him, and hear of him, but Rustem will be his father, as Krush was, and is, father to me – every day – and that is as it should be, not some half-legend who appears out of the sky from time to time, who is there for some of the big things but none of the small things that mean so much. Ah'nora deserves to be a first wife, as Io is a first wife, not a second wife, or a wife who either stays in a strange place far from home, or in a familiar place far from her husband. She deserves a good man who adores her. If she loves your brother, then that is who she will have. But if we don't get that letter stopped, it's going to make a mess of what they have planned, and that is the last thing I want."

He reached to his right at the center of the table and tapped a small circle with his fingertips. "What is your first officer's name again?"

"Kiger."

Ardenai nodded. "I should have remembered that." A spiral appeared in front of him and he said, "Computator relay routing, high priority, to Seventh Galactic Alliance Ship, Sweetwater, from Imperial Stormclass Tactical Cruiser, Dragonhorse Thirteen. I am Ah'krill Ardenai Morningstar, and I am Firstlord of Equus. Acting Captain Kiger, a packet was given into your keeping from me personally, to be delivered to a certain party on Calumet. I need you to find that packet and, in front of witnesses and with Captain Mecklin watching, I want you to destroy that packet with the seal unbroken. Under no circumstances can that packet reach Calumet. When you have done as I ask, I want you to send a duplicate history, by crys-tel, to me at the Great House. Please do this immediately, with the thanks of the Equi government and myself." He tapped the circle again and looked up at Mecklin, who had no trouble reading the grief in his eyes and the set of his mouth.

"Are you sure you want to do this?"

Ardenai nodded. "Want, not being the operative word, but yes, I do. The least said of this the better, and certainly nothing is to be said to your brother about whose baby Ah'nora is carrying. That is her story to tell if she chooses. Would you rather I set my head against you and left you remembering only a disembodied packet?"

"No," Mecklin smiled. "I prefer to cherish the memory of a leader choosing the joy of two simple people over his own happiness."

"As long as you keep it to yourself I don't care how you remember it," Ardenai muttered. "I've taken enough of your time. You may go back to your ship. And Captain, keep sending that message until you get a reply, and then contact me, because if that letter gets through, you're the one who's going to have to fix things between Ah'nora and your brother. I'm out of it."

Mecklin nodded respectfully, turned on his heel and walked out, leaving Ardenai alone in the conference room.

The Firstlord put his elbows on the table, dropped his forehead into his hands, and spent a long time with his eyes closed, seeing Ah'nora, and trying to figure out whether he was relieved, or broken-hearted. He sighed deeply with relief when two arms came around his chest and Io's familiar mop of curls came to rest against the side of his head. "Hard afternoon, Love?" she asked, and kissed his cheek.

"Gideon?"

"Kehailan. I was through with my meeting and your sons thought you needed a hug. So, Mecklin's brother is marrying Ah'nora?" Ardenai nodded. "And you're going to step aside and let him?" It wasn't asked as a challenge, merely a question, and Ardenai nodded again. "Why?"

"Because it is more the right thing to do than marrying her would have been." Ardenai sighed, kissing her hands. He sat up, patting the chair beside him. "Io, I told you I was going to fight for the right to have just one wife, and the second it felt more convenient not to fight, the second I thought you approved, I was ready to go back on my word. I have some very real feelings for Ah'nora, but I wanted to marry her because it would have been easy. She would have been at the far end of the alliance and I would be home with you. What kind of a life would that be for her?"

"Women have given up more to be with less," Io said, but she leaned into him, and he put his arms around her as she dropped her head under his chin, rocking her slowly back and forth as he stared out the window.

"I promised Gideon a flying lesson," he said after a bit. "I better get at it."

"If you're sure you're all right I will stay awhile. Kee promised me a tour of his ship, and I want to see it. I'll scramble down and be home for supper." There was a pause. "Ardi?"

"I, Sweet Wife, will be just fine. I'll see you at dinner."

▲ ▲ ▲ ▲ ▲ ▲ ▲

If anyone else knew about the Firstlord's afternoon they didn't mention it, and the conversation at dinner revolved around Kehailan's ship, Gideon's near collision with a space buoy, Criollo's confidence that Jasreth was going to be caught up with her class before the end of the school year, and Ah'din's assurances that Ah'krill seemed in no way influenced by any sort of herb or potion.

The wind began to howl around the edges of the ancient structure as another storm blew in from the Straits of Viridia, and the family retired to the bathing pools for a hot soak and quiet conversation. It seemed so normal, and Ardenai felt his stress beginning to melt away in the warm, gently circulating water. "Ah'brianne is feeling a lot better," Gideon said, flipping a little water at Lionel, who snapped at it from one of the rocks at the edge of the pools. "Pythos says she can go home tomorrow, and on Hormigyre she will be back in school."

"Timor and Ah'mae have gone back to Lee keep?" Ardenai asked, pulling his shoulder away from the corner of the boulder he was leaning against. Why was his shoulder sore? Ah yes, he'd bounced off a wall breaking someone's neck, hadn't he? Pleasant thought.

"Ah'brianne chased them off right after lunch," Ah'din said, lounging in front of her husband with her head on his collar bone. "Timor thinks there's a protoped in the neighborhood and Ah'mae is worried about her beautiful woolies. Ah'brianne is made of stone, they know that."

Ardenai tilted his head and looked at his sister. "Weren't you going to go home this afternoon? I mean, really home?"

"I have one more thing to do," she said, snuggling closer to Teal. "Once that's done, you are all one hundred percent on your own."

"As it should be," Ardenai said, and the talk drifted to the afternoon meetings, and what had been decided, and what strategies were going to come into play.

In the pre-dawn hours of the morning Ardenai heard his sister's quiet footsteps going by his study. He reasoned that whatever it was, she either didn't want to worry him or didn't want him to know what she was up to. She'd spent a large part of the afternoon with the Eloi, and it probably had something to do with them. In any case he trusted her implicitly, and his thoughts were deeply wrapped around a computator program that would lay down a pattern of astricting pulses as well as wave cannon fire to best effect using just telepathy, so he pushed it to the back of his mind.

Ah'din made her way to the apartments of the Eloi, and having been admitted, to a place where they adjoined the apartments of High Priestess Ah'krill. There, she waited. Just at dawn, when both priestesses and Akoliti awoke for morning prayers, Samarra came down the passage carrying a pot of tea and two cups on a tray. Ah'din fell in silently behind her and followed her to the chambers which Ah'nis shared with Eridi.

"I have tea for you from High Priestess Ah'krill," she said, and was admitted, though the door was left slightly ajar. She put the steaming pot of tea on the small round table which each room held and asked, "Would you like me to pour?"

"Thank you," Ah'nis said, seeming busy with her long blonde hair. "You say this is from Ah'krill?" Ah'nis turned from the mirror and looked at Samarra face on. "You're sure it's not from your little bag of tricks, compliments of Halaf and Naram?"

Samarra put the pot down and took a step back, hands reaching into the sleeves of her flowing robes as she bowed. "I do not know what you are talking about," she said, still nodding deeply and stepping back again. "Halaf and Naram are gone, sent home by the Dragonhorse with the body of Prince Addur. This is your usual morning tea, sent by Ah'krill to honor you and Princess Eridi."

"Well, thank you, but since Akadia said you might try something like this, I think I'll just have it tested," Ah'nis said, and suddenly there was a long, lethal looking knife with a curved blade in Samarra's hand. Ah'nis stepped quickly back and Samarra regained the step she'd taken earlier.

"What a shame," she said in her singsong voice, "that you pushed poor little Princess Eridi so far from her own true beliefs that she thought she had to take your life to save your soul. And then, grief-stricken over what she had done, she took her own life as well. Poor child. How sad. How sad that your Dragonhorse did not accept our gift. None of this would have happened, no lives would have been lost if he had taken Eridi to his bed as he was supposed to, and then taken her and her baby home. Now, he will have to take her home anyway, and he will have to bury you, which will make him very sad, I know. I am sorry to do this, but we need room to grow, room for our faith to grow, room for food to grow." she was moving ever closer with the knife, and Eridi opened the door to her sleeping room just as Ah'nis's back hit the wall beside it.

"Close the door!" the priestess exclaimed, and Eridi did, momentarily distracting Samarra.

"I am sorry," Samarra said again, turning back with the knife, and the next second she was crumpled on the floor.

"I'm sorry too," Ah'din said, and looked at Ah'nis with tears welling up in her eyes. "My husband said knowing how to do that might save my life someday, but I didn't think..." she burst into tears and Ah'nis ran to enfold her. "I didn't mean to kill her!"

"You saved us, Ah'din. She would have killed us both. You saved us," Ah'nis said, and in her head she was calling, *Dragonhorse, please come at once! Dragonhorse!*

"I just came to test the tea," Ah'din was sobbing, "I just came to test the tea."

One minute later Ardenai was in the room. "What happened? Dini are you all right?"

At the sound of her brother's voice Ah'din turned from Ah'nis and flung herself, sobbing, into his arms. "I didn't mean to kill her, Ardi, I just did that…thing…you know..."

"She saved us both," Ah'nis said, and about then Samarra groaned softly and twitched a little.

Ardenai burst out laughing and covered his sister with kisses. "It's always the quiet ones you have to look out for," he said. "Din, stop crying, the woman's not dead, you just knocked her out. Look. Ah'din, listen to me." Ardenai held her at arm's length and realized she was now laughing. He pulled her close again and held her head against his shoulder with the palm of his hand.

"And you, Ah'nis, are you all right as well?" he asked.

"I am," she said. "Oh no, Poor Eridi is probably scared to death." She turned to knock on the girl's door and Ardenai reached out to Teal.

Teal, kinsman, wake up.

There was a moment's pause. *This isn't another schematic, is it Ardi? Because I am dead tired.*

There had been enough alarums in the night of late; this didn't have to be one of them. *No, it's not another schematic. Get dressed and come to the apartments of the Eloi. Ah'din and I have something to show you.*

Eridi opened her door at the sound of Ah'nis's insistent voice saying, "The danger is over. Everything is fine. Samarra is down and the Dragonhorse is here. The danger is over."

Eridi hugged Ah'nis and crept cautiously over to peer down at Samarra, both arms still around her protectress. "Is she dead?"

At that point Ardenai let go of his sister momentarily and knelt to feel for a pulse at Samarra's neck. "She is not dead." he stood up and put his arms around Ah'din, thinking with the darker part of himself that he should probably wash his hands.

"Oh," Eridi said, and after some thought added, "That's too bad. I mean, she was never happy anyway, and she did some pretty awful things to me over the years. All in the name of religion, of course."

"Do let's test the tea," Ah'krill said from the doorway, "though the knife is pretty convincing on its own. Good morning, my son. Good morning, Ah'din Physician."

"Good morning, Mother," Ardenai replied, smiling at her over Ah'din's head. "Nobody touch that teapot, anything on that tray, the knife, or the woman. We don't know what all is poisoned."

"Din, are you all right?" Teal's voice, charged with worry, and Teal himself, very wide awake, long black hair loose down his back, reaching for his wife. "And Samarra?" At that point he was really alarmed and held his wife at arm's length as her brother had done. "Look at me," he said, more sharply than he meant to. "Ah'din, look me in the eye and tell me you're all right."

"Very much so," Ardenai chuckled, gesturing with his chin to the person on the floor. "Samarra was going to kill Ah'nis and Eridi and Ah'din saved them with her magic fingers – laid her right out."

"That's my girl," Teal laughed, hugging her close to his chest.

She relaxed a moment, then pushed herself away, wiped her eyes rather fiercely and marched over to the tea tray. "Fabric?" she asked, and Ah'nis handed her a towel from just inside the lavage. Using the towel, Ah'din picked up the knife, added it to the tray, then picked up the tray with the towel, stepped over Samarra and headed for the door. "Teal, Ardi, do not touch that woman again without gloves on, you don't know what she might have on her clothing or her skin. I will be in the sanecere, and when I'm through testing this, and I mean it this time, I am going home to Canyon keep." With that she disappeared.

"If you will remain here for a few minutes, I will go get some protective gear and a couple members of the Horse Guard," Teal said, still chuckling, and at Ardenai's nod, left him with the Eloi.

"Would you like some tea?" Ah'nis asked, looked at the expression on his face, and for the first time, Ardenai heard her laugh. "Seriously, would you like some orange and cinnamon tea?"

"Priestess, I have been up for two days and three nights, and I would love some tea," he replied, and looked down as Samarra moaned again. "I didn't want to tell my sister, but I won't be surprised if the Anchoress has a broken neck."

"Break it now, break it later, treason is treason," Ah'krill said quietly, but there was nothing placid about the look she gave the body on the floor.

"I don't think treason carries the death penalty," Ardenai was saying when suddenly the Anchoress rolled onto her knees and in a flash she had scurried to the corner of the room with her back to them, shoving something into her mouth.

Ardenai made a grab for her, and Eridi for him. "Don't touch her!" she cried, yanking back on his arm. He hardly felt her weight, but it did bring him up short of touching Samarra, who looked furtively over her shoulder and began chanting something very quietly in her high, nasal singsong.

"Anchoress," Ardenai said, "Samarra. You do not have to be afraid that we will do to you what you have tried to do to us. Our God doesn't teach us as yours does. Samarra?" But she had already crumpled, foaming at the mouth and twitching as the poison she'd swallowed took effect.

He turned away with a grimace, half sorrow and half disgust, and realized Eridi was clinging to him, not as a wife clings to her husband, but as a child clings to her father. "It's all right, you're safe," he said, taking her in his arms, and at that point, the girl began to cry.

He stayed, sipping tea and trying with some morbid amusement to ignore the body in the room until Teal returned with help, wrapped the corpse and left. "We will just take her with us when we go," Ardenai said. "Her life was on the Lebonathi worlds, perhaps it is there she will finally find peace."

"I hope it is there that all Lebonathi, including me, will finally find peace," Eridi said, now calmly seated while Ah'nis fixed her hair for the day.

Ardenai got down on one knee beside her and looked her in the eye. "Is it your wish to lead your society in that direction? It's going to be a long, hard road, Princess."

She returned the strength of his gaze. "It is my wish. I know that my guardian is going with you to Lebonath Jas, and I wish to go as well."

The Firstlord's eyes shifted from the girl's face to Ah'nis, who gave him a slow nod. "My specialty within the Eloi is emergent governance, Dragonhorse."

His eyes widened a little. "You won't be coming back with us, will you?"

"No," she smiled. "I will be staying. If Eridi is willing to take that risk, I think we owe it to her. She has spent her whole life preparing to be the wife of a powerful leader. In that training she has learned many things which will help us steer a new government, plus she has knowledge of the wealthy, ruling class, and they are the ones who will trouble us most."

"I don't know a thing about anyone else," the girl said, and her face registered embarrassment.

"That, you were not allowed," Ardenai said, patting her hand. "Now, you will be." He looked back at Ah'nis. "Have you concerns about being a woman governing aspects of a planet ruled until now by men?"

The priestess looked a little startled. "I had no notion of being one of the major Interposing Governors."

"Why not?" he asked, "You are a brave, no-nonsense kind of woman. What better example could they have than you? You have a fine head for organization. Who could possibly embody our beliefs and represent us better than the Eloi?"

She shook her head. "They will not listen to a simple priestess, even one put in place by the Dragonhorse."

"If you bear the indelible stamp of the Dragonhorse, they will listen, I'm quite sure," Ardenai said.

"You could marry her. Surely there is no better indelible stamp than being wife to the Thirteenth Dragonhorse."

Ardenai didn't even turn in acknowledging the comment. "And this conversation just jumped the fence," he sighed. "Ah'krill, I have a wife. She is smart, she is kind, she is beautiful, and when it is necessary she is lethal. She does many things well, and I adore her."

"But Ah'nis has made request of the Eloi to remain a virgin in the service of the Creator Spirit and the Great House," Ah'krill replied, reaching over his shoulder to take his tea cup. "I thought that might suit the two of you just fine."

Ardenai turned and stood up at that point, smiling at Ah'nis and at his mother, as well as the others who occupied the room and the doorway. "I want all of you to consider the fact that on this planet a person is allowed one partner. Once they are married they are expected by law, by faith, and by social mores, to remain faithful to one another. Two people equal one marriage, not three or four people. That is the way I was raised and the way I have, and want to continue to raise my children. How can I do that if our most pious and most respected citizens force me to be the exception to a rule that everyone else has to follow? How can I set an example for our people if I am expected to break the rules for the sake of an ancient custom that no longer makes any sense?"

Ardenai held his breath for about a minute before his mother said, "Oh, fine. Whether it no longer makes any sense or not remains to be seen, and I'm betting you're going to change your mind. But, I'll bring it up with the Council of the Eloi, and I will stop nagging you, at least for now, Dragonhorse. Just remember, the word of the dragons of Achernar and the powers of Mountain hold will have equal and sometimes ultimate sway. In the meantime, don't think this lets you out of matings sanctioned by the Great House. And if the situation changes, my thoughts on the matter may change as well." She turned on her heel and walked away, crimping a smile and nodding to herself. "Many things – customs, laws, legends – which are ancient, no longer make any sense," she said to the priestesses walking with her. "Mountain hold thinks he is the one, and I certainly think he is, don't you?" They nodded their agreement, and Ah'krill's eyes softened with pride in her only son. "Have him brought before the Council this evening. We shall offer him our … full assistance."

Ardenai looked wide-eyed at Ah'nis. "Did she just say yes?" he asked, hardly able to believe his own ears.

"Tentatively, I would say she did, at least to the extent of giving you some breathing room. You can bet that she, or the dragons themselves, are going to want something in return one of these days, and you'd better be ready to give it, Dragonhorse."

"From elated to uneasy in ten seconds flat," he sighed. "I wish I had a polo pony that fast. Ah'nis, again I thank you, and…do I need to apologize for being constantly shoved at you in one form or another?"

"Since you are not doing the shoving, you do not," she smiled. "Best get some rest. You'll need your wits about you in short order."

Ardenai knew he needed sleep. He could feel it in his responses, and in his reflexes, but he also felt an agitation, a drive to get things ready – every strategy – every plan in order – every talent in the right place to keep the most people safe. He was not the only one feeling the pressure. Teal was tired, Io was tired. Ardenai hadn't touched his wife sexually in nearly a week. He thought about that as he went quickly from the apartments of the Eloi back to his own. He needed food, then a wash, a brush, and fresh clothes this morning. Thinking about Io was pleasant, and had he found her at home, he would have enjoyed spending time with her, but she was off someplace using her expertise, probably with the Eloi. That's where she'd been most of the time the last few days.

He did find Gideon and Criollo just finishing breakfast, and had a chance for some guided conversation as he joined them. Ardenai assumed Gideon was going to want to go with the interposing forces to Lebonath Jas, because Ardenai was going, and Gideon hated being separated from the Firstlord. But Ardenai wasn't about to take the boy someplace that might turn into a hot war zone. They'd been through enough like that together. One son in the line of fire was unnerving, two was unacceptable.

"I want you to take good care of Ah'din, Ah'rane and Krush while Teal and I are gone," he told the boys. "You need to go home as often as you possibly can and try to keep them from worrying too much. Keep an eye on Girsu and Jasreth as they get used to being here, and for pity's sake, try to keep Ah'brianne out of trouble. Also, Gideon, you'll be the only member of the family here in Thura in case someone needs something ceremonial done. I hope that doesn't bother you."

Gideon studied him for a bit. Subtle as an atomic bus this morning, but amazing nonetheless. The Firstlord was bone tired but straight-shouldered under the weight of taking a heavily armed incursion force to another world. Much as he hated violence, he could see no options, and the complexity of the construction he was bringing into play left Gideon's head spinning. So he listened, nodded politely, knew why his father wasn't taking him, and accepted it without comment or argument. When it was time to leave for school he got up from the table, kissed Ardenai lingeringly on the temple and said, "I love you, Dragondad. I'll do my best."

Had Ardenai been a gambling man he'd have found a game at that point. No argument about number one wife, no argument from number two son – it was almost too much to hope for, much less have happen before the sun had been up an hour. He promised himself a nap, put on a winter Dragonhorse uniform and trotted off to Dominus.

"Imperial Equi Clipper Dominus requesting permission to launch into deep space and jump to light speed," he said. "Destination, Anguine II. Initial terminus flight control, please," he added.

"Usual destination coordinates?"

"Yes, thank you, Cutter," he said, and when he was safely launched and out of traffic he abandoned his chair and sprawled on his bed in the forward cabin for the forty-five minute flight, hoping he could turn off his brain long enough to sleep.

The snow was deep on Anguine II. He was still stomping it off his boots when Ah'rika opened the door and took his cloak. "Mother has been expecting you," she smiled. "She told me you would be here when you finished up with the Eloi."

Ardenai gave her a questioning look as they walked toward the prow of the house. "Did someone contact her?"

Ah'rika shook her head. "No. You'll see, Firstlord."

The room was pleasant as always, decorated in shades of blue with a little gray, and brightened by the sharp white of the snow falling outside the big windows. There was a subtle fragrance to it that Ardenai always liked when he came. Not quite floral, not quite spice. He found Ah'davan in her usual spot on the day bed, propped up with pillows, a knitted throw across her legs, doing needlework and watching the snow fall.

"Dragonhorse," she smiled, extending her hand, and Ardenai took it and kissed it as he sat lightly on the edge of what had become her prison.

"Are you enjoying the snow?"

"Nik loved it, you know," she said, still smiling fondly at this young man who made the time to come and see her often, no matter how busy he was with other things. "He ice skates beautifully, and he loves to go sledding with the grandchildren. And now you think you know where he is, and you want to know if I want to come along, just in case you're right."

Ardenai gave her a slightly startled and searching look and her smile became a soft chuckle. "It seems the weaker this body of mine gets, the stronger my telepathic abilities become. I really don't know why that is, and I don't know why I hear the things I do, or the people I do, but you, Ah'krill Ardenai Morning Star, I hear you whenever you think of my husband. Isn't that odd?"

"It is odd," he smiled, patting her hand, "and rather wonderful at the same time. I hope the things I'm thinking aren't disturbing to you."

"Some do and some don't, but any thought of him is welcome. The fact that you have not given up trying to find him, even for one day, has been such a blessing to me, Ardenai. And now you are wondering if you should ask me to come, because if he is not there, you can sense that I will not return here alive, and you are correct." Ardenai just dropped his eyes and said nothing. Ah'ree had died like this. By inches, by days. "Don't be sad, Dragonhorse. I have said my goodbyes to this part of my life, many times over. Konik is not here. If there is any chance, one in a million, one in ten million, that he may be where you think he is, I am willing to take that chance. I need to see him, Ardenai. I need to have him hold me one more time, so that is my last memory of being alive – my years with my good husband."

Ardenai nodded and blinked back the tears in his eyes. "Then you shall go, Ah'davan. This mission needs more strong telepaths. If things stay on schedule we will leave for the Lebonathi worlds in two days. A shuttle will pick you up as we go by. What can I do to make your flight more comfortable? What can I provide for you?"

"Hope," she smiled. "Hope of finding my husband."

▲ ▲ ▲ ▲ ▲ ▲ ▲

"I want to be sure you understand," Ardenai said, pacing the length of the chamber of the Apprising Council and turning again to his mother, who sat with Cavalry Captain Abeyan on one side and Sta'dan of Corvus on the other. "I do not want this to begin as an interposing campaign. This is a delivery and rescue mission. I am going to take them Samarra's body as a way of getting in, and I am going to get Senator Konik out. If I get him without a fight, I am going to offer our help, as you did, Ah'krill. Scientists, agronomists, economists, but if they move against us, which I'm positive they're going to do, I want to be able to stop them before they can even knock the sand of their world off their boots."

"You think they're allied with the Telenir?" asked Ambassador Drakkyus.

Ardenai paused in his restless pacing and put his hands together as he spoke. "I think…they think…they are allied with the Telenir, which is why they're attempting something as foolish as war with the AEW. It is also why I'm very nearly positive they have Konik."

"And that lone man, that Telenir, is worth all this?" Abeyan asked.

Ardenai smiled at his old friend and father-in-law. It almost always made him want to snicker that they were the same age, and it always scared him a little that he'd married the man's daughter. He still harbored half a notion that he was going to get a knife in the crotch some dark night when he least expected it. "Given everything else that goes with it, yes, I do. He is invaluable as a catalyst if nothing more."

"So you are going to declare war only if they fire on you?" Ah'krill asked.

"It will probably go like that, yes, only I have no intention of declaring war on them. Too much paperwork," the Firstlord said, and began to pace again, as much to keep himself awake as anything. He'd spent hours in the Council of the Eloi, and he was exhausted. "I plan to do exactly the same thing Vanner did when, as the Seventh Dragonhorse, he took the Terrenes into the AEW. We will disarm them, try to reason with them, remove as many of them as we deem necessary to receive the appropriate amount of cooperation, and begin to help them rebuild as a Tribute World of Equus."

"The Terrenes were one thing, but why in Wisdom's name would we want the Lebonathi?" Abeyan asked.

"I suppose at this point we don't," Ardenai replied, "but they are worlds on the verge of exploding into the galaxy in search of food and territory. All they need is a little help to do it. There are ten signals recognized by the United Galactic Alliance that a planet is about to become a threat to the larger whole. Lebonath Jas is demonstrating at least seven of the ten, and in their path of immediate expansion lie Amberia and Menorquin, both Affined Equi Worlds, both of whom have SGA neighbors, both of whom are capable of annihilating every man, woman and child on the Lebonathi worlds. Whether they destroy others or are themselves destroyed, it is a tragedy we can help them avoid. Furthermore, I have it on very good authority that the Potami are looking at the Lebonathi worlds with an eye for conquest, though what they're after is beyond me. Whatever it is, they won't be gentle in taking it. If we get there first, they can just ask for it."

"It would help you solve the Lebonathi's population problems," Drakkyus joked. He was Potami, and while Ardenai's comments had been overtly offensive, Drakkyus had taken them for the warning they were. "But we will not stand in your way, Dragonhorse."

"If we can save the planets, we can save the people. We have the power to do it, the wealth to do it, the experts to do it. I know it will not be completed in my reign as Firstlord. A hundred and fifty years isn't really much time to rebuild a world and reshape a people, but it's a start, and it will strengthen the SGA."

"So will those thirteen Dragonhorse Cruisers," Sta'dan laughed. "Cadence took me for a little spin yesterday and I was most impressed, Ardenai, most impressed."

"Thank you," the Firstlord smiled. "We will send word by relay if there is need of a declaration. Until then, please say as little as possible. I doubt that any society as xenophobic as the Lebonathis has any real allies. Their delegation pretty much said so, and their broken-down ship was further evidence, but I don't want to find out they have an extra cinch on their saddle."

"About their delegation," Dahman asked in his dithery little voice, "Yes, their delegation. What exactly happened to all of them again, exactly? Because they can't be very happy about that, can they?"

"Princess Eridi is with the Eloi. Girsu and Jasreth defected to Equus and are living amongst us. Prince Basra is in the sanecere wards and when he is released it will be into some sort of guarded situation. I killed Prince Addur for raping Ah'brianne, Samarra committed suicide, and the rest went home in a Lebonathi ship that Cadence said looked Narga in design."

"And what about Samarra?" Dahman persisted. "What is her... disposal to be?"

"We will deliver Anchoress Samarra's body to Eridu when we ask for Konik."

"And if they don't hand him over?" Ah'krill asked.

"If they have him, they will hand him over, I guarantee it," Ardenai replied, and his jaw muscle rippled slightly under the light olive skin.

SGA Representative Cornwallis Mettenger sucked air through his bottom teeth for a bit, as was his habit before speaking. Everybody knew and accepted this oddity. Though it annoyed a few people it bought time. In this case he was giving the Firstlord time to cool down a little. The stress wasn't really obvious unless one knew Ardenai well, and Cornwallis did, had for many years. A delightful man in most ways, but not a man to mess with. Never had been, despite his reputation. "You don't mind if the SGA sends along a few ships, just to observe?"

"I was hoping you'd offer," Ardenai replied, and flashed that charming, disarming and largely misleading smile of his.

Cornwallis knew better. The man wore unlimited power on those sinuous, tattooed arms of his, and just now, he wore death in his dragon's eyes.

"Be ready," Ardenai said quietly, nodded to his mother and left the council chambers.

THE ELEVEN PLANETS OF THE AFFINED EQUI WORLDS (AEW)

Equus
Menorquin
Corvus
Amberia
Demeter
Anguine Prime
Anguine II
Papillia
Phylla
Calumet
Terren

IMPERIAL STORMCLASS TACTICAL CRUISERS

AEW planet of assignation and commanding officer

ISTC XIII "Dragonhorse"– *Equus.* Flagship. Ah'ree Kehailan Ardenai

ISTC I "The Dragon's Teeth" – *Amberia.* Ulric Hamar

ISTC IV "The Dragon's Claws"– *Calumet.* Ah'calla Mecklin Pentro

ISTC V "The Dragon's Hide"– *Corvus.* Cadence Holofernes

ISTC X "The Dragon's Tail" – *Terren.* Marion Eletsky

ISTC II – *Anguine Prime.* Under Construction. Unassigned

ISTC III – *Anguine II.* Under Construction. Offer on table

ISTC VI – *Demeter.* Under Construction. Unassigned

ISTC VII – *Menorquin.* Under construction. Unassigned

ISTC VIII – *Papillia.* Under Construction. Unassigned

ISTC IX – *Phylla.* Under Construction. Unassigned

ISTC XI – *Equus*. Under Construction. Unassigned

ISTC XII – *TBD*. Under Construction. Unassigned (Speculation has it that this ship will be assigned to control Lebonathi space, though no announcement has been made.)

CHARACTER LIST
(Alphabetically)

Abeyan – *Equi*. Master of Cavalry. Father of Ah'riodin, husband of Ah'kra, who is his second wife

Addur – *Lebonathi.* Son of Halaf's sister, one of Eridu's subordinate wives. Nephew of Halaf

Ah'brianne – *Equi.* Daughter of Timor and Ah'mae, neighbors to Ardenai. They lease Lea keep

Ah'clare – *Equi.* Director of Education for a school on Taraxia. Wife of Gidran. Mother of Teal

Ah'cora – *Equi.* Stepdaughter of Saremanno, stepsister to Sarkhan. Being held at Mountain hold

Ah'davan – *Equi.* Wife of Konik, mother of their twin daughters, Ah'rika and Ah'nia

Ah'din – *Equi.* Physician and Master Weaver. Wife of Teal, Mother of Criollo, sister of Ardenai

Ah'jin Kehailan Morning Star – *Equi.* The Twelfth Dragonhorse. Ardenai's biological father

Ah'kra – *Anguine/Equi.* Wife of Abeyan. Stepmother to Ah'riodin (Io)

Ah'krill – *Equi.* High Priestess of Equus. Ardenai's birth mother, though not his biological mother

Ah'lauren – *Equi.* Telemetry specialist. Wife of Rounce. They befriend Girsu.

Ah'mae – *Equi.* Master Weaver. Raises exotic, long haired sheep. Wife of Timor, mother of Ah'brianne

Ah'nis – *Equi.* Priestess who becomes the guardian of Princess Eridi

Ah'nora – *Calumet/Equi.* Carries Ardenai's son

Ah'rane – *Equi.* Friction Analysis Engineer. Ardenai's foster mother. Wife of Krush, mother of Ah'din

Ah'ree – *Equi/Terrasian.* Deceased. Ardenai's first wife, mother of Kehailan.

Ah'ria Konik Nokota – *Equi.* Senator from Anguine II. Possibly a Wind Warrior. Husband of Ah'davan

Ah'rika – *Equi.* One of Konik's twin daughters

Ah'ti – *Equi.* Priestess. Member of the Education Council.

Ah'vel – *Equi.* One of the wives of the Twelfth Dragonhorse, and Ardenai's biological mother

Akadia – *Lebonathi.* A servant

Anseri – *Equi.* Master Composer to the Great House of Equus

Anseri – *Equi.* Master Composer for the Great House of Equus

Ardenai – *Equi.* Ah'rane Ardenai Krush / Ah'krill Ardenai Morning Star, the Thirteenth Dragonhorse

Ardenai – *Equi.* The Tenth Dragonhorse and Ardenai's great grandsire. (Website for further details)

Asturian – *Equi.* The Eleventh Dragonhorse. (Website for further details)

Balearic – *Equi.* The Eighth Dragonhorse. (Website for further details)

Basra – *Lebonathi.* Son of Halaf's sister, one of Eridu's subordinate wives. Nephew of Halaf

Bonfire Dannis – *Phyllan.* Second in command of the good ship Belesprit. Friend of Kehailan

Brak – *Lebonathi.* Standard Bearer for the Lebonathi Delegation to Equus

Breton – *Equi.* Elderly Master of Education

Cadence Holofernes – *Corvi.* Wife Merri. Captain of Imperial Stormclass Cruiser Dragonhorse Five.

Chirion – *Equi.* (The Eldest). Ancient and wise Androtech being from Mountain hold

Cornwallis Mettenger – *Terren/Coronian.* SGA Representative to the Great House of Equus

Criollo – *Equi.* Son of Teal and Ah'din. Nephew of Ardenai, Grandson of Ah'rane and Krush

Cutter – *Equi.* Communication/launch and vector officer for the shunt bays of the Great House of Equus.

Dahman – *Taraxian.* Ambassador to Equus from Taraxia. Member of the Education Council

Devario – *Menorquin.* In line with wife Strea to captain an Imperial Storm-class Tactical Cruiser

Drakkyus – *Potami.* Ambassador from Potami and member of the Education Council

Eider – *Equi/Demetrian.* Master of Distribution for the Great Stables

Eridi – *Lebonathi.* Eldest living daughter of The Most Wise Lord Eridu. Presented to Ardenai

Eridu – *Lebonathi.* The Most wise Lord Eridu. Ruler of the Lebonathi Worlds. Father of Eridi

Gallios – *Menorquin.* Wife Isla. He oversees the huge farm ships that move as needed around the SGA

Gideon – *Declivian/Coronian/Terren/Equi.* Ardenai's adopted son

Gidran – *Equi.* Wine Master. Ambassador to Taraxia. Husband of Ah'clare. Father of Teal

Girsu – *Lebonathi.* Secretary of the Minority Party, Lebonathi High Council. Uncle of Jasreth

Hadrian Keats – *Terren.* (Dennis Strathmore) Serving a sentence on the island of Dorset, Declivis

Halaf – *Lebonathi.* Secretary General of the Lebonathi High Council. Uncle of Addur and Basra

Harrier – *Equi.* (Androtech) One of the changeless ones of Mountain hold. He loves to cook and garden

Hassuna – *Lebonathi.* A servant

Hirzai – *Equi.* One of the senators from Equus to the Great Council

Io – *Equi/Papilli.* Abeyan Ah'riodin Morning Star. Wife of Ardenai, Prim-uxori of Equus

Isla – *Menorquin.* Husband Gallios. Pilots and maintains orbit for the farm ships individually and as units

Jasreth – *Lebonathi.* Niece of Girsu

Jilfan – *Equi/Papilli.* Young son of Ah'riodin by Salerno, stepson to Ardenai

Josephus – *Terren.* Captain of "The Grand Old Rust Bucket." Friend of Ardenai and Gideon

Kabardin – *Equi.* The Ninth Dragonhorse. (Website for further details)

Kehailan – *Equi*. Son of Ardenai and Ah'ree. Third in Command of SGAS Belesprit.

Kehailan – *Equi.* (Ah'jin Kehailan Morning Star) The Twelfth Dragonhorse. (Website for further details)

Kestrel – *Equi* (Androtech) oversees the affairs of Mountain hold and all the Dragonhorses so far

Kiger – *Coronian/Equi*. Acting Captain of Seventh Galactic Alliance Ship Sweetwater

Krush – *Equi*. Bloodlines specialist. Keeplord of Sea keep. Ardenai's beloved foster father.

Landais – *Equi*. Master Farrier for the Great Stables.

Lark – *Equi* (Androtech) Changeless and wise, she cares for the denizens of Mountain hold

Mahruss – *Equi*. One of Ardenai's creppia nonage students

MalDor – *Kohathi*. Ambassador. Represents the Parasectra of Kohath Zadok

Maremmano – *Equi*. Saddle Master for the Great Stables

Marion Eletsky – *Terren*. Captain of SGAS Belesprit. Friend to Kehailan and Ardenai

Mecklin – *Calumet*. Captain of Imperial Stormclass Tactical Cruiser Four. Brother of Rustem

Merri – *Corvi*. Astrometry and Stellar Cartography. Wife of Cadence Holofernes

Naram – *Lebonathi*. Nuntius d'affaires for the Most Wise Lord Eridu and the Lebonathi Delegation

Oona Pongo – *Terren*. Protocol Officer aboard SGAS Belesprit. Friend of Ardenai and Kehailan

Pen Darus – *Demetrian*. In line to captain an Imperial Stormclass Tactical Cruiser

Pochard – *Anguine Prime/Equi.* In line to captain an Imperial Stormclass Tactical Cruiser

Pottuck – *Equi*. Master of the Great Stables

Pythos – *Achernarean*. One of the ancient order of sea dragons. Ardenai's personal physician and friend

Rounce – *Equi*. Documentary Historian. Husband of Ah'lauren. Friend of Girsu

Rustem – *Calumet*. Saddlemaker. Brother of Mecklin

Salerno – *Equi*. Late husband of Io, father of Jilfan

Samarra – *Lebonathi*. Anchoress of Womankind. Member of the Lebonathi Delegation

Saremanno – *Equi*. (Telenir) Father of Sarkhan. Being held at Mountain hold

Sarkhan – *Equi* (Telenir). Pretender to the role of Dragonhorse. Slain by Ardenai on Calumet

Seglawi – *Equi*. Captain of Arms for the Great House of Equus

Skyros – *Equi*. In line to captain an Imperial Stormclass Tactical Cruiser

Sta'dan – *Corvi*. Ambassador from Corvus to the Great House of Equus

Strea – *Menorquin*. In line with husband Devario to captain an Imperial Stormclass Tactical Cruiser

Taki – *Equi*. (Telenir). One of the Telenir who spoke for peace. Being held at Mountain hold

Tarpan – *Equi*. Captain of the Secondary Squads. Former student of Ardenai. Husband of Ah'keena

Teal – *Equi*. Master of Horse for the Great House of Equus. Husband of Ah'din, father of Criollo

Thatcher – *Calumet/Hectorian*. The mine boss on Calumet.

Timor – *Equi*. Master Farmer. Leases Lea keep from Krush. Husband of Ah'mae, father of Ah'brianne

Ulric Hamar – Amberian. Captain of Imperial Stormclass Tactical Cruiser One

Vanner – *Equi*. The Seventh Dragonhorse. (Website for further details)

Winslow Moonsgold – *Declivian*. Physician. (Winnie) Head of the Science Wing, SGAS Belesprit

Wren – *Equi*. (Androtech) Ancient, wise and incredibly beautiful, she is Ardenai's hetaera and friend

OTHER NAMES OF IMPORT

Eladeus – the Equi name for the Creator Spirit

El'Shadai – the Declivian name for the Creator Spirit

THE ANCIENT LINES OF THE GREAT HOUSE

Equine – From which most of the Dragonhorses have come, including Ardenai

Waterfowl – More ancient than Equine. Teal is from this line

Aviarium – More ancient yet. Represented mostly by the ancient beings of Mountain hold

Arboranthus – An early line which has fallen into obscurity, but is still represented

Achernarean – Represented by the venerable and powerful sea dragons

HOW EQUI NAMES WORK

A woman carries her father's name first, then her given name, then her mother's name. For example: Ah'din was Krush Ah'din Ah'rane before her marriage to Teal, at which time she took his given name to become Krush Ah'din Teal.

A man carries his mother's name first, then his given name, then his father's name. This does not change when he marries. Hence Ardenai was Ah'rane Ardenai Krush. When he rose to become Dragonhorse his name became Ah'krill Ardenai Morning Star. Morning Star being the designate of all the named Dragonhorses.

Ah' prefaces nearly all women's names. It is an ancient designate meaning, "lady, woman or female."

ABOUT THE AUTHOR

Showandah S. Terrill is an award winning speaker and storyteller, as well as a lifelong writer and equestrian. Steeped in Native American culture, she was raised as the only child of an itinerant cowhand on sprawling ranches in Southern California during the turbulent 1960's.

She is currently writing two extended series: the epic science-fiction *Dragonhorse Chronicles* and the fictional autobiographical *Peter Aarons'* novels.

www.ingramcontent.com/pod-product-compliance
Lightning Source LLC
Chambersburg PA
CBHW020305030826
48979CB00027B/2137/J

* 9 7 8 1 7 3 2 8 0 5 2 3 1 *